DRAGONS

LEXICON TRIUMVIRATE

DRAGONS
LEXICON TRIUMVIRATE

A Novel By

KENNETH CHE-TEW ENG

NARTEA
PUBLISHING
A DIVISION OF DNA PRESS, LLC

For information regarding permission write to: DNA Press, LLC, P.O.Box
572, Eagleville, PA 19408, USA or contact: editors@dnapress.com.

Library of Congress Cataloging-in-Publication Data

Eng, Kenneth C. (Kenneth Che-Tew), 1983- Dragons : Lexicon Triumvirate
/ by Kenneth C. Eng.— 1st ed. p. cm.
Summary: Dennagon, a lowly dragon sentry, leads a band of dissident
dragons in facing cyborg Technodragons, the forces of time, and the
corrupt dragon king, Drekkenoth, as they seek the source of infinite
knowledge known as the Lexicon.

ISBN 0-9748765-0-X

(alk. paper) [1. Dragons—Fiction. 2. Knowledge and learning—Fiction.

3.Cyborgs—Fiction. 4. Technology—Fiction. 5. Science fiction. 6.

Youths'writings.] I. Title. PZ7.E6974Dr 2005 [Fic]—dc22

    2 0 0 4 0 2 8 5 6 1

Printed in the United States of America on acid-free paper

DNA Press, LLC

PO Box 572

Eagleville, PA 19408 USA

www.dnapress.com

editors@dnapress.com

Publisher: Alex Nartea
Executive Editor: Alexander Kuklin
Art Direction and Production: Studio N Vision (www.studionvision.com)
Cover Art : David Cabot (CabotArt@aol.com)

This book, the emerald facet of my life's work, is in honor of my family, friends...

...and anyone who acknowledges that in a realm of infinite possibility, the pursuit of perfection is the meaning of life!

Contents

PROLOGUE

Circuits lined the preserved carcasses of countless dinosaurs. Like monuments of the past, the mechanized fossils surrounded an entire chamber of medieval architecture, still and cold and dead. Along the stone walls, computerized enhancements ran throughout, wiring lamps and torches that illumined the environment. It was a frigid place, one that had not been touched in ages. Yet, in the center, a single mobius strip constantly spun, emitting silver rays that shone upon the walls and made them transparent in its wake. Space could be seen where the strip's light met the stone, and every star of the cosmos twinkled like a watcher, a spectator of time. The essences of many ages ran across the air, letting the voices of eons echo.

"There's no time. We have to get out. Now," said a female.

"What about the sentry?" responded a male.

Flames roared, but there were no fires to be seen. It was as if they had come from a place very distant.

"We can reach him later. The present is what concerns me."

"I thought you said there was no time. How can there be a later?"

Growls shuddered the place, yet there were no beasts from which the growls could emerge.

"None of your riddles. Just fly to the Pedorian Forest."

A spherical metal orb blanketed the entire stellar mural outside. It was a globe of planetary magnitude that was adorned with landscapes far and wide.

"I don't know Lyconel. We might not make it."

"Too late, Dradicus. We're already in."

The chamber of robotic dinosaurs started to fragment whilst the walls disintegrated into nothingness. The mobius strip evanesced like a spectre, and all that was left was the gargantuan green-blue orb – the World.

———————————

Trees floated above the Everkin Forest. Their roots hung in the air, reaching down like pale green veins to the bizarrely twisted landscape below. The leaves upon the branches were circular and ovoid like those of plants that came from an era long past, yet the air was hardly prehistoric. Upon the Mesozoic verdure, the sun cast its dawn light, giving life to the hovering woodland realm in the form of photosynthetic vitality that sparkled betwixt the morning arbor. It seemed like a peaceful new day, one that was full of promise. However, nothing on this planet was stable.

Scales ripped through the plant life, shedding blood across the twigs. A drake, a dragon without wings, charged through the placid shrubberies, her life fleeting with every gallop she took. On all fours, she dashed desperately past the hanging roots, digging grooves into the erratically warped dirt underneath. Death was near and she knew it. There was no slowing down or the enemy would consume her. Albeit the only thing on her mind at the moment was retreat, even she knew that might not be possible.

"Keep moving, keep moving," Lyconel reassured herself.

Wood splintered behind her as two beasts followed her path. They too were dragons, one a wyvern and the other a behemoth. Their claws ravaged the terrain in devastating blows, tearing up anything and everything that got in their path. Rapidly, they were catching up, as quickly and menacingly as one's own shadow.

Lyconel hurriedly tried to make a sharp turn, but a root caught her leg abruptly. Rolling on her side, she knew she was in peril and that fleeing was now futile. As she hit a large stone, she reached for her belt and slung out a spiked mace. She was prepared for battle.

Almost immediately, a giant reptilian talon came down upon her. Wielding her mace high above her head, she clashed against it, deflecting its claws in sparks of metal. She whirled the weapon about, trying to strike upon the behemoth's abdomen, but a colossal axe swooped down upon her and parried her attack. She swung around, twirling like a dancer as the enemy tried to take her down, feverishly dodging every assault that came her way. Alas, she pounced into the air as the blade arced under her. Catching onto the trees, she continued running.

"Try again," she dared.

The trees started collapsing in her wake as the behemoth rammed his fists into them. Crashing trunks fell upon the ground, but she persisted in her furious stride. Wings might have been helpful at the moment, but unfortunately, nature had not endowed her with any. She hurried out to the canopies of the forest.

Standing upon the very apex of a tree, she glimpsed the landscape to the horizon. Far in the distance, whitish, pointed hilltops reached to the sky, forming a chain of mountains. The Fangs of Astinor. She was headed straight to them, and if she went there, she would never come back. Not with two of her greatest enemies on her tail, anyway.

Suddenly, a rapier lashed at her face. She ducked just a split second before it could hit her. The other draconic opponent flew over her, flapping its wyvern wings as it swiped its weapon madly downward. Too close to her enemy, Lyconel thrust her talons out, blocking the rounded foil with her forearms. Her dermal layer chipped as it struck her, and she tried to gain an opportunity to counterattack. Nonetheless, the wyvern was too fast, and delivered a slash that wrapped the foil around her arm and sliced her across the cheek.

A splash of silver blood spurt out from her wound. Lyconel dropped her mace, and then dropped herself deliberately. As she descended back into the woodland, she gripped a branch with her tail, grabbed her mace in midair and swung around to her opponent's rear. Her legs slammed his back, but did little more than knock him away. He instantly darted in for another sortie just as she rushed back into the verdure and continued to flee.

For three seconds, she heard not the crushing of trees behind her. In a flash of optimism, she thought they had left. Nevertheless, just as fleetly as the silence came, it perished with radiant explosions that erupted all around. Plasma shots were fired at her, detonating into ever-expanding orbs of energy that toppled the airborne plants. Now she was certain she would not escape.

Then, something caught her eye. To the flank, a rocky outcrop rose from the ground like a marble web of caves. Stretching up into the air, it formed a mosaic sculpture of stony veins that branched like a living network of pure, solid earth. The light of morn shone against its varnished surface, and she knew she could escape. She was safe from her enemies -- but was she walking into another threat?

A plasma shot blasted the ground to her side. There was no time to consider the options. Without another thought, she leapt to the webbed caves and scurried along their glossy surfaces. Coming across a dark orifice, she took a breath.

"May the darkness not consume me," she prayed to no one in particular.

Quickly, her serpentine form slithered through the opening. Into the cavernous veins she delved, swimming through the bleak unknown as blackness consumed her body. As fleet as she entered, she was gone. Without a trace, and without a path to follow.

The plasma emissions ceased. The behemoth and wyvern perfunctorily crept up to the air-dwelling stone network, their claws clanking against the rocky surfaces as if they were made of metal. Their composures equally metallic, they located the orifice through which their target evaded and espied the ebony depths. They came to the same conclusion simultaneously. Knowing exactly what to do, they exchanged glances and waited.

Fires lashed the air before them, seemingly coming out of nowhere. However, these flames were not of light spawned, but of pure darkness. The black conflagrations grew before them, bubbling like liquid flares, until alas, a shape formed. It was another dragon, average in stature, but of a hellish essence that far transcended its apparent size. Dark fires wrapped around its every muscle, licking the air with hot blazes, yet not a single feature could be seen beyond its general contours. Baronial in dread, it looked to its two watchers.

"Is she annihilated?" inquired Drekkenoth.

The wyvern, Arxinor, and his behemoth colleague, Gorgash, processed the question within their mechanical heads. Gears and circuits turned about in their brains.

"Unknown."

Drekkenoth peered into the opening of the Supersurface Cave Network. Neutrally, he accepted the fact. Cocking his forearm, he looked at a wristwatch attached to his talon, one that was built with a face of countless iterating membranes and ten dials that pointed to the thirty hours of the day.

"The Key," stated Arxinor in his snakelike accent, "is sssstill in existence."

"Affirmative," replied Drekkenoth.

"Their next objective is to reach the Archive sentries," added Gorgash.

"The marked sssssentry identity is: Dennagon."

Drekkenoth looked up to the morning sun at the apex of the sky. Wires, robotic in nature, coursed through his pupils, spreading through his body of pure fire as if to make the flame cybernetic. The very bleakness of his gaze burnt the light and made it as black as a laser of shadows.

"We must make certain that the Lexicon is demolished," he declared.

"In time, time shall be oursssss."

All at once, they cocked their heads up. Cyborg wings burst out from their backs and they took to the heavens above. There was much to do and much to destroy before the closing of the World. Before time ceased its bidding.

CHAPTER 1

T ime is not a concept. It is a word. And like any word, it can be manipulated according to one's subjective state. Just like quantum mechanics and relativity are unified in that they require perception to create reality, every passing trice can be toiled at one's will – or against one's will. Yet, in the tides of linear moments and unfolded space, there is a realm beyond which any ordinary creature can reach. One must forget everything he has learned and retain only the one thing that matters in existence if he is to attain the ultimate state of omniscience – the essence of the Lexicon.

Across the lands of the ever-changing World, between the globe's poles and past the dying terrain of Aurahelm, there laid the prominent kingdom of Drakemight. It was a civilization as grand as it was elegant, a place where knowledge towered above all else. Architecture stretched to the skies in the forms of simple geometric shapes, complex and intelligently crafted, but untainted by the opposing thumbs of man. No, this was a kingdom of dragons, undimmed in splendor amidst the fabric of glorious earth, striving to survive and striving to understand all that laid within comprehension.

In front of the walls that surrounded its perimeters, there

was a single dragon that stood guard under the dusk sky. Perching upon the edge of the stony barricade, he watched over the mossy, rock-speckled plains that lay past the city, making certain that no attackers breached. Or, at least he was supposed to be watching. Instead, however, his green eyes were fixated on a book in his emerald-scaled talons, deeply engrossed in the physical and scientific laws it dictated upon its pages. He was aware that his actions were an explicit violation of collective code, but he wasn't worried. His battle-scarred plate armor and tarnished scabbard were enough to remind him that he had quite enough experience to combat any poor soul that dared to assail his post.

"Interesting," muttered Dennagon to himself. "The force of gravity is 9.8 meters per second squared on this planet, but not in space. I wonder if 'space' actually exists."

His eyes crawled down to the bottom of the page. He did not want to stray in his thought, for he felt that he had not read enough today.

"Oh well, I'll probably never travel there anyway," he said to quell his imagination.

The wind flipped a page just as he finished it. At the same moment, a clutter of footsteps rumbled the terrain. They were metallic, banging against the stones upon the field and tearing up the moss upon the dirt. A loud cranking sound churned as well, wooden and monstrous. However, Dennagon did not even budge. He knew what was coming and how to handle it.

A train of human knights with shimmering armor and horses of aegises adorned marched forth. Wheeling a catapult amongst their lines, they loaded a boulder. Equipping their shields, they fell into combative positions, orderly as they were taught to by their predecessors. Reptilian bones decorated their tunics, granting them their only source of bravery in this battle.

"And I wonder," pondered Dennagon whilst he continued browsing, "if these worldly variables are actually constant."

The commanding paladin trotted up front.

"Desist beast!" he shouted under his cage-visor helm. "Prepare to be vanquished!"

"Could you attack me later? I'm in the middle of a tome."

They armed their lances.

"Charge, valiant knights! Destroy this abomination!"

With that, they charged forth. Lances pointed, they rushed to run through their target like they had run through so many other creatures in their path. Blood boiled in their veins, fueling their avaricious anger.

Dennagon nonchalantly dropped down from his perched position to the ground. Without even taking his eyes off his book, he casually thrust his fist out, punching a hole straight through the head of one of his enemies as it charged. The decapitated body still hanging off his forearm, he merely shifted his fist to the side so that the others could run into it. Expectedly, they did, blasting apart their own skulls against his scaly knuckles.

Shocked, the remaining knights armed their archery equipment and fired a volley of arrows. Their draconic prey simply snatched the hilt of his scabbard and ripped out a sword of pristine green metal. Whirling the blade about, he deflected the shots, shattering shafts into wooden shards that spurt across the air in splintered clouds. When they ran out of ammunition, he thought they would finally leave, but these humans were a bit dumber than most he had met. They drew their close-combat weapons.

Sighing, he set down his book and faced them.

"All right, let's get it over with."

Hominid war cries were bellowed. The knights attacked all at once, and in an instant, Dennagon found himself in the center of a bladed flurry. Swinging his sword around, he clashed against multiple weapons, parrying them to the ground and into the air. Albeit he was only twice the size of a human, his brute force was not enough to defeat their highly coordinated onslaught. Nevertheless, he was one that did not rely on strength to succeed.

A knight leapt onto his back and held a halberd above his cranium. Taking a roll, he crushed the adversary under his weight and threw the body at an incoming swordsman. Another unit tried to throw a spear at his flank, but he slid onto his side to let the projectile fly over him and hit a human behind him. Spinning around, he then swept his sword in bladed and bloody arcs, paving through his enemies in a gory surge. Severed human parts flew everywhere, and red painted the terrain.

The catapult then launched. Dennagon sprung into the air, flapping two wings that batted down a few more men in his way. Heaving his entire bodyweight, he slammed into the flying boulder, catching it before it could collide into the wall. Gyrating like a top, he hurled it back at his opponents. The massive stone rolled across their lines, running them down like insects until its bone-crushing path ended in a collision with the catapult. The launching mechanisms exploded into wood and metal fragments.

As he descended back to the ground, a sword was thrown at him. Blending to the side, he let it skim by his chest. It cut through the air, grazing the ground as it reeled, and hitting his book. The blade penetrated through the cover and out the back, dragging it across the dirt until it was pinned to the wall. The bookmark fell out.

Dennagon growled.

"Oh, that does it."

The humans hurriedly gathered their things, frantically trying to decide whether to retreat or fight. Dennagon bore his fangs and spread his jaws, creating a heated ignition from his esophagus. With a huge grunt, he let out a burst of green-hot flame from his nostrils and mouth, casting hellish heat upon his adversaries. Those in the center of the fire were cooked instantly in their armor. The others, who were perhaps not as lucky, had their metal shells melted in the blaze, and liquid iron streamed through their flesh. The few that survived did not have moment's time to think before fleeing into the night, screaming like little girls.

The leading paladin was left alone. Battered and beaten by too many hits with the draconic sword, he still held his sword high.

"Your gold is mine! MINE!" he roared.

The foolish man dashed in for a final attack. Dennagon pulled his book out of the wall, and with a mighty swing, he swatted the predator. A splat sounded and there was only gore upon the stone barriers. Lifting his tome, he brushed off the remains of his adversary and blew the dust off the bloody pages. As the smashed remains fell, he continued reading.

"The only forms of gold I own are the bars of knowledge, simple human."

Just as he found his lost page, horns blared from within the walls. Reluctantly, he shut his tome again.

"Drakemight calls. This day is over."

To the calling, he flew to the inner city.

———————————

Polyhedrons, all simple in shape, stretched up from the ground for several miles into the sky. It was a vast maze of geometric shapes built of stone, metal and glass, not unlike most medieval constructions. However, there was something oddly advanced in the architecture, something strangely futuristic about how it was designed. After all, it did reach ten times higher than most castles of its era.

Crowds of dragons flew through the aerial streets, draped

in armor and equipped with weapons. Dennagon was amongst them, another creature trying to make his way through the World, trying to find his way home. His armor was identical to all the other sentries that surrounded him in every direction, and he appeared no different than any of the hundreds that inhabited the kingdom. The very atmosphere of the place often sickened him, for he detested his likeness to the rest of his comrades. Nonetheless, it was not his position to question anyone. He didn't even want to talk to them.

Speedily, he found his way through the masses and located a particular dodecahedron that was built into the city. Opening a hatch that lay at its base, he crawled into his domicile and slammed the door shut. Peace and quiet at last.

Inside the ten-sided stone chamber, books were stacked everywhere. From volumes of science to catalogs of mathematics, history, and the languages of many species, they littered his realm. Each of them had been browsed at least once, and he knew it was time to get some more books. However, he rarely had a moment to spare, as he had a life to lead and a war to win. A war that raged across the entire globe.

Stained glass windows lined each of the faces of the chamber, yet all of them were intentionally tarnished with charcoal. He had burnt them long ago because he knew there was nothing to see outside. Only the kingdom that he was unfortunately too familiar with. The charred markings, however, were fading, and perhaps it was time to blacken them once more. Then again, if they stood one more burning, they would probably fracture.

Stepping betwixt piles of books, he reached down through many sloppily organized scrolls and pulled out a crystal ball. Stroking it with his talons, he let streams of energy run through his claws, recharging the magical item with the mana of his mind. It lit up as if given the breath of life.

"What new events have emerged?" he asked.

The crystal ball illuminated even more with every word it spoke.

"The sapiens have advanced. Worldly data is continually receding into nothingness."

Dennagon rolled his eyes. Conjured objects were always so fickle with meaning.

"I said what NEW events have emerged?"

He took a black marble out of his belt. It was a tiny ebony sphere that dripped with liquid just as dark, seething with knowledge embodied in material form. It was as soft and supple as caviar, and he almost felt like consuming it himself. However, he had resisted the thirst for such luxuries for a while. He would not give in now.

Casting it forth, he let the crystal ball devour it in a ring of silver fire. It had been transported to another place far from his home, somewhere it would be out of his sight. The crystal ball read the marble's data and analyzed what he had accomplished that day.

"Your daily collection of data: 8 million liters of information."

Information could be quantified by material essence, and that was what Dennagon sought everyday. The World was frothing with knowledge, and it was his duty to gather as much as he could, just as it was the duty of every other sentry in the collective. Knowledge was not something that could be left in the mines across the planet, for cognition was under threat by the humans that wished to eliminate everything that could facilitate thinking. Why they wanted to do such a thing was really an unknown piece of info in itself, but he pretty much surmised that it was the inherent evil of the hominids that really caused all the ills of existence. Nonetheless, he knew only one thing – he had to know as much as possible before it was too late.

Out of curiosity, he stroked the ball again.

"Who is the day's most efficient sentry?" he asked.

"The day's most efficient sentry is Sentry Dennagon."

As usual. He had taken the role of the best info hunter in the entire collective, and for that he was both despised and loved. The attention he liked, for it often made him feel significant, even amongst dragons that he didn't really care for. It was a wonder that he even cared about comparing himself to others in the first place, but he was aware of precisely why he did want to stay above them. It was for himself. Not for the advancement of his ego, but for his own good. He wanted to make himself proud.

Before his mind could wander, he focused on his mission once again.

"Did anyone hail my wrath?"

The crystal ball let out a beep.

"You have three unheard messages," it stated. "Message one – "

Dennagon grabbed a random book and started searching through the masses of literature at his four feet.

"—sent today at 8:10 and 26 seconds."

Someone else's voice resounded. It was a recorded directive.

"Sentry Dennagon. I bring word from the Archive Lord. A wisdom gathering is commencing later. You should come. For your own good…"

Dennagon touched something very cold on the floor.

"No thank you," he mumbled to himself.

"Message two – sent today at 3:10 and 8 seconds."

The cold substance was ice. Fortunately, it was still solid and he could feel the chilled carcass of a lion underneath. Wrapping his claws around its furry hide, he pulled it out. The second message started playing.

"Are you tired of being a dolt? Then try our new and improved memory spells! Crafted by our most superior magicians, these scrolls are guaranteed to enhance your recollection or your gold pieces back! Approved by the Drakemight council."

"Definitely no thank you," responded Dennagon with a jowl-full of lion meat.

"Message three – sent three minutes ago."

Reclining, he opened up a good book, only to find that it was a good book he already read. Tossing it away, he took another one, as well as another bite out of his lion.

Meanwhile, an ominous heaving breath was emitted from the crystal ball. It bore the desperate tone of a creature near death, which meant that it was probably a prank call.

"I speak for the fate of dragonkind," it declared in a female voice.

He opened another book that he had read before. Knocking it away, he flipped through countless others that were piled up all around. Each one flashed him with an aggravating sense of déjà vu. Theories On The Macrocosm/Microcosm Unity. He read it. The 0th Evolution. He read it. The Anatomy Of Existence, The Theory Of Nothing, The Infinitieth Dimension and Holographix. Read it, read it, read it. All of it.

All the while, the last message played.

"We've not many trices left. The very existence of life may soon end."

Dennagon finished up the last bit of his lion, excluding the rear end of course. With a mouthful of carrion, he grumbled.

"Crystal ball, delete this message."

The crystal ball started to process the request, but as it did, the female voice made a declaration.

"The Lexicon is in peril," it said.

The words walloped Dennagon like a ton of maces. He snapped his neck forth, hurling out the chewed carnage in his jaws. With slaver dripping over his chest he thrust his open claws desperately out to the ball.

"Ignore that command!" he shouted.

The crystal ball did so, and the message resumed. Dennagon, his head perked, listened intently. Nothing else seemed to exist.

"From the edges of the sky, I call to you," stated the unidentified female. "You are all we have left. I impose nothing on you, but please consider our request. The World is in your talons, Dennagon."

Silence. There was no more. He seized the ball and started wringing it madly.

"That's it?! That's all?!"

"Affirmative," it replied.

"Trace that call! Where did it come from?!"

Another beep. The mana flowed through the crystal structure, letting it reach out to the landscapes of the planet and find the traces of magic left by all those who used sorcery on the World. It streamed across the globe, but marked only a broken trail left by the broken creature that called upon it not long ago. That trail was displayed within the shimmering orb.

Dennagon examined it. It was quite a distance from his locale, about a hundred miles away near the Cadin Dunes. "From the edges of the sky" she said, so she must have been high above the surface. He could be there in a little over forty minutes at best. Nonetheless, his capability of arriving there did not account for an important question indeed – Should he go there?

His frozen thoughts suddenly melted as the crystal ball let out a ringing sound. Snatching it, he put it to his ear. A deep, ominous voice spoke to him.

"Your lord summons you. Meet him in an hour," it demanded.

"Who is this?"

"Your lord himself."

A deep roar accompanied the fading vocalization as it

disconnected. Dennagon set the crystal ball down and touched the temples of his cranium. There would be no way to reach both the Cadin Dunes and the Archive within the span of sixty minutes, and there was no defying the lord to which his decree was ultimately bound. Then again, he was never known as one who followed any beckoning.

Alas, he came to a conclusion, for there was no time to falter with decisions. Knocking piles of books out of his way, he opened the hatch and took to the air. Gliding through the dusk atmosphere, he soared toward the city walls, outside of Drakemight and to the unknown. Mystery lured him with every passing breeze.

Crystalline clouds separated the murky stratosphere of the desert from the orange and purple bands of the celestial zenith. Rain had not fallen upon the Cadin Dunes in well over a thousand years, yet these clouds did not signify that there was any moisture to come. No, they were there merely to linger as emblems of false hope, teasing the inhabitants of the long-forgotten death fields with the promise of water. All the while, the glass ozone layer laughed at them above the silver linings of the wispy winds, rolling the airborne perspiration about; but never letting it go. Glumly, it frowned, a murky jester, under the descending sun enshrouded in gloom. It allowed none to pass its damning gaze.

That was not to say that no one ever approached. Draconic wings soon pushed the foggy clouds away, rising from the scorched lands below. Dennagon, sentry of the collective, tore through the floating condensation, his tail lashing about like a fishy fin and his scales speckled shiny by the drops of water they gathered on the way. He was a hundred miles from his homeland, and a thousand miles above the ground, which would make him very late for his commanded meeting.

There had better have been something good there, or someone would pay the price and face his wrath.

"Is anyone out there?" he echoed across the atmosphere. "Who here hath summoned my presence and drove me from my duties?"

Some of the gaseous precipitation began to churn. It looked almost as if a creature were trying to sneak up on him. He pretended not to notice.

"Who? Is there anyone out there?"

Finally, the bubbling patch of vapor tumbled before him. Bursting out from underneath, a female drake emerged, her scales as blue as the sky would be at noon, and her body as lithe as it was sinewy. She bore no wings, as her subspecies naturally did not, yet she loomed amidst the sky and stood upon the clouds as if they were ground. Even as her body was damaged by the gashes of battle, her face was still as pristine and innocent as a gem, untainted by her disheveled and unkempt appearance. But he knew better than to judge a book by its cover. There was certainly some sorcery involved, some form of energy behind those seemingly weary eyes that had just witnessed vast streams of death. Or, at least there was another beast in the vicinity.

"Yea," she replied almost sarcastically.

"What is thy name?"

"I am Lyconel. Lyconel the azure drake."

Dennagon furrowed his brow, searching his memory.

"Lyconel. That sounds familiar…"

"I am known here and there, maybe everywhere. Dennagon."

"And how do you know me?"

"Because we share one thing in common. We both seek the same entity."

Dennagon snorted green fire from his nostrils. He wasn't going to be led in a roundabout riddle.

"I am a sentry of Drakemight. I will not be hassled with paradoxes or lengthy doctrines of poetic nature. You will tell me what your purpose is in speaking, lest I cast you forth into the gorges of doom whereupon my emerald fires shall rip past your scaly hide and smite you with great force upon the desiccated dunes down under. Thence shall your corpse remain, a battered, broken ruin upon the wretched earth from whence you were spawned."

Lyconel smirked.

"You guard knowledge?" she asked.

"I live only for that mission, yes."

"But I'll bet that's not what you really want."

He couldn't see where this was going.

"You desire, sentry, as I do, the one thing that can never be found. It is the possessor of all data in the universe, the source of everything that can be known. You are aware of what I speak."

Now he could. However, he was unmoved.

"Of course," he bluntly snapped. "But such an entity doesn't exist beyond the mind. It is but a fancy in a million, an illusory toy for the cerebrum."

"Then why do you still dream of it every night? Why don't you attend the wisdom gatherings with the other dragons in the Archive? How come you never want to remember anything the Archive tells you, and how come you hate Drakemight with all your ardor?"

Her presuppositions were truthful, and he did not comprehend how she could have understood. Somehow, he suspected that she already knew the answers to her rhetoric.

"It is all for this one unattainable entity," she continued.

Dennagon could not deny the inevitable. There was no escaping his subconscious, what with its desires hidden from his waking mind.

"The Lexicon."

The words came out almost mechanically, as if some force had driven him to utter the truth in all its light.

"It exists, Dennagon. It is your choice whether or not you wish to find it. Follow me or stay with your collective."

With that, Lyconel turned about. Trudging toward the sun in the horizon, she slowly walked away, shrinking with every step. She was not turning back, not in space and not in time.

Dennagon watched, his expression almost numbed by the unbelievable experience he had endured. There were so many questions he wanted to ask, but there was no time to resolve them. If he followed, perhaps she would put a spell on him. If he did not, he might forsake his very freedom from his already forsaken life.

Then, a glint of the sunlight on her scales flashed through the stratosphere, glimmering upon the glass ozone until it struck upon his eye. The blue light immersed him with memories of something he had learned long ago. Recollection surged through his mind, granting him that which he needed at the moment – certainty. As the engrams poured through his brain, he knew exactly what to do, for he now knew who he was really talking to.

"Wait," he said composedly.

She did. A hopeful expression formed on her face. However, it just as quickly began to recede as she saw Dennagon reach for his hilt.

"Now I remember you."

In an instant, the scabbard stretched out into an unsheathed blade that whirled around as an incoming overhead slash was delivered. Lyconel lunged forward, her claws digging into the vapor as the sword narrowly missed her from behind. Both warriors took combative posture.

"But we've never met before!" she proposed.

"The Archive informed me of your activities. You once tried to decimate Drakemight City."

"You don't understand."

"I don't need to. All I need is knowledge."

Charging forth, he took another swing at her, his two tons of muscle wildly hurling the blade. Lyconel drew her mace and clashed just before the metal could meet her bone. Feverishly, they exchanged a furious series of attacks and parries, every blow as thundering as it was devastating. Metal flew across the air, along with occasional punches, kicks and chops. The flurry of assaults was equaled by the number of blocks, but only Dennagon was truly gaining the advantage of the offensive. Lyconel squeezed in what hits she could, hoping that her enemy would tire out. Unfortunately for her, he seemed almost limitless in endurance.

Finally, she lost her concentration. In a disoriented moment, her opponent's sword sliced her across the abdomen, creating a gash of blood as silver as liquid metal. She bore her fangs in pain, but did not give her enemy the pleasure of her scream.

"Not bad," she commented.

"You're right."

He wailed a frenzy of claw slashes at her.

"It's excellent," finished Dennagon.

As he came at her, she crouched. Sliding along the gaseous ice of the clouds, she slipped underneath him and threw a tail sweep. The small spikes at the tip of her tail whipped him in the back of the cranium, jarring him to the ground. He fell onto his side. Growling, he pushed himself up and gave her a menacing snarl.

"Really?" Lyconel inquired.

Dennagon rushed in again. Lyconel, cocky at her quelling of his arrogance, flung her mace at his chest, arcing it downward so that it covered enough area to prevent him from jumping over it. However, as it came, he torqued in the air, spinning to her side in a way that almost defied the laws of physics. Before she could let out a confused grunt, his fist rammed into her face, and she was floored onto the cloudy ground. Dizzily, she wavered in her pose.

At this point, Dennagon had had enough. Reaching for his belt, he pulled out something he used often to slay pesky beasts, a nice little package he kept for efficiency and fun. It was a spellbook, worn and torn at its edges, but still bound together by its unwavering metal book spine. Flipping open the cover, he browsed its pages and stopped at several that he had bookmarked.

"All the universe's hellish wonders," he read with the ire of a draconic wizard, "give me the strength of mighty thunder!"

A lightning bolt surged from his palm, ripping across the stratosphere like a liquid stream of electric current. It flowed to his adversary in graceful rage, knocking her in the chest as if to steal the air straight from her lungs. Lyconel collapsed. He flipped a page.

"In the lighted cosmic halls, lend me the craze of azure fireballs!"

Comets as blue as the ocean burned the air, blasting their target, whose equally sapphire torso became even further scarred in the meteor shower. Dennagon turned to the last of his favorite pages.

"Strongly does the World ensnare upon its grounds the dreaded air!"

A mental storm of wind exploded from his mind, unleashing a heavy torrent. The gust struck Lyconel like ten tons of metal, heaving her body off its stance. Cast in the violent tempest, she tumbled around to the very edges of the cloud. Desperately, she caught onto the rim, the silver lining, before she could plummet to the dunes a thousand miles down.

Dennagon closed his tome of sorcery and stepped up to his clinging enemy. Holding the sword high above his head, he was ready to kill her.

"It'll be quite a fall," said he, "especially when you don't have wings."

"I got up here just fine without them."

He delivered a final slash to her face. Just as the blade neared her claws, she let go, plunging to the surface below. It was almost as if she planned to release herself, yet it did not seem as though she intended to die. As she fell, her last words to him faded.

"The World is what you make of it…"

Dennagon watched as she shrunk in the distance. He wanted to pursue her and finish her off, but decided that it was best to save his energy. After all, she was obviously a lunatic, right? Who would drive themselves off a cloud and expect to live, save for an imbecile who was willing to sacrifice his existence for the whimsical indulgence of a dream unattained? The very thought was ridiculous, and it perturbed him even greater that his paranoia fancied she might survive. He tried to relinquish the thought, and surrender all nonsensical worries. He wasn't afraid of phantasms as a whelp and he certainly would not concede to fear now.

Alas, she vanished completely as a vapor stream passed before his vision. He had other duties to attend. Judging by the position of the sun, he could tell that it was precisely 18:29, which marked the eve of a thirty-hour day. He had spent ten minutes here, ten minutes of his life wasted. Even worse off, he was late in finishing those books he intended to read later in the day. But even worse -- he was late for his meeting with the Archive Lord.

"Crud," he thought to himself.

Without another second wasted, he darted into the distance, wings flapping with urgency. There was not a moment to spare, for as he flew, his master waited for his arrival. He could almost feel the anger building, the impatience tearing through the fabric of the World as if the dragon king's decree were all that mattered in reality. He just hoped it wasn't too late. For what hope was worth…

CHAPTER 2

The Archive rested in the center of Drakemight, for it was the most important structure of the kingdom. It was a grand sphere of metal lined by stone that appeared strangely organic in structure, as it winded around iron chunks like nerves of rocky substance. Every dragon collected data for the purpose of storing it in this informational core, yet few often pondered why it appeared so odd. No one in the medieval realm had ever experienced such erratic architecture, not even the artists that manifested their surreal imagery in the forms of paintings and sculptures. Then again, not everyone who questioned the dragon lord's wisdom ever made it very far. He had secrets to keep, and he had a purpose in doing so. Thus, the Archive's creation remained a mystery that was both beautiful and disturbing at the same time. Its walls were a marvel to look at, encompassing the craft of the ancient world and the craft of something yet unseen. Something almost...cybernetic...

Inside the cognitive castle, the sacred Archive, millions upon millions of circular dishes floated throughout a gargantuan area that rivaled the cosmos in spaciousness. Each one contained a gooey, soft, black orb submerged in liquid crystal fluid that sparkled like sugary tar and swirled with countless megabytes of data – the speed of light, the Planck constant, the Schrodinger Wave Equation, the radius of a carbon atom, the structure of organic molecules – each bit of wisdom as important as the next. They were the embodiments of information transformed from the raw data essence that lined the World's lands and air, to the core of the planet and beyond, collected by the dragons that lived to support the kingdom. The orbs all looked like giant caviar, dripping with dark fluids from their supple surfaces as if to contain embryos and cerebral nutrition within shelled walls of savory, salty substance. And assuredly, they were just as tasty as they appeared. The dragon lord promised so, and so they would be.

Dragon sentries amassed in the hundreds, returning from a hard day's work. Black orbs magically appeared in empty dishes, sent via conjury from domiciles within the city. Those that didn't feel like expelling mana just physically dropped off their daily collections by coming there themselves. Afterwards, elders tended to each of the newly added inventory, careful with each and every morsel of information that was dropped off. Nothing could be wasted, for although they had the data in their possession now, the knowledge was still not safe. Not until it was consumed.

Amongst the throngs, Dennagon flew, once again feeling sick at having to remain with all of his low-life colleagues. What made him even sicker, however, was the thought that he was now half an hour off schedule from his appointed time to encounter the master that endowed him life in the first place. Passing through the lanes of floating dishes, he hurriedly bustled through the crowd, trying not to knock anything over as he moved. His reputation was already falling apart as it was.

As he moved, his eyes sometimes wandered to the dark,

wet spheres that were spread throughout the realm. At the sights, his mouth watered and his tongue slithered, longing for the flavor of knowledge, thirsty for the sanguine sapidity of information. When he was younger and had just taken up the art of the sword, he used to sample the black orbs that the collective gave him. Indeed, they tasted richer than the most concentrated vanilla flowers on the planet. Their savor must have become embossed in his unconscious like the scars on his scales, leading his pupils to the ebony caviar like magnets to metal.

With great strength, he wrenched his mind away from them. He knew they tasted like the finest bloody meat whilst sending surges of orgasmic information to one's head. He knew they were accepted by the majority as the only way to salvage the World's intelligence and to achieve success. Nonetheless, he had to stop longing for them. Deep in his thoughts, he was aware that there was something not quite right about them, and he would not let himself resort to indulgence before figuring out what that was. For many years now, he had been starving, living off frozen carrion hunted in second-rate forests, and it would probably be many more years until he could again quench his desire. He would not stray from his path, even if it was agonizing.

Something jarred him. Another draconic sentry bumped him in the shoulder, nearly pushing him into a dish. At first, he thought it was accidental, but then he saw who it was.

"How's it going, Dennagon?" asked Thargon sarcastically.

Dennagon cast a stone-cold glance at his mocking "comrade". Several more draconic sentries surrounded him, glaring at him with disgust. Their words, like poison, shot at him.

"Still on a diet?"

"Wow, you look like you've lost a lot of weight."

"From your reduced brain size."

They enjoyed a good laugh, clasping their talons around each other's shoulders in grouped conformist ardor.

"I take it you didn't get my message," continued Thargon.

"Of course I received it. Why do you think I didn't come to the wisdom gathering?"

"Heh, heh. You're at a loss, my friend. Knowledge is power, and power is what matters in life. Right?"

"You're one to speak. Especially when I collect more knowledge in a day than you can collect in a lifetime."

Everyone stopped laughing. More sentries gathered, all drawing their weapons in insulted demeanor. Thargon drew a halberd.

"It's a small World. We'll find you eventually."

"Why find me? I'm already here."

Dennagon drew his own sword.

"If you want to kill me, give me your best shot," he challenged.

The brutish comportment of his antagonistic colleagues lessened at the sight of his weapon. Attempting to maintain their masculinity, they shirked, hiding their cowardice behind euphemistic visages. Thargon spit out reptilian slaver.

"You might be the best sentry now," he said. "But persistence wears away any challenge. In time, when we have enough knowledge, we will breeze through this globe like gods amongst gods. You will remain a pawn, shadowed in nothingness until eternity croaks. Then, we'll see who has the last laugh, my friend."

With that, they sheathed their weapons and flew off. Thargon snatched an orb from a dish and gladly licked it up, letting its rich juices spill over his tongue. The fluids seethed into his abdomen, coursing through his veins and nerves as he drank. Every morsel of its information gradually appeared in his eyes as flashing glints of light surrounded by dark haloes whilst the data was assimilated into the very fabric of his brain. Physical laws, astronomical constants and chronological facts filled his consciousness. His smirk gleamed in Dennagon's eyes in an attempt to swarm him with jealousy, an attempt that was fueled by intense jealousy in itself. Dennagon, however, cared little for the thoughts of such insignificant beings. He knew the future did not belong to them, for if there was anything that was certain in the World, it was that he created his own future. Thence, he moved on.

As he reached the top of the environment, he neared a colossal throne that stood at the apex of all. Currents of illumined magic surrounded it, flowing through the spacious area down to the very nadir of the Archive itself so that they could connect to every dragon and orb in the place. This was the lair of his master, the point at which wrath would most likely wrench him for his tardiness. The sorcery surrounding the air there was extreme, emanating from the mind of the one creature that every serpent owed its life to. Guilt and anguish further imbued Dennagon's heart as he approached.

Straightening his battle gear, he floated before it. The magic gushed past him, but he could not detect any emotions in the conjured tides. The dragon king's mind was too shielded from the minds of others, and no one ever knew what he was thinking. Some even rumored that the king had no emotions, which was not that ludicrous of a proposition. Dennagon himself had never seen him display any sentiments, and it was his wish that no rage would swarm over him today.

"What do you ask of me my lord?" he addressed in composed nervousness.

The throne lit up with dark flames. Dark flames that seemed to have been in existence forever. A silhouette formed around them, cloaked in a shadow eternal, until alas, it could be understood that the unseen shadow itself was the final form of the dragon lord. It flared out its blackened blazes, spiraling above its throne in an omnipotent dance of conflagrations that echoed the mystery of a thousand riddles. It was somewhat glorious, yet its artfulness did not negate its fearsome nature. When it was done, the silhouette settled at its own beckoning, sitting upon its throne so potently. So prominently.

Drekkenoth almighty waited a few seconds before allowing his voice to be heard. He looked at the wristwatch that was strapped onto his forearm, the one timepiece that no one else was allowed to look at. Whether or not it told the time of day Dennagon did not know, but there was one thing he did understand for certain – Drekkenoth was aware at all times of almost everything.

"What I always have, Sentry Dennagon," said he. "The World is being ravaged, and the sapiens roam the lands, burning the earthen knowledge in their hominid horror. Soon, there will be nothing left of the globe's wisdom, and ignorance shall reign supreme. It is our quest to gather all that remains of the planet's knowledge before man can destroy it."

Arxinor and Gorgash flew by his sides like reptilian angels designed to guard their lord. Dennagon straightened a final plate that was still crooked.

"With all due respect," he politely stated, "you have not answered my question."

Drekkenoth twisted his wrist as quickly as a machine. Amid his claws, colored flames emerged, forming from a rainbow of fire the three-dimensional image of the World in its entirety.

"I hath called upon you because you are our greatest warrior. Each day, you collect more data than any other sentry."

"Of this I am aware," replied Dennagon humbly.

"Then why do you not join us in the wisdom gatherings?

We need as many minds as we can to store all the World's information. The information that may no longer exist after the sapiens raze the planet."

A talon of dark fire motioned toward a group of dragons in the distance. They gathered around the black orb dishes, slurping the cognitive rations and bantering as if intoxicated by ale. Like idiots they were, enjoying themselves far too much when they had far too little.

"I don't think I am wise enough to hold the insight of the Archive's cells…"

Drekkenoth was not pleased with the answer, but his neutral expression remained, red eyes gleaming behind a veil of bleak blazes.

"Spare me the false modesty. Knowledge in itself is not permanently saved until it is wired into the brain of a dragon. Dragons are the only species capable of attaining enlightenment, for we've reserved ourselves from rapacity for eons. Will you let those eons go to waste?" Drekkenoth leaned forth. "Will you let Shevinoth's will die as he died many ages ago?"

Dennagon hated rhetorical questions, especially when they did not address the true issue at talon. Drekkenoth ranted on, yet his voice commanded a respect that shielded its rambling attribute from consciousness.

"The future must be heeded. There is not much time left in this World. Can you feel the essence in the air, the unchanging fate of the World that shall draw it to its inescapable end? The future must be heeded, for the rise of Totality is coming. It will not be long before all living things are eliminated."

Totality. It was one of the most powerful words that could be used, aside from profanities and threats. It meant the merging of the World into a single unification that would ruin all differentiation. If time were to cease, so would life, and thus, everything would fall into an eternal darkness. Albeit it was often viewed as an omega far, far in the future, Dennagon knew that it was his responsibility as well as the responsibility of all beings to stop it. And the best time to do that was now.

"Let's meet the sapiens head-on," he declared.

Arxinor and Gorgash exchanged sharp glances.

"Wreck them before they can strike," continued the highest-ranking sentry. "The humans are infatuated with trinkets of gold and gems and whatnot, for avarice guides their every flaw. They should not be difficult to destroy. In fact, I believe they have already destroyed themselves. Consider their history of warfare and torture, how they lost everything to their own havoc. But consider what matters most – The future is ours only if we take control of the present."

For a moment, there was an ominous silence. In that foolish instant, Dennagon thought he had impressed the lord with his portrayed zealousness. Nevertheless, that thought died as soon as Drekkenoth rose, a threatening snarl rumbling from his jaws.

"Have YOU, Sentry Dennagon, ever faced a sapien?"

Dennagon shook his head, petrified.

"They have retained the avarice and alignment of the humans, but are not at all human anymore. Far more powerful are their souls. Should we attack, they will bring us to death as the waves bring shored stones to the ocean. Speak you to me about the future? I am an eternal ancient. I have had many, many futures. How can you advise me of what is to come when you have sampled nothing of the past?"

It was the first time he had ever heard Drekkenoth speak in such a way, yet the perfunctory inflection of his voice still did not change. Nor did his faceless visage appear to display any emotion still. It was strange to hear such words uttered without any hint of ire.

"Perhaps if you had spent more time assimilating information, you would have known that already. Be gone."

With those words, Dennagon immediately about-faced. Descending back down to the depths, he floated past the rows of dishes, staid in his stride. Drekkenoth cast not another glance at him as he left, but instead, turned those flared red eyes forward to stare into nothingness. The dragon lord was meditating again, and it was best to leave as quickly as possible as not to disturb his concentration. Not that anyone could tap into such an incredible consciousness anyway.

Alas, the throne was far above, and Dennagon tried to find his way to the exit again. As he made his way through, he passed the dragon sentry congregation that loomed in the distance like a blur of scales. They ceased their incessant persiflage as he moved by, only to hurtle jeers at his ascetic disposition. With mouthfuls of blackened orbs, they chortled, liquid ebony crystal bubbling from their fangs to highlight the darkness that lined their forms. Their hollers blended into one another, tripping over one another's angst whilst meaningless words spilt from their throats. They were vile, unlike dragons of the past. Unlike the dragons that gave dragons their good name.

Dennagon ignored them, for words were as immaterial as dreams. Insignificant they were, for they mirrored the semblance of man in servile baseness complete. They were already dead, even though their bodies still moved and their hearts still pumped. Dead, even though their brains processed occasional "thoughts". They didn't matter in the slightest, their somas as phantasms piffle in the wind.

Regardless, they were still laughing at him. They remained flying, moving and carrying weapons with the potential to kill him. They could probably kill him if there were enough of them attacking at once, and would perchance torture him if they ever had the chance. To be tortured by one of them…The very thought aggravated him to the core. He couldn't bear it.

"SLASH THY TONGUES, YOU WRETCHED WURMS!" he shouted with a fist in the air. "THOU SHALT BE TRAMPLED BY THE HOOVES OF EVOLUTION WHEN THE TIME COMES!"

His words were as meaningless to them as theirs to him.

"WHEN THE TIME COMES!"

Green fire spilling from his jowls, he snapped around and continued on his path. A black orb hit him in the back on his way out, flung by one of his colleagues.

Night had taken one side of the World. Under the plasmatic eyes of the stars, the kingdom was at rest, serene under the stellar lights that were beaconed throughout the celestial sea. The eve still bore a tint of royal blue in its fabric as if to mirror the ocean, or as if the ocean had mirrored it to bring utter symmetry to the planet. Yet, even as water bore its own inherent sapphire tint, it had islands embedded upon its vistas to break the smooth uniformity that existed not in the universe. For the universe, strangely, did not have any planets this night or any night for that matter, nor any Moon to accompany the glow of the stars or the meager lights of the human kingdom Aurahelm that shone in the far, far horizon. It didn't really need it, though, for no one ever came out at night anyway.

At peace inside his dodecahedron, Dennagon rested, upon piles of books mounted like a reptilian sleeping beauty. The tomes were his life, his food, his water, and his bed. They were his catalogs of dreams, dreamed by others, and now, upon them he created dreams of his own. The evening lulled him with the greatest song of all – silence – and he slept as deeply as a dead squid at the bottom of the sea. His fantasies streamed through his eyes, and his eyes streamed through his fantasies.

Beyond his own pupils and waking mind, he was in his own little world. Here, the Moon laid as lucid as a stained glass window, clear as an astronomical orb of silver. It floated in the middle of nothing, in vacuum space unbound by gravity and any directional coordinates. Hanging in no particular place or time, it rotated slowly, taking its sweet moments for every turn. Was it revolving around anything? Its spectator could not see anything else, but it certainly was revolving around something. Something invisible. Truly, this was the realm of nowhere.

In the voids, there suddenly appeared an entity that flew around the Moon. It was a serpent of silvery scales that was armored to the bone, but was still as fragile as an icicle on a winter twig. In its clutches, it held a hook-ended broadsword that resembled a demon's head with two horns to the flanks protruding and a snout that was the blade descending. Against the lunar light, the dragon gleamed, reflecting in its form the visage of the silver orb whilst the silver orb reflected it as well, creating an endless sequence of images that stretched on into infinity. The sight was glorious, but ominous as well.

Dennagon, all the while, was merely an observer in his dream. He had seen this dragon many times before, and knew his name well. Everyone knew Mighty Shevinoth, first king of the dragons. It was Shevinoth that frequently dominated his thoughts and dwelled in his dreams, a soul of fantasies built that followed him like a shadow in waking and sleeping. Of course, to him, this was as real as anything, for as he lay in slumber, he was neither a warrior nor a god. He was just a watcher.

Shevinoth approached the silver Moon surface, sailing through space's airless, crushing environment. Caution accompanied him with every inch he mobilized. After surveying thoroughly the area, he landed upon the shimmering, polished lunar ground and brandished his sword high above his head. A sparkling coruscation emitted from its hooked tip, casting a dim, but powerful light into the dark surroundings as if to notify all who lived that this was to be a remembered moment. Then, a potent strike fell upon the metallic landscape, digging his blade far into the subsurface. The sharp edge clawed its way round and round, creating a jagged circle amid the floor. Craters bubbled out of every cut, dissolving into nothingness just as quickly, until finally, the beginning of the circle met its end. An orifice was torn into the Moon, and inside, there was a hollow.

The one who watched hoped that the lunar-bound warrior would make it inside. He mentally cheered on for Shevinoth the mighty to rush inside to the very core of the Worldly satellite so that he could find what was in there. His cheers echoed into his subconscious, repeating themselves as many times as they could until fading ardor washed them away. For as Shevinoth stood, nothing happened. Not a single claw budged to reach into the orifice, nor did any talons shift to sample what was inside. The once dragon king simply remained, an image of glory shackled in stasis.

Dennagon pondered. Shevinoth turned as if to face him, the omnipotent master of the dream.

"What is art?" inquired Shevinoth.

No answer.

"There is nothing more beautiful than the self."

With that, an abrupt blast exploded out of the orifice. Yellow fire and light ringed around the silver dragon's figure, tearing away his flesh. Strips of carrion flew from whence Shevinoth stood, ashen charcoal scales flinging into the ceaseless depths of space. All that was left was his skeletal form, burning in hellish wonder as if to beg the question, "why" in its disintegrating vapors. Alas, a horrid shriek ripped even the soundless vacuum of the voids and the body fell to the lunar core in death combusted.

Dennagon burst into waking consciousness, his sweeping talon knocking a stack of books into a wall. Sweat dripped from beneath his reptilian dermal layer, coating him in a layer of saline gloss. However, even as his body lay in shock, his breaths were steady and contained, as was the mind that kept perfect control over his actions. He had never been shaken by this nightmare before, and he certainly would not be shaken now. Excellence was constant, not contained in a singular act.

"Steady," he reassured himself.

Reassurance? How pitiful. If he were really secure, he thought, he would not need to constantly reinforce his composure. He should really stop talking to himself in his head, as well. It certainly wasn't helping.

Wiping the sweat off his head, he took a moment to reassess his thoughts. Reflecting on his nightmare, he had the same cognitions he had always had after experiencing it – curiosity, wonder, slight anger, and some questions he always wished he could ask great Shevinoth had he not been slain over a thousand years ago. There was definitely a meaning to his fantasy, as there was a meaning to everything in life. Many a time he had laid awake just like this when he should be sleeping, trying to figure it all out. After all this time, nonetheless, he had not come to a single conclusion.

Sleep. He really needed it. Or did he? Often, he thought about the necessity of rest in the functionality of dragons. Humans needed to sleep, for they were weak, but why did the World's knowledge pools always state that dragons needed exactly 4 hours of dormancy every thirty hour day and two hours every ten hour day? There seemed to be no premise for such a rule, no absolute link in the chain of causality. Yet, he did admit that he usually felt tired after each day and he did need to rejuvenate himself. Perhaps that was his subconscious' way of telling him that he needed to resolve his problems.

One problem at the moment was that if he did not rest in the next twenty minutes, he probably would not have enough time to replenish his efficiency by the dawn of the next day. It was 1:28 in the morn, so he only had a little more than two hours and thirty minutes to finish his nap. There was no time to indulge in frivolous ponderings when he should be readying himself. Then again, he had been having insomnia much more often as of late, since his recurring dream had been popping up more frequently. It wasn't really affecting his combative habits that significantly, and his "comrades" were complete idiots anyway, so he saw no purpose in having to slip back into unconsciousness. After all, why couldn't insomnia be a catalyst for exploration?

Deep into the mossy, rock-speckled plains beyond the Drakemight walls, Dennagon strolled. A lone dragon on an equally lonely landscape, he meandered, looking to the crystal clear celestial sea above. Stars flickered, as tranquil as the night whilst the rest of the draconic collective remained immersed in slumber. He found his own peace alone in the plains, but even harmony could be beleaguered by discord. As contradictory as it was, the paradox existed in his mind, manifested in his perturbation.

His eyes scanned the darkness overhead. It was well into the night, and at this point, the sun was farthest from his present locale. He liked the sensation of obscurity, for it allowed him to be free of ideas that would otherwise cloud his consciousness. Everything was lucid now without any light but those of the lonely stellar beacons. Some often claimed that there were places in the World at which two suns rose at either horizon and could usurp the lands in eternal daylight, but he didn't really buy into those tales. He had traveled the planet far and wide, and he had never seen such solar duality. Nothing would take his darkness from him, for now, he had some special place to which he needed to traverse.

Luckily, he had brought his favorite book with him as he always did on these existential nights. Superstition never sat well with him, as assumption was always an imbecile's best friend, but he always felt comfortable carrying it as a – dare he admit it – good luck charm. The object itself was not that which granted him good fortune, but rather its inner story. Albeit the tome's title had been scraped off by a human ballista long ago, the tale inside always pulled him through good and bad times. It was almost like a friend in the field of war, something he never truly had. Strangely, though, it had been a while since he read it. Did he even remember the story?

Stumbling upon a stone shaped like a spike, he knew he had reached his destination. Carefully, he looked around to make certain no one was watching. Scenting the air with his outstretched tongue and his fire-breathing nostrils, he detected nothing but the cool smell of flower pollen. When he was certain no one was spying, he moved toward a circular group of stones that surrounded a bumpy patch of earth. Driving his claws into the mud, he burrowed, casting away the upper layers of the ground. Clandestine, he hissed.

How many nights had he come out here? How many trices did he waste on fantasies so trivial? Far too many, no doubt. He couldn't help it. Strangeness always lured him, just like his collection of curiosities lured him to this spot. As a magnet drawn to metal, he was drawn to what lay underneath his digging talons so ardently that he would even risk getting caught outside the kingdom barricades in the middle of the eve. The attraction was spellbinding, and even with his sorcerer's capabilities, he could not resist.

Finally, Dennagon's pupils caught a dull white object embedded in the medieval dirt. Meticulously, he brushed away the surrounding mud, unearthing the first part of his collection of oddities. Like a prize, he pulled it out of the ground, still speckled with bits of moss, algae and underground worms. From the sockets in its calcium-encrusted exterior, maggots wriggled out, falling to the grass at his feet whilst he cautiously blew off the rest of the debris. When he was finished, he beheld its true figure. A large, 15-foot reptilian fossil.

"Wonderful."

Burrowing even deeper, he dredged up several more bones. A few were of rib cages and shoulder blades, others were of spinal cords and tails, and the last few were of arms, legs and claws. As best he could, he fit them together, locking joints like puzzle pieces according to the general draconic anatomy he had studied in many of his tomes. Ischiums connected to iliums and pubises, some of which were birdlike and others which were lizard-like. Prehistory manifested as quickly as he reconstructed the bony frameworks, opening a window to an unknown past. The completed skeletons took the shapes of nothing he had ever hunted.

Dead dragons? Impossible. Dragons, although highly varied in bone structure, limbs, wings, scale color and even head count, could not conceivably have such bizarre frames. No one he had ever met had as enormous a skull as one of the upright-standing skeletons he had in his fossil trove. No one had a neck as long as one of the giant quadrupeds he had in storage. Certainly, there was no warrior alive that was as specialized for aquatic life as the eccentric four-finned reptile skeleton he found a few years ago.

The possibilities were limitless. Considering that sorcery could summon up any potential beast, any reasonable being would just assume that these were just the remnants of conjury left from a war long ago. In fact, he would have complied to such an interpretation had it not been for other items he had discovered. Excavating to the farthest reaches of his private hidey-hole, he sought the last anomaly he had gathered in his many voyages. A metallic glint shone in the dust as he scraped the ground away. At first glance, it would have looked like a helmet, but as he exposed it further, it took the shape of something quite alien. Circuits lined its substance from its outer shell down to its inner joints and wires. It was like a living beast of nerves, veins and bones, except that its flesh and parts were built of pure steel. The parts were all over the place underground, for he had spent many a year collecting them from the bleakest places of the World. Yet, the more he looked at them, the less they seemed like they had anything to do with his World.

Gradually, he began to reconstruct the mechanized fragments just like he had reassembled the bony skeletons. The robotic joints fit together much more easily than the calcium ones, as if they had been perfectly constructed to be redesigned. Metal turbines locked into cybernetic gears. Wire jacks fit precisely into plugs. Everything seemed to have an exact purpose, and there were no vestigial parts that were prevalent in the constantly evolving biological organisms he knew. At the same time, it was extraordinarily complex, for no matter how long he focused his vision, he could never make out the extent to which its inner cables decreased in size. The finished piece was a creature of metal and circuits, dented at its edges, but whole nonetheless. Wholly mind-boggling.

Dennagon had less of an idea of what to make of the weird

machines than he did of the prehistoric bones. They were the primary reason why he came here, for his mind never relinquished an unanswered question. Unfortunately, he could not even think of one possibility that could account for the existence of such incredibly advanced machinery. Even the highest level magicians did not have the capability of creating anything of this magnitude, let alone leave it for other creatures to find.

If only Drekkenoth had all the answers. The dragon lord often claimed that only the limitless knowledge of the World could grant one with absolute wisdom, which was one of Dennagon's motivations in his continuing search for information. Still, even Drekkenoth himself was not omniscient, otherwise he would not have rallied armies in search of all secular data. Hence, there was no way to figure out where the fossilized ruins came from, if anywhere at all. It kind of made him wonder about causality and logic. It forced him to consider the potential for induction and mathematics to be flawed. But most of all, it made him think about… The Lexicon.

The Lexicon was the one thing that lay on his consciousness more than anything else. If only he could touch upon it for just a moment, to experience what it was like to be all-knowing and totally wise. How far would he be able to see, and what would he be able to understand? To have the mind of god; it was the most magnificent dream of all. The rationale of his brain told him that it wasn't real, that it couldn't be found, but the very thought of it elicited a blissful emotion in his heart. He didn't want to let it go.

But he had to.

A sudden tremor rocked the ground to its very bedrock. The prehistoric fossils toppled and the robotic skeletons began to melt. At first, he thought it was an ordinary earthquake that happened every so often around the World, but a blinding flash stung his eyes the instant it appeared. He clutched his head in pain.

"Aaahhh!" he roared.

Heat gusted all over his body, and he knew this was no ordinary quake. Prying his own claws off his eyes, he forced himself to espy the distance, where a massive ball of fire had engulfed a large portion of the wall. An army of magicians would have been needed to create such an explosion, and it was likely that there was an army of knights to accompany them. A battle had initiated, one that sparked more grandiosely than any he had ever fought. He couldn't believe what he was seeing.

But it didn't stop there. The conflagration boiled up from the ground like the expanding sac of a red-warm embryo. Growing upwards in the form of a mushrooming cloud, it scarred the sky as it spread out to the flanks, ripping a gargantuan crater in the ground and ozone. More radioactive emissions burst out from its center, blowing Dennagon right off his feet and onto his back. In a flurry of dust and atomic hellfire, he tumbled back behind a rock. Sickly, he coughed.

"What the blazes was that?!" he blurted.

The entire night sky lit up as if it were day. Now, he was beginning to believe those tales of two suns, but to his misfortune, that sun seemed to have fallen right to the earth. After several seconds, the illumination faded, and the stars began to take the sky again amid a stormy holler of screaming winds. The heat began to lessen as did the roar of the detonation far off. A rain of boulders fell upon the plains like a shower, riddling the terrain with even more shudders from the raging havoc. For a moment, everything was quiet once more.

Dennagon waited for the radioactive winds to stop. He then poked his head out from behind the rock and peered at the cloud of wreckage and dust that engulfed the portion of the wall at which the blast had occurred. The debris was so dense that even the colossal lights of Drakemight could hardly penetrate. Nonetheless, what was penetrating was indeed an enemy force, and he was determined to stop it. Even if it meant ending up like his fossil collection.

"There's no more appropriate time for war," he said as he drew his sword, "than the present, and the past and the future."

The dragon sentry shot into the air, a harbinger of death to all those who opposed his quest.

CHAPTER 3

The sky lit up like a celestial inferno. It was neither day nor night, but something beyond the two opposing sides of a Worldly rotation. The heavens grew crimson with the blazes that erupted all over Drakemight, blazes that detonated out of massive metal rods that came shooting down from the clouds. The sun and the stars were shielded by the intense flares that ripped across them, replacing them with speckled flashes of the incoming storm of projectiles. All over the kingdom, polyhedral towers fell and dragons fled for their lives, uncertain of what was going on – or when it was going to stop.

Dennagon darted through the frenzy, as perplexed as anyone else. The rain of doom bombarded the walls all around, creating an even greater wall that burned of stone and fire to prevent any units from escaping. Mushroom clouds bloomed everywhere, spreading radioactive winds across the entire civilization as if to summon a deadly aurora borealis. There was no place to run, and certainly hiding from the atomic emissions was out of the question.

Just then, two familiar faces passed him amidst the swarms. Arxinor and Gorgash, the two cryptic guardians of the lord Drekkenoth, brushed by his sides, tipping his sword with one of their wings. He twirled around wildly, stopping himself with an outward thrust of his talons.

"What of the enemy?!"

The two guardians turned around simultaneously and identically perfunctory.

"Can you not predict?" asked Gorgash.

It was rather obvious.

"Humans." He looked to the blood-torn sky. "What the hell is this rain?!"

"Let ussss identify it."

With that, Gorgash and Arxinor disappeared into the flying, bustling throngs. Sentry commanders began to amass their frantic forces and lead the draconic battalions into battle above. Gradually, the clamor was receding into raging order.

Dennagon felt no need to wait for orders. Stark raving mad, he bolted into the heavens, gliding swiftly past his slower comrades. With a talon held out to increase his aerodynamic motion, he rushed forth, blade drawn in his other talon. There were cylindrical comets in the sky. Hundreds of them. From where he was, he could not determine their size, but he could sense that these were not ordinary fireballs that could be forged from any old spellbook. These were entities he had never seen before, perhaps something recently written by an experienced spellcaster. There was no stopping this war without finding out what kind of magic did this.

He was halfway betwixt the stratosphere and the surface when one of the projectiles neared him. It was headed straight toward the Archive at the center of the city, flaring like a meteorite that came directly from the sun. He could not let it meet its target. Dashing right in its way, he charged straight toward it, his eyes glowing as his pupils locked onto its fiery tip. The projectile stared straight back at him as a cyclops would gaze at its prey with a single eye, flames lashing out like a beast's fanged jaws. In his mind, all he saw were the pages of his books, dictating to him exactly how he should manipulate his realm.

"Velocity is distance multiplied by time," he reminded himself.

The furious rod-like comet barreled toward him at the speed of sound. However, he swiftly spun to the side just as it came, swinging his blade around to carve a groove into its cylindrical shaft. The projectile jerked up into the air, spiraling off course in a wild trajectory that wound around and about the polyhedral extensions of the kingdom. It fell to the ground, amazingly dodging countless potential targets in the way whilst dragon sentries rushed out of its path. Dennagon raced back down, following its awkward trail of smoke as best he could. Trigonometry and dynamics shuffled in his consciousness, guiding him with the mathematics of physical laws so that he could optimize his efficiency. To his aggravation, hordes of comrades bustled past him, jarring him from side to side as he tried to catch the plummeting entity that could devastate the entire legion. Enraged, he shouted.

"GET OUT OF MY WAY! GO UP, GO DOWN, BUT MOST OF ALL, JUST GET OUT OF MY WAY!"

In the rumbling night, he could hardly hear his own words. Nevertheless, he sheathed his blade and started punching sentries that were stupid enough to get in his path, making certain that they were clear of the potentially explosive range of the descending enemy projectile. Occasionally, punches and bites were returned to his chest and face, but there was no time for vengeance. He had a mission to complete.

Finally, he came within ten feet of the sizeable rod-like object. The smoke blared against him, but he quickly implemented the laws of motion in his mind and calculated its presumed trajectory. With a downward boost of his wings and a strenuous stretch of his limbs, he caught it with all fours. Yanking it upside-down, he put it up in the air whilst his back faced the ground, making certain that it would not erupt upon surface contact. Unfortunately, as the smoke cleared from his vision, he could tell that the ground was actually a lot closer than he originally thought.

"Uh-oh."

Opening his wings even further, he leveled himself out against the currents of air. Parallel to the ground, he maximized his surface area and increased his air resistance to its full potential. Slowing down a bit, but not quite enough, he hit the ground with a thud, skewing himself sideways as well. Blending into a back roll, he let his captured projectile tumble overhead and drop on the ground behind him tail-first. As it clanged against the dirt at the surface of Drakemight, it wobbled around, rolling its two tons of weight along a natural incline. Dennagon sprung to a stance, catching it under his limbs before it could go any further. He took a breath of relief.

"Whew!" he let out, grateful that it did not explode.

His claws scraped its surface. It was hot and smooth, charred on the outside from the friction of the air, but still recognizable as metal underneath. Like an arrow, this missile was elongated and slender, twice Dennagon's length, maintaining a point at one end and steel tail rudders at the other. A propulsion system seemed to be built into the tail end, but there was no sorcery that could have created it, as it appeared to be a machine in itself. As his claws felt the scar that his sword had left in its shaft, he then realized what it was really made of.

Severed circuits protruded from the torn opening like wriggling serpents tipped with electrically charged ends. Sparks flew from their broken edges, lighting up the area with curt pyrotechnics. They were similar to the circuited parts that he held in his collection, except the missile in his clutches was actually alive and operational. Electricity surged through it like blood through veins, and it felt as if he were beholding a power that was truly beyond his realm of existence. It could destroy him if it exploded. Incinerate him so that he himself would become a fossil. Regardless, the question at talon was how it was capable of being set off.

A high-pitch whistle shrieked. Another missile rocketed toward him from above, clearing all other dragons out of its way. His comrades did not even try to stop it, but merely dodged so that it could hit him. Dennagon had no time to think.

"Eeeeerrggh!!"

With a tremendous thrust, he hurtled the missile in his clutches to the one that sailed toward him. The two projectiles collided in midair a mile up, emitting a blast of illumination that scorched all of Drakemight with fierce pulses of light. The eruption tossed him back with a force so whopping that he felt like he had been socked by twelve million human knights all at once. His body lashed through the flaming air, cutting an infernal streak of red flares in the conflagration cloud. Spiraling horizontal, he crashed into a polyhedral domicile and tumbled around as the metal and stone fragments deformed to wrap around his talons and legs.

The radiation filled the air, but underneath the rubble, Dennagon was mildly shielded. Still, he could only rise groggily, limply tearing off his fettered debris with disoriented slices of his claws. He barely had the strength to growl.

Then, a horrific realization hit him. Snapping his head up, he looked to the cohorts of dragons above, fleeting ignorantly to meet the onslaught of missiles from above. Idiots they were not to know by now what the missiles were capable of, but instinct drove him to save them anyway.

"Noooo!!" he cried. "Stay back! Do not engage thy projectiles! They will disintegrate you! They will – "

The sky was bloodier than it was before as detonations cast roses of red fire into the sky, their flaring petals lined by the gore of foolish warriors slain. In the bleeding heavens, hundreds of nukes were set off by morons who decided it was a good idea to strike the warheads with their blades, fangs and claws. Reptilian cadavers fell from the celestial sea, showering the polyhedral networks in carrion burnt.

It was too late for any of his comrades. Dennagon darted into the air, what little air was left about the flaming ruins. He scudded through the aerial polyhedron maze as edifices crumbled all around, casting their shattered fragments from the flanks and overhead. Storms of stone came to his flank, but he yawed to avoid them. A blast of glass flew from the windows of a domicile being crushed by a boulder, so he pitched below it and flew right past. From behind, a gush of liquefied metal poured from the walls of a melting building, shooting right to his back as a chunk of rock raced to him from the front. He rolled in the air and tucked himself at a 45-degree angle to the side, allowing the metal stream to blast the rocky piece to molten droplets.

Chaos surrounded him, but he remained undaunted. As the edifices ahead continued to topple, he pressed forth, thinking only of escape and survival. Alas, in a trail of exploding and collapsing buildings, he ripped past the crumbled city walls, heaving a plume of dust in his trajectory. For a second, he glimpsed the mossy plains and thought he was finally safe, but another atomic explosion struck the kingdom at its very heart, sending a wave of heated air across him. An outburst of dirt rolled against him, sending him reeling to the landscape outside his realm. His massive body hit the ground with a heavy thud, digging a giant groove into the moss-coated terrain.

Hitting a tree, he stopped. The trunk broke and collapsed on him, but it felt rather comforting compared to the scorching heat of battle.

"Ughhh…" he groaned.

Flinging the tree off himself, he looked to the distance again. The situation seemed familiar, since he was just here about fifteen minutes ago. Only then, he was ready to head into battle, not away from it. In the horizon now, there was hardly anything left but smoldering devastation ringed by hellish blazes that were more blood red than any fire he had seen before. It was going to be a while until the dragons could return to the kingdom. If ever.

Just then, a rumble of footsteps quaked the ground. Judging by their metallic resonance and their light pressure, he could tell that they were not of his own kindred. Rolling, he leapt behind a growth of shrubberies that just barely concealed him as he lay on his side. Through the webbed leaves, he could see what approached.

Metallic bodies marched toward the kingdom. Knights in shimmering armor and simian form headed to Drakemight, some on horses mounted and others on foot prepared. They held in their hominid gauntlets lances sharpened to their tips, crossbows locked and loaded with arrows, and halberds whetted to the finest edges. Indeed, the humans had never stooped so low, yet amassed so highly at the same time. This time, they actually stood a fighting chance. Nonetheless, Dennagon was not going to let them take his kingdom, no matter how many units they had.

It was irony that always plagued his life whenever he made a promise. Just by merely declaring his resolution to himself, he was expecting an entire legion of ten thousand men to storm the castle, thereby forcing him to fight nearly impossible odds. However, as they plodded forth, he saw the enemy forces in their entirety, and there were little more than a hundred strong. Cocking a brow, he decided to stay back to see what they were planning.

One last unit backed up the rest of them. At first glance of its shadow, he thought it was a high-level magician and that for once, he would be able to face a challenge. As it came into full visibility though, it revealed itself to be a mounted knight no greater than any of the others. Its tunic was more adorned with the symbols of gold, but other than that, it looked like an ordinary man. Even if it was a paladin, Dennagon was not certain what the humans were planning to accomplish with such a puny attack. Even hominids were not usually this dumb.

A monstrous roar sounded. The paladin craned its neck back, shaking its head wildly from side to side. In a mechanized voice, it spoke.

"Increase mobilization speed. Annihilate everything."

The tone of its speech was droned, similar to that of an insect's buzzing. It sounded synthetic, as if each of its vocal cords vibrated in tubes of metal. But how was that possible? Humans were of flesh and bone not unlike reptiles, avians and krakens. If this was a knight, it was certainly augmented with an enchantment.

And the enchantment was viewable as the paladin turned its head again. Built into the back of its skull was a chip of metal lined with wires, circuits and mechanical nodes that he had no idea what to make of. Integrated into the very cerebrum of this creature, it was unlike anything in his private collection or the missiles he had examined at Drakemight. This enemy was perhaps their secret weapon, a new type of magician on the front lines.

Or was it? One more shadow followed it from behind, shaped like a creature that had a slithering neck and a serpentine head crowned with horns. Cocking its jaws open, it let out another roar, and it was then that he understood where the deafening clamor came from. It was a dragon. Amongst the enemy lines, there was a member of his own species, attacking the kingdom just like a human would. Now he knew there was something potent about his opponents, for few spells, save for those of draconic sorcery, had the puissance to coerce a serpentine intellect.

Dennagon shifted through the shrubberies, trying to get a closer look at the creature from which the reptilian umbra emerged, but as quickly as he moved, a stone struck him upon his cranium. He almost growled as he fell to the ground, clutching his aching skull. At first, he thought he had been hit by a catapult shot, but as he rolled onto his back, he looked up, only to see a wurm, a dragon with no limbs, slithering on the ground before him. Instantly, he reached for his sword, unsure of whether it was a comrade or adversary.

The wurm picked up another stone, preparing to knock him over the head again. Withal, he was surprised at how quickly Dennagon rose, and backed down at the sight of the sword.

"Sorry fellow," said the wurm, "but this has to be done."

It was an enemy. Dennagon delivered a cross-slash that grazed the shrubberies, yet completely missed the target, which hopped into the air like a coiled spring. Dizzily, he tried to turn around, but by that time, it was too late. The second stone already hit him in the forehead.

He flopped over, unconscious. The wurm poked him with the end of his tail to make sure he was out cold.

"You'll feel better when you wake up. Or maybe you won't. Or maybe – "

The wurm shut himself up. Wrapping his limbless body around Dennagon's comatose soma, he dragged him silently into the night. All the while, the human hordes rampaged into the remnants of Drakemight, followed by the beast that backed them up. The gargantuan tremors shook the ground as it marched, dark as the night without a star.

Dennagon's worst nightmare had come true. In the midst of war, he could now only dream.

———————————

The bounds of the World were converging. In a landscape rife with archaic verdure, dinosaurs traipsed the terrain, killing at unwilled instinct, surviving for the sake of survival. Tyrannosaurus rexes trampled triceratopses whilst plesiosaurs roamed the seas with sharks and prehistoric fish. Slaying and breeding, breeding and slaying were the only two things that went on during this era, the Age of Reptiles. The World was ruled by animals, unknowing of why they behaved in such a manner, yet continually acting on the whims of their unconscious. Were they weak or just ignorant? Probably both.

After an apocalyptic asteroid raged across the lands, only the peons of animals survived, evolving into yet another species of beasts – men. Men who were so easily tainted by avarice and cowardice dominated the planet, infesting it with their greed and bloodlust. Their technological contagion spread throughout the globe, computers lining every inch of the sky down to the very planetary core, creating a gargantuan multicellular organism composed of multicellular organisms. In their mechanical flare, they were stuck in the middle of time, along with the observer that watched them in the dreams. Thence, the middle of time burned, the simian realm melting amidst cybernetic havoc.

Alas, another center of time sprung forth. The Middle Ages covered the lands in mystical topography as imaginative as it was majestic. However, even its majesty bore a dark essence that could neither be seen nor heard, only felt. Mana brimmed around the magical brain of the World, Gaia manifested in the form of the liquid of life bubbling around the souls of every conscious being. It stretched far indeed, for everything in the

World and Universe was as conscious as any life form, biological as the creatures on the earth and the sun that let them thrive. These were medieval times, a time of chivalry and honor, an era of darkness and dusk, an endless string of eons bound together in an undifferentiated chain of the temporal realm. They were the only realm that could be known of by beings of the dark age.

Whilst creatures traversed the terrain like shadows on a dune under the dark blue sky, a murky cloud loomed over all existence. The onyx sky charred the vision for all, even more ominous than the jet blackness that smote the dinosaurs in their animalistic mortality. Thunder as black as the depths of vacuum space scarred the heavens against the silver clouds, bleeding dark flames to the surface below. Albeit, this was no meager prophecy, for there was no future to be foretold in the fields forbidden to temporal flow. It was the present, the past and what was to come. It was the word unsaid, the term untold, for everyone knew.

As ebony flames ripped across the dominions and oceans, a ghastly shadow formed over all. A mechanized dragon soared over the World, its biotechnological eyes scanning everything that lived so that its cybernetic brain could process the info underneath its metal-plated body. The knowledge of the World, liquid in sable saturation, boiled out from the earthly mantle up to the surface, drowning out the lands and seas in a sheet of oily residue. All creatures struggled against it, but not even the most adept warriors could survive this evil tide. The mechanical dragon swept over the jetty waves, surveying its subjects as they were battered under the currents of hellish raven bleakness. It was difficult to tell the difference between the eve sky and the knowledge-coated planet, for even the stars of the Universe burnt with the same inky fire that floated along the surface of the murky flux. The light of the sun also became black, firing dark streams of purely ebony lasers down to the earth to kill everything in its range. Soon, nothing thought, and thus, nothing lived.

The mechanized dragons dominated the air between the heavens and the knowledge-ridden lands. In the devastation, they all bore the same thought on their minds. They all knew what they were hunting.

"Dennagon". They knew the name, but were unaware of the nature of the creature to which it was assigned. Dennagon the lone sentry was still somewhere on the terrains unwashed by information, and he was the only thing that stood in their way. Like a pebble lodged in the gears of the omnipotent machine of time, he was disrupting everything, yet they could not find him. Nonetheless, they soon would. As long as he was alive, they could feel him, and his doom was not far.

Time moved forward again, as it always did.

Dennagon wrenched open his eyes, terrified at the visions that bombarded his mind. In horror, he roared, blood and sweat dripping from the gashed scales of his battle-scarred body. Feverishly, he scurried about, trying to flee from the tides of darkness that loomed in his imagination, snarling aghast at every plant leaf that he saw. Despite his terrorized posture, the dark ocean of his dreams only existed as dreams, and nothing more. It took him a second to realize that fact.

"Where am I?! What is time?! Certainty lies in one's mind, but how can I know anything for certain?!" his random thoughts rambled. "Why am I talking to myself?"

After a second, his breaths calmed. Looking around, he noticed that the verdure was inverted so that all tree branches lurked around the ground like roots and all tree trunks and roots poked up toward the sky, which was littered with stars. Shrubberies adorned some floating patches of land above, hanging transposed like the larger plant life that surrounded it. At first, he thought he himself was positioned upside-down, but then noticed that the force of gravity still drew him down feet first. The entire woodland was upside-down. This must have been the Pedorian Forest.

A stark contrast to the enshrouding foliage suddenly appeared as his wurmy captor dangled over him, facing him with a goofy expression.

"You're not talking to yourself," answered Dradicus, the wurm.

Faster than lightning, Dennagon grabbed the opponent by the throat and slammed him into a ground-dwelling canopy. Dradicus' googly pupils ringed around his rounded eyes disoriented.

"Ah!" he screamed. "Watch the scales! I just cleaned myself and that's hard to do when you don't have limbs!"

Dennagon had no intentions of complying.

"Do I know you?"

"You know nothing yet," came a voice from behind.

Two more dragons entered the vicinity. One, a wyvern, grabbed him by his left shoulder while the other, an ouroboros, seized his right shoulder. They yanked him off and threw him to the ground. Initially, he thought they were Arxinor and Gorgash, but then saw that they clearly bore differing attributes. The purple wyvern was much slimmer than the reddish Arxinor, and the orangish ouroboros always kept his tail in his mouth, unlike the behemoth Gorgash. Regardless of their appearance, nonetheless, Dennagon understood only one thing. They attacked him, and thus, were the enemy.

He reached for his scabbard, but his talon cut through thin

air instead of clasping a hilt. His sword was gone. Surprised, he looked to see the ouroboros dangling it in its index claw, casually taunting him.

"Looking for this, vile sentry?" it asked.

The ouroboros whirled the blade around, his attacks fueled by the hatred of a hundred souls. Dennagon stolidly dodged as best he could, the metal flashing all around his body in merciless assaults. Although the wyvern snickered, this was no joke. They really were trying to kill him.

"We don't like those who keep secrets," noted the wyvern.

When he saw an opportune instant, he threw a backhand at his adversary. The ouroboros blocked with a forearm plate and returned a roundhouse punch. Dennagon parried the offense, catching the enemy by the wrist. They snarled in each other's faces, about to finish each other off before two more dragons entered the scene.

"But I think we'll make an exception in this case."

Lyconel snatched the sword away from the ouroboros' grasp. They all backed off as a mutilated elder hydra followed her into the grove. She walked to her captive, her bluish scales still shimmering as if she had not even taken the slightest damage from her fall off the cloud. Dennagon wasn't certain what to make of her apparent survival, let alone everything else he had seen within the past day. She should have been dead, but she walked as lively as any healthy drake.

"You'll have to excuse my comrades," she started. "As you probably guessed, we're cautious around members of the draconic collective. I'm sure your lord told you about our treachery, of course."

Dennagon spit out a wad of silver slaver. Although it was a very pedestrian and lowly gesture, he had to discard any knocked-out fangs before he swallowed them and scraped his own throat.

"You're Errants. Dissidents," he stated. "What do you want with me? Actually, it doesn't matter, since I'll die before handing anything over, but just for the sake of quelling my curiosity, what is it that you want? Rations? Recon? Knowledge? What?!"

Lyconel's reply was as calm as a spring breeze.

"You."

Dennagon looked at her. His eyes were straighter than the path of the fastest light ray.

"Me."

She nodded.

"You want me and only me, nothing more. What is this? The Draconic Inquisition?!" he blared with squinted eyes and shrugged shoulders. "Go ahead, blackmail the collective! See how far you get before a thousand laughs pass your ears. They want me back as much as they want to suck the bladder of an incontinent minotaur."

Lyconel wagged her index claw.

"Oh, no, no, no. You really don't get it. We come not in malice, Dennagon. We're here to help."

"Well, if you want to help, start by getting out of my way."

He headed for the forest depths, but the ouroboros stamped a foot in his way. Another fight was about to break out.

"Nomax, back off," commanded Lyconel.

The ouroboros, Nomax, reluctantly complied.

"Look, Dennagon, if you want to know the truth, the attack on Drakemight was not meant for the elimination of data," she continued.

"What else does man crave, aside from gold? Humans do not think, which is why they seek to destroy all knowledge."

"The words you speak are truthful, but tell not the entire story. The attack you just witnessed was brought about for an even more secretive purpose."

Dennagon crossed his talons and listened. For some

reason, he thought this was going to be entertaining.

"Long ago," Lyconel spoke with a deepened tone, "when the World was first spawned, there was a point that encompassed all moments in time. That point was the center of all being and it was that that the sapiens truly desired."

A yawn.

"I've heard the myths."

Lyconel could tell that her one-dragon audience was losing interest, so she pulled out from her belt a sleek metal weapon. Tipped with a cylindrical barrel, it was composed mainly of a firing mechanism, a chamber and a breech system that was mounted with a retractable tripod. Connected to the chamber was a magazine of ammunition that contained several rounds of leaden bullets ready to be fired. Her claw on the trigger, she held it as a human would, pointing it up for safety.

Dennagon tilted his gaze, unknowing of what the 20th century machinegun was.

"They've already tapped into the source of time. Already, their powers are beginning to grow. That's how they managed to initiate that onslaught so easily. And that's not where they'll stop."

She gestured to the wyvern.

"Lefius."

Lefius, the wyvern, cast a metal helm into the air. Lyconel unleashed a stream of bullets at it, rattling the firearm in her grasp. Explosive crackling filled the atmosphere as a volley of gunfire tore the helm apart and dropped Dennagon's jaw. All that was left was shrapnel that fell to the ground and the smoke from the machinegun's barrel.

"This is but a sample of their capabilities. No sorcery can battle the tides of temporal flow if their powers continue to expand. Only the dragons have the intelligence to bring upon them doom. We evolved to be the most advanced species in heart and mind, and for that we act as their bane. It's thence our responsibility to stop them from attaining the center of time."

Dennagon stooped to view the machinegun's engineering. It was so complex in his eye, even more complicated than the grand clock towers of Glackus, kingdom of the thunderbirds. Gears wound about churning tubes filled with a dusty, unidentified powder, all centered around a seemingly important hammer positioned behind the loaded bullets. He was sincerely impressed with the artful construction, even though he didn't fully understand it. However, he was not as impressed with the weak story his captor had concocted.

"Every being with enough brain cells," he uttered with an air of arrogance, "knows that we, the dragons, are the keepers of wisdom. Certainly, we are beyond the meager whims of the humans, and it is undoubtedly our duty to keep them under control. Yet, I hardly believe that their 'powers', what little they have, were a result of tapping into the source of time, unless you meant to say that time granted them enough evolutionary strength to develop into such vileness." Despite Lyconel's groans and rolled eyes, he resumed in rubbing his point in. "You're a nice story teller, but I'm afraid you're not a very convincing general. So, if you'll excuse me, I've got a kingdom to return to, as well as some knowledge to collect."

"They aren't trying to destroy knowledge. They intend to annihilate the one thing that can stop them – the Lexicon."

There it was again. That accursed word that nearly prevented him from meeting with the lord Drekkenoth many hours ago. He wouldn't have it.

"Is that why you brought me here?! Don't you think I have better things to do than kill you all?! I'm a defender of Drakemight!"

She gestured to Lefius again. The wyvern drew a crossbow

and fired a shot upward. The arrow hit a sheet of foliage above, scattering the leaves in the air to reveal the sky. Although the stars twinkled against the night backdrop, the ashes of Drakemight still lingered in the atmosphere like blackened stellar entities. The heart-shattering truth fell upon him as if the earth were ripped right out from under his feet. It was such an impact that Lyconel could not help but utter it.

"Drakemight is no more."

Dennagon stoically accepted the obviousness of it all. Like a warrior, he bore the pain without a single frown to show for it.

"Believe us or don't. You haven't a home to return to."

Lyconel held out a blue talon.

"Follow us and we can take you to the only hope you have left. Or you can wander the lands, an errant of a species fallen."

He sensed a lack of sincerity in her words, as he did with most creatures that had the cognizance to choose. No creature he had ever met was entirely truthful, for every intellectual being was inherently imperfect. Besides, those that were completely honest at all times were usually slain by the claws of brainwashed masses or by the guile of those beings who knew how to utilize the secrets of dolts foolish enough to divulge too much. Albeit he could detect the same treachery in her tone, he had all but any more strategic plans.

Thrusting out his talon, he viciously displayed all sharp claws to show just how friendly he was.

"Fine," he forcefully said. "I'll battle by your side as long as you do me one favor."

His pupils shot at Nomax.

"Give me MY BLOODY SWORD BACK!"

Nomax, wearing a nasty grimace, chucked it to him with the underside of his ouroboros tail. Dennagon snatched it in the air, twirling it until it fell into a comfortable grasp. With a handkerchief of human skin, he wiped off the filthy claw prints. If it was one thing he kept clean, it was his blade and the logical element of his mind. Both were as essential as rations and water to him, for war was what mattered in life.

Suddenly, a familiar sound in the heat of war alarmed him. Hundreds of flapping wings filled the air with an aerial rumble similar to a thousand flags whipping in the wind simultaneously. They all looked up, only to see minions of draconic sentries soaring above the woodland, all plated in the armor of the recently decimated city. Lyconel immediately slid under the forest's inverted foliage.

"Duck!"

They all did. The rumbles increased in magnitude, spreading to the ground and the areas all around. The battered sentries wearily plodded across the entire environment, drained of their energy, but of grim vigor nonetheless. Their bodies were fueled only by the ire and fear that filled their veins, the two emotions that drove them away from their homeland that had just been riddled with the cadavers of their fallen companions. Upon their faces, mindless expressions were sculpted as if from stone carved, and it was difficult to tell whether they lacked food or the ebony crystal liquid of knowledge. Through the verdurous growth, they flew in the livid air, galloped across the lands and swam where streams allowed. Thirsting for vengeance. But more importantly, information.

The dissident clan huddled together under the shadows. Their scales pressed against one another as the fleeting lightless silhouettes of their draconic hunters passed all around, unwary of their presence. Dennagon had fought alongside many of them in battle, yet even he could not recognize a single face. Perhaps he just could not view them in such bleakness, but more likely, it was just because he didn't give a blasted blight about their visages. He knew only one thing now – he had to stay hidden.

Or did he? Why didn't he ask himself "why?" before coming to such a conclusion? Shame, shame shame. He shouldn't have acted on his instinct, he thought. To do so was to be no more than an animal. The fear that Lyconel's coercion incited in him almost drew him to a plight most mad and cost him his reasoning capabilities. Swiftly, he regained his mental composure. He was again aligned with the collective.

However, just as he reached out a talon to signal for his loathsome Drakemight comrades, he halted. It wasn't the threat of being assaulted by these rabble dissident units that were so close by, but rather, the thought of falling for the same mistake he had just made. He could not just act on instinct and trust the collective again, for his reason told him to trust absolutely no one except for himself. Thus, there was naught a single reason why he should believe that Drekkenoth's purposes were anymore benign than Lyconel's, even though the dragon king did always appear wise. Both choices were equally dangerous. His mind froze, as did the rest of his body.

The tension virtually permeated the air. He could feel one of his new allies immersed in terror, another that was stooped in clandestine, covert thoughts, another that pondered meticulously, and the last that just plainly wanted to kill him. Dennagon ignored these sentiments, for he wanted to take his time. Time that was slipping away as the dragons continued to pass without a sign of when they would completely mobilize beyond his range. Their sheer volume was extraordinary, and he was surprised there were that many inhabitants of Drakemight. He could easily kill Lyconel and her band by himself, let alone with a fleet of dragons. He would probably prove himself to be more of a hero than he already was by doing so, and hang her head as a trophy of nobility.

But, then again, she gave him his sword back. And even as he crouched, overtly pondering whether or not to betray them, Lyconel stayed as placid as a spring dawn. It was as if she did not care to stop him, even though she was aware of the peril. At the same time, she was neither apathetic nor hostile, but rather, of a strange, organic neutrality. One that was enough to convince him that she was just as, or maybe more propitious than the collective.

He withdrew his talon. The swell of tension was suddenly released. The rest of the draconic legion rushed by, trailed by a few weaker units that lagged behind. Lyconel nonverbally motioned for everyone to stay amidst the guise of the shade for a minute before rising once more.

"Follow my lead," she advisedly commanded.

She started toward the east, where the dragon army had turned. Behind her, her warriors followed her trail, careful not to strike any sounds in the air and not to leave any massive clawprints in the dirt. Even though the forest was upside-down, there was no reason to assume that the foliage hanging at the floor would conceal any blatantly clumsy marks. Marks that were haphazard enough to leave permanent scars in the ground were frequent of reptiles.

Reptiles like Dennagon, who had left a scar upon something immaterial in the stead of something upon the lands. He had already shown his new clan just about how loyal he was in that near-miss treachery. The feeling always made him feel like a furnace had been lit up in his chest, for he always sensed the pain and anguish of others. Thence, he could touch upon the discomfort he had generated just now. There was an uncertain air all around of what everyone was thinking to themselves.

Then again, the situation was always uncertain in the

theater of war. He had to do what was strategic, considering the variables he was aware of at the time. Only weaklings moaned at the agony of battle, and definitely at the injuring of a potential enemy. There was no time to brood over such meaningless individuals whom he was probably going to ditch later anyway. Taking back his warrior's heart, he pressed on to find out where his new friend was taking him.

At the center of the Pedorian Forest, there was a lake that many creatures journeyed to in the past. Inverted like the rest of the woodland, it was unbound by gravity and hung in the air like a floating dome. Its flat, rippling surface faced the ground below as if to act as a mirror or a watery lens, yet there was nothing but the stars in the sky to see. The same stars that appeared every night just as the celestial maps stated they should. There were no planets, asteroids or meteors, let alone the occasional fireballs that quarreling idiot magicians used against one another in the fields of petty human battles. Most of all, though, there was no Moon, which was something the World missed dearly. That was why the lake was there, for the globe coveted its sister, its companion to join it in heavenly harmony. The liquid lens watched the skies every night to linger on that hope.

However, as so many religious fools of the past, there were many who came here that had no hope. At the present, the remnant army of Drakemight congregated, shaken under their armor. Coolly, they tried to regain their equanimity so that they could bare themselves of the humility of being units that could hardly keep a steady claw at the sign of devastation. Their homeland was destroyed, and they grieved less in their strategic loss than in the fact that they were also losing their vaunted images amongst their colleagues. Instead of thinking of ways to improve their situation, they only thought of ways they could pretend to be suave about it. The only parts of them that appeared to be okay were the parts that weren't – their outward aspects.

"How goes thy night?" uttered Thargon to an amphiptere, a worm without wings, who appeared less secure. "Are you in the need of comfort, brethren? Perchance I can be of assistance, lesser one."

It snapped its fanged jowls at him.

"Slash thy breath, oh putrid one. I am stronger than you ten times ten!"

"What does that mean?"

"That means that if I had ten units of strength, you would only have one."

"If that were the case then I would only be ten times as strong as you, not ten times ten as you said."

The amphiptere opened its mouth for a rebuttal, but his immediate response was a sock in the face. Under the wavy waters, a brawl ensued, and the two grappled almost as purposelessly as men drunken with the addiction for dominance. Other sentries gathered around to gawk at the fight, males and females alike shouting in ardent displays of false zealousness.

In the underbrush surrounding the perimeters, Dennagon crept, lured by the unambiguous ruckus that had broken out. In front of him, Lyconel, Dradicus, Lefius, and Nomax peeked through the shrubs, careful as to not be seen. Death would be instant if they were caught, and the mission they had on their heads was far too significant to fail. So significant that Lyconel hissed under the audible range of the sentries.

From her throat, a vacillating whinny whispered into the auditory organs of her group. Everyone heard the message loud and clear.

"We have to stay out of sight, no matter what. Got it?"

Dennagon was not familiar with the language of the primordial reptiles, but he got the jist of the message anyway. Her tone of voice was enough to warn him. Quietly, he asked the question everyone else was always afraid to ask.

"Why?"

"The Drakemight collective organized that attack upon itself. They're as much the enemies as the sapiens are."

"How can that be? I served them."

"Then perhaps they didn't let you know everything."

The moronic sentries began to brawl their way to their concealed spot. Luckily, they tackled each other away before coming too close. Alas, Thargon walloped his opponent away into a cluster of waiting sentries, knocking him unconscious against a wall of scales. When it was clear that the amphiptere was not going to rise, the spectators rallied and stomped on the defeated unit, shattering the little glory it once had. All the while, their animalistic grunts drew forth yet another visitor.

A vast shadow swept over the hovering water like an eclipse of draconic form. The dark umbra of Drekkenoth soared to the center of the gathering, lightless as it was haunting. Silence befell all the inhabitants as they watched the sable flames flare across the sky, neutral and ghastly in their heat's aloof lordliness. The king descended from above, reflecting his blackened fires against the rippling surface of the airborne body of water. Ebony light streamed over all the sentries of Drakemight.

Dennagon now thought he understood. They were probably here in temporary transit to an auxiliary outpost he had heard of often. He couldn't remember the name, though. It was of no importance what it was called. He remembered only the most significant fact, that it served as a safe haven in the case that Drakemight was taken. Drekkenoth seemed to be taking on his mechanically patient carriage as usual.

While Dennagon almost viewed the king as a silent hero, Lyconel shirked at the sight of him. It was as if she were in the presence of a demon bent upon deceit in the most cunning of ways, for it was apparent that she was not afraid of his sheer power. There was something else she despised about him and the expression on her face conveyed a form of anger he had never seen in any dragon. Certainly never on the face of lord Drekkenoth, whose unmatched stoicism had many believe that he was a clockwork machine.

Dradicus, the wurm who had taken Dennagon earlier, poked Lyconel with his tail.

"Should I scout?" he asked, true to his duty.

"It's too dangerous. Recon is of the utmost importance."

And recon they sought. Eyes locked forward, they watched the legion before them as the dark lord hovered above like a demi-god. Drekkenoth said not a word for a few seconds, as if every spoken vowel and consonant was worth waiting for. Loyally as canines, the sentries did wait, every moment their pupils focused upon their master.

Then, in a mighty thundering voice, he started his speech.

"Silence," he commanded even though there was already silence to begin with. "Our walls are destroyed, but we have not yet lost this battle. We must advance upon the human armies lest they wreak their havoc upon the remainder of the World. The World that is our home and matriarch."

For a few moments, there was an awkward shuffle as the sentries looked to one another for guidance. One mildly brave unit spoke up.

"B-but they've grown too strong. We cannot hold them off." Others joined in.

"We'll not be able to withstand another attack! Didst you not experience their new sorcery?"

"Those projectiles from the sky came as if from hell itself!"

Drekkenoth raised a talon high over his head. All units

cowered, expecting for it to blast them away into the night. However, as he drove it down, he hit not one of his subordinates but instead ran right through the floating lake. The airborne water splashed into the air, warping his massive image as he streamed down through it like a bombshell. The liquid never seeming to touch his black fires, he drilled directly into the ground, slamming his claws right through the surface. A potent yet non-lethal quake shuddered the lands and he ripped out something from the earth.

Ebony fluid crystal dripped down his drenched palms to his forearm like oily tar of saccharine glimmer. The sugary substance spilled from the hole in the terrain that he created, yet it was hardly of petroleum produced. It was the knowledge of the World, the veins that lined every inch of the globe from pole to pole so that humans could attempt to eradicate it and dragons could strive to fight for it. Pure, untainted knowledge in tangible form.

"They are mightier than you are as of now. Their craving for ignorance draws them to destroy this existence as metal is drawn to neodymium. That is why we need this, the data of the World, to seize the lands that belong to us."

A dissatisfied clamor loomed about the crowd.

"What is that word? 'Data'?" inquired a sentry.

Dennagon was just about to ask the same thing. He had heard the term used frequently, and had even attempted to use it himself a few times. It seemed to have something to do with wisdom.

"Yes," added another sentry. "Why do you keep using it?"

Drekkenoth did not answer. This time, his quietude was not in awe seen.

"I say his leadership wavers," said the last sentry. "He cannot command us any longer."

They started to draw their weapons. Visions of glory suddenly filled their minds as they dreamed about killing the one who controlled them for so long. Despite the fact that they thought he had saved their lives for so long, the only thing they thought of was triumph. In fantasies deluged, they prepared for an attack.

"Kill him."

Drekkenoth was as still as a mountain. Violently, the hordes unleashed a storm upon their master, blades smashing against his sinew, claws scraping against his shadowy scales, tails lashing his face and biceps, and flames tearing from the mouths of the masses attempting to incinerate him. It seemed so incredibly vehement that even Dennagon was ready to believe that the lord would collapse under the insanity, since no creature in his long years had he ever seen survive such an assault. He prepared for a gory mess, one that would herald the end of a dynasty.

However, as dragon sentries began to tire, they receded, revealing the draconic leader, who was still as solid as a living monument. Not one attack had even scarred his dark scales, and there was not a hint of disturbance in his face. The attacks, if he even felt them, had about as much effect as a pebble striking a grand sequoia.

"Heh, heh, heh," he chuckled in mechanistic pace.

From tranquility to emotionless rage, he suddenly burst with hellish havoc. His colossal talons ripped through the air, smashing his assailants away until they all knew that they had instantaneously become the prey. With ease, his claws and fangs tore through metal armor like knives through paper scrolls, and reptiles flew even without their wings. Their weapons dropped as they scattered, completely disoriented in the chaos wrought. It was like they had been hit by a tidal wave the size of an ocean.

They tried to retreat into the woods even though they knew it was futile. As fast as lightning, Drekkenoth crossed his talons and drew from his scabbards two swords with blades that were forged of onyx crystal. Thunderously, he heaved his weapons at them, several tons of crystal and metal soaring across the air as quickly and easily as a feather swiped through the icy winter torrents. Blood splattered all over and severed body parts were cast in all directions, the duress of a bestial fury untamed directing the wrath without care for life. There was no heed in the destroyer's eyes as he struck, killing some and mutilating others. There was only a sentience that lived on a secret hidden within the dark fires. A sentience that drove him like the clock he was theorized to be.

Horrified, Dennagon could only espy as the severed limbs and hacked torsos flew through the air and splashed into the hovering lake, painting its water with shades of dark, silver blood. Of course, the lake itself never shattered, for the force of gravity that seemed to lie in the middle of the air suspended it as a passive observer. It simply absorbed the gore until the massacre came to an end.

Carrion littered the landscape. The vast majority of the sentries were still alive, but struggled in agony in their writhing postures.

"Do you comprehend?" questioned Drekkenoth. "Information endows me with the strength of a million dragons. If you choose to remain ignorant, you shall perish."

A slow rotation of his head let him survey his fallen forces. Randomly, he grabbed one of them and chewed off its head. Casting the body away, he threw it toward the shrubs. The decapitated soma landed right behind Dennagon's crew, splattering some of its innards upon them.

"Else, you can be as I."

Drekkenoth reached into his belt pouch. Sloshing sounds resounded as he retrieved a talon-full of soft black orbs. Each one dripped with precious knowledge, concentrating the might of erudition into rations. In one whirling motion, he flung them into the air, letting them disseminate in the atmosphere like flying spheres of caviar. As if to imitate pollen, the orbs soared into the horizon and the unseen distance of the celestial sea, spreading out to vast stretches. Every sentry immediately got up off its war-torn belly and took to the air, desperately chasing the entities that they knew of as their source of strength. They ran as if their lives depended on it, and their wounds seemed trivial as compared to the need to understand the physical laws of the universe.

Finally, Drekkenoth was alone. He did not even crack a smile at their cretinous behavior. His flames were completely soundless as he sat meditating in the middle of the woodland, holding something within his heart and mind that not even the five units that spied on him could detect. Dennagon did not dare to speak, but could only hold his breath and view the dragon king whose raging conflagrations let not one decibel of noise into the vicinity.

Lyconel was almost as still as the enemy she watched. She had obviously done this before. Thus, it was not a surprise when she heard the hums of rockets coming from above, encased in two balls of fire that shot down from the sky like shooting stars.

Drekkenoth looked at his wristwatch. His angels of doom were right on time, as he always expected. Arxinor and Gorgash flew to his sides as they were ordered to, plunging through the floating waters in streaks of liquid bubbles. Obediently, they bowed.

"That went as calculated," remarked Arxinor.

"Their pace in downloading has quickened," descried Gorgash.

"Their minds will grow weak with the cognitive venom we have implanted."

Something shone in their eyes that were unlike anything in the medieval realm. Circuited veins bled into their corneas as they processed their data. Arxinor and Gorgash spoke simultaneously.

"And our grasp over all will thicken."

Arxinor then happened upon a thought a second before his slower colleague did.

"But what of the target sssssentry?" he asked.

"The one called Dennagon," finished Gorgash.

Drekkenoth delved into his internal database.

"He is irrelevant. As long as the Lexicon is kept from their reaches, the mission will continue on," he concluded.

Arxinor and Gorgash comprehended. They flashed their circuits through their sinew and took to the sky, serpentine wraiths of cyborganic nature born. As comets, they streaked across the heavens, traveling to accomplish their next duties.

Meanwhile, their programmer continued meditating under the Pedorian Forest's central lake, neither praying nor blaspheming. He was just thinking, for that was what he was best at. Neuromech wiring piloted his intellectual coordination so that he could see his own mind's workings with utmost clarity. Serenely sinister, he waited.

Dennagon, having been exposed to so many anomalous weirdities in such a short time, was completely numbed. He began to implement the age-old question of what was real and what was not, and came to the conclusion that this was as absurd as any dream he had at night. After all, who was to say that anything he perceived at the moment was as tangible as it appeared? It was much more reasonable to assume that he had just been toiling with too much mana, and that the magic had poisoned his thoughts. Yes, that was it wasn't it? What was real? 'Real' was a word like anything else.

The ludicrousness of it all propelled him into a state of nihilism, and he thought he was still asleep. The only way to come out of a dream was to die, as he had once read in an ancient text. Thus, the only way to escape was to dash straight into his enemy so that it could free him from this whirlpool of the subconscious. Again, he was compelled to move toward the collective. To move toward this false Drekkenoth so that he could be extricated from this madness and awaken to his former realm. Then, he could live again to ponder whether or not that realm truly existed.

Fortunately, a sharp blow to the head with another stone knocked him out. Nomax had seen him edging toward visibility and acted as quickly as he ordinarily did. Lyconel, this time, agreed with the decision, and together, they quietly dragged their unconscious comrade away from the scene. Their moves were as silent as the stars twinkling above, and in clandestine sleekness, they swiftly skulked away. Their enemy was left in a state of true solitude — but not a state of true ignorance. For Drekkenoth did not need to see his enemies in order to detect them. He needed only to feel them through the wristwatch that was wired to his very spinal cord, transmitting information through space and time into the mind that wanted to seize everything. He had battled eternity, and it was eternity that he wished to eliminate. Time was his prison, and in his causal shackles he had plotted for many an eon. Totality would be coming soon…

…and he would ring in its arrival.

✗✗✗✗✗✗✗✗✗✗✗✗✗

CHAPTER 4

An aerial river stretched out from the center of the Pedorian Forest, snaking over a vast grassy plain amid the morning sun. It was a tube of transparent liquid that hovered above the fields, an aqueduct constructed neither of machine, dragon, thunderbird, kraken, nor man, but of nature in its infinite wisdom. Such oddities were commonplace in the realm of the World, for the environments of the planet were spawned forth from limitless imagination. Such creativity could only have been crafted by the mind of a dragon or a demon, or perhaps both united. No one knew where or how everything began, for that was the essence of the cosmos. Uncertain. Chaotic. No matter how hard they tried, few warriors could challenge the tested temperament of entropy unbound. Few could defy the endless variation of the earth and catalog everything there was to know about it.

However, if no one tried to accomplish omniscience, no one would have existed in the first place.

Dennagon trudged through the grass, his noggin aching from having been twice stricken at close range. Lyconel walked in front of him, but he could not do anything to her, for the rest of her comrades had their weapons drawn at his back. Nomax and Lefius, the two grunts, kept a close eye on him, ready to strike him down at any time. Behind them, the elder hydra that followed Lyconel into the grove of the Pedorian Forest seemed to be lagging greatly, slowing them down. He wondered why they didn't just abandon him, since he was evidently too old to fight and too mutilated to heal even with the most powerful of spells. Regardless, judging by his looks, he appeared to be important.

Dradicus slithered warily around the area, jumping wildly from side to side. He could move faster than any of his colleagues, and for this speed, they made him the scout of the group. Constantly, he was assessing the peril of the environment according to enemy footprints, bestial scents and anything else that might indicate the presence of a malignant force. So far, on this fine morning, there was nothing to incite defensive actions, but they kept their guards up nonetheless.

He decided to take a short break. Wriggling across the ground to Dennagon's side, he poked his new friend's shoulder with a wurmy tail.

"By the way, I'm Dradicus, sibling of Lyconel and scout of this dissident company. Good to have someone else on our side. That's what we're here for, to bring those without the sight of consciousness to the realm of understanding."

He was beginning to sound like a religious acolyte, and he knew it. Desisting in his pitiful tone, he resumed.

"Nice spellbook you have there. I personally never liked spells, since I don't usually have the same mana capacity that most other dragons do. Magic makes me thirsty as a desert in its drought season. Don't ask me to cast any spells, nosiree-bob…"

Still no response. Perhaps he should focus less on himself.

"The ouroboros is Nomax and the wyvern is Lefius. Nomax likes bladed disks, but Lefius is more on the long-range side with his crossbow and all."

Dradicus then pointed to the hydra.

"Old Ballaxior is the name of the hydra. He guides us through difficult times. His thoughts lay out our paths along this journey, for he has known war longer than any of us. Perhaps we like him because he does all the thinking for us."

Dennagon's face was as icy as a stone locked in frigid carbon dioxide. He was considering clocking the idiot over the head just as forcefully as he was knocked out twice last night. His aggressive stride made no effort to hide that.

Dradicus' goofy smile receded off his visage. It was time to shut up again.

A wave of warped light flashed across the tube-like river from the distorted sunlight passing through the water. The contorted illumination washed over them, breaking the image of the solar entity into fractured fragments that melded together slightly at the connectedness of the fluid body. The sight intrigued Dennagon himself, for albeit he had traveled far and wide in his years as a knowledge hunter, he did not frequently see these types of bizarre landscapes. By rationale, if such places were common, then he should have witnessed far more of these kinds of terrestrial structures. Unless of course, he was being led somewhere unique.

That would not have been all too surprising. After all, in the past thirty hours, he had just lost his entire kingdom and was sent on a quest with a bunch of bandits who he was now too weak to kill. He hadn't had rations in a while, but it was not the disorientation of hunger that made him delusional. There was still a good amount of knowledge in the World to be salvaged and it was the need for such intellectual stimulation that was driving him nuts. He needed to learn something. Fast.

The first thing that came to mind was his enemy.

"What were those things?"

"What?" chimed Lyconel, even though she already suspected the answer.

"Those three dragons of steel veins that commanded the collective?"

"Technodragons. Futuristically enhanced reptiles."

"Futuristic? What do you mean?"

Dradicus could not help but jump in. His mind was riddled with riddles and there was nothing more preponderant in his pondering brain than paradoxes preposterous.

"Yes, Lyconel. Tell us. What does the future mean? Is this not the future now constantly budding from the stems of the past? Thus, should we not think of the future as analogous to the present and the past likewise melded with what is the ultimate 'now'? Why then, do we even need a term annotated as the 'future'?"

Lyconel rolled her eyes and tucked her head down at her inquisitive brother.

"Assuming that we ignore this oaf," she said to Dennagon, "then we can assume that the future is composed of the unseen depths that lay ahead in the path we travel along time. Those Technodragons were augmented by a time not yet arrived in this World."

Dennagon had read time travel stories many times before. They usually bored him out of his mind, what with all their senseless contradictions, and he hoped that this was not going to be another false myth told by an ignoramus.

"So what are they capable of?" he pragmatically questioned.

"Like all things in life, it matters less what they can do than what their ultimate purpose is."

"And what would that be?"

"To take control of dragonkind and reap the spoils of victory alongside…the sapiens."

The words nearly knocked him flat on his back. The sapiens were the nightmare race of all existence, feared by everyone in the collective since the time they were hatched. He could hardly imagine any sentry working peacefully in the presence of a human, let alone in the presence of the sapien subspecies that evolved from men. In fact, no one alive had ever seen a sapien and lived to tell about it as far as he knew.

Despite his shock, however, he was not completely weak-minded. He was open to other conceptions, even if his will strongly attached him to another.

"Are you surprised, Dennagon? Have you not noticed how knowledge breaks the free will of any creature, even a dragon?"

"That I have seen with my own two eyes, yet even mine eyes can lie."

"As can mine, but for now, you have nothing to believe in. So hear me. The enemy collective is conspiring with the sapiens to corrupt the minds of all dragons so that the Lexicon remains forever hidden."

"That implies that all the knowledge I was hunting was actually no more than mental contagion."

Just then, he stepped on something squishy. A black orb splattered under his feet, spilling its sugary fluids all over his feet. Drekkenoth had actually thrown one of them that far, and it now painted his lower body in ebony. The putrid substance dripped off his abdomen, and he sampled it in his claws.

"Precisely," confirmed Lyconel. "We're hunted because we refused to accept their data and their collective."

Dennagon scented the sticky substance. Inside, he could feel that it contained the atomic number for uranium, something that the Archive had not yet discovered, along with other information about chemistry that the sentries would have desired. In addition to its valuable facts, it had a pleasant aroma, but now that he actually examined it closer, he could feel a swell of dark mana rolling around its atoms. It was so faint that it was barely discernable, but he could detect it anyway. A lesser organism would not have been able to.

"These black orbs. They're meant to grant one knowledge of the workings of the World, but they bear an evil essence." He shot a confused glance at Lyconel. "Why would the Drakemight collective want to damage its own units?"

Lyconel drew her mace. Running one of its spikes against her shoulder, she gave herself a small cut.

"A damaged organism heals itself with greater potency."

Silver blood dripped from her wound.

"You see, Dennagon, now that they have tasted the dire holocaust of nuclear fire, they have hastened their absorption of information. Information, once wired into the draconic nervous system, can never be deleted. The more they work at gathering and consuming data, the more their minds grow corrupt and unwavering, as if their brains were water being frozen into unmoving and unchangeable ice. That's why we need you."

Dennagon, flattered and suspicious, cocked a brow.

"In order to defeat them, we must tap into the sole source of omniscience – the Lexicon."

"And what have I that you don't?"

"The Lexicon can only be acquired if one attains an object known as the Key. There are many obstacles on the way to this item, countless trials of difficulty that are meant to test the creatures that dare seek the ultimate goal of existence. These challenges, wrought with the influence of imagined physical laws from the powerful minds of the most potent magicians in all the lands, can only be surpassed by one who has extensive expertise on the laws of physics."

Dennagon felt like taking a dump. Luckily, he hadn't any fecal matter left in his empty stomach.

"Y-you must be jested once more."

"Enough with the false modesty. We've been watching you through telepathic means. You spent all your life reading those mountains of books that were piled up in your domicile."

"I'll even wager that he knows the gravitational force on the sun," butted in Dradicus.

Dennagon was always prepared for battle. However, by the tone of their voices, he could tell that those "tests" he would have to encounter were all but easy to surpass. He wondered what kind of beasts he would have to fight later on…For now, nevertheless, he was just trying to absorb and accept that which seemed to be his fate.

"Are you certain about these things you say, warrior Lyconel?"

"As certain as one can be," she replied with a twinkle in her eye.

Ballaxior cranked his necks up, including the ones that had been severed. All his heads looked up to the aerial river, which had turned greener whilst they mobilized. He pointed up, and everyone viewed the algae and vegetation that thrived in this part of the body of water. Finally, there would be rations to restore their much-needed nutrition.

"About time," commented Dradicus.

Most of the crew could fly up thirty feet to reach it, but Lyconel and Dradicus weren't blest with wings. It was a wonder how the former managed to soar to the sky without the aid of such bodily apparatuses, let alone how she survived the plunge from the clouds after she and Dennagon fought. Notwithstanding, they all continued moving to find a spot where they could stop close enough to reach the water from the ground level.

As they walked, the terrain began to slant. Tilting by 90-degrees, it curved around as if to wrap around a spiral formation, yet they were all still bound to it by gravity. Dennagon displayed a quizzical expression.

"Something wrong?" asked Lyconel.

As if she couldn't tell just by looking.

"This land is twisted upon itself."

"Like so many things in existence."

"Yet, we're still standing on it."

"Space and time are relative. Direction and meaning are defined by relations."

"Space…I do remember reading about space."

He looked to the sky, wondering whether or not he should doubt the certitude of the outer vacuum that supposedly encased the entire globe. Before he could come to a conclusion, they ceased at a point where the land inverted by 180-degrees and the water was within talon's reach. This part of the river practically bubbled with greenery, and the dragons dove their limbs into it. Algae started to collect on their scales.

Dennagon did not bother to gather any morsels of plankton, though. He would probably have expended more energy than he would have gained by doing so, since underwater verdure was generally not the most appetizing of foods. He was more interested in the twisting land, seeing as to how the sky was now oriented toward where he used to be standing.

"I've never seen this element of the World before."

"Believe me, there's much more to be seen," Lyconel said as she licked up some clumps of algae on her arms.

Spontaneously, she dove into the river and paddled through the liquid with her drake talons. Her actions frivolous, Dennagon grew impatient.

"What are you doing, bathing?! Where the heck are we going anyway?"

"Direction is relative. I'll tell you when I'm done."

"This is ridiculous. Shouldn't we be heading forth now?"

"I'm not moving on an empty stomach," growled Nomax.

He too joined her in the waters. Shortly, Lefius dived in along with Ballaxior. Amidst the waters, they more easily consumed the aquatic vegetation floating throughout.

"Well, my friend," said Dradicus as he patted Dennagon's back. "Truth may be subjective, but one thing's for sure – we need rations to survive."

With that, he slithered into the liquid stream and joined the meager meal. Dennagon watched as they swam about like fish in a tank, bound to their need for nutrition. He had starved himself of Drekkenoth's black orbs long enough, and considering the circumstances now, he did not regret doing so. There was no reason not to forego the satisfaction of hunger in place of the necessity for progress.

"Then I shall find what must be found," he muttered to himself.

He looked to the direction they were headed toward and espied the river up ahead. Squinting his eyes, he could faintly see what lay a mile away, and a crimson patch filled his vision. There was blood in the waters further on, which meant that there was meat. Savory carnage that was recently killed and probably plentiful enough to appease his extraordinary craving. He was generally inclined to handle his duties before devouring rations, but since there were no assigned tasks to him at the moment, there was no reason to remain ascetic. If he couldn't assimilate any more knowledge, he might as well have a snack.

Licking his lips, he turned to inform his comrades of his departure. However, they appeared too occupied in their bantering and algae "feasting" to heed his leaving.

"I'll be gone for just a moment," he thought as he started toward the other end of the river.

The Aerial River stretched many miles into the south, as far as the inexact maps of the World could tell. At its end, it was thought that there laid a swamp whereupon few traveled. Fewer even knew this place existed, for its scent drove many warriors away before even coming within a single mile's range. Blood saturated the mud as if it were water, for the entire marsh was composed of bodily circulatory fluids brimming in their most concentrated form. The soil could hardly be seen in its original color, for the crimson tint of innards had been infused with its very substance just as robustly as nature had originally hued it with earthen shades. A ruby fog lingered above the surface, blurring out red puddles under a veil of gaseous gore. The smell was not at all rank, yet it bore the tinge of iron in it. Iron that had been forged at the hands of hominids, whose fingerprints still loomed like specters upon swords long broken. That was why so many fled from these places. No one wanted to go near the Red Marsh.

Except for Dennagon, of course. Unaware of its history that so many sentries knew, he lurked about its scarlet topography, searching for any signs of carrion. His mind remained rational despite the fact that his stomach spoke to him constantly. Obviously, violence had blanketed this place, yet he could find no remnants save for the bleeding essence of the swamp itself.

"What have we here?"

He looked to the side. Even the shrubs that lined the perimeter were ruby in color, their leaves like gory antitheses to photosynthetic material. With the little knowledge he stored in his mind, he contemplated why they did not die as a result of a lack of light absorption.

"Most unusual."

Lowering his head to the ground, he sniffed a leaf on the ground. Before sampling it by direct contact, he wanted to make certain that it was not a trap created by another predator. The redolence was subtle, but he didn't sense any form of venom in its veins. Carefully, he jerked it out of the ground, making certain not to tear its roots off.

The herb dangled in his claws, non-draconic blood dripping from its fractal pattern-like roots to the ground below. The mud looked almost like bits of flesh hanging off its base, and the remains of a seed shell clung to the part of the plant from which it sprouted. The leaves were splayed out from a central stem like any modern shrub, reaching toward the sunlight above. There was nothing apparently odd about it, other than the fact that it was feeding on animal fluids.

Dennagon tilted his head. The curious herb's anatomy was too ordinary to be able to support the use of blood as a life source, considering that the liquid contained as much salt as ocean water. The xylem and phloem transported fluids, the buds and nodes sent out new growths of leaves, and it seemed to be carrying out carbon dioxide assimilation just fine. There must have been something about the gore that caused it to thrive and carry out osmosis even with the high presence of salt in its soil.

Just then, a stem sharply shot out from one of the younger buds. It extended out toward his face, cells dividing a hundred times more rapidly than cancerous cells until alas, a flower burst out from its tip. The petals flashed outward in brilliant redness, casting a bouquet of stamens and pistils in his snout, each with a likeness to the entire flower itself. It was fully blossomed in less than three seconds, ready to be fertilized to the depths of its ovary womb. Pollen spurt into the air, tickling his nasal receptors.

Instantaneously, he sneezed. His dragon germs flung a prominence of mucous mist upon the fog at his feet, drenching it with his phlegm. The vapor abruptly changed color where his breath touched it, altering it to a silvery hue as if the air in his body were foreign to the haze all around. Like bacterium around a malignant virus, the fog spread out away from his sneeze in a manner that resembled that of a conscious being. Metallic, his snout's germs floated downward, hitting the ground with a slow, but impactive puff. The very blood it met turned dark, cold and dead, killed like so many strains of diseases in an alchemist's petri dishes.

It was then that he understood. The ground he stood in was not of the carcasses of regular animals, but of the most horrid animals of all. Men had fought here in a war that must have been as violent as the marsh that kept their ruins. Their reddish circulatory fluids were now recognizable in their odor, except that the land had granted the liquid with some of the World's fragrant aroma, nullifying some of the stench. There must have been hominid bodies in the hundreds once, yet there were none at the present. Only the untainted blood of men lay all around him.

Curiously, he dipped a claw into a puddle. It rippled with the visions of wars long past, displaying transient images of humans in armored splendor clashing with weapons medieval. Blades to lances, they slew each other, pouring organs upon what used to be a field of emerald grass. In little time, they eradicated one another, smashing each other's wills and weapons till shards remained of all that represented life in the soma and armaments. Those fragments disintegrated into the blood that now surrounded him, keeping the presence of the bipedal humans in the fog, shrubs and dirt. Their essence remained with what little souls the dead ones carried.

Dennagon looked to the medieval sky. It was painted with celestial grayness, clouds lining it in cirrus strokes. The heavens were eternal, he thought, as the tragedy of the humans filled his heart. He always did feel a pulse of sympathy for their path along the tides of time, for their story was a sad one. Evolution wrote their lives to advance to self-awareness and technological might, yet greed was the primary fuel that drove them. In a wheel of progress, they rolled toward ultimate dominance, enhancing their machines so that they could place their hands over all the World. However, like every wheel, the creatures had to end where they began. Avarice drove them to their doom, thence the end of humanity was sculpted in the desire to have everything. Including their own deaths.

They walked but were no longer alive. Their hearts were beating with biological functionality and their brains still took in external stimuli, but none of them truly thought anymore. They did not ponder philosophy and meaning alongside the dragons and krakens as they once did many ages ago, for their weakness had taken all but their simplest and basest existential states. Then again, no one ever pondered truth with anyone else anymore. Everyone was too far in the evolutionary line to act in accordance to alliance, for it was accepted that social orders were the prisons that locked minds out of intellectual musing. Unfortunately for man, the path to solitude was one that required another form of social shackling – the very bonds that ensnared their minds to a passion for gold.

The Drakemight collective was indeed different than the civilizations of men, for dragons intrinsically sought wisdom, not material trifles like mellifluous metals and rare minerals. Yet, even they were not without their flaws. The sentries fought for a noble quest, but their efforts were misguided by the one he once called master. Legend once said that men now lived on the ingestion of gold. Was it just as possible that the dragons in their collective vaunted thrived on the black orbs of "knowledge"?

"What have I been fooled into? Am I but an imbecile for believing in Drekkenoth or believing in Lyconel? Only one can lie, and only one can be trusted."

The clouds stirred above until they were shaken into staccato strokes of altocumulus formation. The sun began to darken in their midst, washed over by the condensed water of the heavens that signaled rain was about to fall. Such weather reminded him of his mission and that he had best meet his comrades again. They were probably frantic over where he went, which would be an added bonus of entertainment upon his return.

Of course, his initial reason for coming here was in search of food, and in that he would not fail. Such a measly task was not to be failed by one with such an outstanding record of achievement. However, even with his skilled hunting affinity, he could not detect anything edible within the range of ten miles, let alone a dead rat whose scent seemed to come from the horizon. He was running low on time and on patience, and his hunger was edging his mind even further toward an inevitable action.

He looked into one of the puddles of blood. His reflection was but a silhouette upon its surface, crimson opaqueness against the translucent backdrop. It looked like it still contained some nutrition in it, even though it had been sitting there for several decades. Aside from the grime upon its surface and the scant parasites, it shouldn't have been that bad.

"Eh, why not?" he said to himself.

Cupping some of the gore in his talons, he lifted it. The ruby fluid spilled between his claws quicker than the finest sands, running along a hastened temporal flow in an hourglass that did not exist. Strangely, the space around his environment did actually seem to be accelerated in time, for the sun above was moving faster than normal, as well as the clouds and the mists. Fleetly, the choppy altocumulus winds spread out from the solar entity in the skies, letting the noon light fall upon the marsh once more. However, the light was not as bright as it used to be. It was the illumination of an eclipse that now overcast the mud, blanketing it in bleakness undimmed.

Fiercely, the blood in his talons started to lash out. It became an amorphous organism, slashing with tentacles of liquid gore and octopus-like suckers upon flagella as malleable. Dennagon snapped back, flinging the fluid away in a spray of droplets that continued to wriggle even in the air. All around, bladed figures emerged from the shapeless masses of sanguine liquid, slicing wildly with the precision of a mindless beast. The bloody plains had become alive, rippling with the muscle and duress of an ireful animal, red liquid limbs scourging into nothingness.

Whilst he prepared to move away from the madness, the herb in his grasp twitched in his claws. He almost forgot it was there until it began writhing like a botanical worm, shrieking from its flower with a tongue of stamens. The blossom closed upon itself, cocooning into a bundle of petals that just as quickly withered into decaying tongues of brown. The entire plant exploded before he could let go of it, casting seeds everywhere. Each one of the verdurous embryos scattered, sucking in the blood from the air and soils to feed an insatiable craving for iron. Most of them sprouted before even hitting the ground, their roots branching down to the ground like thunderous bolts of umbrage born.

They grew toward the sun, straining toward it with foliage of crimson. Dennagon looked up, only to see a solar entity that was as black as the night, perhaps even darker. At first, he thought it was an actual eclipse, but that would have been impossible, since there were no known satellites that traveled around the World for over a millennium. The sun itself had become sable, an umbra of dark light cast upon the earth, as nightmarish as it was real. It was a totality without a moon, a complete anomaly that had arisen out of nowhere. The red plants loved it, and reached as far as they could to photosynthesize the negative luminosity.

Dennagon tumbled to the ground, nearly splashing into one of the puddles. Closing his eyes, he would not look into the dark solar entity, for he had read that eclipses could render one blind. Hopefully, his perception was wrong and he had just seen a totality of the sun.

The sloshing of the blood sounded all around. Underneath his palms and eyelids, he could see the glow of the dark radiance coming from the sky passing through his flesh. He would wait till it receded, but in the meantime, he sharply avoided the slashing tentacles of gore that came from every direction. Using only his auditory organs, he agilely maneuvered his way out of incoming attacks. With a somersault, he bounded over a sideswipe, and followed through with a flank-side twirl that dodged an overhead strike. A duck saved him from being beheaded by a blade of pure gore.

Alas, some more light seemed to be spilling between his claws. He opened his eyes again as the sun returned to its ordinary state, bright as the noon at the heavenly zenith. At the same time, the puddles stopped contorting, and all their tentacles fell back down, splashing into their original, shapeless figures. For a few seconds, he remained in combative posture, ready to take another attack. When tranquility abounded, he took a steady breath of relief.

"Whew," he let out.

He took one step forth. His peripheral vision peeked at a puddle to his side and caught not only a silhouetted reflection of himself, but of another dragon behind him. He probably would not have seen it if there weren't a gigantic axe held at least 25 feet in the air.

Dennagon took a roll. The massive blade slammed the

ground in his wake, heaving two tremendous waves of dirt on either side of its double-edge surface. Gorgash the behemoth towered behind him, wailing the weapon with a roar that was as bestial as a hundred lions combined. The shrubs shirked back to their ordinary growth postures whilst gargantuan feet stomped betwixt puddles in horrifying rumbles. He lifted the axe again.

Dennagon immediately cupped another talonful of blood and tossed it in the air. The gore splattered in the enemy's eyes, temporarily distracting his vision. The immense blade came down at its target's side, knocking Dennagon twenty feet away, but not directly striking him. Gorgash fumbled around for a few moments whilst the ruby liquid seeped beneath his scales and into the circuits that structured his body. He tumbled around, flapping his wings violently in a crazed disorientation. One of the wings batted the ambushed target yet again, tossing him even further.

"Ah!" shouted Dennagon as he was walloped.

The behemoth steadied himself and rearmed his weapon. Locking his focus on the mark, he bore his fangs.

"Target acquired," he declared. "You will be annihilated."

With that, he bolted in, galloping on his two hind legs whilst wailing his weapon wildly from side to side. Dennagon charged on all fours, dashing across drier patches of mud and zigzagging away from the axe as it came below and above him. The behemoth was amazingly expedient for its size and even at max speed, he could not outrun the rampaging assault. Steel shined on all sides, wide flashes that gleamed of the blade's metal that swung at all flanks and angles. The pursuit was relentlessly ferocious.

Finally, the axe came toward his midsection again. Dennagon pounced up, torqued and jammed his legs into the blade's flat as it passed underneath. Thrusting himself off the metallic surface, he drew his sword and threw a right swing right into his enemy's face. Steel carved through cyborg iron circuits, renting a bloody trench in the opponent's visage.

Gorgash flinched, but did not fall. Instead, he grabbed Dennagon in midair with a giant talon and hurtled him backwards toward the remains of a dead tree. Although the force was stunning, it would have been more effective if Dennagon did not have wings with which he used to slow himself. Halting his motion in flight, he hovered down atop the tree, three stories above ground level and at the height of his adversary's head.

Gorgash came in once more, this time more cautiously. Dennagon carved his sword through the foggy mist, clashing against the giant axe as quicker melee strikes were delivered. All the while, he weaved his way through the rotting arbor, snaking between branches and behind the mossy trunk. More than once, the assailant thought he hit him, only to realize that the target had been mistaken for a branch. A few minor slashes were easily parried by the comparatively smaller sword.

Finally, the battle drew the impatience of the opponent. Gorgash lifted his weapon high above his head, heaving it down for a mega-smash. There was no point in trying to deflect this attack, so Dennagon swiftly leapt out of the tree, letting the massive steel armament tear it apart into fungal chunks of shattered wood. Nearly falling into a puddle of blood, he stumbled onto the ground and clumsily regained his posture.

Immediately, he then jumped straight into his enemy. As he expected, the axe sheered at him again, creating mammoth gashes through the beclouded vapor rising from the swamp. Rolling in the air, he clashed against the enemy weapon, using its unrestrained forces to toss himself up, down, and all around. It just kept coming, and with each attack, he thrust his way closer to the opponent's body. Gorgash, in a crazed attempt to ravage his pesky little prey, was bringing the blade dangerously close to himself as his target drew near. Each time he assaulted, aggravation built up tenfold.

Suddenly, the behemoth ceased, stopping the axe from striking his own abdomen. Dennagon had come close enough to launch an onslaught on his enemy's brain, but he was much too smart for that. Whilst Gorgash instantly lifted an elbow to defend his own cranium, Dennagon slipped under his forearm and hacked the enemy's side deltoid with a backhand slash, following through with a stab to the wrist ligaments. The monumental dragon snapped back at the two-pronged maneuver, clenching his slit mechanical veins as silver robot fluids spilled. Tripping on the stump of the fallen dead tree, he slammed headfirst into the bog, squeezing from its mud several hundred gallons of human blood upon impact.

The gore drenched his circuits. Horrifically, he screamed, but it was less a wail of pain than a cry of war. As the hominid gore slipped into his chips and metal armor, Gorgash's true form became apparent. The Technodragon anatomy coursed through every bit of his flesh and bone, becoming temporarily transparent in some areas. An entire exoskeleton of platinum lined his skeleton, surging with electric currents that guided every thought in his metal-cold brain of plasma-hot neural synapses. It was utterly shocking to see a comrade he had known so long enchanted with the strange technology he had seen in his private collection, yet Dennagon felt inside that he should not have been too surprised.

Without another second to waste, he rushed in to finish off the cyborg reptile before it could rise. Stomping onto Gorgash's back, he hurled his sword straight down, a terminating blow that he usually used on even the most aggressive of his past enemies. Unexpectedly, the blade hit the scales of the spinal cord, only to resound with a metal ring. The dermal layer was composed completely of steel. Its vibration shuddered the hilt and shook Dennagon to the core.

Gorgash shot a menacing half-turn.

"Uh-oh."

A sharp elbow whacked Dennagon in the chest, knocking him away like a fly. Gorgash rolled onto his front side, clenching one of his immense fists. His entire forearm dismantled itself into jointed mechanical parts that started to realign. The claw bones receded back toward his bicep to form the barrels of a firearm, the wrist bones turned into junctions that connected various elements, and the palm, ulna and radius portions of the arm turned into a cylinder studded with switches. Firing mechanisms fell into place with what was left of the knuckles, completing the new weapon that had formed – a plasma cannon.

"What the?!"

The question could hardly be processed before a radiant orb of energy encircled by flying rings of electrons ripped toward him. Dennagon craned his neck back, barely dodging it as it burned the red fog above his head. It hit the ground thirty feet behind him, erupting into an explosive blast. He spun around, spinning his sword to fan off the droplets of blood that rained down.

"Annihilate Sentry Dennagon! Annihilate!"

A barrage of plasma shots came. Dennagon first tried to blend out of their way, but their velocity proved to be far greater in magnitude than that of a current of electricity through copper. Twisting his sword in awkward positions, he feverishly warded off the offensive by knocking away the atom-shaped projections with batted strikes and upward cleaves. Howbeit, the storm was ruthless, plasma lightning raging from torrents of crimson, gaseous gore. The pressure was growing as quickly as the expanding space of the cosmos.

The metal of his sword rapidly became charred. In its relative flimsiness, it abruptly fractured at the very edge, letting an emission pass through its bladed gate and into his chest. A spurt of silver carnage accompanied a shower of burnt iron fragments from the chipped weapon. He collapsed.

A splash. At first, he didn't know what it was, except that he felt wet from all sides. For a moment, it seemed like plain water, but after a second a chilling sensation ran through him. It was not of temperature frigidness, but rather, of tactile and mental cold. The semblance of ice rippled up his spine, ricocheting against his nerves and sinew until every cell of his body detected it. Gelid fear coursed through him, touched with the garnish of avarice and the repugnant taste of hate. Stripped from his regular state of consciousness, the essence of the dragon fleeted away from him for an instant, ghostly and passing as the distant galaxies in the night sky. It returned only to let him know one thing – he had fallen into the human blood. The redness seeped into his scales like worms in a carcass, liquid wriggling forms that resembled the solid objects of the earth burrowing into his mind and soul. The penetrating evil was everywhere, ruby in color and just as hard as the stone that gave the hue its namesake. His heart nearly stopped, but only in that it spent all his energy and focus to break away. To rise from the depths.

The puddle was only two feet deep, but he felt like he was drowning. Frantically, he ripped himself out of it, slashing his talons around and sending red waves into the surrounding dirt. Frenetically, he climbed out as gory liquid tentacles reached for him in friendly gestures, beckoning his whim to return to the plight of men destroyed. Mightily, he refused their bequeathed and sinister amicability, running as far from them as possible. A trail of blood splotches followed his wake as he dashed, soaked in sanguine carnage. Unwittingly, he hit something with a hefty collision.

Accidentally ramming into Gorgash's belly, Dennagon fell onto his back. The behemoth did not even budge as he raised the axe for a killing blow.

"It was not wise to defy us," came the deep-voiced comment.

Suddenly, mankind's gore seeped into Dennagon's cranium, fusing with the nerve cells at the edge of his cerebral membrane. Oozing into his cerebellum and brainstem, it instilled the aspect of a hominid in his biological functions, inciting a flare of ire in his thoughts. Enraged, he sprung up and slammed his fists into the ground before his enemy's stroke could fall, sending a wave of mud forth. The tide burst up like a fanned tsunami, washing over Gorgash's face and visual organs, throwing bleakness upon his sights.

The blade swooped down. Dennagon scooted to the side, letting the axe fall to his flank whilst he rushed directly into his opponent. Headfirst, he bolted at full throttle, butting the adversary beast straight in the weakest parts of the draconic abdomen. Surprised, Gorgash lurched, reeling back at the heavy clout that beset him. The force practically wrenched his feet from the ground and his talons from his weapon, crashing him onto his side to create a trench that stretched a hundred feet. Dennagon careened with him, sliding off and into a group of shrubs as Gorgash came to a stop. Springing off the ground, he leapt back in the direction from whence he came, over his disoriented adversary.

The axe spun in the air, an enormous bulk of several tons of metal wheeling slowly in the air. Dennagon flew right past its downward-swiping blade and propelled his legs down with a drilled plunge. Contacting the weapon by its handle, he drove it further toward the ground with an incredible strength, leading it at an angle toward its former owner. Gorgash tried to stand again, but his eyes dilated as he saw the axe rocket straight toward him. The blade buried itself in his Technodragon skull, deactivating him instantaneously. He flopped over with a quaking rumble, extracting even more gore from the bleeding ground as his prodigious body hit the terrain like a gauntlet around a soaked cloth.

Dennagon victorious perched upon the pommel of the axe that was mounted at an angle blade-first in his defeated foe's forehead. Sliding down its tilted handle, he scraped his fangs against the incapacitated dragon's head and popped up onto the ground once more. It was nice to admire his work.

"Perhaps it was not wise to defy you, but wisdom comes in so many shapes and forms. Besides, who needs knowledge when you have victory?"

He shook his head. Did he just say that?

More footsteps emerged from behind. Lyconel and Dradicus hurried in, weapons drawn in combative stances. They viewed their comrade, who was strangely frozen in a maniacally quizzical visage with his veins immersed in the reddened blood. It was unusual for a sentry to behave this way, and even for the short while they knew him, he never acted in such a strange manner. Nonetheless, the most important attribute of him was that he was still alive.

"What happened?!" blared Lyconel.

Dennagon could not answer.

"Why did you –"

Sooner than she could finish, Dradicus pointed a tail at the comatose Gorgash. It was a wonder they didn't notice him before and instead were drawn to view Dennagon first.

"A Technodragon!" they both shouted simultaneously.

Dradicus slashed out from a sidepack strapped to his lower midsection a pair of whips with which he lashed the air. Lyconel armed her spiked mace and hurtled it at the beast as quickly as she could. Unfortunately, Gorgash, speedier than either of the two, lifted a talon to deflect the sharp-studded weapon with the iron side of his forearm. He rose, thrusting out both clawed upper appendages to let out a deafening roar.

Everyone clutched their heads. The hellish sonic emission tore through the fabric of space, piercing their eardrums. Gorgash expeditiously burst open his wings, sending a gust of wind that blew the crimson fog behind him with the flare of fission energy. Two rockets extended out from the top of his tail, tipped with cones of conflagration as blue as the deep ocean. In a flux of stellar energy, he emitted an eruption of nuclear pulses, sending circumpolar shockwaves out to create a crater around himself. In a thundering boom and clap of pure light, he lifted off, racing into the sky at the speed of a jet. Smoke trailed behind him, burnt with the fury of atomic physics and the loss of a medieval battle. He was gone.

"Blast!" cursed Dradicus.

Lyconel galloped to Dennagon and helped him up. Her benign face was tinted with the marks of amazement.

"How did you defeat him?!"

Even he did not know.

"Why did you wander here?" she lowered the tone of her voice.

Dennagon searched himself. Then, he realized the answer he sought was the answer itself.

"To find something."

"What?"

"I don't know."

Dradicus scanned his eyes across the skies. He was a fool at heart, but not in vision and environmental awareness.

"The enemy will be here shortly. We can't let them find our trail."

He motioned his comrades to follow.

"We have to keep moving."

Lyconel tried to assist Dennagon in his stride, but he lightly pushed her away. This was going to be a long battle, but he wouldn't submit to a dependency on others. He stood alone and he always would. Now and forever.

CHAPTER 5

Everything was alive to a certain extent. Even the World itself had its own form of sentience, for it too was a biological organism. Gaia theory never held much more credence than it did for those who actually understood it, for in everyday existence, one could easily see that the globe did in fact live and breath and think. The waters and the lands were the flesh and blood, the skies and air were skin and bones, and the Supersurface Cave Network was the nervous system that linked to the spine and core brain. That was why cavernous structures extended far out into the air above the lands that speckled the seas to form marble, stone and lime tubes that branched out like a web of earthen roots. Spanning acres, they dove in and out of the rocky terrain in gnarled, branched corridors. These grottoes served as conduits to the inner planet and lined the globe from pole to pole, essential to the World's survival. However, they were only useful to a select few. Those that dared brave the inner workings of the planetary machine were the only ones that could utilize this aspect of the earth as an advantage. Peril was never more prevalent than it was within those walls.

Dradicus snaked along a massive outcropping of the supersurface caves. Warily, he slithered his wurm body everywhere to survey the exterior of the rocky tunnels. Of course, there was no point in searching inside of the pathways, as to do so would be to place oneself in danger to begin with. Searching the outside was the best he could do, and from his vantagepoint, there was no threat.

He gestured to the rest of his party, who moved up at his signal. Lefius and Ballaxior entered first, for their combat skills outmatched those of the others. Lyconel and Dennagon stayed in the center, followed by old Ballaxior, who slowly marched behind. His heads were bobbing with every step he took, and heaving breaths accompanied his motions.

Dennagon carefully held his scabbard still, for within it, the shards of his chipped sword were held in place. When he had the strength to breath fire, he would re-forge the fracture, but for now, he did not want the charred metal to take any more damage. He had taken enough damage himself and he didn't need any other weaknesses to get in his way.

"So how," he asked Lyconel, "do we intend to get this gate to the Lexicon? This item you called the 'Key'?"

"The World has two poles. One is called the Alpha and the other is called the Omega. Only we, the ones who have the gift of open-mindedness, can traverse to either."

"So which one is it?"

"To obtain the Key, we have to go to the Alpha Pole, where frost reigns supreme."

"Then what's this?" he asked, pointing to the overworld caverns.

"The Supersurface Cave Network."

"I thought we were going to the Alpha Pole."

She smirked at Ballaxior.

"Not without sufficient weaponry," he said.

Ballaxior smirked back, advisor of the crew who was the one who suggested that they came here in the first place. His grin was on many of his hydra heads, curved and wrinkled through many ages of smiles and frowns. The sight of his faces lightened up Dennagon's heart in their blunted fangs and kindly eyes. Albeit he viewed the visages of an elder, he could see inside the pupils a whelp as carefree as the midsummer night and innocent as a young, half-century-old bonsai. There was something soothing about the old dragon's semblance that made him feel comfortable, like he was back at Drakemight. However, it also seemed like there was something behind that inculpable appearance, information he was forbidden to know. A clandestine essence lived beyond what he saw in those hazel green eyes that fronted every head with shades of oddness. Then again, perhaps it was best that he never knew what the elder hydra was hiding. Sometimes, things were best kept in secret.

Lyconel seized a stone that was positioned precariously in front of a crack in the wall of one of the supersurface caves. Rolling it out of the way, she revealed an orifice large enough for Nomax, the largest of the group, to fit in. She waved her talon.

"Come hither, new comrade."

Dennagon approached the seemingly normal orifice. Lyconel casually slipped into it, and as soon as she passed its walls, the caves engulfed her in total darkness. The shadows within bore neither umbras nor penumbras, but were instead swabs of total darkness that lingered in three-dimensional space. Even as sunlight struck the interior of the grotto, the illumination did not follow her in. It was literally a sightless realm.

Dennagon was hesitant for a second. Nomax crossed his talons, a bladed disk armed in his clutches.

"What are you? Afraid, hero?"

Dennagon decided it was best to ignore the brutish serpent. Calculating, he entered the bleakness as well.

The web of winding, rocky corridors turned in every which direction, chaotic and spontaneous. Yet, Dennagon only knew this through touch as he tried to traverse inside. His claws scraping the glossy, smooth walls, he tried to feel his way through in the depths of the totally blacked out chambers. In all directions, everything was tactilely alike and there were no landmarks. He didn't even know where he was supposed to be going, let alone how to get there.

"Um, Lyconel? Lyconel? You there?"

He wished he had an eye-seeing falcon like blind dragons did.

"Where the hell are we?"

A tail whacked him over the head.

"Sorry," came her voice. "This way."

"Which way?"

"This."

"What's 'this'?"

"Which?"

"This."

"The way?"

"Yes."

"This way."

She held his talon and started leading him through. Great. Now he felt like a whelp in its spawner's clutches.

"These places hold many secrets," she stated. "Hidden secrets that can only be found by those who are willing to risk life and lobotomy through blade and boulder."

"If you have something so treasured here, why not just bury it and speckle a bunch of stones around it?" he asked as his personal collection of items came to mind.

"Because there is no certainty that it is safe out there. In here, no one knows where to look, so I can be sure that it is concealed from the searching eyes of thieves and gold-tongued humans."

"Certainty? How can you be certain of anything in here? It is pitch-blackness unlike any dungeon I've ever explored!"

Lyconel was grinning right in front of him, and even though he couldn't see her, he somehow knew.

"Oh, wipe that stupid smile off your face. I'm only here for my benefit, 'comrade'."

"No, I'm not laughing at comradeship, I'm snickering at your ignorance, dolt. In uncertainty lies certainty. They're one and the same, twins of opposing nature."

"Certainty is uncertainty's brother? I may as well say that I am my father's father!"

"Theoretically, you could be. Certitude implies that something is irrefutable, yet in complete darkness, I can say that anything is certain."

"Why?"

"Because I can never be certain that anything is happening, so all possibilities must be happening at once."

There were too many thoughts bogging his mind. She had just about contradicted herself in every way, yet by the tone of her voice, she thought she was right. That very fact was troubling. This he could not ignore, seeing a member of his species so moronically illogical.

"You need to get your head checked," he said.

Just then, his cranium smacked right into a stalactite. He bumbled back, clutching his forehead. After getting up, they kept moving and he continued his diatribe, a headache lingering in his temples.

"How can multiple realities be happening at the same time? It defies logic and the very nature of the idea is pure absurdity. Reality is reality, be it in a dream or in the material world, for what one observes is essentially real. The oldest philosophical pondering in the history of the World, good Lyconel."

Her talon abruptly wrenched from his grasp. He slashed around in the air for a while, almost desperate to find it.

Silence took him for a moment as he wondered what happened to her.

"Good Lyconel?"

"I'm still here," her voice resounded from the left.

"Oh good, because I was growing concerned."

He reached for her, but she wasn't there.

"Or maybe I'm here," came her voice from behind.

He growled. His sonic patterns echoed throughout the stony walls and he could paint in his mind a mental spatial picture of her location. Although it was a blurred and flawed detection method, he still gathered enough information to determine that she was scurrying along the walls from one place to another.

"This is no time for games," he asserted.

"Who's playing?" she asked.

He continued to look around. Her motions became more erratic, as random as the twists and turns of the corridors through which he mobilized.

"Why are you doing this? We're wasting trices," he declared.

"To show you something."

"What would that be?!"

"Nothing."

Dennagon buried his claws in the rock walls. His scales chipped of a bit as they penetrated the mineral surface, but it was worth it. If he could find no landmarks, he would make some.

"Have it your way, wench. I'm out of here."

He started heading back toward the general direction from where he entered, carefully plotting his claw marks as he went. Around his vicinity, he could hear the other unseen unit scuttling about him.

"Do you still need a guide, Dennagon?"

"Not at all. I know there's only one way back and I'll find it."

"How do you know there aren't two?"

"If there were two, even better."

"Three? Four? Five?"

"In the bleakness, I shall strive."

As he proceeded, he saw a faint patch of light in the distance.

"You know, a dragon in a box, if left unobserved for three days, might die," added Lyconel.

"Then again, it might not. I'll get out of here in less than a minute, so don't worry about me."

"I'm not concerned. But if the dragon in the box cannot be observed for three days, how would one know it was alive or dead without opening the encasing tomb?"

"Induction. Probability. The same science that drives the strength of the dragons and opposes the weakness of the religious."

The light spot was getting larger. He was coming closer to the exit.

"Can you ever be totally certain with probability?"

He furrowed a brow. Even he had to admit that the answer was –

"No."

"So how can you assert that it's definitely in one particular state?"

"I can't. I can only estimate."

"Then if no one can say for certain that the dragon in the box is dead or alive, then it must exist in both states simultaneously."

He took another step. The light spot suddenly vanished out of his view. Complete darkness usurped his view once more. Circumspect, he backtracked, his hind leg touching the ground behind to locate his last claw mark.

"That's impossible. There is no way something can be in two places at the same time."

"How about a light wave?"

Dennagon shifted back to where he was, but the light spot still was not there. Or maybe he wasn't in the same place he wanted to be. There was no way he could tell, surrounded by nothing but blackness and the sound of that irritating drake's ramblings.

"Light waves," she resumed, "can be spread out across a grander range, unlike particles, which are supposedly fixed in one place and time. Just as the stars are painted onto the celestial sphere unchanging, particles can occupy only one point in spatial and temporal currents."

"So why did that light disappear? Why can't I find my way now?" complained Dennagon, who was now struggling to trace his route.

Lyconel ignored his pining.

"However, if you were to cast the mellifluous light upon a particle, its cosmic position would change by order of the light's granting energy."

"So?!"

"How can you ever find the journey of a lonely particle if that particle remains forever dim? Should you radiate it with the currents of the sun, then it would stray from its path, leaping onto the flanks of the road upon which the universe bound it. Thence into the forest of uncertainty it would wander, lost amidst groves of senseless observers."

Dennagon nervously straggled in the entombment. He lost the path of his claw marks and was completely unaware of where he should be facing. Disoriented, his quest to escape was hopelessly lost. With nothing left to do, he considered what she had to say and came to his own conclusions about the nature of the cosmos.

"So if I cannot observe something, then it is not real," he correctly stated. "Therefore, in a state of total nothingness, everything would be equally real."

"Thereupon, all possible realities would exist at once."

The truth was inexorable now. The uncertainty of the universe could be molded according to the certainty created by the perception of the mind – the unification of quantum mechanics and relativity that he had read about long ago in a book now burnt in the ashes of Drakemight. Lyconel was concealing her valued items in this dark realm for the sole purpose of leaving it only up to her mind to create the reality amidst the fog of war. This was her fortress, crafted by her mind, for her mind and of her mind. That was why she wanted it. To be ensconced in shadows eternal.

Still, she would not reveal herself yet. Dennagon touched something familiar, and his claws sampled something they had created. It was the first marking he made as he tried to leave himself a trail to be followed. Recognizable by its distinct deepness, he remembered jamming his pointed digits in fairly far into the varnished wall. He had come back to where he had started, much effort exerted, but no fruition ultimately reaped. He had been cheated by no hand other than his own.

"Very well, Lyconel. You win. I hath concede to your superior intellect, oh mighty drakess, so if you don't mind, would you please lead me to wherever you wanted to take me? I am getting claustrophobic."

He heard some scuttling, but he wanted to make certain that it was her. Clenching his larynx, he squeezed the flammable fluids in his throat to secrete chemicals that mixed to spark a flame. A heated orb formed down the back of his jaws, green in hue. He was ready to breath out and lighten the entire area.

The scuttling became urgently quick. Two talons clapped his mouth shut just before he could unleash the fire. In a brief instant before his flame was quelled, he saw Lyconel clasping his jaws as if it were a life and death situation.

"Then don't breath fire, lest you want this cave to collapse you into a space so small you wouldn't be able to move the width of an atom. Or a human brain."

Placing her tail in his talons, she once again led him through the paths. A silent sigh of relief resonated in his mind.

———————

Outside the orifice of the Supersurface Cave Network, Nomax and Lefius stood guard whilst lounging like unwitting grunts at the same time. After all, that's what they were if not for the discipline of purpose. Warriors meant for the kill they were designed by who knows what in the when. Their weapons were their minds, for they traveled the World with nothing else but death on their thoughts, slaying at will and scavenging like sordid animals on the incessant prowl. That is, until they found Lyconel. For some reason, she had a reason for living, one that went beyond the menial quest for rare minerals and glorious artifacts built by the hands, talons, tentacles and brains of many creatures. Instead, she sought something far beyond the realm of materialism and hunted the one thing only dreamers went for. The Lexicon was indeed a commendable object to acquire, one that most would regard as ludicrously difficult to find if it even existed at all. They called her asinine, witless, simple and even whelpish to trample upon her morale with the hooves of venomous words. Yet, words meant nothing to her. They were like matter. Nor did they mean anything to these two brutes, for they knew that finding the Lexicon meant finding omniscience. And finding omniscience meant finding all the material entities their hearts desired.

"The Geveshtor Crystal," blurted Lefius.

"Yes," was the blunt reply.

"The Firilax Blacklight at the Sollen Plains."

"Fine."

"How about the entire kingdom of Menovis in all its radium substance?"

"Okay."

Lefius could tell his friend was distracted from the game they usually challenged each other to.

"Fine. How about a pile of minotaur fecal matter in the middle of a labyrinth?"

Nomax was obviously not paying attention.

"Suit yourself."

Lefius slithered his wyvern head right up next to the preoccupied ouroboros' ear.

"NOMAX!"

Nomax snapped back. He pushed Lefius' face away.

"What?!"

"I was giving you a roster of the most valuable items in all the World and you just said 'yea' to all of them. You're the most relentless guy I know. You can't possibly be that jaded."

"Slash your tongue, piffle wyvern. I have not garnered over a thousand kills to be called a jaded jester. I'm thinking, that's all."

"What's angering you today? You're biting your tail more than usual."

Gnawing the tail that was always in his mouth, Nomax squinted his eyes fiercely.

"That damn sentry."

"Ah, Dennagon. I can't believe he took that Technodragon down."

Nomax bit harder. A chomp like that would have taken the head off of any unlucky beast.

"You think he is still loyal to the collective?" continued Lefius.

"I don't think. I know."

Ballaxior bustled in, stretching his gray-scaled necks to

relieve them of the wrinkled postures they were usually in. He carried with him a stash of herbs that he had recently plucked from the ground near the bases of the overworld caves. Heartily, he offered some to his friends.

"It is wise," he noted, "to mind the decisions of our leader Lyconel. She is the greatest warrior amongst us."

"True, she possesses a free-spirited mind, but she still requires you for advice," said Lefius factually.

Nomax growled, offended by the statement the elder hydra dared to make with an implication that everyone in the group, including himself, was inferior to Lyconel.

"Say what you will, old one, but I'm only here on a bounty hunter's decree – Make the kills, hack the heads and take my share of the glory. End of story."

"The stories never end, or at least not the good ones. The cosmos is eternal, and all time is what is really substantial. Every moment is thus precious."

Enraged, Nomax seized the elder by his throats. Ballaxior had many heads that were still free, but his sinew was too decrepit to fight back. Even if he could, he wouldn't, for he had fought in the past already. There was no need to perpetuate the violence, especially when the underside of Nomax's oral-bound tail began to protrude numerous lines of cartilaginous spikes, shielding his body with an aegis as belligerent as it was defensive.

"Do you mean that I am not intelligent, elder guide?!"

Ballaxior spoke with all heads at once.

"Meaning is derived from subjectivity. In fact, the meaning of 'meaning' is subjective."

Nomax peered into the many heads of his momentary captive. Ballaxior did the same, except he saw farther into the psyche than his assailant could. There was very little depth in Nomax's mind, for it had been taken by swarming hatred for everything that lived. Then again, every being always had something beyond the surface, no matter how far one looked into its brain. Everyone had something to hide.

"I think," stated Nomax firmly, yet insincerely, "that you led that Technodragon to us."

Ballaxior did not refute the accusation, for he knew that uncertainty rendered anything possible and it was therefore pointless to make any argument of it. Nomax simply threw him into a wall and clenched his fists. Crossing his arms, he leaned against the wall of the supersurface caves and brooded in rage.

Lefius shrugged as Dradicus entered, having completed another scouting cycle. His pupils shifted from side to side, wide-eyed and wondering.

"Did I miss something?" he quaintly asked.

───────────────

They had been traveling for over two minutes now, but alas, Dennagon and Lyconel reached their destination. Although he still couldn't see anything except shadows, Dennagon knew as he slid down a rounded floor that he was in a particularly special place. His tail grazed against cold, smooth metallic surfaces as it swung about, tapping the rock walls occasionally. Judging by the echoing of his breathing, it was spacious enough to fit ten dragons of his size, and since Lyconel was only three-quarters his mass, there was plenty of room. It was probably a library, and not a moment too soon. He was dying to read something.

"Almost there," said Lyconel with enthusiasm.

"Is this a chamber of books?"

She reached up for a dangling chain. Tugging on it, she sparked an energetic reaction in a magnesium filament at the center of a glass container hanging on top of the area. A spherical space was revealed in a sudden burst of illumination emitting from a 20th century light bulb, which also illuminated everything else in the room. Weapons of all sorts lined the stone from the floor to walls to ceiling, from every era past, present – and future. It was an armory secretive, an arsenal of battle gear hidden. Artillery to hand-held armaments, he recognized many of the objects as sabers, halberds, lances and diadems. However, the vast majority of the items he had no idea what to make of. These strange weapons were mostly composed of metal parts, elongated on their ends by thin barrels connected to central mechanisms that seemed to contain pellets of powder and solid lead. Each one was built with complex inner chambers that contained little rotary hammers that seemed to react at the pivot of a trigger. Oddly, a few of them were even wired with the same circuits that he saw in that horrid creature he fought at the Red Marsh, only on a much smaller magnitude. It was all very interesting, seeing as to how he now had a chance to see pieces of these "futuristic" works in their completion.

"Aha," he muttered, fascinated.

With the darkness washed away, he looked to the shadow-cleansing light bulb that granted him the ability to finally see in those wretched grottoes. Tapping on its glass surface, he examined the inside filament. No traces of mana were detected.

"What sorcerer can summon light without White Magic?"

Lyconel clicked the bulb on and off.

"One that's mastered the physical laws of this World."

"Then how can you say that knowledge is venom?"

"Because perhaps it is better to create our own laws than to comply with those that we are given."

She was still clicking the bulb. He got the idea. Annoyed, he seized her wrist.

"Would you cut that out?"

Lyconel let go and motioned toward the arsenal.

"These are weapons of all ages. Although we as dissidents can't travel through time as easily as the humans now can, we can gather the scraps of other warriors to build these machines. We reconstructed these firearms from the remains of fallen enemies and most of them are pretty functional."

She showed him a machinegun again.

"Remember this?"

He nodded, still not quite sure how these "firearms" operated. To add to his befuddlement, Lyconel pulled out an even larger, more complex machinegun that was composed of multiple rotary barrels that alternated between discharging. She spun the barrels around, making certain that they were working properly before taking it into battle. Holding it out, she showed it to her comrade.

"It's called a gun. It existed in the future, or rather, a future."

"Again with this 'future' rubbish. Who can define what such a term means? If that thing, that 'gun' as you call it really did come from the future, then what happens if it is used to destroy its inventor? If it hadn't been invented, then how can it have been there to destroy the one that caused its existence?"

The temporal paradoxes were the ones always thought of by children who knew no better. Strangely enough, however, the simplest questions were usually the most difficult ones to answer.

"As I said before, there are countless possibilities where one's eyes and mind do not fall. These multiple realities can allow for the existence of seemingly impossible occurrences, since one does not always have to stay in one reality."

"So if I contradict one reality by eliminating the existence of a particular cause, then I end up in another?"

"Precisely."

Dennagon's cackle resounded through the entire cave

network. It was one of the silliest things he had ever heard.

"Oh, I get it. You're an indulger of fantasies. Laws may be illusory in many cases, but you can't defy logic."

"And why not?" retorted Lyconel, her arm bent akimbo on her hip.

"Because it's logic!"

"What if I were to say that the only truth in the universe was the infinitely reflexive acknowledgement that there is no truth?"

"Then I would say that your infinitely reflexive nihilistic conjecture requires logic to live. Thus it dies the moment it is born. A beginning and an end in one tight little package."

Lyconel could not find a refutation. For once, her jaws hung open only in offense.

"Causality," continued Dennagon, "is the line that keeps the World turning and the stars from falling off their eternal celestial sphere. Without causal occurrences, there would be no time and thence, no existence. So you can't tell me that I could eradicate the cause of an event from the shores of reality's ocean and expect to remain untouched by a violent tide of nonexistence. There is a reason why certain laws cannot be altered."

Sullen, she frowned.

"Show me a proof and I shall concede."

"Show me a multiverse and I shall recede."

She tossed the huge machinegun at him. It clunked as he caught it, jerking him back with a heavy tug. It was either a lot heavier than it looked or she was a lot stronger than she was making herself out to be.

"Let's get back to the mission, shall we?"

Surveying her wondrous collection of militaristic engineering, Lyconel rummaged through the various piles of weapons. The search for the perfect weapon was what her mind was locked on at the moment, and she would find one that suited their current needs. Unfortunately, the environment immediately following this stage of her journey would not be suited for weapons at all, so she took that into account as well. She just hoped that they would be able to pass to the Alpha Pole without having to lose any of their firearms, artillery, ammunition or lives so that they could be able to do some massive shooting. A bloodbath was what she really looked forward to.

In the middle of her armament forage, she yanked out a rocket launcher.

"Hmmm… Not right now."

Restraining her bloodlust, she placed it back and continued searching. Every weapon she tossed back was accompanied by a "no" that incessantly repeated as she rummaged. There had to be an ideal weapon somewhere.

A grenade launcher flew out as Lyconel cast back the ones she did not want. Dennagon liked the design on that particular weapon, what with its enlarged barrel and sizeable firing mechanisms. The shape reminded him of a serpent's, for it was bulky, yet compact enough to be maneuverable at the same time. A group of rounded balls were nestled inside its chamber behind the hammer, occupying most of the center of the piece of technology and were probably used as gears of some sort. Or so he thought. To test it out, he retrieved it.

Lyconel had burrowed through most of her armory, and all the complex weapons were apparently not suitable for this scenario. Though the worst and puniest weapon of her collection was rarely used, if ever, she decided that it was necessary in this case. Everything in life was situational, and this was no different. She retrieved the pistol.

"Dennagon, I found the –"

Just as she turned around, Dennagon dabbled his claws against the handles of the grenade launcher. It was an alien sensation to hold a weapon in this way, for the closest thing to it was an archer's accouterment. Nevertheless, he was unable to determine how to use it. To search for clues, he turned it upward toward his face so that he could look into the barrel.

"Hmm."

Lyconel lunged in. Torquing the weapon away from him, she pointed its barrel at an angle just as his claw accidentally tripped the trigger. It fired a shot that tore out like a comet engulfed in silver fire. The discharge barely missed the light bulb and hit the wall at the other side of the chamber, blasting out thick sheets of granite. Dennagon stared stunned for a moment, blinking in petrifaction. Now he understood why he was not supposed to breathe fire in here. There was enough firepower already.

With her index claw and pinky, she lightly yanked the weapon away from him.

"I don't think that weapon is for you."

She was about to hand him a pistol, but as the dust from the minor explosion settled, skeletal fragments were revealed within the shattered wall. They were those of giant reptiles, neither of the present-day dragons nor the futuristic breed he recently learned about, but of the prehistoric serpents that no chronology book ever recorded. Mystified, he approached them as if he had never seen them before.

"I've seen ruins like these before."

The fossilized claws were gnarled and bent in anguish, bestowed with a touch of glory from an era of tragic doom. It was almost like a mirror into the past.

"What are they?" he finished.

Lyconel walked toward them as well. She lightly caressed the dinosaurs' aged, mineralized forms. One of them was carrying a sword made of diamond that seemed to be more fit for a bipedal organism than for a massive reptile.

However, it was not placed there by her, but by the geological tides that buried it several eons ago.

"Time," she began, "has no divisions. There's neither a past nor a future, but only what is."

"You said that before."

"I'll say it again."

"So what 'is'? The present?"

"Not necessarily."

A metallic glint dully shone in earthen tarnish beneath the fossils. They were the remains of cyborganic limbs, the flesh turned stone, but the wiring still in tact. Plastic and steel lined its infrastructure.

"Of course," he continued. "After all, what is the present when it unfolds constantly from the past into the future?"

He pulled one of the cyborg limbs out of the wall.

"What is time?" Dennagon inquired.

Lyconel knew not the answer, but knew an answer.

"A word."

She tossed him the pistol. This time, he knew that the trigger was not just an unnecessary adornment.

"One that happens to mean a lot to us," she declared as she turned off the lights.

The sun was setting, casting its obscure luminosity upon the ends of the Supersurface Cave Network. There, under the fading solar winds, the draconic dissidents mobilized, not a moment to waste and not a trice to spend on targets trivial. Totality laid heavy on the minds of those that knew Drekkenoth's mind well, for the darkness was falling all around them. They felt it…The evil rising and the vileness frothing. It was like a fantasy they had all dreamed of at one time or another, yet a fantasy that bore a brain as solid as the sky and oceans. They had to move fast, for too fast was not speedy enough.

Much as the horizon was engulfing the sun, there was a sudden increase in illumination throughout their environment. They galloped, slithered and flew as fleetly as they could toward it, for they knew what it was. All their weapons were drawn, for they were now not only equipped with conventional medieval apparatuses, but also firearms as well – Lefius with his six-shot revolver, Nomax with his roaring grenade launcher, Ballaxior with his ragtag shotgun, and Dradicus with his versatile rifle. Dennagon, unlike the rest of his ardent team, was confused, for the light appeared to be emanating not from the sky but from the lands itself. The heavens were dark, royal blue, yet there was more brightness than a noontime cloudless day.

"The light is rising. There is peril near."

His words were not heeded. The lustrous incandescence, once occulted by the grotto webs ahead, now spilt through the fingered caves in refulgent gusts of radiance. At first, it looked like a rainbow gone mad, but soon, the multicolored lucency spread out so greatly that only a dying wizard could have summoned it. He tumbled in his trot, collapsing in his tracks whilst bracing himself with both talons.

"A magician!"

The other five team members plodded on, unwavering. The sun set as they moved, handing the celestial realm to the stars and revealing underneath the guise of daylight the true nature of the lambent entity that blasted its beams upon them. It was a wall of fire, colored with every tint of the visible spectrum and spanning across countless miles past the edge of the cave network. It lashed out like a conflagration should, though it was swirling with pyrotechnics of unexplained chemical origin. There seemed to be nothing fueling it and no reason for it to perpetuate in the middle of nowhere. Yet, here it was out of nowhere in the midst of nowhere.

"Dead end," professed Dennagon, ignorantly bold.

"Don't be so sure," responded Lyconel.

She tucked up her chin at Ballaxior.

"This is the only way to the Alpha Pole," he offered his wisdom in a manner that was not arrogant.

The fire lashed at them like a conscious beast, angered at their apparent hostility. They recoiled at the unfriendly indication. Dradicus looked around for any alternate routes, but from what he could observe, old Ballaxior was right. They would have to traverse through this flaming barrier.

"What does it want?" asked Dradicus.

"Peace. Yet we are at war in a necessary fashion. I say we sheath our weapons under the veil of harmony. These flames are as living as the trees, so we must be careful not to instigate them," advised Ballaxior.

Everyone locked their firearms and artillery in their holsters and strapped their blades and talon-to-talon weapons in their scabbards and belts. Dennagon locked his weapons down, but instead drew something else from his sidepack – the spellbook. One of two things he always kept with him, the other item being his sword, which he carried into every last battle since the day he was hatched. Focusing, he flipped through its pages, browsing for any suitable spells.

Nomax's nostrils flared. Blazes spilt out of them like mucous geysers. He drew a bladed disk and prepared to launch it straight into Dennagon's skull.

"Cram that blasphemous tome down your throat," he demanded.

Lyconel elbowed him.

"Let him be, Nomax."

Nomax reluctantly disarmed. Dennagon continued browsing the pages for an appropriate enchantment. The spells were arranged according to color type, yet there was no alphabetical order to anything since most sorceries did not have names. It was too cumbersome to assign labels to every single conjuration because many of them were very similar in effect. A picture was worth a thousand words, so the creator of the spellbook simply used pictorial references that were supported by brief verbal descriptions of mana cost, effects, and the types of organisms that could cast given spells. Near the end of the tome, he found one that he rarely used.

"By the mind of the heavens and abysmal blight, grant me a shield of untainted light," he read.

A shell of energy extended from a coruscation in front of him. From nothing came a powerful aura that surrounded him in an encasing forcefield easily capable of repelling an attack from a thunderbird assassin's strike. After touching it to make certain it was functional, he turned to the book again.

"No need to cast it upon us," Lyconel stopped him. "There's no rudiment of the World we're afraid of."

With that, she led her warriors into the blazing barricade of flames. The rainbow of flares devoured them as quickly as they touched it, roaring as their silhouettes passed deep into the hellish heart. Dennagon stole his breath and dove in as well.

Inside the Fire Elemental, infernos of all colors swirled about in a graceful dance. It was an ocean of fluid flame as vast as the seas themselves and as teeming with life as any body of water. Fishes of pure fire formulated out of enkindled scintillations, complete with fins, organs, eyes and sentience that were not at all different from those of regular material organisms. Familiar aquatic biology was present everywhere, embodied in the pyrotechnical shapes he saw, igniting out of whorls of flowing flames and receding into the lighted abysses of whirlpool conflagrations. The resemblance to a real underwater environment was so striking that he was expecting to see a kraken materialize.

As weird as it was, it only appeared natural. Only his protective shield separated him from sampling it directly, and he almost wished he hadn't summoned the aura. His comrades, however, streaked through the realm with ease, gliding as effortlessly as they would through any liquid. They had no aegises to accompany them, yet they were totally unharmed.

"You're not taking damage," said Dennagon perplexed.

"The Elemental will not harm us lest we wield our weapons," answered Ballaxior.

A silver flame breezed across them. Mingled with it were infernos of red, blue and green.

"Another oddity. My head is beginning to spin. How can these fires be induced without any substance to ignite them?"

"Who says anything requires an origin?"

"Science," he declared mightily. "Causality is the base of all things, so everything requires an origin. Everything has a meaning." He furrowed his scaly brow. "If you are so sagacious, shouldn't you know these things already?"

Ballaxior chuckled wholeheartedly.

"There are many things in life that 'shouldn't' be, but exist nonetheless."

He took out a trinket shaped like a slab of stone. Upon it, inscriptions were written by the hands of man. Inscriptions dictating moral laws.

"Take the laws of morality, for instance. Humans were once bound to them, built to be benevolent. But after they became conscious of fire and steel, they were devoured by avarice. Now, power is all they think of."

"But why should moral laws be placed with such esteem anyway? They only exist as a side effect of evolution. Social orders survived more effectively than loners, but only if such social groups operated so that dissidents were eliminated."

"I wasn't saying that ethics should be placed in any

credence."

"They should not be placed in any credence, as they bind one to a realm without free will."

"Tell me, why should morals hold any more value than the knowledge you absorbed from those countless hours of reading?"

They shouldn't. That was the logical answer, but Dennagon felt that there was still some value in gathering erudition.

"As I said, there is always a reason for everything," he retorted. "There was a purpose the universe had in mind when it caused me to draw in all those volumes of information."

"Perhaps that reason was to deceive you from the real truth."

"What truth?"

"The Lexicon."

Circular reasoning, he thought. There was no point in continuing this conversation. Nonetheless, there was one more thing he wanted to clarify from this elder.

"That doesn't answer the question of why these fires exist perpetually without anything from which to grow. It violates the first law of thermodynamics, the conservation of matter and energy."

"Ought all matter and energy spring forth from other matter and energy?"

A silly question.

"Of course!"

"Then where did the first matter-energy come from? If everything is based on causality, or at least causality as determined in most texts, then there must have been a predecessor to everything that required a predecessor in itself."

Dennagon felt his argument crumble like an anthill at the

boot of a sadistic hunter. The oldest paradox in the universe had just struck him like a lightning bolt that he could neither outrun nor hide from. He searched the canyons of his wrinkled brain, scouring his intellect for an answer, but it would not respond. He let Ballaxior finish.

"If causality holds true, then it must have emerged from nothingness. Unless you wish to succumb to the dungeons of nihilism."

Dennagon shook his head.

"Nay, I'll not accept nihilism. It makes no sense. Causality is inevitably real. It drives the machine of time."

Therefore, everything did come from nothing. It was the scientist's nightmare, which also happened to contradict everything he was trained to believe. He could not believe that although he resisted the usage of the black orbs of knowledge, he was still foolish enough to submit to the writings of the libraries of books he had read.

"Why do you fear a vacuum?" asked Ballaxior as if he knew what Dennagon was thinking.

"Doesn't the universe abhor one as well?"

"Why should you think as the conscious universe does?"

"Because the universe created this World and I."

"Just because the laws of conservation of energy and matter do not hold true in the strictest sense doesn't mean that there is no truth. You ought not fall to the plight of men in their self-loathing surrender."

"I thought you said man was corrupt by the will of technology. If science is malignant, then there would be no reason to resume this quest."

"I wasn't saying science was malign."

"Then what? Are you telling me that one should abandon technology?"

"No. I am merely saying that one shouldn't say 'should'. To bear neither the rules of physics nor morality is to possess no bounds."

He put a talon on Dennagon's shoulder. The touch of the elder's skin was rough, yet soothing at the same time without the force of mana. Ballaxior said one final sentence.

"To have nothing is to have everything."

The words stuck to Dennagon's mind indelible. They echoed through every neuron in his system, reprising the hope he once had in his journey. There was something mystical about the phrase, aside from its infinite possible meanings, that led him to crack a smirk on his face. He had a feeling that everything would work out for the best.

Dradicus' pupils unanticipatedly twitched. He caught the sensation of being pulled toward a certain direction as he viewed a whirlpool of fire amassing in the distance. The vortex spun around like a tornado amid the infernal sea, dragging in most everything within a mile's range. At first, he thought it was a minor eddy that could be easily broken away from, but then he realized that he too was being hauled in.

He was the first to notice. Soon, Lyconel, Nomax, Lefius and Ballaxior also realized the presence of the inescapable force. It was far mightier than the earth's gravity and clearly more controlled than that of a random anomaly. With every second, it grew increasingly stronger, until even their flapping wings and paddling talons could not resist the immense pull. They began to become alert.

"Dradicus," announced Lyconel. "What do your wurm eyes see?"

He squinted his eyes. No one else could see as far as he could, but after a moment, the expression on his face was enough to warn everyone. Direly, he darted straight into Dennagon, tackling him out of the way. Initially, Dennagon thought it was a mishap, but as soon as he regained his steadiness, he saw a plasma shot lash right through the place he was just flying in.

"Incoming enemy!" shouted Dradicus.

From the center of the flaming tornado, a draconic silhouette of raging blue fire rocketed out with two jet propulsion systems attached to its tail. Backed by a streak of radioactive plasma fuel, it raged across the fiery sea with the havoc of a nuclear storm. Following a magnetic field, the vortex ripped behind the hellish figure like a spiraling tail, propelling the enemy as it bolted toward its targets. Abruptly, the trajectory snapped at a 90-degree angle, and the wreathe of rainbow flame swept over the dissident party, bowling over all the dragons with an intense torrent turned.

Dennagon fumbled chaotically in the Elemental as his comrades were knocked everywhere. Even through his shield, he felt like he was being punched from all sides and kicked in the face with every twist the currents cast him in. For ten seconds, he fumbled, his inner balancing techniques and wings useless against the forcible flaring waves.

Finally, he ceased, but not by his own skill. He had fallen out of the twister, left alone in the middle of the living flame realm. Howbeit, his colleagues were still trapped within the crazy cyclone, rattled like dice within a gambler's crystal ball. They were tossed like so much refuse amongst the colored winds of blaze, until alas, he saw with his own eyes the storm fling them into the distance. They were lost. He was in solitude.

"Dennagon," sounded an asphyxiated voice from behind. "We missssssed you."

A rapier lashed at him from above. Dennagon blended out of the way as Arxinor the wyvern Technodragon descended upon him.

"So I guessss this time we'll improve our aim. Prepare to be annihilated!"

He delivered another series of attacks. Dennagon rolled

and turned in flight, dodging the malleable, pointed blade with approximate success. Occasionally, the tip sliced him, for he was unaccustomed to these conditions of flying. In fact, he almost drew his sword when he remembered what Ballaxior had said. Thrusting himself upward, he mobilized as far from his enemy as he could.

"Thou art a gudgeon, vile Arxinor! Know you not that the flames will devour you, chew you to shreds, and spit you out like so much trash?!"

Flames bolstered around Arxinor. The Fire Elemental roared from its non-central vocal cords, throwing fists of multicolored infernos at the reptile that dared to arm himself in its realm. Prominences as hot as the sun rent through the heated ocean, cleaving upward and downward slashes at the wyvern Technodragon. Violent was the barrage, full of heart and hate. Notwithstanding, it was all too futile. Every wave and membranous scourge of pyrotechnical blasts could not stop the circuited beast as his mechanical endoskeleton showed through its deceitfully organic exoskeleton.

"Aaaahahahaha!" laughed Arxinor at the puny attacks.

Dennagon darted in, waiting not for his enemy to make a first strike. With a fist and kick, he hurtled his knuckles at the opponent, utilizing all his strength and agility. However, the lithe adversary sinuously manipulated through the flaming space, easily avoiding every assault. Uppercuts, backhands, front punches and combinations of the such could not even touch the winding, slithering robot serpent.

A sharp jab to the abdomen sent Dennagon reeling back. It was not with as much momentum as Gorgash's punch, but the concentrated impact was just as damaging. Arxinor leapt in, arcing his weapon's point down for a deadly stab.

"I will spill your silver blood and paint my programmer's name with it!"

A flying talon suddenly whizzed into the rapier, averting

its foil from its target. The spiked underside of a mouth-clenched tail then struck the biomechanical assailant in the torso, knocking him back. Nomax and Lefius rushed in from the beclouded distance of the Fire Elemental, encircling the enemy Arxinor.

"Where'd you come from?!" wondered the astounded Dennagon.

"Shut up and fight!" responded Lefius.

Nomax charged, running his thick, spiked tail toward the opponent.

"Let's wreck this techno-rabble!" he ardently proclaimed.

Even though his tail did not budge from his jaws, Nomax was still a surprisingly proficient fighter. His entire body careened at the adversary with the potency of a wrecking ball, each move solid, deadly and focused. Arxinor, cold in his robotic sentience, made sharp erratic motions to avoid the unblockable onslaughts, yet could not pass the infuriated grunt.

Nomax had had enough of this weenie dodging. For the first time in many a month, he took his tail out of his mouth and revealed the part that was always in his jaws. It was tipped with a ball of metal spines honed to whetted edges by constant and precise chewing. Each spine was augmented with the venom secreted from his salivary glands, adding an extra layer of lethalness to its already souped-up armament. Wildly, he swung it around, a wrecking ball upon a wrecking ball.

Arxinor himself had not anticipated this, and could only duck the first two swings. The third one hit him in the torso, crushing some of his inner circuitry and battering a sizeable portion of his outer dermal layer. His supple body lurched at the clout.

"Take that, you biomech runt!" railed Nomax.

He tried to throw its underside down with an overhead blow, but Arxinor slipped around the circumference of the tail as it passed. Gouging Nomax in the eyes, he swiftly pitched down and headed straight for his primary target again. His rapier jammed into the top of Dennagon's energy shield, piercing the forcefield deeply enough to slice the dragon's face. Dennagon recoiled as his magical aegis crumbled into a thousand pieces, speckled with droplets of silvery blood.

An insane series of slashes immediately ensued. Dennagon could hardly move, so he used his forearms to block the furious whips of the rapier as best he could. Scars scourged his scales with every slit that came, leaving marks that burned more than the conflagrations all around. Arxinor's incredible fencing techniques weaved the foil around in ways that seemed to violate the laws of physics at times when they twisted around and about every which direction. Stabs, slices, fake-outs and arcs came from everywhere, making it nearly impossible to block without taking a cut.

Abruptly, he parried a speedy cross-slash. The foil bent upon contact, wrapping around his talon in a coiled shape. He pulled on it, but only accelerated Arxinor as he reeled in for a roundhouse. A talon clotheslined him in the face with both his enemy's strength and his own. Dennagon's snout broke, spurting a shot of blood.

Lefius whirled his tail at the adversary to save his comrade. Arxinor, instead of ducking the attack, followed the tail as it spun around, confusing the unwitting Lefius. A mechanical fist punched him in the back of the head before Arxinor grabbed him, gyrated him around, and threw him away. Arxinor then turned back to face his prey, only to find that Dennagon had risen with a roundhouse kick of his own. The clawed hind talon clocked the biotech skull in the cheekbone, knocking out a few fangs.

Dennagon seized his enemy's neck. Without a moment to

lose, he grabbed it by its arteries and twisted, snapping it off at its base. Arxinor's neck was severed from his head, which smoothly spun around by 360 degrees. Automatically, the spinal bones realigned, reattaching themselves with the nerves, brainstem and circuits of his nervous system.

"Huh?!" growled Dennagon stunned.

The robotic foe administered a sharp peck to his chest, jamming a piked draconic beak straight into his sternum. It became stuck in his flesh, and Dennagon hectically tried to pull it out. Arxinor himself was also trying to extricate his head from the wounded sinew, scratching at his target's deltoids. Dennagon returned a barrage of close-fisted punches directly into the metallic enemy head.

Astounding both of them, a bladed disk flew by them. They shifted their bodies to the flank as it streaked across, seeming to originate from Nomax and Lefius, who watched fifty feet away. Nomax conspicuously had another disk prepared in his talon.

"Where did that disk come from?!" blared Lefius.

He then noticed his comrade holding one.

"You idiot!" he exclaimed.

Nomax had no idea what he was babbling about.

"What?!

"No weapons in the Elemental, moron! Let go of it now!"

As if he were not even aware of his senses anymore, Nomax looked dumbfounded. He saw that he was in fact holding a weapon in the realm of the Fire Elemental.

"Oh crap," he uttered.

The blazes condensed around them. Like a red, blue and green vise, they crushed with immense weight upon the ones that challenged the decree of the inferno. As the Elemental did with Arxinor, so too did it strike down on Lefius and Nomax, washing them out in a tide of fluid flares. Swept away were they in the flaming flood, their screams drowned out by the cataclysm's spate, silenced by an undying deluge of dire fire.

Dennagon alone exchanged blows with the opponent whose head was still embedded in his broken sternum. All the while, the flaming realm was still bombarding Arxinor with burning barrages, none of which harmed him, but much of which bled over to the other fighter. Fueled by the need to distance himself from the enemy, he surged with strength and pulled the wyvern jaw out of his torso. They circled each other once more in combative posture.

"What a pricccce to pay for omniscience," taunted Arxinor.

"What price do you speak of, old colleague?"

Arxinor moved nearer again, bringing with him his encompassing blaze. Dennagon unleashed a breath of his own inferno to counteract the heat from the Fire Elemental's useless attacks on the foe.

"Your life," answered Arxinor.

With that, he too disgorged a ball of silver flame. Dennagon flapped his wings, lifting himself over it whilst clawing the mechanical wyvern's cranium with his feet as he passed overhead. The skull, lacerated by several dozen dead-on punches, was torn off completely, exposing the cyborg brain beneath in all its CPUs and finely tuned machinery. Misfortunately, it remained undamaged.

"A good try," half-sincerely complimented Arxinor.

In a flash, he transformed his forearm into a cannon. Splaying his talon in an arc, he released a spray of plasma pulses in the general direction of his enemy. The radiant emissions scudded more apace than those of the previous Technodragon Dennagon had fought, and in the fury, Dennagon promptly contorted his body to avoid them. Nonetheless, even his dexterous adroitness could not prevent the heat from igniting all the plasma shots that bulleted at him. They all exploded, sending blasts of energy all around. His scales scorched, he was thrown back into the storm of detonations until his will and body were both vitiated to the core.

"But you are meant to die," Arxinor rubbed in.

Impaling him through the chest with the rapier, he plunged the foil right through Dennagon's heart. The flames that lashed at Arxinor also heated up his circuitry, thereby increasing the potency of his hit. Flames spread through his mechanized body unperturbed, spreading through the foil and into Dennagon's cardiac system. A demon of metal and blazing streaks of fire, Arxinor grinned sinisterly. His programmer's will would be fulfilled.

Dennagon tried to pull the foil out, but it was blown clean through his entire midsection, the circuited metal melted into his liquefying sinew. There was only one thing left to do.

"Not likely," he rebutted his technological enemy's statement.

Reaching for his scabbard, he slashed out his sword, carving a nova of light around the nebulous flames. The charred blade flung out the chipped remnants of its fractured edge, casting away all blazes where it sliced. The realm of flame boiled everywhere, for the Fire Elemental was now seething with fury more dreadful than the thirst of a desert. Its need to quench its hatred was centered upon the two warriors within its embodiment that defied its one and only rule.

Dennagon jammed the sword into Arxinor's throat. It cracked down the middle of its blade, but was still held in tact by the base of the hilt. A mechanized shriek filled the sultry air.

"Aaaarrr!"

With both their weapons drawn, the Fire Elemental's rage was tipped over its top. It boiled the realm of fire around them, encasing them in an infernal shell of colored fire that roared in liquid madness. Like a waterfall, ten acres of fire blazed across them, congealing around a point betwixt their locked armaments in the heat of a young sun. Even Arxinor was beginning to feel pain.

Suddenly, a detonation erupted. Plumes of rainbow fire exploded from it, striping across for miles in the fiery voids. These rainbows had no gold at their ends, for they were sending both warriors flying in opposite directions at mach 3. Their own screams could hardly keep up with them.

"This hasss not ended!" promised Arxinor as the deluge carried him away.

Dennagon bustled through the inundation. Overwhelmed in heat and haze, he soared like a missile across the Elemental, swamped in a cataract of flaming fury. His consciousness slipped away from him like a spectral ghost lost in his jet-speed trajectory, yet he tried for as long as he could to keep a hold of it. Nevertheless, unconsciousness took his valiant will, and he spiraled endlessly into the abyss of the Elemental, descending further and further toward its lowest nadir. It seemed as if he were rocketing forever into blazing infinity, enfolded in a shadow of sleep that was his only amenity.

———————————

At the edge of the Fire Elemental, the living flares met an icy terrain. The stark contrast was only equaled in magnitude at Lyconel's surprise as to how quickly she was tossed here. Along with Dradicus and Ballaxior, she tumbled out of the inferno, gradually falling to the ground. She hit the terrain with a thud, pouting up dirt as she landed. Dradicus fell next to her, rolling on his wurmy side to decrease the impact. Ballaxior came down next.

"Steady," she cautioned her brother as they prepared to catch him.

With a considerable weight, he dropped on them as

languorously as a stone. They both collapsed onto their backs, cushioning his plummet with their bodies. Brushing himself off, the elder casually rose to his feet, feeling not a thing.

"Thank you, Lyconel," he said kindly. "I would not know how to survive without you."

Lyconel, rubbing her aching head, sat up. Dradicus' pupils dizzily jumped around his eyes in ways that were not possible.

"We have to go back," she declared. "Dennagon, Nomax and Lefius are still in there."

"With a Technodragon," added Dradicus.

Ballaxior raised his palm as if to stop them without a touch.

"The past is done," he stated. "One cannot take a retrograde condition along time, and similarly, one should not do the same in space."

She glared at him. His utterance bore the heart of a craven.

"Then again, who am I to say 'should'?" considered Ballaxior.

Lyconel looked again at the flames and knew he was right. There was no point in going back, for if her comrades were still alive, it would take an extraordinary effort to find them. All the while, the enemy could be hounding their backs, placing their own lives in danger. She could not risk the lives of the colleagues that were with her for the sake of pursuing a wishful fancy. As much as she favored her dreams, it was too great an expenditure to be wagered in the tides of war.

"No, you're right, guide. If they were alive, they would have returned by now."

Somewhere in there, Dennagon laid. She knew it. However, what she didn't know was whether or not he was still breathing. Perhaps it was best not to know, as she always remembered the philosophy of the dragon in the boxed tomb and how it could potentially be alive and dead simultaneously. Yet, the uncertainty principle could not offer her any comfort now. Her hopes on finding the Key were in great jeopardy, lost within that wall of fire that she despised and admired at the same time. That sentry had everything she had spent years searching for, and now, in an instant, he was gone. Of course, there were hundreds of other sentries out there that were similarly knowledgeable…but she wanted that specific one…

Just then, to her delight, two entities were rising from the rainbow barrier. Swagging, they were severely injured, and she galloped forth to help them. Dradicus lifted a tail to stop her.

"No Lyconel! They could be Technodragons!"

They were not. It was Lefius and Nomax, charred to the bone. Burnt blood lined their wounds where the fires struck them so mercilessly that they could barely open their eyes without their corneas stinging with pain. However, progress was not the first thing on Lefius' mind but for the one swell of retribution upon his old grunt colleague.

"He armed," he vented with smoke coming out of his ears, "his disks!!"

Nomax shrugged his shoulders perplexed.

"I don't know how they got in my talons!"

"Oh really? Maybe because you forgot that you weren't supposed to equip them?!"

"Cast your words back from whence they came!"

"I'll cast you back from whence you came!"

Strangled in a clutter of cheap threats, they started to brawl. Not in the mood for trivial bickering, Lyconel pushed them apart.

"What of Dennagon?" she demanded.

Lefius straightened what was left of his ragged armor.

"The enemy took him down to the bottom of the blazing ocean last we saw."

"What else did you notice? Was Drekkenoth there?"

"Only but an extension of his body. One of the Technodragons was present, yet no more no less," noted Nomax.

Lyconel thought. There was something different about this attack than for the others. She couldn't put her talon on it, but it seemed as though there was an evil presence somewhere in her midst.

"So Dennagon is lost," she concluded. "He stands alone, as we do."

"We would've been able to defeat that techie and retrieve the sentry if only he," Lefius pointed at his colleague, "didn't nearly kill us by drawing his weapons!"

Nomax repeated his action. He slipped a disk out of his belt and prepared for combat.

"If that was the intention, then maybe I should finish the job," he threatened.

Lyconel stared at him coldly.

"What?" shirked Nomax, putting down his guard.

He appeared too defensive in this case, even for his usual attitude. Guilt was written in his eyes, but Lyconel was no psychic. She could not tell if he was merely hiding a dullard goof or if he was concealing a secret far more wicked. Either way, there was a time and place for everything, and now was neither the time nor place for quarrel amongst the group.

"Save your ire for the attainment of the Key," she imperatively suggested. "We're near the Alpha Pole."

They started for the tundra that laid beyond the conflagration wall. The icy plains stretched far toward the top of the World, layered in sleet, hail and snow. They had reached this part of the journey with many a casualty, but luckily no definite fatalities had transpired. Fortunate they were, for the quest ahead was far more menacing than what they had already been through, and any warrior would certainly call them divinely blessed if they did not suffer the loss of life sooner or later. No creature knew what secrets rested at the Alpha Pole – or what entrapments awaited those who came anywhere near those secrets. They were bound to find out sooner or later, whether it would come at the loss of their life or freedom.

But what secrets awaited them in a place beyond their time and space?

✗✗✗✗✗✗✗✗✗✗✗✗

CHAPTER 6

A landscape of computerized metal stretched as far as the eye could see. Futuristic architecture lined every inch of the endless miles, towering up to the stratosphere thousands of leagues above. Technological monuments built of gears, circuits, wires and advanced central processing units riddled the very fabric of the environment, for neither a speck of sand nor stone nor water lived here. This was a place of inorganic silicon, steel and copper topography terraformed to appear as an enhanced city of computers. However, it was not in itself inanimate. The grounds maintained a striking resemblance to earthen terrain, despite being made completely out of metal. Even the towers, which were constructed of hundreds of gigantic cybernetic terminals, looked like giant sequoias that gnarled and twisted as chaotically as any biological organism. It was difficult to tell whether this was the past, present or future, but in actuality, it was none of the three known time frames. It was the Technorealm.

Dennagon lay unconscious in the middle of the mechanical dune. Gashes riddled his soma, revealing scathed muscle under flayed scales. He was completely deformed. How long he had been laying there was indeterminate, for he was completely without awareness for the entire time, rendering uncertainty to forge its own truths of entropy. It didn't really matter, though. There were more pressing concerns at the moment.

His eyes cracked open at the onset of sentience. Trembling, he rose as if to have awakened at Drakemight upon his bed of books. Stretching out his talons, he casually thrust out his chest, yawning whilst flexing his muscles. The joints of his bones cricked as he sprung them about. His tail slashed horizontally, loosening the ligaments betwixt the tendons of each skeletal juncture. The horrid tincture of plaque coated the inside of his jaws and he was wondering where his bottle of water was so that he could wash it out. Aside from that, though, the rest of his body felt refreshed, as if it had just come out of packaging, its fibers still twitching and edging for the taste of a new morning's set of tasks. He was ready for another day.

"How much knowledge shall I collect tod –"

His eyes finally opened completely and alas he woke up for real.

"What the?!"

The Technorealm blasted him like a dream, except if it were a fantasy, he would not be aware of it as he was at the moment. Torrentially, all the memories of his recent journey spun through his consciousness, reminding him of why he was here. Yet, even though he knew why he was here, he still didn't understand why he was here.

Astonished, he slung out his trusty spellbook. There had to have been something in there that could explain this. Browsing through the pages, he searched every single color type mana to find out the reason for his inhabitance of this place.

"Green, Blue, Red, White. Never pity the magician's plight. Brown, Orange, Purple, Black. Never use the mind rack."

The words of a whelphood song rolled off his tongue to

ease the shock of his predicament. Green magic was used for life spells, and came first in the arrangement of the book. Blue was related to water in its fluidity supreme and followed Green as the second category. Red was for fire, White was for light, Black was for death, Brown was for earth, Orange for material strength, Violet for venom, Gold for air, Silver for metal, and Clear for the mind. Unfortunately, his mind was anything but clear. None of the color types could account for the universal element of "insanity".

"Okay, maybe Silver magic? Nay, no mage can craft something this complex," he said as he espied the tremendous mechanical trees.

Desperately, he flipped the pages, until at last, he reached the back cover. There was nothing left to see in that book. Clenching his fists, he started sweating.

"Hold your head, keep your brain functioning."

He considered the possibilities. Perhaps it was best to just wait it out and see what happens. Then again, the universe never played kindly with those who were too apathetic to take action, so perchance his best option was to explore. The latter seemed more accustomed to his persona.

"Ready or not, here I come, fantasy realm. Whatever you are..." he talked to no one in particular.

The wired floor scraped against his feet, unfamiliar with his medieval, carbon-based form. An anomaly in the middle of an even more anomalous environment, he plodded across the lands, struck with wonder at every step he took and every sight he saw.

He traversed for several hours, as far as he could tell. There was no sun in the sky, only darkness without a single star. The "space" he had read about in so many encyclopedias did not appear as it was described. The ordinary universe as he was taught was composed of countless stars that emerged from a center of time that spawned forth innumerable webs of protostellar nebulae. These stars amassed into spinning whirlpools known as galaxies that were centered by sentient rips in spacetime known as black holes. Whereas the cosmos he was used to had only scant traces of these dark gates of the voids, the celestial sea he now observed seemed to be completed consumed by bleakness. Maybe his prior suspicions were right. Maybe there was no space at all...

Dennagon really wished he had a wristwatch like his former master Drekkenoth. Or, at least a compass. He had no idea when or where he was in this foreboding weird scenery. For all he knew, he could have slept for ages only to have awakened in some distant future where everyone was already annihilated. It happened before in science fiction literature he had read, so there was no reason why it couldn't happen now. Was there a north or south? Forward or backwards? Now and then? Did it really matter?

Not really, considering that all that mattered was that he was where he was and he had no clue as to how to escape. Which made him wonder why Drekkenoth always kept that blasted wristwatch with him anyway. He had examined a great many timepieces crafted by the timesmiths of the draconic collective, but none of them even appeared remotely similar to the dragon lord's item. It wasn't that it was more technological and elaborate than any ordinary watch or that it was gem-encrusted with onyx as sable as the sordid sea, but that its very engineering was oddly designed. As he remembered, it had ten hands that pointed to thirty hours of the day, yet most dragons agreed that time should be divided into hundred-minute hours that were in turn divided into hundred-second minutes. Were the other hands for smaller degrees of time? To add to their strangeness, they moved about a face that echoed with endless membranous sheets of time much like two mirrors facing each other reflected one another infinitely. What the hell was that supposed to be used for?

The only thing he could conceivably sum it up to was idiosyncrasy. Maybe Drekkenoth just had an unusual fetish for the abnormal. So too did Dennagon, as he always enjoyed analyzing oddities and escaping from the prisons of societal bounds, but this current situation was going way too far. He always liked to slip into imagination, not remain entombed in it.

He looked up to one of the mechanical sequoias. Around its warped trunk of cybernetic construction, the wires surrounded a central, ovoid gem that constantly changed color. It looked like an eye of crystal embedded in the computerized arbor, continually shifting as if to scan the environment. There was not much else aside from the lone curious dragon and the rest of the boundless terraform.

"Maybe it was best to stay with the collective," Dennagon was beginning to regret.

He saw his own reflection in the gemmed eye as it turned to him. A metallic vibration resounded through the air, massaging his feet. His green scales shone against the crystal surface as it became flushed with a rainbow of color as varied as that of a chameleon's chromatophores. The emerald of his dermal layer was distorted by the fluctuating colors that backed his image, mixing it with hues of blue, red, brown and yellow – all the colors of sorcery. After several seconds, the gem's surface settled at a silver tint and he could see himself clearly; only without his wounds.

"You know, I have really nice scales," he complimented himself.

Suddenly, the image contorted yet again. It now displayed his body for what it really was – damaged beyond the repair of medieval dragons' medical procedures. At the sight, he gasped, for he had not even noticed the pain until he observed it with his own eyes. His wounds were buried deep within his "nice scales", and charred burn marks tattooed him with irreversible scars. Horrified, he looked at his talons.

"Damnit!" he shouted. "I knew this was going to happen one of these days."

A voice came from nowhere.

"You can't know the future by longing for the past."

Dennagon equipped his scarified sword. It was on the brink of crumbling, having been through the tortures of the Red Marsh and the Fire Elemental.

"Still thinking in the present, eh?" came the vociferation again.

"Who are you? Where am I? What have you done to me?!"

A robotic arm suddenly swung out from a gall nodule in the mechanical tree. Jointed and clawed, it was held together by plasmatic balls of energy that streamed through it like a system of radiant blue ligaments and nerves. The energy poured from within the tree itself, driving the mechanical arm like a battery of mechanized life.

"So many questions. No wonder they want you annihilated."

The robot arm slashed at him. Dennagon somersaulted over it, only to be surrounded by even more mech appendages rising from the ground. They all attacked at random, seemingly uncoordinated for such advanced machinery. He weaved from side to side, up and down to avoid the assault, eventually blending into parries and counterstrikes. His talons blocking the relentless barrage, he flapped his wings to escape to the sky. Nonetheless, several arms barricaded his retreat from above. Perhaps they were not all that disoriented.

Abruptly, he felt his rib cage crush. A giant circuited talon grabbed him by the torso, squeezing him with the perfunctory ruthlessness of an unrestrained CPU. There was no mercy in the force of its contracting, and it was clear to him now that this was no sick joke of a test. This was a real assassin at hand. Luckily, his forearm talons were still able to slip between the cybernetic fingers, allowing him to whirl his sword around and deflect incoming appendages. When he had a moment to spare from blocking the attacking arms, he turned his blade to the wrist of the one that was holding him in place. Slamming the chipped edge into its joints, he severed its plasmatic infrastructure, blasting it apart in an eruption of blue fire. In a silver halo of heated air, the entire mechanical hand fell off and he wrenched its digits off his broken ribs.

Staggering, he lurched down as several more flew overhead. Four arms came from the front and grabbed him by the chest, but he arced his sword across them, hacking them to shreds. The rest of them amassed ahead of him and came in for a unified onslaught, charging all at once.

Dennagon held his sword over his head. Thrusting himself forward with a sharp flap of his wings, he spun in the air, arming his sword as a jagged protrusion above his skull. Like a whirligig disk of havoc, he wheeled at them, slicing them at full throttle with his momentum and centripetal force. Minor plasma spurts detonated all around as the robot appendages fell in his wake.

However, just as he struck the last one, his sword's blade fractured from a chink in its edge. The crack spread across its metal like a bolt of lightning, reaching down to its hilt and out to all corners of its flat. Upon impact, the final mechanized arm broke, but so too did his sword, which shattered into a shower of scintillating shards. The metal debris burst out like a silver array of fireworks, falling upon the ground in a hundred clinks. He landed on his feet, stolid and unwavering as the warrior he was, but bereft of the weapon he had carried into battle for so many years.

Stoically, he stared at the remnants of his armament. All that remained was the handle that bore the protruding ruins of a once shimmering blade. Like icy outcrops of an arctic cave, the metal fragments jutted out from the hilt's top as if to imitate the stump of a fallen tree. The orbed pommel remained in tact, the only surviving relic of a once great sword, albeit it could not bring its glory to life once more. Taking a breath, he lowered his weapon, knowing again that this day would come. He turned to face any more enemies.

There were none. Only the voice stayed.

"I must commend your valor," it sincerely complimented.

A dark figure rose from behind a mechanized mount of computers not far away. The silhouette Dennagon felt in his tactual senses immediately, guiding him to snap around instantaneously with his broken sword readied. Whilst the creature that taunted him remained as still as stone, he stared into it, prepared for battle and analyzing the reasons why it was just standing there. It would have been wise to attack on sight, for a being unmoving before a former Drakemight sentry was a dead enemy indeed.

Dennagon did not assail, though. Peering deep into the soul of the opponent, he could apprehend why it did not move. To remain stable was to be dead, but that would not really matter if the said creature was already amongst the perished.

"An undead," he murmured.

Its skeletal incarnation was draconic in shape. He had never witnessed the revitalized cadaver of a reptile in his journeys before. Yet as astonishing as it was, it stepped forth to reveal even more of its stunning attributes, lightened by a source of illumination still unseen. From the mechanized mount, it marched, exposing its entire anatomy from cranium to tibia. A walking fossil it was, still wearing the remains of a tattered suit of plate armor upon its quadruped spine and bearing the faceless skull visage of a dragon ghoul. While in the cold dark sockets of its eyes there was little recognition, its stride did emanate an essence of command touched with the blessing of fortitude and myth. However, above all the shocking aspects of its appearance, it had one thing that indicated its true identity without a doubt –

-- a hook ended broadsword in its clutches. One that was drawn in every last history book in the known World. The weapon's formal name was the Exarius if he remembered correctly, but it needed no nomenclature to enhance the renown of its simple image. Everyone knew what it meant and who it belonged to. Dennagon kneeled to its owner.

"Shevinoth," he saluted to the ghost he could neither believe nor deny.

The cadaverous skeleton dragon Shevinoth approached him benignly, ghastly as he was petrifying. Without explanation to his existence, he answered.

"He."

He lifted a bony talon, signaling Dennagon to rise. Dennagon did so, shoulders shrugged in confusion.

"But you died! Many ages ago!" he said in frantic incomprehension. "How can it be that you exist now before my very eyes?! Have I done something to deserve thy presence?!"

A phantasmal chuckle resounded.

"Haven't you stopped reading those whelp storybooks, Sentry Dennagon?"

Shevinoth flapped his bony wings. Without flesh or membranous surfaces betwixt his joints, he boosted to the sky.

"Come," he welcomed. " I must show you some fine literature."

Dennagon quickly darted up into the celestial sea as well,

chasing the mythical dragon. Bounding across the landscape, he ascended to the sky, soaring past the towers that rose miles to the heavens. He could now see the lands in a panoramic view, and as circuits grew small in his perception, even larger circuits that encompassed the smaller ones took their places in his large-scale sight. Truly, the entire realm was endless, for as many times as he passed the horizon, there was always another horizon that still contained the exact same type of mechanized terrain. All the while, not a single star lingered in the sky. Thence, he tried to ascend even further, reaching up as much as he was reaching toward his spectral reptilian guide. He rose continuously, never stopping, until he came to where a stratosphere should have been. However, there was no barrier to the ozone. It just kept going, boundless in space as if the skyborne sphere bore but an infinite number of azimuthal degrees. There was no zenith at which meridians could converge, for the heavens bore no top. There was no space.

"Would you like to see my library?" sounded Shevinoth's voice from a distance.

Dennagon looked down only to see the entire Technorealm from several thousand miles high. The entire landscape and all its grounds appeared just like it did when he was down at surface level, only that structures had increased in magnitude. The tiny patches of ground he now saw contained entire clusters of towers, and looked identical to the tiny patches of ground he observed when he was walking the terrain. It was infinitely iterating, containing the whole within every part, every modicum of its surfaces encapsulating clones of its panoramic view. It was the ultimate embodiment of microcosmic-macrocosmic unity.

Then, past the entire realm, he saw a flash as brilliant as it was fleeting. For an instant, everything became pixellated as if to exist across the interface of a computer monitor, a wave of cybernetic strokes that centered upon a colossal tower that seemed to lie at the center of the centerless place. Upon it was Shevinoth, waiting for him as patiently as any spectre would. Dennagon descended, ready to hear a tale from the hero he had admired since birth.

The Technorealm Mainframe was a tremendous cylindrical tower that scraped the limitless heavens of total darkness. An enormous screen wrapped around its radius, founded upon a prodigious control panel that was studded with keypads and buttons. Dennagon had no idea what to make of it, what with all its alien symbols like "Alt", "Ctrl" and "F5", yet he surmised that its familiar icons of the alphabet were used to cast spells. Perhaps finally, those spells would allow him to understand what this mysterious "technology" really meant in the tides of his reality so that he could make sense of everything that was going on. Standing on the edge of the panel, he awaited Shevinoth's speech, still locked in disbelief that the draconic legend was still alive, let alone in his presence at the moment. Maybe if it were a dream, it would be more acceptable to his rationale…

Shevinoth pressed a switch next to Dennagon. A smaller control panel rose from the smooth, glossy floor, positioning itself in front of his skeletal claws. Rattling the bony digits across the tinier keypad, he caused the keys on the grander control panel to move. He then touched a button marked with an emblem composed of a zero spliced with a one, activating the mainframe screen. It displayed the words "Starting: Windows 1200 AD".

"This place is the Technorealm," he dictated. "It is an area that no sorcerer can find and no map can mark.

"Then where is it?"

"This place is nowhere but here."

"I don't understand."

"You will. Soon."

The mainframe screen opened up with a clear, silver interface. There were no icons on it save for a single circle centered by a dot in the exact middle. The image was pixellated like the environment in which they stood, the only difference being that the view on the screen was two-dimensional. Nevertheless, both the three-dimensional realm and the membranous realm were both virtual.

"Why," he asked Shevinoth. "Why are you here? How long have you been trapped?"

"Trapped? This is not a game of dungeons and dragons, Sentry Dennagon. I am here for a very specific mission."

"I can't apprehend how you are still alive. All those myths, those legends I read since being hatched. They said you died in flaming glory upon the Moon that once was and never will be again."

"Can you not think beyond what simpletons say? If anyone is dead, it is he who acts on his emotions, not I who has but a heart of bone."

Shevinoth pressed an arrow-shaped switch. A disk outlet popped out of the panel.

"What is this entity?" Dennagon pointed to the mainframe.

"Is it alive?"

"Everything is alive, and you know it."

"I don't know anything anymore."

"Sure you do. The knowledge you learned, I agree, was not wholly accurate, but at least some of it was useful."

"The World is dominated by uncertainty."

"However, in the chaos, there is order. There are things that are tautologically certain."

"Such as?"

Shevinoth's tone abruptly changed to a mechanical one.

"Logic, consciousness, causality, a timeless genesis, a temporal genesis, destiny, time, space, spacetime, relativity, macrocosm, microcosm, quantum mechanics, uncertainty, unconsciousness, symmetry and asymmetry."

Evidently by his immediate and crafty complex response, he thought about his response beforehand. Dennagon was curious as to whether he had a corresponding explanation to each one.

"And why are these elements necessary in existence?"

"Logic cannot be defied, for even the infinitely reflexive acknowledgement that there is no truth requires logic. Causality is real because logic is based on cause and effect, premises and conclusions. An infinite number of causal events still cannot contradict causality because infinity can be quelled by the essences of limits. A genesis in time would be necessary as a causal predecessor to timed existence, yet that too would need a genesis of its own that would not itself need a temporal premise."

Dennagon was trying to absorb the information. He wasn't sure if it was more astounding that Shevinoth was alive or that he was stating this all in one clump as if rehearsed for all eternity.

"Thus, there would be a non-temporal genesis from which all purpose emerged and from its being, one can conclude that destiny, time, space, spacetime, relativity, the macrocosm, the microcosm, quantum mechanics, and uncertainty are real as necessary elements of irrefutable space and time. Space, of course, would not necessarily have to be real in the sense of tangibility, but would include the duality between dreams and reality. In addition, as you definitely know, the origin of the World encompassed all moments in time, expanding until it was linear so that causality could exist, along with its inhabitants. Therefore, there would also be a symmetry to the World, one that balanced all things in accordance with causal purpose, yet in order for there to be differentiation in the holographic globe, there must also be asymmetry balanced within this symmetry. This is the circle of existence, the ring of all that is."

Dennagon was still on the non-temporal genesis from which all purpose emerged. Practically giving up on ascertaining the rest of the information, he pondered that one peculiar idea.

"And what is the meaning of life? What can be derived from all this that you speak of?"

Shevinoth inserted a CD-Rewritable inside the disk outlet.

"In good time, Sentry Dennagon, all shall be explained. My startling existence from nowhere, time in its total glory, and the meaning of existence."

"You say that causality is a lifeforce of existence. But who can say that purpose is a requisite of causality itself?"

"A life without a meaning is one not worth living."

The tremendous screen lit up. Computerized code streamed across its pixels, radial from the central circular icon. The entire monitor warped like a cybernetic sheet of liquid crystal, morphing into a circular screen from its original rectangular shape. From its middle, a dialogue box was projected forth, at first appearing only along the two-dimensional surface, but then extending out into three-dimensional space as a laser hologram. It was a cybernetic holograph projector whose mechanical spirit stretched even into the lighted photons that composed the spatial sculpture. Difficult it was to determine the rift between the virtual World and that of the Technorealm space.

A message appeared within the box's substance –

"Connect to internet?" it asked with options "Affirmative" and "Negative".

"Internet?" asked Dennagon.

Shevinoth clicked "Affirmative". Ignoring Dennagon's inquiry, he spoke.

"I did die, as the stories tell. However, death is but a word, and a word is changeable by the laws of relativity. After my destruction, I still had a purpose in life – to ensure the flow of time."

"Time. You control it as a lord of chronology?"

Shevinoth paused. There was something in his expressionless eyes that spoke for his despair.

"Affirmative…" he muttered in a conspicuously insincere tone.

"And what face of time is this 'Technorealm' made of?"

"The only one that matters."

Dennagon did not know how to respond.

"The future," finished Shevinoth.

Another prompt lit up across the mainframe hologram. "Enter password" it demanded.

"I found omniscience eons ago," Shevinoth said in a reminiscent voice. "It cost me my life, but the price was certainly worth paying. Now, Drekkenoth threatens to take it from all. That is why I must endow you with the same gift."

"If you're omniscient, where's the Lexicon?"

Shevinoth pointed at the Mainframe. Another keyboard popped up out of the edge of the control panel in front of Dennagon. The blinking cursor pulsated on the screen password prompt, beckoning him to answer its riddle of infinite possible solutions. He stared at it as blankly as it stared right back.

"It's all yours if you can find the password."

"What's the password?"

Dennagon realized the stupidity of his question only after it spilt out of his forsaken jaws. Shevinoth did not seem to take notice to his ignorance and answered it.

"You know it. You've known all along."

Dennagon stole his nerves. Searching his mind, he scanned through his memories with the intellect that made engrams purposeful. His processing capabilities ciphered through hundreds of memorized facts, trying to remember what it was that would be the logical set of alphabetic letters in this situation. He could only think of one thing.

Clamping his eyes shut, he typed in Shevinoth's name. The letters riddled the prompt as a string of asterisks that coruscated as if to replace the stars nonexistent in the night sky. For a moment, he kept his lids closed, afraid of the consequences of being wrong and imperfect. The screen went completely blank as he pressed "Enter", and even though he could not directly see the illumination sweep away from the monitor, he could detect the lack of light penetrating his eyelids. The tension in his muscles built.

Transmitting the data through its motherboard, the Mainframe CPU analyzed his information and made its decision. A window opened up, revealing storms of icons that covered the screen and the computer's holographic projection. Each one symbolized a field of cognition – a celestial sphere for astronomy, a vector for physics, calculus operators for mathematics, a DNA strand for biology, a molecule for chemistry – a specialized icon for each and every potential classification of study. A swell of relief washed over his spirit as he saw what was apparently a successful entry into the database. Even though he knew nothing of cybernetics, he deduced that these were vast storages of wisdom compiled into compact spaces. In wonder, his eyes glistened against the brilliant flickering of the passing cybernetic emblems, trying hard to keep track of them while being so mesmerized. It was incredible how many there were to choose from, seeing as to how he was not really certain how anything could possibly contain that much information. Not even dragons with photographic memory could keep track of this.

"Are these—"

"Affirmative, Sentry Dennagon. They are volumes of information designed specifically for you. I once saved the World, but now, I am but a watcher. Only you can defeat Drekkenoth and his evil minions."

Dennagon, as mystically fascinated as he was with the entire spectacle, was befuddled as to how he was supposed to memorize all this information before his body withered into that of an elder. Just as he was about to ask about any requisite spellcasting, several cables extended out from the control panel and slithered around him. Like mechanical serpents, they snaked through the air, coaxing him to take one of them.

"Now finish it. Download the knowledge and save the World."

Despite Shevinoth's demands, Dennagon was still hesitant. The cables were beginning to look more like worms than friendly serpents.

"I said finish it. Now."

Shevinoth's tone was growing impatient in a way that sounded almost desperate. Nonetheless, Dennagon caved in to the pressure and took one of the cables, wringing its neck as if it were an overgrown maggot. The instant he touched it, it took a mind of its own, overpowering his hold and jamming itself into his cranium. He did not have the will or the decree to fight back.

His skull lit up like a glow-in-the-dark endoskeleton. Soon, the same radiance spread through the rest of his bones, brilliantly flashing with illumined blasts. Torrents of computerized code ran into his mind, carrying with them megabytes of information that were contained within packets as compact as quanta. Flowing like a stream of cybernetic intellect, the Mainframe database began transmitting itself directly into his cerebellum, not even bothering to waste the energy to maintain a copy for itself. There was so much to teach and so little time, so all the knowledge was for Dennagon.

A sense of doubt overwhelmed him as the process was starting. It seemed like a familiar instance, one that resembled his refusal to download the black orbs of Drakemight.

"Isn't this—" his brain froze his stuttered speech slightly, "not any different -- than the venom of the black orbs – Shevinoth?"

Suddenly, a rush of data surged into his cerebrum, fusing with his brainstem. He suddenly knew everything there was to know about advanced string theory.

"RRRRRR!!" he roared.

It was an ecstasy far different from that of ordinary information consumption. Whereas black orbs were savory and putrid at the same time, this downloading was far quicker and completely bare of any traces of evil. It was pure, unadulterated knowledge as free of corruption as the white snow of crystal winter. As more of it came in, his eyes spangled with innumerable visions – physical variables, mathematical constants, chemistry formulae, draconic DNA gene isolations, and equations that spanned the limits of his boundless imagination. A decade's worth of data came into his consciousness in less than a minute. He didn't understand why it felt so great, but he surmised that in the endless streams of wisdom he would eventually find out the reason. His sinister grin held that faith.

"Yeah! I feel it! The power! Millennia of data flowing into my sentience! This is truly omniscience."

Shevinoth snickered. His talons rubbed together, plotting.

To add to his intellectual rhapsody, melodies of futuristic

technological data stormed into his waking mind. Files on computer languages, binary code, engineering software, hardware info and operating systems melded with his consciousness, granting him the capability of fluently understanding any cybernetic construction. Where the ideas came from, he did not know, but he didn't care. He now knew what the term "data" meant and how to program a simple arrangement of silicon transistors and generators to do his bidding by decree of C++ and Java. He just wanted more info. More power.

"I feel the future indeed!" he shouted, declaring himself god.

Just then, as he was expecting to learn more about how to travel to space, the smirk on his face perished. A sharp pain shot through his head, racking every one of his neurons. Every byte of data had clasped onto his cerebrum, biting it like billions of living quanta. They were living quanta, each one bent upon ravaging his brain.

"AH!" he screamed. "What's happening to me?!"

Shevinoth grinned. His benign selflessness transmuted into a sadistic growl that would make even fools feel foolish in that they fell for his ploy.

"You," he said in an accusatory taunting way, "are acquiring the aspect of the Mainframe."

Dennagon writhed in utter agony. It was an infinite torture device attached to his brain; and it was just warming up.

"Mechanical," continued his deceitful foe.

Desperately he tried to yank the cable out. However, at a mere tug, he could tell that it was lodged deep within his cranium, its metal almost as one with his brainstem.

"All-knowing."

With the jagged stump of the blade of his broken sword, he attempted to sever the link. His efforts were to no avail.

"But ultimately without free will."

Shevinoth started to transform. Dark flames engulfed his skeletal figure, wrapping around his bones like fiery flesh of total blackness.

"You have failed, Sentry Dennagon," its biomechanical voice stated.

Splaying his claws, the Shevinoth-morphed doppelganger raised an ebony talon over his enervated victim. It was a killing strike Dennagon had seen before, used only upon those who defied the collective. Dennagon jolted, parrying the strike with a desperate wail as it came down. Bereft of a second to spare, he then reached for his belt, grasping the one thing that he thought he would never use.

It was the pistol that Lyconel gave him. The database had just taught him everything he needed to know about the weapon, and he slung it like an expert gunner. Pointing it at the Mainframe screen, he fired, renting the circular monitor apart in sprays of bullets. The holographic model started to shatter, creating fragments that were merely smaller versions of its whole self. The more bullets he discharged, the more miniscule the hologram pieces became, until at last, a silver explosion destructed the entire machine. Hectically, he fired a few extra shots at the control panels, popping off their keys with sharpshooter aiming. The cable detached itself long before he stopped shooting.

In his frantic rage, he didn't realize that he had just spent most of his bullets on a mechanical cadaver that was already decimated. Snapping around, he threw a roundhouse punch as the false Shevinoth rushed at him. The fist nailed the skeleton dragon in the face, blasting apart its bony form to reveal what truly lay underneath.

Drekkenoth.

"Oh no," Dennagon uttered.

In hellish bleak flame, the enemy rushed right back. Two fiery fists walloped Dennagon in the torso, knocking him into the horizon. His body ripped across the air, something he was beginning to get familiar with, except this time, his back was crashing right into the cybernetic edifices that inhabited the terrain. Straining, he tried to weave away from the tower walls, but his velocity, as he knew from physics, was too great to prevent himself from ramming through every structure. As a reptilian asteroid, he rocketed through the atmosphere, letting towers come crumbling down in his path. After half a minute, he ultimately slammed upon the ground, carving a trench of broken circuits as he impacted.

Battered, he rose trembling from his mauling. Surveying the distance, he viewed the havoc he had constructed. He could hardly believe that he actually brought down that many structures.

"Whew…"

Another comet came jetting in like a black meteoroid. Drekkenoth, talons crossed about his chest, soared mightily above the Technorealm to reach his prey.

"Victory is impossible," he declared as the machine he was.

The dragon king bolted straight down. Dennagon galloped out of the way just as the ground behind him exploded into fragments.

"For you," Drekkenoth rubbed in.

Dennagon, even with his vast knowledge of the universe, was helpless. The only plan he could concoct was the use of his pistol in direct assault. Hence, he thrust the gun forth and blasted away madly, only to find that lead projectiles bounced off dark flames like rubber balls against a wall. Meanwhile, Drekkenoth surged with circuitry, his wires merging with his sable blazes as they ran together like biomech flame. He waited until the puny gun ran out of ammo.

"Surrender or be annihilated," were the conditions of the dominating party.

With that, Drekkenoth charged at full throttle. Throwing a lightning barrage of thunderous punches, kicks, chomps and tail sweeps, he vehemently sought to give his former subservient a death most violent and gory. Dennagon manipulated his way between his adversary's enormous fists, hiding under the debris that came bursting out from punches and stomps that barely missed him. Thick layers of steel were crushed like paper scrolls as the massive assailant slammed his tail and clawed the lands. Slashes flew toward the comparatively meager target, sometimes accompanied by immense jaw chomps. Dennagon was in a hopeless position. He could only see one strategic thing to do.

As Drekkenoth snapped at him with a hellishly mechanical bite, he dove forward, sliding underneath the enemy legs. The opponent's reptilian beak smashed right through the ground, burying its entire head under tons of broken, twisted metal. Dennagon took immediate advantage of the opportunity and trotted away on all fours, fleeing like the cravenly humans he once smote so easily. At seventy miles an hour, he galloped, running for his life.

Drekkenoth effortlessly lifted his head from the ground, letting tons of metal roll easily off his back. Robotically, he turned about, locking onto his fleeing prey with his optical targeting sights.

"Your annihilation is acceptable."

He lifted his precious wristwatch. Perfunctorily, he adjusted the knobs around its circumference, twisting the analog dials around. The machine of time churned its ten hands, ignoring the thirty hours that seemed to vanish off its limitless faces. The very fabric of space warped, and along with it, time was altered.

Dennagon slowed. As the temporal dimension dilated around him, a gravity field emerged from the mighty timepiece of his enemy, drawing him in with bent spacetime.

He tried desperately to refrain from its pull, but the strength was too great for his sinew. Everything around him seemed to be moving faster than he was, including the tree-like towers that watched him with their cyborganic gemmed eyes. Spacetime was indeed a certainty, one that could be molded according to the specifications of one's mind. Or in this case, the specifications of the watch that was wired directly into Drekkenoth's spine.

"It can't end like this…" said Dennagon, striving for life.

Drekkenoth lifted his one free talon. He was never in the mood for tormenting his worthless prey, for even to him, time was of the essence. Instead of killing him with his swords, it would be best to kill the pitiful unit with his forearm cannon. His plasma artillery morphed from his cybernetic flesh faster than the blink of an eye. Of course, to the time-trapped enemy, the blink of an eye was quite slow at the present.

"Farewell, Sentry Dennagon," said the Technodragon ruler as he aimed the plasma cannon.

Dennagon speedily searched his mind. His consciousness was still moving along ordinary time, even though his body was trapped in dilated space. Rapidly, he scanned through his engrams, his intellect struggling to find a solution, until he ultimately stumbled upon a saving answer. The equations of relativity, which the Mainframe had taught him, granted him an idea that he derived from the formulas that supposedly depicted the behavior of space and time on this World. Of course, his concept would require a bit of insanity, but at the moment, psychosis was just what the battle demanded.

Crazily, he charged straight into the path of the gravity field. Straight into his enemy.

"Hmmm," wondered Drekkenoth.

The warped spatial fabric exponentially accelerated the

gravity-bound captive. Dennagon's speed increased at an incredible rate, fueled both by the contorted time and by his own physical galloping. Drekkenoth launched a leviathan plasma orb more sizeable than those of his inferior minions, but even with his supreme aiming systems, he missed. This was something he had not calculated.

Approaching the speed of light, Dennagon bolted straight toward his adversary. Drekkenoth stood as still as a mountain, ready to take any blow with his divinely designed bodily mechanics. However, just before Dennagon could dive into the wall of scaly titanium that was his indestructible foe, he abruptly reeled back. He had broken the speed of light, and the World's organic soul could not allow him to do so without falling backwards in time. His body rolled into the sky like a cosmic timeline played in reverse, sending him far into the distance. Faster than anything on the planet, robotic architecture was rent apart in his path whilst he shrunk in the horizon.

Dennagon was gone.

Drekkenoth looked around, unfeeling and cold. The havoc that littered the entire realm was grander than most battles he had fought here. Nonetheless, he remained unimpressed. There was nothing that could shift his metal-icy heart nor alter his indifferent aloofness to everything irrelevant to his mission. Neutrally, he disarmed his plasma cannon and took to the sky.

The future never looked so beautiful as from the aspect of the past.

ズズズズズズズズズズズ

CHAPTER 7

A tundra of pure crystal lay near the northern pole of the World. It was the only place on the globe that was cold enough for ice to cap the lands, save for the freeze spells that powerful Blue Mages used to lock down their targets. Here, however, all the gems were naturally occurring, taking the place of snow in their crystalline forms. It was jeweled arctic, glittering in the setting sun and overcast by a slight snowfall. The scant flakes of precious stones that fell from the sky gradually built up the lands for eons, smoothening it to a pristine, white blanket.

Dradicus carved a sinuous line across the landscape that had not been touched for ages. The chill was beginning to seep into his scales and he wished he had brought some manskin with him. Then again, he was no barbarian that needed to harvest the ruins of his prey. He was a dragon, a wurm that would hold his own with his own leathery hide. Even if the frostbite was numbing him from head to tail.

"Are we there yet?" he asked aggravated.

Lyconel, Nomax and Lefius followed him.

"I can't answer that, brethren," replied Lyconel. "You're the scout."

Dradicus looked to the horizon. Darkness lingered in the coming of dusk.

"Eve is falling," he remarked. "Perhaps the stars will guide us to our rally point."

"No," denied Lyconel. "We'll not need the stars tonight."

The sun crept below the horizon, almost noticeably fast enough on this part of the World. Releasing a stellar flash as the edge of the landscape occulted its solarization, it descended beneath the terrain, casting darkness to the sky at the opposite side of the environment. There, stars began to twinkle across the royal blue night, accompanied by yet another grand whiteness rising from the depths of the horizon.

"Oh my," commented Dradicus.

Nomax and Lefius squinted their eyes at the evening illumination.

"It still exists," said Lyconel in contained joy.

A grand orb of silver ascended opposite the descent of the sun. Gleaming in splendid brilliance, it emitted a halo that ringed its outer layers, one as ancient as the legends that gave it renown. Although many accounts stated that it was supposed to be speckled with craters, this sphere was as smooth and perfect as can be. Refulgent, it hovered in the sky as it hovered in their imaginations for so long.

It was the Moon, a surreal celestial object that had just materialized before their very eyes. It belonged only in fantasies, yet here it soared above them, casting its luster all over the landscape and refracting its incandescence through the snowy crystals that covered the entire terrain. The entire tundra lit up, a blanket of ice and sleet that glowed with turquoise green-blue hue encrusted in auras of pure white light. Sharp leaves of illumination stretched out from the gemmed grounds as blades of grass would have extruded from a floor of dirt. The dragons' eyes glimmered in the magnificence.

"Wow…" they gaped all at once.

However, the spectacle was not over. Nature's performance was only half done, for as the solar light evanesced completely, more lunar lucency bathed the environment. From the other side of the azimuth, 12 hours right ascension from the first Moon, a second Moon rose counter to the paths of the stars and planets. It was identical to its predecessor, smooth, silver and pristine, its only differing exception being that its trajectory was completely opposite. How two twin global satellites got positioned at either side of the sky, no one knew, but the simple idea countered all the laws of physics that so-called "wisemen" were trained to believe. The dragons supposed that was why their lone serpentine band constituted the only creatures to have witnessed the phenomenon in ages.

Lyconel felt particularly grateful that she was blessed with the opportunity to experience the World in its freest grandeur. However, despite the fanged grin on her face, she was not completely unaware of the time. She noticed that both Moons traveled toward one another along the sky's local meridian so that their ways would eventually cross at the zenith, the crown of the sky. No doubt, this was no mere coincidence, for if she knew anything, it was that causality did not allow for anything arbitrary to happen. This natural occurrence was an artificial timekeeper.

"We must make haste," she assertively informed her team. "The Alpha Pole is near."

They plodded through the snowcapped territory that acted as the diadem of the spherical World. Night had befell their position for a few hours now, and the frost was beginning to creep beneath their scales. Even Nomax, whose dermal layer was so tough and calloused through the tides of battle, was beginning to curse at the numbing chill of the unrelenting arctic. Nonetheless, they knew of only one direction to move in time and space – forward.

"Are we there yet?" whined Dradicus again, half-kidding.

"It has to be close. The Moons did not show themselves just for the sake of cleansing us with their lunar light," returned Lyconel.

"Are we there yet?"

"Still, I don't detect any strong sources of mana. Either the Key is hiding itself from us or we've come to the wrong place."

Nomax started edging his frostbitten claws toward his disks. If she even dared to say that they were going the wrong way all along...

"But we couldn't have gone the wrong way," she assured herself. "Ballaxior said that this was the location of the Keygate, the tundra of the forbidden satellites."

"Ah, but location is non-extant, a mere construct of the mind. In a way, we can teleport just by thinking," teased Dradicus.

She turned to him, not in the mood for jokes.

"Did you do proper recon?" Lyconel shot.

"Yes, and the Alpha Pole is near as you say."

"How near?"

"Errr...As near as one would like?"

"What does that mean?"

"That proximity is relative?"

Lyconel glared at him, brows straighter than a linear geodesic.

"You have no idea where it is, do you?"

Dradicus pursed his lips, curling up the corners of his jaws uncannily. Lyconel slapped her forehead.

"Great. This was the only place Ballaxior told us it could be. There's something not right here."

As her teammates groaned, she lifted her head with a precipitant realization. She looked amongst her party and saw only three other units aside from herself.

"Where is Ballaxior, anyway?"

Everyone was so used to having him lag behind that they had completely forgotten about him and missed his absence. Spooked, they looked around, shocked at how they could have so easily lost a comrade in their journey without even taking notice. There were no tracks of his hydra footsteps, which was fairly obvious even amidst the clutter of their own talon trails. Blood was nowhere in sight, and if it were hidden they would have scented it. Had they been covertly attacked far back, they should have at least been aware much earlier that he was nowhere in their vicinity. Now, they were left with nothing but clueless confusion touched with the madness of inner chaos in its quietude venomous.

Lyconel scanned her companions' eyes. Although it was rare, there was a slight chance that they could have been enchanted by a secretive mental curse. Magicians wandered the World frequently, some in search of quarry, others in search of belligerent glory, but most in search of mischievous entertainment amidst their immortal existences. If they had passed one, they might not have known, and they could have been locked in a spell at that very moment. For all she knew, the World could have passed a million ages whilst she was trapped within an illusion.

Nonetheless, there was no time for her mind to wander. Though everything in the universe was theoretically possible, there was a factor of probability she needed to consider. At the moment, she caught something in the eyes of one of her comrades. It was not a rancid odor of mana coming from his orange pupils or a tightening sorcery around his mouth-clenched tail. Rather, it was a psychological stench that reeked of guilt pervading his very soul. Nomax, it seemed, was hiding something.

"H-he must have gone astray," he said so stiffly that a tree would have appeared more animated.

Lyconel considered her situation.

"Those Technodragons intercepted us too easily. Dennagon was lost in the Fire Elemental. Now our guide is missing for no apparent reason. It seems a bit improbable this would happen by chance…"

"Maybe Ballaxior was a traitor," suggested Nomax.

She shot him a glance. It was enough to pierce diamond.

"Maybe," she accusingly rejoined.

Lyconel looked into him for a second, nonverbally disclosing the warning, "I'm watching you". Then, she searched her belt, pulling out a compass. It was a circular instrument centered by a needle that spun round a ring of directions labeled in calligraphy. Built beneath its depleted plutonium outer shell and its clear, stained glass face, gears and wires were integrated to form a system of medieval and futuristic electromagnetic detectors that sensed when the globe changed its magnetic alignments. It was a crazed planet, and she had to be prepared, even when the World itself altered its own energy fields through the conscious Gaia mind she had seen only as a whelp. Thrusting the instrument out before her face, she traced her locale.

"Stabilize," she told it.

A dilute stream of mana rolled out her head like an aural mist. It influenced the material essence of the compass, shifting the needle to point in the right way. It fluctuated wildly, pointing in every which direction.

"The planet must have taken on a multimagnetic field," suggested Dradicus.

She reached under the stained glass bauble and tweaked the knobs. More directional coordinates rose, sliding over west and east so that they were much closer to north. Since the

World often altered its own electromagnetic orientations, it was necessary to have more orientations than north, east, west, south, northeast, southeast, northwest and southwest. Hence, the directions dorth, leth, drex, teth and doam were created. Lyconel, with a serpentine tongue stuck out and an eye keenly closed, examined the oddly transformed compass.

"Looks like we're due dorth."

The needle started to arc away from the flat face of the compass. Translucent angles of right ascension and declination appeared on the glassy outer casing, denoting the coordinate system of a celestial sphere. It angled up, pointing toward the top altitude of the bauble.

"And we're at the Alpha Pole itself. It's here."

She pocketed her instrument. As she was about to turn to her comrades to assign new orders, a sudden geyser of snow caught her eye. Initially, it looked like a trapped ancient gas chamber that had just burst, scattering a shower of whitened crystal ice over her band. The natural havoc seemed benign, but they were wary nonetheless.

"What the hell was that?" bluntly asked the obvious Nomax.

"Are there supposed to be geysers like that at the Alpha Pole?" inquired Lefius.

Lyconel felt a tiny tremor tickle her tail. She flapped her wings, boosting straight up into the air as the ground underneath her fractured apart, releasing another vent of frozen gems. The frigid spring, although composed completely of crystal, was fluid in nature, swirling in the air to form a spiral pattern in its wake. Branching down like a deranged root of some horrid creature, it curved down to the ground again, wriggling its way back into the terrain. Chunky icicles hailed upon them, grouped together as liquefied and flowing as the freest fluid. Even though it was still solid snow in its most condensed form, it felt as warm as the sands of a dune, hot as the tar of an onyx torture chamber.

Lyconel was only speckled by the debris as she flew a hundred feet away. Her comrades, well attuned to her amazingly quick reflexes, followed her immediately, unscathed by the winter snow that burned like coal.

"I guess there are now," she rejoined her fellow dissidents.

The geysers sprouted all around them, creating prominences of white arctic resembling those of the red sun. Soon, they started to form a nerve network, extruding vein-like tubes of chilled liquid crystal beneath the powdery surface. The dragons were being surrounded in circular formation.

Lyconel leapt into the air again, and her warriors did as well. Hovering over the lands, they looked down, only to see the land that they were standing on transform into a gigantic lens that was built of permafrost and snowy gems. Soon, it mutated to contain an iris, capping its pupil with the cold bluish tint of its equally gelid stare. It was a gigantic eye constructed of the arctic, sliding across the layers of ice that stretched down to the very core of the World. Complete with eyelids of glacial tundra, it blinked, then viewed those who dared to disrupt its slumber.

"In the name of Shevinoth!" cursed Dradicus.

"The glacier! She lives!" blurted the stunned Lefius.

Lyconel drew her mace.

"Then we must make certain she dies."

Fangs protruded from the undersides of the snowborne eyelids. They fluttered like the lips of a beast, reaching out to chomp anything above. The draconic dissidents scattered, tumbling at all sides to leave their enemy without any unthreatened flanks. Lefius drew his crossbow and Nomax equipped his bladed disks.

They swooped in one at a time, delivering sorties to the lids. Trying to stay clear of the pupil, Lyconel grazed her spiked mace across the edges of the optical mouth, scraping off some of the snowy fangs. Dradicus lashed out two bladed whips, ripping them along the corners of the beast's eye to weaken its vision. His flagellations triggered the tear ducts, which squirted out streams of heated snow at either end. Everyone rearranged their positions.

"To the left Nomax! Lefius, to the right!" commanded Lyconel.

The creature tried again to bite, missing as the dragons crossed each other's paths in a confusing manner. Lefius scudded directly over the predator as it pulled back from its assault, and fired an arrow straight down to the pupil. The projectile ricocheted off the outer whiteness of the eye, but he fleetly torqued, spinning around so that the crossbow was held behind his back. Launching another shot, he struck the lid, penetrating its flesh-like mineral snow.

However, he wasn't quite done yet. In one last spin, he slung out the revolver holstered in his belt and plugged the trigger with rapid clicks of his claw. Bullets were hammered out from the semi-automatic weapon, blasting through the enemy monster in bursts of pearly eruptions. All six shots were expended quickly, but they met their marks, satisfying the marksman.

"Yeah!" he zealously shouted.

The glacier roared. Lefius departed from its sight whilst Nomax entered to finish it off. Cocked with a disk, he pitched downward slightly toward the interior of the damaged eyelid. His comrades first thought he was going to try to rupture the injured ice, but unexpectedly, the ouroboros turned orthogonal to the ground, heading straight for the pupil. He held his weapon high above it just as the fangs were about to close on him.

Lyconel, in a fit of urgency, rushed in and snatched the edge of the eyelids with her bare talons as they were collapsing. Dradicus joined her, pulling on the organic frozen crystals with his own mouth while plunging his tail's whips into its flatside. Lefius dashed in last, grabbing whatever part of the edge he could. In his lack of foresight, he did something he regretted. Pain shot through his palm as a fang busted through his hand.

"Ahhh!" came the sharp bellow.

"Dradicus, cast a heal spell!" blared Lyconel.

Dradicus, even though he was desperately trying to prevent Nomax's life from ending, could not comply.

"I can't!"

"Then cast a ring of blood or a rain of metal, or something!"

He still couldn't. Magic was his bane. It made him sick just thinking about it, let alone conjuring it...

Meanwhile, Nomax landed on the cold ice of the blue pupil. His feet nearly slipped upon the glossy surface, but he maintained his posture and cast down all his might and rage upon the beast. Slamming his weapon into the iris, he cracked it like a mirror, sending thunderbolts of fractures through its whole lens. Yanking out his grenade launcher, he then launched a final explosive right into the humungous sight organ, detonating the core of the corneas into broken chunks. The grenade tore crystal snow apart, letting the devastating disk sink into the chilled optical abomination, and causing it to shriek in horror and agony unrelenting.

The glacier did not rumble as they expected, but instead, stopped instantly as if time had ceased its bidding upon it. The jaws that were its eyelids melted away, liquefying as if the very swords of the sun's light stabbed them in the middle of a mooncast eve. Fangs turned to fluid gems and the nerves that constituted the grand eye crumbled back into the diamond permafrost from whence they came. Slowly, the creature died, receding back into an unconscious sheet of white. As everything settled, the dragon party descended back to the surface upon the evanescing ruins of their defeated opponent.

For once, they were glad this glacier stopped.

"Never seen a glacier move that fast," jested Dradicus.

Lyconel was disappointed in his lack of fortitude in spellcasting. Even a simple heal spell was not too much to ask.

Just then, an abrupt eruption exploded between them. The force cast them a hundred feet away in all directions, and as they flew, another geyser tore up into the air, shooting to the sky like a tendril of tundra snow. They all reached for their accouterments again, but stood still and watched as the pearly tentacle reached to the heavens, striking the stratosphere to point to a constellation that was at their zenith – the Eye of Arcadin. When it was certain that they had all seen it, it boiled back down to the surface, all of its snowy essence crumbling into the hole where a pupil once was. Once more, there was silence.

The wind blew in her face. Lyconel looked up to the zenith constellation, the arrangement of stars that bore a striking resemblance to the eye they had just fought. It rested in the heavens as if to watch over the World from an almighty view, spectacular in its place amongst the center of all. However, as astounding as it was, she could have sworn that it was not there when first she arrived. In general, stars moved across the sky gradually, but she was sure it could not have moved there that speedily in the time she had been in the arctic.

"It's trying to tell us something," she commented. "We didn't fight that ogling thing for no reason. It was a test, and now that that test was passed, it gave us a hint." Even she had to admit what prize it had given her. "Knowledge…"

She rose from her feet, her inspiration in her mission rekindled. Ardently, she raised a fist.

"Come, my warriors! Let's move on! There are more challenges to be fought before we can reach the Keygate!"

Dradicus was two hundred feet away from her. He waved his tail against the backdrop of the lethward Moon.

"Um, I think I just found the Keygate."

Her auditory organs perked. She galloped across the distance, treading snow in her wake until she reached his location. A wurm-shaped hole was punched into the surface where Dradicus fell, leading to a hollow interior. Somehow this all felt familiar. It felt like discovery.

Dradicus gestured for her glance. She fervidly looked inside, but did not stick her head in just yet. Inside, she could see a hall made of bluish diamond, adorned with gemmed ornaments of books and engraved with symbols of keys and locks. Certainly, the markings were enough for most warriors to infer that they had found their target, but Lyconel was not satisfied with this alone. She had to be absolutely certain that it was her objective.

She scooped up a clump of crystal snow. Compacting it in her grasp, she rolled it into a tight snowball before patting it down between her palms. The substance flattened out to a sheet of reflective moonstone agate, slightly tainted with the brownish bands of dirty nitrous gems, but still acceptable enough to act as a mirror. Wrapping the end of her tail around it, she lowered it down into the hole.

Cranking her neck around almost by 180 degrees, she peered down to see the reflection of the entire subterranean corridor. The book ornaments upon the walls and the engravings that accompanied them all led to a single door at the end. Ominous, it was tilted slightly forward as if to have been deformed by some geological event, yet from what she could see, it was unguarded.

"I'm going in."

Before Dradicus could contest, she dropped down.

Skulking slowly down the path, she kept her mace at her side.

"But we can't enter without Dennagon," worriedly said Dradicus from outside.

She had no time for doubt.

"We have to."

Elsewhere upon the polar tundra, a whitish light lashed across the sky. One might have thought it was a comet in its nebulous coma, but on a second viewing, it was clearly bound toward the planet's surface. As it came closer to the ground, it became increasingly hellish, screaming into the night like a banshee-haunted pyrotechnic. Grazing the terrain like a red-hot iron, it instantly liquefied a groove of crystal into the topography. Any observer would have expected it to stop instantly at the magnitude of its impact upon the ground, but contrary to accepted wisdom, it kept hurtling, eventually arcing in circles as if it were guided by a navigational system. Inside, a faint scream could be heard from someone desperately trying to cease the endlessly propelling projectile.

"What the bloody fuck?" appropriately asked Lefius.

"You said it," added Nomax, who stood beside him upon a hilltop.

Insanely, the comet started to speed around them in circles. Confused, they listened to the constantly oscillating cries coming from within the astral entity. They could faintly see Dennagon's face inside the fire.

"The sentry," remarked Lefius.

Gradually, it slowed in its centripetal motion. A stop only came after half a minute, at which point the flame continued to burn like a pyre to no one. Eventually, it cooled, leaving a patch of archaic ice exposed. Dennagon lay in the center of it. No longer encased in his celestial fire, he stumbled dizzily, pirouetting for a second before flopping over. His two companions casually walked to him, nonplussed.

They looked down at his scarred body. He snapped to life, grabbing Lefius by the collar.

"When am I?!"

"At the Crystal Realm Alpha Pole."

"WHEN am I?!" he reiterated.

To the two unwitting dupes, his words were incomprehensible.

Inside the Keygate entrance, Lyconel and Dradicus slid closer to the door. The crystalline azure of the book-shaped trinkets hanging on the walls twinkled amidst the light of tiny torches that floated above them. The shadows of writing were projected from their semi-transparent surfaces as the illumination passed through, superimposing a mural of shaded literature upon the key symbols. Every step they took made the door even more threatening, and the creepy carvings at their flanks certainly did not help.

"I wonder if those crystal books can be read," uttered Dradicus to alleviate the tension.

"You can read them from their shadows on the walls, stupid."

Baleful roars sounded from within. They halted for a moment, then continued. Their nervousness came about as a result of their knowledge, for they were aware that the Key had three tests of wisdom behind its entrance door. Only one who had extensive knowledge of the World's physical laws could bypass, yet neither of them had ever consumed a black orb and assimilated the liquid wisdom within the globe. It was curious that if they had gathered data, they would have become as weak-minded as the sentries of the collective, but since they did not, they were powerless to find their objective. By their insurrectionist nature, they generally did not appreciate the workings of the planetary machine, whoever created them. Perhaps this was their castigation for their blasphemy. The wrath of a cruel puppeteer deity.

Good for the deity, Lyconel thought. Let him have his revenge if he wants it. He'll never have the worship of a TRUE warrior.

She now stood before the door that would lead to her challenge. Reluctantly fearful, she drew her talon toward the knob, edging inch by inch. Dradicus almost felt like fleeing from her, which he would have done if she were not of his genetic alignment. Since she was chromosomally related, he was essentially screwed if anything went wrong.

It was a touch colder than ice. She made contact with the knob. As if to summon a fireball, she wrapped her claws around it, clasping it as firmly as she could.

"Here goes everything," she reassured herself.

Stealing a deep breath just in case it was her last, she let all her phobias rush away with a blast of her forced will. There was no turning back now. Valorously, she twisted the doorknob and pushed.

Nothing happened. It was locked.

"Silly me."

Again, she stole the nerves that she once owned. Extending her talon, she slowly turned the knob one more time. Thrusting her shoulder forth, she rushed in to ram it down with all the strength of her sinew, a growl broiling fury in her skull. With her momentum, she could have taken a castle down.

However, something grabbed her before she could make contact with her target. Dennagon pulled her away just in time. His charred flesh hung enervated off his limp, battered body, but he was still ready for battle.

"Dennagon. How did you –"

"We can get to that later. Right now, we need that Key."

There was something different about him, an attribute of stunned potency that was evident in his face. However, he was right. They could get to that later.

"Are you certain you want to do this?" she asked because she wasn't.

Dennagon looked at her with expressionless eyes that were dimmed by melted flesh.

"As certain as one can be."

More easily than he would have broken a twig, he turned the handle and casually pushed open the door. There was complete darkness within it, but this time he had no fear. Anything was possible, which meant that he might even win. Might...

He slipped into the darkness as quickly as the most serpentine of creatures. The darkness engulfed him and the door slammed shut, locking out his comrades from the realm that would have killed them all. As soon as he entered, he landed in a muddy chamber where stalactites and stalagmites were synonymous, as they protruded from all sides equally. The dirt all around was blue in color, so saturated in tint that one might have thought it was an earthbound sky. However, it was mud like anything else, and it was as stable as any inanimate entity. This was supposedly the first challenge.

At the center of the chamber, two objects suddenly materialized. From gears and parts embedded within the dirt, two clocks self-constructed in midair, one as large as Dennagon's head and the other twice as large. As soon as they were finished, they started ticking immediately from 15 o'clock midnight. It was a test of time.

Dennagon took combative posture, but lurched in his stance. Suddenly, he couldn't breathe. The air of the environment was sucked out through the tips of the stalactites, creating a void of airless space. It was a vacuum trap and there was no way of getting out. He turned around to run for the door, but found that it wasn't even there anymore.

"What…is this…?" he strained to speak asphyxiated.

Another mysterious voice in his quest came out of nowhere.

"I am the Key," it announced in a tone that implied it was not manifested within the vacuum. "In order to surpass this test, you must determine the speed at which the larger clock will fall if the smaller one falls at 10 meters per second."

Dennagon strained to vocalize in the thin air.

"Freely falling objects…move at the same speed regardless…of mass or size in a vacuum."

Those were the last words he could expel before the air in his lungs ran empty. Collapsing onto one knee, he was prepared to slip into draconic meditation, but even in a reptilian unconscious state, he was not sure how long he would survive without respiration.

The clocks fell in front of him, twirling as they plunged to the ground. They hit the floor simultaneously, each one carrying a different mass, but both composed of the same atoms. Thus, all their atomic particles struck the surface at the same time, as they all accelerated at the same rate. Dials and gears shattered around fragmenting glass, returning back into the ground from which they emerged. The machines of time melted away.

Air filled the chamber in a gust as potent as it was refreshing. Dennagon took a breath as deep as he would if he were just about to submerge himself in water. However, this was all but an aquatic test of hydrodynamic skills. This was an examination of intellectual might. Another door opened up in the middle of the floor, welcoming him to his next challenge. Without even waiting to regain his full strength, he plodded forth.

Into another chamber he spiraled whilst the horizontal door above him closed itself forever. Gravity abruptly vanished, and he found himself tumbling like a cosmic wrecking ball or an asteroid that had lost its wayward way. Slashing his claws around, he tried to steady himself, only to find that he could hardly exert enough force to counteract his acceleration. Helplessly, he rolled through the space, unknowing of what was to happen.

A crystal ball appeared in the center. It looked like the one he had at his old domicile, but this one appeared to be wired with magical energy that commanded it to carry out something malign. As its mana churned, a claw of water slashed out of it, crustacean in nature. It grabbed the hapless draconic challenger by the torso, pinning down all his primary muscles. Even though his limbs were free, he could barely move them.

"The only way out of this chamber is through the orifice," stated the Key as the claw began to spin Dennagon slowly in centripetal motion.

An orifice appeared in the middle of the wall approximately 100 feet from the crystal ball, aligned with the plane of centripetal motion.

"However, as you detach yourself from the claw," continued to brief the bodiless Key, "it will only remain open for 1 second."

The Water Elemental claw swung him around in a circle with a radius of 10 meters. Numerals materialized upon the surface of the ball from the streams of sorcery that flowed within it. Like a digital meter of magical mechanisms, it denoted increasing units in Newtons of force. Dennagon knew what to do.

Centripetal force was equivalent to mass times velocity squared divided by radius. He was rapidly accelerating, so from that he would have to determine the speed at which to dislodge himself from the claw. The central meter currently read at 500,000 Newtons. Focusing, he visualized the tangential distance from his circle of motion to the orifice. $F_c =(mv^2)/r$, he kept in mind.

By his observation and keen draconic eyes, he could tell that the tangential distance from his circle to the orifice was 100 meters. He needed to exit within one second, so therefore, it was necessary to move at 100 meters per second to achieve escape velocity. Now, the only issue left was how many Newtons of force he would require to achieve such a speed. Unfortunately, he could not remember how much he weighed.

"Bloody hell," he cursed at himself.

The meter rose to 2,000,000 N. He couldn't tell how much time he had left unless he knew his own mass, so he frantically searched his thoughts for traces of memories that might indicate this information. The last time he measured his heaviness was a year ago, at which time he weighed approximately 4,352 kilograms. The two times before that were two and three years ago, when he was at 4,740 and 5,001 kilograms respectively. Considering that his fasting from black orbs of knowledge reduced his mass by about 350 kilos every year as they had apparently done in the past, he should now have weighed about 4,000 kilos. Albeit he didn't like using inductive reasoning, it was the only choice he had right now. He couldn't change the laws of physics in this arena.

His force was now at 3,000,000 N. If he were 4,000 kilograms, the required speed was 100 meters per second and the radius of the circle was 10 meters, then he would have to solve for $F_c =((4,000 \text{ kg}) 100^2)/10$, which was exactly – 4,000,000 Newtons.

He wrenched his neck forward as best he could, chomping the water claw and severing it just at the point of his motion where he was directed toward his destination. It released him, sending him flying. Rocketing through the gravity-lacking space, Dennagon shot through the orifice at 100 m/s just as it closed. Into the final chamber he entered.

Falling from the ceiling of an unfamiliar room, he landed upon a metal ground. Rising from crouched position, he looked up, only to see an immense glass prism sitting before a colossal laser projector that orbited around it like a star around a galactic center. It rotated up to the apex of the chamber, shining down on the prism from above with a high-intensity beam of green light. The laser bent through the glass, following the indexes of refraction that controlled it so that it could spread out in all directions as a rainbow. The walls came alive, but not in a comforting way. Every inch of the room was lined with plastic explosives, which had been activated by way of the light illuminating them. Their countdown meters started to drop, giving him only sixty seconds to complete the mission.

"You must shift the light to the only place where explosives are not planted," ordered the Key.

Yet, there were explosives everywhere. Dennagon only saw one option. Stolidly thinking, he contemplated the factors of his situation as variables that could be translated into pure mathematics. Judging by the heat, the wavelength of the light was about 5×10^{-7} meters and its frequency was 4×10^{14} Hertz. However, it was moving through the prism at a slower speed, and he estimated by the degree of the heat that the velocity was 2×10^8 meters per second inside the glass. That meant that the index of refraction was about 1.5, and that if he wanted to bring the light together, he would need an index of 1.

He flew up to the laser emitter at the top of the chamber. Punching a hole through its outer shell, he seized the lens inside and started to turn it. He adjusted the angle so that the light emitted was altered to a yellowish hue, changing its wavelength to 7.5×10^{-7} meters. At this modification, the laser bent away from the explosives, deactivating them. He was safe.

However, as the illumination changed its orientation, it bathed entirely upon Dennagon, suspending him in the air. He felt his bones lock down and his brain freeze as the photons grabbed him in their sentient luster. Immobilized, he absorbed all the luminosity, preventing any of the incandescence from reaching the detonators. He had completed the mission, but he was unable to do anything more.

At first, he felt incarcerated. Anon, howbeit, he relished in the powerful laser beam as it mightily surged through his body. Light swept across his flesh like liquid salve, fusing with his muscles and healing the places where he was wounded. Demigod strength coursed through his mind, making him feel like his primitive material form was being transformed into pure illumination that granted him the invincibility of an unbreakable hologram. This was a true type of enlightenment, yet not one that was ultimate.

"So you have wisdom," complimented the Key. "The bounty is forthwith yours."

The glass prism below cracked open. Bursts of pure energy expanded from its fissures like parasites of auras borne. It detonated itself, revealing a sapphire crystal ball that floated up into the clutches of its new possessor, ringed with the ribbons of glorious scintillation untainted by matter in its ascendant embodiment. Dennagon readily accepted his warrior's prize, his bone free from the clutches of the laser. Prying open the lid, he peeked inside, face bedazzled.

Yet, there was nothing inside.

"Nil. It's a bloody void."

Or a sick joke. He looked around, searching for the creature whose voice taunted him.

"Where are you, Key? Where is thy Key?!"

There was no response. It was like he was talking to himself.

"It was promised to the victor of this test!"

Then, he noticed his voice had changed. It seemed to be integrated with the one that had announced all the parameters of the challenges to him.

"Wait a minute. What's wrong with me? I'm talking to myself again."

Lyconel and Dradicus entered. The exterior of the Keygate unlocked itself half a minute ago when the challenges had been accomplished. Dennagon huddled the sapphire ball close to himself, perplexedly pondering what his change in tone meant. He sensed another consciousness buried deep inside of him, one that seemed to have come out of nothing.

An epiphany struck him. His own reflection was the only thing that lay inside the crystal ball, the only thing that was visible in the many cut faces of the orbed jewel. He was his own prize, the gift that the always sought. Only he knew where the Key was.

"I was always talking to myself," he said.

"No Dennagon. We heard you," responded Lyconel.

She knelt. Nomax and Lefius entered.

"What are you doing?" wondered Dradicus.

"He IS the Key," she declared.

Dennagon knew it to be true as well. Dradicus tucked down his limbless body in respect for his leader's proposal, and Lefius did the same afterward. Nomax hesitated to comply, but at the sight of Dennagon in his crystalline scales and brightened eyes, even he could not deny the truth. He bowed his ouroboros head.

As if reborn, Dennagon cocked his head up in the brilliance of the laser. The high-intensity light did not even sting his newly gemmed eyes as it glittered through his body of pure emerald. This was not the same dragon that had been spawned amidst the Drakemight swarms. This was Dennagon the Key, and he intended to bring forth the one thing that could complete his journey.

The Moons were at 45-degree altitudes in the sky, still on their path to convergence at the zenith. The gem tundra still sparkled in the lunar illumination, but even more so through Dennagon, who appeared as a draconic beacon in the middle of the arctic pole. His new body of pure emerald crystal glistened more fervently than the glassy snow, sparkling with every move he made as if his stride were an endless haiku that constantly evolved along the line of time. He was a walking jewel, a crystal dragon, gemmed scales lining his muscle with ten times the hardness of diamond and a hundred times the brilliance of the most finely cut stone. As he scintillated, his party traversed merrily across the snow, cheering for their victory.

"We've done it! The Key is ours!" applauded Dradicus, who was so immersed in blitheness that he couldn't even come up with a stupid riddle.

"We have only to take it to the Omega Pole," appended Lefius. "There, the Lexicon awaits us."

Dennagon seemed perturbed. He was not omniscient yet, but he was powerful enough to sense that there was something wrong with the fabric of time through which he was traveling at the moment. There was nothing he could do about it but think. That was even more disturbing than the problem itself.

Reaching for his belt, he pulled out his old nameless storybook that he always kept with himself as a good luck charm. Glaring at it with loathing eyes, he flipped through its pages haphazardly before slamming it shut. At the impact of his force, he puffed out gusts of dust from the old tales he hadn't read in ages, burying his claws into the back and front covers. His decree solid, he flung the tome away, letting it bounce across the snow like a skipping stone. Not even a farewell glance accompanied its ousting from his life.

Dradicus wished that he had discarded the spellbook instead.

"You've seen something," deduced Lyconel from the expression in his green eyes.

Eerily, he gave her a half-turn.

"It was called the Technorealm," he started. "A place born of the future, yet of no future spawned. I acquired more information in a minute than in my entire life."

Everyone's grins suddenly turned to astonished visages of shock.

"Is that how you overcame the Keygate tests?" questioned the envious Nomax.

Dennagon nodded. That was where he downloaded most of those files on the behavior of light through a prism.

"I only managed to escape that Technorealm by the laws of relativity. Travelling faster than light, I contorted the fabric of time."

"You went to the past?" asked Dradicus.

"No, where I went, there was no past."

He remembered where he was. It was a void out of this World in which sights of various eras could be seen – prehistoric eons, the human stone age, Precambrian Earth, and spatial installations on other Worlds. On second thought, they were not mere sights, but actual membranes of realities that had become intermingled with one another. He did not know how to elaborate it in words, for words were so limited.

"It was a realm like this planet, only space and time were inverted," he explained. "Temporal moments were embedded in the voids, and space was merely a thing that flowed forward to maintain change. In our realm, time elicits change, whereas spatial entities occupy the voids."

In his own mind, the memories of the timeless visions flattened out into two-dimensional planes. They melded together chaotically like a jigsaw puzzle bereft of linear arrangement. It was a timescape that he had been trapped in, composed of various random moments that were mixed together without order or sequence. It was like an almighty deity had forgotten to put them together into coherent worldlines of destiny so that nothing made sense and there was neither a rhyme or reason for any event. Reminiscing his presence amongst the timescape, he recalled that objects were passing from one brane to another, one particular entity being himself. Unfortunately, he could not remember how he managed to escape from that horridly bizarre place, let alone how to further elucidate it to his comrades.

"I strayed across the branes," he tried as best he could, "a wanderer in nothingness, until alas, I found myself here."

He shook his head. The memories were too disquieting, so he released them for now.

"Something drew me back to you."

Lyconel cranked her head forward. Right away, she charged ahead to their next objective, fueled by the emergency of what she had just heard. Her talons buried deep claw marks into the permafrost as she ran as fast as she could.

"We have to get to the Omega Pole at the speed of sound. Our enemies are ready to unleash their ultimate wrath."

Dennagon was the only one that exchanged glances as everyone else bolted forth. Even as an enlightened being whose soul contained the Key itself, he did not understand why they were mobilizing with such urgency. Then again, one could never move too fast. He had a feeling he would found out all the "whys" soon enough.

Kingdom Drakemight lay in ruins, its polyhedral domiciles wrecked to the very surface of the wretched earth. The splendor it once boasted was no more than a vast stretch of rubble strewn across countless miles in a blanket of charred metal, stone, glass, and all the other substances from which the city was built. Carrion of its long dead inhabitants still reeked their stench in the bonfires that continuously burned, filling the atmosphere to the sky with odor unmatched. It appeared that nothing could survive in this devastation. However, as the chronology of earth implied, there were always survivors in every extinction.

The Archive, the grand steel orb in the center of the city, still remained in tact. Inside, hundreds of surviving draconic sentries furiously assimilated the knowledge within the remaining black orbs that floated throughout. With every orb they consumed, their minds grew weaker and weaker until they could barely feel any sentiments other than those of a mechanical desire to destroy. Knowledge was poisoning them, yet they were too puny to stop their own self-destruction. They were becoming the slaves of man, who wished to herald the control of time forever. Soon, humans would not only be able to tap into time; they would be able to control its very center.

Drekkenoth sat atop his dark throne, surveying his minions as they relinquished their free will. They were but machines of scales encased to him, extensions of his mind that contemplated every moment what his objectives were. Dark flames roared through his body as he meditated deep and mysterious thoughts.

He was as old as the universe itself, and the endless passage of ages coursed in his nerves. His mission was to battle the one thing that kept him from seizing the diadem of time – eternity. For countless eons, he had fought to reach the Origin of all, yet in every age, he was cast back to where he was, where he was born – the present. Here and the "Ultimate Now" were his supreme prisons. The present was the dungeon that he ruled as master, yet could not himself escape from. Perhaps the more slaves he created, the less imprisoned he would become.

"They will die. All of them," he said mechanically. "The World shall fall to the humans, but time shall be mine. They cannot operate the center of temporal flow, so I shall seize it from them. I will take eternity."

For a moment, deep within his mind, he felt something he had never overtly sensed before. It was hatred for something, but he could not tell what it was. He did not want to know anyway, for his will was one of a robot. He quelled this malfunctioning virus known as an emotion to maintain his neutral composure.

Arxinor and Gorgash soared before him, holding various futuristic tools of mechanical repair. Wrenching and tuning their inner circuits, they fixed their damaged parts, attaching new plates where their scales had been torn. Gorgash injected liquid metal into his fractured cranium to fuse it shut whilst Arxinor used plastic adhesive to reinforce his scorched bodily vehicle.

"What is to be done?" worried Arxinor. "Thissss dragon is too powerful."

"He has already tapped into the Lexicon's essence," supported the doltish Gorgash. "Soon, he will transcend our control."

Drekkenoth grumbled, quaking the entire Archive.

"Then the moment has come to activate our greatest weapon."

Arxinor and Gorgash exchanged nervous glances.

"We calculate that our forcccccces are not yet prepared."

"They are still too violent. Too avaricious."

"Affirmative," confirmed then dragon lord with dark

flames blazing around his eyes. "That is the source of their deadliness."

He lifted a fist of fire, forming a flared diagram of the World in his talons.

"Deploy," he commanded, "the SAPIENS."

At the depths of the Archive, past the hordes of mindless dragon sentries, horrific roars echoed, indicating the presence of something terrible harbored below the structure's foundation. The Technodragons had been breeding them for this occasion, and soon they would be free from their spawning grounds. Even as machines, the two subservient mechanical reptiles felt the terror that the creatures below could cast upon the World, but they had no choice. The war was just beginning and all true wisdom had to be annihilated.

CHAPTER 8

Mountains of bone spanned for countless miles beside the comparatively tiny woodlands that surrounded them. Gnarled and jagged, the skeletal hills jutted out from the ground level many acres down, creating a chain of valleys and alps that studded the World as a natural wall. All the stones were made of pure calcium, but not the same type that ordinarily occurred in regular landscapes. The mounts here were built of the very same matter as the endoskeletons of any man, dragon or thunderbird. Like dental protrusions of a leviathan mouth, the peaks ranged the terrain into the horizon, sharp to their very tips, whetted like they had been carved recently. However, the Fangs of Astinor had stood upon the World for many an age, so prominently that they were visible from space.

The draconic dissidents were not interested in the cosmos right now, for they had more pressing matters. Dennagon and his comrades trudged through the mountain ranges, heading only by the directions of their lone scout.

"The Fangs of Astinor," Lyconel stated the name of the area she had avoided several days ago as she was pursued by Technodragons. "Dradicus, see if there's a safe campsite up ahead."

"That depends on what you mean by 'see'. I can 'see' it in my imagination, but does it exist if I cannot observe it?"

"JUST DO IT."

Dradicus hurriedly snaked across a bony mountainside. Lyconel knew they were in a rush now, but also considered that they needed to regenerate before expending all their energy. She could jump from clouds and not die, run through fire without a single burn and tread through water deluges as forceful as a meteor shower, but even she was not strong enough to counteract the first law of thermodynamics and third law of motion. There was a balance to all energy and an equal and opposite reaction to every action. Thence, her expenditure of energy would not go unnoticed by a universe that operated on symmetry.

She halted her team. Taking from her belt a flask of water, she took a drink.

"What's the sudden hurry?" inquired Dennagon.

"The Technorealm is the Technodragon dungeon. If you escaped from it, then they probably know."

"About what?"

A clutch of calcium rocks tumbled off a peak. Nomax and Lefius warily drew their weapons. Nevertheless, Lyconel was unmoved by the possible threat, for what lay on her mind was heavier than any monstrosity the World could unleash upon her.

"I lied to you," admitted Lyconel with the utmost strength in her truthful will. "I didn't take you on our quest because of your status as a sentry."

Dennagon gravely stepped forward.

"I took you because of your mind," she resumed. "The consciousness that guided the beginning of time also built the linearity of temporal flow, thus creating destiny. However, it still kept within itself a timescape in which all the World's events were unbound."

Dennagon touched his head. He thought he knew she was hiding something.

"The Lexicon," he murmured.

"No, you. That timescape you were 'trapped' in was yourself, your own sentience at work. I searched the World, looking for a source that could disrupt causality. Break the tides of fate. I found it in your mind and your mind alone."

More stones fell from the peaks. It was now definite that something was watching them, for the mountainous fangs began to shift like teeth across gums. Although the terrain rocked, Dennagon and Lyconel did not break from each other's gazes in their deep conversation.

"We all dream, but you Dennagon, are different. You don't fancy in time's conventional code."

Nomax and Lefius took offensive positions. Something emerged from behind one of the mountain summits near them, hissing putridly. Lyconel severed her engrossing speech with Dennagon and also armed her weapon. They all stood ready to fling their blades and spikes at the incoming beast, and trigger the wrath of the living landscape they inhabited. The mountains were dangerously easy to anger, but what lay behind that peak seemed more threatening.

Just as they were all about to hurl their weapons, the creature showed itself completely. Reptilian heads, all identical to one another, slithered around an elderly dragon body that climbed down wearily. The bony ground chipped in its staggered stride, yet it was aware enough to notice its band near. It was the hydra Ballaxior, their lost guide.

"Ballaxior!" said Lyconel surprised.

As she held out her talons in a welcoming gesture, Nomax growled. He threw a bladed disk at the incoming dragon and chopped off one of its heads. Ballaxior shrieked as best he could with his decrepit vocal cords, tumbling down the flank of the hill in a small avalanche of pebbles.

"What the hell are you doing?!" berated Lyconel.

She trotted to the elder as he rolled battered before his comrades.

"I'm all right."

"What happened to you, Ballaxior? Why were you lost?"

He swallowed his own blood.

"I was ambushed. A disk just like that one struck me when we were mobilizing to the Alpha Pole."

Lefius turned to Nomax, nonverbally blaming him for the assault. Disks still accoutered, Nomax pointed incriminatingly at the victim.

"He lies! He tried to ambush me first!"

Lefius positioned himself behind his former colleague, preparing to take him down.

"I'm telling you, he will kill us all!" Nomax continued to wail. "I did the right thing, I did! If only he were dead!"

"You'll fall before your disk can leave your claws," menaced Lefius.

Now he turned around, situating himself to swing his ouroboros tail at the accusing wyvern. Lefius, although relatively smaller, did not budge.

"Enough," Lyconel demanded. "There are doppelgangers throughout the World. It could have been one of them playing its mischief upon us. We need not battle one another when we can save our fighting spirit for the humans."

Dradicus then returned, again missing out on what had just transpired. Judging by everyone's tense faces and the fact that the lost member of their party was amongst them once more, he deduced that it was probably something he did not want to learn about. Anger was not his favorite emotion, for he preferred blissful ignorance as opposed to the harrows of ire. Perhaps it was best just to state his findings.

"I found a groove near Astinor's tongue."

And so they went to the Tongue of Astinor. Daylight shone through a fleshy grove rimmed by trees of pure cartilage. The illumination shone through their translucent trunks, letting ghostly, semi-lambent shapes dance across the grounds like wraiths in the middle of the noon. Large taste buds protruded from the floor, warping the weird shadows of the whitened verdure with their bulbous figures that sampled the flavor of everything that passed. Luckily, dragons tasted good to the giant terrestrial beast called Astinor, so it let them make their encampment there.

Dennagon threw down a pile of bone fragments, heaping them together in a small cluster. Breathing green fire upon them, he set them ablaze, warming himself in the coolness of the air. They were well out of the Alpha Pole, but it was still a bit chilly since their latitude was not far off from the northern cap of the planet. Deep within these mountains, the atmosphere was even colder, as their altitude was halfway toward the sky.

Dradicus gnawed on a tiger he had easily caught in the skeletal wilderness. It was an evolved species of feline that scavenged specifically on the bone fragments of slain animals, one he had rarely seen with his own two eyes. Albeit, it still tasted just like any tiger, which tasted just like chicken. He wondered if this was true for all felines, but then remembered that truth was subjective. What was savory to him could be refuse to another.

While Nomax watched everyone in paranoid demeanor from a corner he decided to brood in, Dennagon pulled out from amongst his equipment a bag of metal shards that constituted the remains of his broken blade. From the taste bud underbrush, he grabbed a slab of stony bone and suspended it over the flame by mounting it atop two lesser stones. Placing the fragments of his sword on top of it, he realigned his blade the way it was supposed to be when whole.

Dradicus contracted his throat muscles. He tried to blow flame on his stale tiger, but his breath was of ice from those pine tree leaves he ate on his last recon mission. It frosted the carnage with tiny icicles and a thin, frozen skin.

"Damn," he muttered. "I knew I shouldn't have eaten those evergreens."

He turned to Dennagon.

"Can I use your fire?"

Dennagon finished lining up the cracked weapon. He placed the hilt, the final piece, at the base, its pommel adorned with the trinket of a dragon symbol. Stoically, he adjusted the stone slab upon which it rested, further blocking the flames of the makeshift furnace.

"Okay," agreed Dradicus, knowing when to take a hint. "I'm fine with cold cuts."

Hammering his claws into the metal pieces, Dennagon began to re-forge his sword. Sparks flew with every massive impact, molding the shards as the emerald fire heated them. Green-hot slashes scarred the blade as his talons melted the fragments together, fusing them as one in strokes that liquefied steel. Flames licked his new crystal dragon body, but served only to make him glow.

Dradicus watched as the weapon gradually took its original form at the blacksmith craftsmanship of the lone warrior. However, as intriguing as it was, it was taking a while, and he got bored. Hence, he pulled out from his sheath a nameless book whose title had been scratched off, and started reading its inner tales. It was the same tome Dennagon discarded at the Alpha Pole.

"You know," he remarked after browsing a few pages, "this book isn't bad. I don't know why you threw it out."

He scanned his eyes through the paragraphs, speed-reading through the first chapter. It depicted the tale of a human skeleton warrior whose life was misfortunately ridden with treachery and deceit in a ploy to seize control of something called the "Gateway".

"Or why you kept it with yourself in the first place…"

Dennagon stopped forging for a second.

"And why did you bother to retrieve it after I cast it from my sight?"

Dradicus shrugged without arms.

"It looked like an intriguing book."

"How could you tell? It has no title."

"Do you judge books by their covers?"

"Yes."

"Oh."

WHAM! Dennagon started to manually repair his blade again, which was now radiant in jade luminosity. Dradicus squinted an eye and carefully studied the torn lettering between the claw marks on the cover. He could barely make out a phrase.

"'Epics of the Ages'," he recited.

Dennagon wasn't sure if he was just making it up or if that was the real title behind the rips.

"How can you tell?" he asked.

Dradicus showed him the cover. Pointing out the placements of the remnants of the lettering, he noted where the words once were.

"See? E-P-I-C-S of the A-G-E-S."

Even Dennagon had to concur that that was the most logical answer. Still, he was a bit humbled that he had the book for so many years and didn't even notice that himself.

"Ah. How did you figure that out?"

"I'm a recon expert. A scout, remember?"

Dradicus continued to immerse himself in the story, his googly eyes quickly breezing through the sentences.

"Thence, I ask again – why do you keep this tome if you've already downloaded data from the Technorealm?"

"Because it dictates neither rules nor unfounded facts. It's just a collection of fictitious tales. Uncorrupted. Pure."

"Forged from nothingness. Creating a plenum from a vacuum." Dradicus snorted a chuckle. "I just love this paradoxical World."

Dennagon fermented a light green fire in his jade diamond chest. Tightening his lips as if to whistle, he breathed a thin rod of flame that precisely melted the metal where he wanted it. The steel splinters were welded together at the intensity of his concentrated inferno, which resembled the exactitude of a laser. Wholly emerald in glowing jade incandescence, its blade pulsed with heat, completely unified into a single piece once more. Notwithstanding, it was still not finished, and with strokes of his calloused scaly talons, he added the final touches.

"You know, words are queer," Dradicus observed. "They can depict everything in existence, yet they're merely symbols upon pages."

"Simplicity's the secret of language," rejoined Dennagon. "Words and icons are the basest ways of communication, and thus, can be extremely versatile. However, in a strict mathematical sense, they are meaningless, assigned significance only by our thoughts. Celerity in exchange for literary nihilism."

"Then who can say what words should objectively be? Is there a way to communicate without the use of symbols that can be interpreted differently by disparate beings?"

"Use fewer words. Get to the point."

The blade was beginning to take its original form again. Dennagon sheered the steel against his fangs, sending lighted sparks bursting against the friction. The edge was sharpened.

"Dennagon, Lyconel, Dradicus," listed Dradicus the triumvirate of creatures in the World he found most interesting. "These names are but sounds. No more, no less."

Lyconel stepped out from the foliage, carrying a dead, two-headed lion of her own.

"As I always say," she joined the conversation, "the World is what you make of it. Those names are endowed with meaning by the agreement of many conscious beings."

"In other words, they are also knowledge created out of nothing," contemplated Dennagon. "No more substantial than any scribe's tale."

"And why should epics not be universal?" retorted Lyconel.

"Epics are written in the language of drama, not in words necessarily."

"Oh?"

"Think about it. A paragraph can only describe so much, and a reading audience must fill in the blanks that lie betwixt every phrase with his own imagination. Who then, is the actual creator of the literature – the scribe or the reader?"

"Obviously the scribe."

Lyconel was surprised at how quickly her response came. Expectedly, Dennagon had a quick rebuttal.

"As you said before, observation creates reality. Even the ancients said that quantum mechanics and relativity were united in that they required perception to design reality, thus coming up with their 'conceptual' Theory of Everything. Akin, if no one reads a tome, why should it even exist? If no one can imagine the words coming to life, then there is no reason to state that it is real. Therefore, the reader, in a sense, creates the book as he reads it."

"An organism creating its creator..." said Lyconel fascinated. "Interesting. Still, that doesn't explain why epics shouldn't be universal."

"Again, the answer hath lies in the words. The less description there is in a book, the less the scribe actually has to 'create'. One might say that a sufficient amount of description would paint a detailed enough picture so that the creator could claim most of the credit for building a given story, but to truly describe anything in reality, one would have to expend an infinite amount of words. Infinity is a ridiculous concept, and no one can write forever."

The blade was honed to a fine edge now, but Dennagon wanted it even sharper. He continued to sheer it against his pointy teeth.

"So what does it mean to create?" wondered Lyconel.

"Try painting a picture. After all, a vision is worth a thousand phrases."

Dennagon, whilst sharpening, accidentally slit his lip with the whetted sword. It did not really sting, as he was used to blood spilling from his body. However, the kind of gore that came out this time was alien to his soma. It was red, not silver. It was evil, not neutral. It was –

"The blood of men," pointed out Lyconel.

Dennagon touched his wound. He saw it to be true.

"Untainted," he added.

"You touched it back at the Red Marsh."

He remembered the fateful fight with Gorgash and how he had plunged right into a puddle of sentient innards. It was discomforting just to think about it.

"I'll be all right," he assured her.

Just as he uttered the certitude he had in his health, his abdomen cramped. Clutching it in pain, he growled. Lyconel looked at him dubiously. Nonetheless, he rose from his enervated posture and lifted his sword from its forge, letting it gleam in the sunlight for all to see. As it cooled, the radiance faded, letting its true emerald tint show through in the luminosity of day. Although still blemished, it was a nearly perfect blade, one that most experienced blacksmiths would have been unable to forge with such meager equipment. Then again, its owner was always a perfectionist. The sword's steel smooth sheen that it had attained from mere fragments of metal demonstrated the craftiness that built it.

As Lyconel and Dradicus looked at the dazzling weapon, Ballaxior then came from the woods.

"I promised we would find carrion for all," he proclaimed.

At his side was Lefius, who carried loads of dead beasts. From skeleton wolves to felines to strange species of skeletal zombie fish that lived only in these sectors, they piled up their trophies upon the ground for all to feast on. The spoils of victory shone at the expense of the perished animals, of course, but that was the way the World turned. Morality was as meaningless and subjective as words were, for the only mission that was really at the heart of every last action of every living being was the attainment of happiness. Whether by the aiding of others or the hording of treasures for one's own indulgence, bliss was the ultimate goal to be sought. In their minds, the only quest worthy of living for was the journey for the Lexicon.

Nomax skulked in the bony hills, shadowed by the cartilaginous groves. He found pleasure not in omniscience, but instead in a twisted form of indulgence – vengeance. Ethics existed only as constructs to create a more coherent society, but he was free from such trite bounds as civilization and cooperation. Noble he was in this sense, yet vile was he in that he expended his moral nihilism on pointless quests of sadism. His hatred drove him, and nothing else. Whilst the party replenished their nutrition on the masses of corpses, he plotted in the darkness, waiting for his moment to strike. It would come in time, but hopefully not too long a span to delay his bloodlust.

———————————

The Lip of Astinor was not but several miles from its Tongue where they had set their last encampment. It was a fleshy cliff rimmed by muscular shrubs that branched out to reach the sun from the nerve-lined terrain. The ground was cracked with the curled up peelings of chapped skin, textured with the rough, scaly patterns of simian dermal layers. It was like a microscopic portion of someone's hand magnified into a macroscopic form. Like any microscopic surface on the uncleanly globe, there were bacteria on its surface.

The draconic dissidents huddled behind the shrubs like germs on the terrabeast's oral parts. Meticulously, they crept toward the edge of the cliff, nearing the scene of something violently loud far down.

"This situation is as fragile as a diamond is when being cut. Move not but the claws you need to, and if possible, creep on your digits alone," warned the strategic Ballaxior.

Thundering rumbles sounded from below. Dennagon shuffled as circumspect as the guide advised, his eyes only catching glimpses of gold coruscations high in the sky. The place reeked of evil, and everyone scented it with their draconic nasal-oral receptors. What was to come should not at all have been surprising, but still, Lyconel had to say it.

"There is a human kingdom near."

She chinned up. Dradicus accepted the gesture and poked his limber head out of the shrubs. Although he knew what he was going to see, it took his breath away nonetheless.

"Damn…"

Lyconel tore a cluster of the plants away so that all could view what lay ahead. A lordly castle was revealed in the distance halfway to the horizon, standing grandiosely to be taller than any of the skeletal mountains it neighbored. It resembled a medieval stronghold despite its size, yet the attribute of greatness lay not in its colossal proportions. Lined with circuits, generators, factory systems and missile silos, its yellow, shimmering walls hybridized a cybernetic military compound with a fortress of the middle ages. Stone towers were replaced with crenellated plasma cannons as large as twenty behemoth dragons, the courtyard was supplanted by a moving platform that could ascend and descend to and from the underground manufacturing networks, the baileys were superceded by catwalks of machinegun turrets, and the walls had been upgraded with so many computer complexes that the whole structure appeared as a gargantuan motherboard CPU. It was the ultimate representation of time's bridging, fashioned into a warfare stature to suit the bidding of its devil-hearted masters. Oddly artistic, it maintained its antiquity even with the abundance of 25th century technology.

The drawbridge lowered, letting out computerized cranking sounds. Armies of armored humans marched out across a moat of molten gold, surrounding the castle in square lines. They numbered in the hundreds by the time they had covered half the perimeter, thousands by the time they poured out enough units to encircle the entire fortress in a ring of clanking, cluttering cavalry. Footmen and horsemen comprised a vile swarm of hominid fury, congregating to assemble a multicellular organism fabricated of multicellular organisms. All faceless under their helms and visors, they stood as still as monuments, waiting for orders from an unknown kind.

Dennagon clenched his fangs. He feared the worst, for no one knew that there were this many humans on the planet. More so, these humans that he now espied seemed much more stable and valiant than those he usually fought when he was guarding the walls of Drakemight. They were almost inhumanly steady.

"Is this – Aurahelm?"

Lyconel put a reassuring talon on his shoulder.

"Feel lucky that it isn't. This is a minor stronghold called Grandyre. Not that the name really matters."

"I had no idea humans had the intelligence to…do this."

A futuristic satellite tower escalated from the inner courtyard, craning itself up to the apex of the castle upon a limb of jointed iron. A dish topped it, rotating about to search the skies for recon and any enemies. The fortress' entire defense systems were linked to it with a vast detection database.

Ballaxior drove his claws into ground, causing the fleshy surface to twitch at its edge. The cliff curled up slightly, giving them a hiding space in case the humans decided to turn the satellite to the ground. Lyconel gave a thumbs up to the elder.

"The Gateway to time rests within the walls of Aurahelm," she told Dennagon. "That is the source of their power, and with it, they seek to possess the center of time. Right now, they can only tap into it, but I feel that something has changed. Their powers are expanding. Do you not sense it too, Ballaxior?"

Ballaxior nodded sincerely.

"What are they amassing for?" inquired Dennagon.

The satellite tower sent a rain of electromagnetic signals to the hominid forces. They all turned to it as if their very helms were wired with broadcasting and internet receptors. A wide shadow swept across their lines, wings beating in the atmosphere with slow, horrific flaps as giant as forty of the stronghold's largest flags. Technodragons soared high above the minions, watching over all humans as one would watch over pawns on a chessboard. Arxinor perched atop a tower crenel, gloating slyly over his dominion. Beside him, Gorgash roosted upon an adjacent tower, a dumb expression covering his visage. They shouted at their forces, voices resounding for miles.

"The dissidentsss have obtained the Key! Your mission is to locate and annihilate them at the Omega Pole! Dessstroy the Lexicon and those who sssseek it!"

Gorgash swept an authoritative talon over the knights and footmen.

"Leave none alive!" he dictated.

More vile units marched out the gatehouse. Mechanized Technoknights, which were human warriors integrated completely with cyberneural operating systems, rode out on robotic horseback. Loads of firearms decorated their garments, along with countless unseen enhancements built into their chromium plates. They were humans, only inhumanly advanced. The greatest augmentations in strength and processing capabilities had been endowed to the worst of all the World's species.

Dennagon squinted his eyes. He never knew that humans were capable of designing machinery that he himself did not understand. Not so greatly was he humbled as much as he was afraid.

Nomax had a contrasting sentiment. Equipping several bladed disks, he would not withhold his carnage much longer. Blood had to be spilt and it would be spilt right now.

"Let's be done with them," he requisitioned.

"Are you insane?!" replied Lyconel.

"Not insane enough to wait for them to annihilate us."

With that, he threw a disk straight out of the shrubberies, letting it fall within clear visibility of the thousands of adversaries below. Dradicus gasped in horror, but Lefius took more pragmatic action. He sprung himself out into the air over the edge of the cliff, catching it before it could fly far. His purple reptilian body was a clear target for any missile to hit as he was suspended in flight out in open, but he would rather have sacrificed himself than let his band suffer the inescapable wrath of an entire legion of augmented humans. Straining his talon, he pulled the disk back inward toward his own body, cradling it under his abdomen to prevent any more light from hitting it. Immediately, he flapped his wings, tumbling back beneath the shrubs.

Lyconel bolted into Nomax, tackling him to the ground. Holding her spiked mace over his head, she restrained him with a forearm under his chin.

"Are you trying to get us killed?!"

He shoved her off. Driving a knee into her stomach, he put a bladed disk to her throat. Just as fleetly, Lefius fired a crossbow shot right into his shoulder, piercing straight through his collarbone. Nomax roared and fell on his side, only to be met by another clobber over the head. Lefius leveled the crossbow to his skull for a finishing shot. It all happened so rapidly that Dennagon could hardly process the information as it was transpiring.

"Cease!" prescribed Ballaxior.

His ancient claws weakly parried the crossbow. Lefius was reluctant to follow the elder's ordainment.

"But he tried to decimate us in the Fire Elemental! He tried to demolish us just now!"

"He was merely seduced by anger. I detect no evil in him and deem his decree not one of malice. Besides, practical one, we need all the talons we have if we are to survive this coming attack."

Lyconel was more concerned in making sure the attention of the enemy was not drawn by their little brawl. Fortunately, if the humans did know they were watching, there would have been an immediate onslaught. They remained oblivious while they listened to the hollers of Arxinor and Gorgash. Thus, Lefius backed down, not wanting to trigger any more clamor. Surprise was the greatest resource in the field of war and they had to remain clandestine at all times.

Dennagon continued to watch as the Technoknights took positions at the heads of the human cohorts. One amassment of a hundred footmen was given to every mechanical paladin, each of which had not a single subservient sergeant to carry out tactical commands. These creatures of the "future", he reasoned, must be highly skilled or adept in the workings of strategizing and micromanagement, for there was no foreseeable way that an ordinary human could assign orders as quickly as they appeared to. They must be sapiens.

"Most of those sapiens look almost like ordinary knights," he remarked.

"Those aren't sapiens," corrected Lyconel.

Dennagon's heart skipped a beat as it was filled instead with a rush of dreaded heat. If those abominations weren't sapiens, then…

Lyconel pointed to one last entity that emerged from the gates to cross the Grandyre drawbridge. It was a grand metal orb pulled by harnessed robotic minotaurs that appeared to have been built only for the purpose of hauling that mysterious sphere. However, it was not the minotaurs that struck fear into the dragons, but what was inside their haunting cargo. Inside the orb, something screamed so loudly that its shriek pierced the very air with sound waves from the depths of the abyssal infernos of the underworld. Not only were sound waves released, but also a tide of direful essence. A soul as appalling as the abhorrent stench of a torture chamber rippled the fabric of space all around the castle, seeping into the nerves of carbon-based organisms and the wires of cyborg-founded creatures alike. The awfulness was so intense that the sound caused tongues to taste diseased vileness, the skin and genitals to feel all the terrors of rape, and the nasal parts to scent the most horrid odors of all. What kind of horrific creature was inside was unimaginable.

Dennagon clamped his auditory organs shut. He could

still hear the screams right through his consternated eyes, as loud and clear as any war cry. Somehow, the shriek melded all his sensory organs into one, unified whole that could feel everything that all other parts were.

"If they knew we were here, they would have attacked already," said Lyconel to ease the agony. "Obviously, we can't pass through this castle, but we can reach the Omega Pole before they do if we travel by the sky."

"Won't they see us?" was Dradicus' concern.

"Not if we pass through the Air Elemental."

They looked up to the heavens. Behind the smoky atmosphere, there was a small patch in the celestial ocean that looked like a cosmic nebulae but for its subtle motion against the starry backdrop. That was the way they had to go to reach their objective. It looked serene in the sky, ringed gaseous clouds lined not by silver, but consumed by silver instead, and tinted also with striations of violet and blue and green. The path was not distant and appeared too placid to be true in its welcoming visage. As with all things in life, nothing but death was peace. There were dangers in there they had to be ready to face, for it was the one and only path.

✗✗✗✗✗✗✗✗✗✗✗

CHAPTER 9

The celestial sea was darker than it was last time Dennagon had been there. Even with the sun at its peak, the glass ozone layer barely shimmered, as if the shadows beckoned its favor more than the logic of light. Perchance it was an eclipse, but then one would ask, where was the Moon to occult the solar orb's smiling face? Why did the World tremble so as the earthen illumination of day ignored the lands, seas and airs? There was something to frighten everyone, animate and inanimate, for as all things were conscious, all things could be racked by the harnesses of terror. The final hour was coming, yet it would take longer than an hour to arrive. Perhaps even…

…an eternity?

The dragon dissidents in their sparkling scales followed the ghostly vapor trails that the conscious atmosphere left for them in the global firmament apex. Before their flapping wings and slithering tails, the Air Elemental swirled, a colossal torrential vortex in the middle of the heavens that roared lightly as if to grumble from a deep slumber. There was a fissure in the glass ozone as clear and open as a scar in the sky, ripping outwards in two directions for miles like a canyon empyrean. From it, a tornado churned down, acting as an umbilical cord to the spiraling aggregation of clouds below it so that it could fuel the airborne whirlpool with gusts of wind more powerful than the greatest terrestrial storms. The cyclone there sat, an immaterial beast bewildering that beckoned the arrival of more prey. Only those that dared enter stood a chance of passing.

Lyconel could not truly fly, but only lift herself for brief moments of time, as she was still trying to forget the whelphood idea that creatures without wings could not take flight. Carried from her wrist by the talons of Nomax, she set her eyes upon the target path amid the ludicrously colossal twister. Albeit the Elemental was a silver cloud, it had a dark core deep within its outer gas shells. There she had to go.

"At the eye of the vortex," she dictated, "there is a portal to the Lexicon gates."

Dennagon knew by their preparatory hesitation that there would be peril. Luckily, he had been saving up his mana via subconscious meditation, ergo he took out his spellbook and searched for his most strategic aegis enchantments. Lyconel, however, wagged her index claw.

"You'll have to drop that."

"Why?"

"The thunderbirds thrive on magic. We can't let them touch any mana."

Thunderbirds? In the Air Elemental? It made sense that the atmosphere would be their most frequent habitation, but he didn't know they would send their spies to annex the trails of the nebulous whirlpool. He was more concerned with his mechanically enhanced enemies down at Grandyre. He could only hope that the Technodragons were not following.

"Isn't magic the bane of technology?" he postulated.

"When you reach the Lexicon," answered Lyconel in a bold, yet warm tone, "you'll learn that there is no rift between technology and sorcery."

Reluctantly, he heeded her words. He let go of his spellbook, letting it drift off into the stratosphere. Should he find omniscience, he supposed that he wouldn't need that old tome anyway, so along with his comrades and a wary perspective, he headed into the aerial maze. Smoky silver fog snaked around their forms before a wave of condensed vapor bathed them, devouring them in a bleak fog of war. To outer observers, it would have appeared that they vanished.

Nonetheless, inside the gaseous maelstrom, colorful storms of vapor swirled around in a massive eddy. Lightning bolts ripped through the vehement clouds like electrical veins, coursing through the wispy whips that lashed out like hellish claws of a demon. Lyconel tugged on the claws of her winged carrier, Nomax, to direct him in which ways to follow so that the rest of the team could follow as well. However, although she was skilled at deducing weather patterns and finding which routes to travel in the storm, neither she nor the ouroboros supporting her could withstand the strength of the random wind gusts. In little time, the sentient air tore them away from one another.

"Lyconel!"
"Dradicus!"
"Nomax!"
"Ballaxior!"
"Dradicus?!"
"Dennagon!"
"Ballaxior!"
"I said Dradicus!"
"I'm Lyconel!"
"Lyconel?"
"No, Nomax!"
"Dennagon!"
"Here, Ballaxior!"
"That's Dradicus, Nomax!"

"That's Dennagon, Dradicus!"

"Ahem," came a forgotten voice in the havoc.

"Oh, um – Lefius!"

Like dice on the gambling board of battle, they tumbled everywhere. Blitzes of one another's bodies passed their eyes as the torrents snapped them from side to side. They kept their weapons in their scabbards not because the air would attack them, but because they might run one another through unwillingly and lethally. The only true weapon they had at that moment was balance, for the only way to stabilize oneself in the rumbling chaos was to overcome the might of the windy forces. Nevertheless, even their wings were useless in the growing magnitude of the storm. The Air Elemental was flying for them, throwing them in places they did not know of, and places they did not want to be in.

"We have to reach the eye," shouted Lyconel somewhere in the vaporous frenzy.

Dennagon had no idea where he was or how he got there, but in the vast distance, he caught the glimpse of the center of the Elemental. There, a point of infinite darkness rested, drawing in masses of gas, fluid, and solid debris with relentless gravity. Impartial to anything that got in its way, it absorbed all matter that came near, reminding him of the metamorphosis of a heavily collapsed star in space that he had read about in his astronomy books. As intrigued as he was, he was completely blown away at what he saw next.

A ray of light emitted from an object to the side of the dark central point. Instead of traveling in a straight line as photons usually did, it bent along a warped geodesic trajectory as it approached the entity in the middle of the violent nebula. First, it was merely deformed by gravity, but after a while, it was completely devoured by contorted spacetime. The light spiraled around the collapsed, sable dot in a ringed path until finally falling straight into it and never coming back out. He knew what this was.

"A black hole," he uttered. "There's a black hole right here in this World."

Now he didn't need to travel to space like he imagined doing whilst reading all those science fiction novels.

"It's not only a super-collapsed rip in space," Lyconel commented as she zipped by him. "It's also conscious."

A living black hole. That was the dark gate that was sentiently guiding the tumult that cast them all around. Desperately, they struggled through the fiercely lashing clouds, but the conscious being they were pitted against was at an incredible advantage. This was its very body. And it would not relinquish its control so easily.

Twisting and turning, Dennagon maneuvered his own body so that he could reach his hilt. Taking the enormous risk of accidentally slaying himself or another dragon, he drew his sword. Wrapping it around his tail, he allowed it to cut through the air as he aerodynamically flapped his wings to fly backwards to the center. A mighty gust of fire burst out from his jaws to propel him whilst he rocketed toward his destination.

"Grab onto me!" he blared to anyone who was nearby.

Lefius, Nomax, Ballaxior and Dradicus all heard his cry and rushed to snatch his back scales. However, their timing was impeccable, for as they charged, they all collided. Idiotically, they bungled back in a knot of clumsy dragons, again lost in the winds.

Lyconel, more dexterous, caught him by the neck. She saddled onto his back, clinging to his shoulders.

"Nice thinking," she complimented.

Although wingless, her experience of being jumbled through the Elemental vortex gave her a sense of what it was like to fly. Howbeit, Dennagon seemed to be a smoother ride as he coursed relatively easily through the maelstrom whose brain was the living black hole. For a moment, she closed her eyes, imagining that she had wings of her own and was soaring on her own accord through skies that she owned for herself. In her mind, the light of morn shone against her blue scales, dandling her in soft dawn as if her blue serpentine form were part of heaven itself. The dream was blissful, for she did not have to concentrate on levitating herself through telepathy or any silly type of sorcery. All she needed was the whim of her fantasies to carry her wherever she wanted. After several seconds of her blithe state, she forgot where she really was.

Lightly, she stroked Dennagon's emerald crystal spinal cord and smirked. Dennagon, even though he was concentrating on his navigation, couldn't help but sense a chill up his diamond nerves at the touch of her talon. It was not one of fear, but rather, one of a sensation he had not felt in a long time. It had been many a year since he had made contact with another being that he wasn't trying to kill or maim, and her caressing claws seemed alien to him. There was comfort and discomfort in his mind, yet his face remained stoic as always. Lyconel continued to glide her hands along his sleek, stone figure, her head stuck in the clouds of her fantasies. Whether or not she had any idea what she was doing, her jaws were beginning to come closer to her comrade's cranium. She started to gesture as if to kiss him.

Just then, a flash was emitted. A stream of lightning shot at them, fast as electrons should be, but completely dark and bereft of luminosity. Dennagon agilely dodged it with a roll to the side, jarring Lyconel off him. They both hovered before the black hole, facing three enemies.

A trio of thunderbirds was poised before their destination, acting as guardians of the dark gate at the center of the Air Elemental. They looked remarkably similar to hawks, except that each was at least twenty feet in wingspan and had bodies that were significantly heftier than those of dragons. Their faces were horrifically sharp, what with their keen, feather-ringed eyes that always locked onto targets like lasers. Much to the dragons' dissatisfaction, they were all geared with crowns of black electricity circling around their craniums, deadly and menacing as their visages.

"Who art thou?" demanded the first avian.

"It is I, Lyconel. I bring the Key."

They squawked. There was no conjurer's energy to be drawn from the trespassers.

"You were wise not to bring mana."

"Wise indeed. And wisdom shall be destroyed unless we unlock the Lexicon. If you don't let us pass, we'll all die."

They contracted their pupils like camera lenses. Their stares were now more piercing than ever.

"Nay, if we don't let you pass —"

Their crowns tilted.

"— you will all die."

Mana surged through their feathers. Ball lightning formed above their craniums, ebony as the black orbs of knowledge. They discharged dark thunderbolts simultaneously, tearing jagged lines of destruction through three-dimensional space. Dennagon and Lyconel rolled to the flanks, avoiding the shots.

Two of the thunderbirds dashed ahead to engage them directly. Dennagon immediately sparred with one of them, reptilian talons to avian talons, exchanging slashes and slices at one another's faces. Their forearms met as they clashed in their lunges, yet the enemy was always a step quicker. The thunderbird hurriedly swiped him in the face several times, its claws not quite powerful enough to penetrate his crystal skin, but still sharp enough to draw blood. Dennagon could not help but squint to reduce the likelihood that his eyes would be gouged out in the flurry of scrape assaults.

"Why do you secure this passageway?!" he shouted. "This

path belongs to all inhumankind!"

The thunderbird chuckled amid its assailment.

"You dragons are always so honorable. That is why Totality will wipe your species off the World and spare ours. For King Cladegannon!"

"Craven! You herald Totality for your own benefit?! Let me show you a dragon's wrath!"

Finally, he saw a moment to deliver a formidable counterattack. Swinging his sword, he tried to behead the creature, but it ducked under his blade in the nick of time and returned a peck to his chest. He was knocked back at the force, his gemmed dermal layer chipped greatly where the beak walloped him.

"A dragon's wrath indeed, vile serpent! Hahahaha!"

Meanwhile, Lyconel exchanged a furious sequence of attacks with the other thunderbird. Although it was quick, she was just as swift, and neither could touch the other in their fleet trade of offensive maneuvers. It was a test of endurance rather than strength and maneuverability, for whoever tired first would be the first to take a hit.

She did not have time for games. Lyconel wagered taking an initial strike by hurtling herself forth with a roundhouse punch. Anticipating the foolish move, the opponent craned its neck back, avoiding the fist. However, as she came around in one continuous circular motion, she armed her mace and hurtled it at the enemy's torso. It was a surprise onslaught.

Regardless, the thunderbird was still too fleet for her ambush. It somersaulted back, thinking itself far too clever to be defeated by such a puny female dragon. Just as it fell back into combative posture to gloat over its intellect, however, she barreled straight into it, seizing its throat. Its bird eyes popped as its larynx was asphyxiated at the clutch. Desperately, it returned the favor by jamming its very sharp lower talons into her abdomen. The claws pierced her flesh.

"Hissss!" she seethed through her clenched fangs.

Dennagon saw that his friend was in peril, yet was still occupied with his own problems. The thunderbird that was harassing him was doing its job well, flying around him like a vulture of great doom and even greater annoyance. His aggravation drove him to keep it from striking him again, but his urgency to help his comrade was an even greater motivation.

"Out of our way!" he bellowed.

Snapping ahead in rage, he bashed a fist in his assailant's face. Its skull was surprisingly weak, and it careened back, dizzied at the impact. Dennagon tried to dart to Lyconel's aid.

The thunderbird he just whopped had no intention of letting him do so. Along with its idle companion, it tilted its crown, and they both fired lightning bolts directly at him. Dennagon whirled his sword, deflecting the emissions with the adroit precision of the warrior he was, knocking the energies elsewhere. It would have been a nice series of defensive techniques if he had not neglected the fact that metal was a conductor. Rapidly, the electricity ran through his blade and handle, shocking him to the skeleton and forcing him to drop his weapon. It would have killed him if he were not made of crystal.

"Blast!" he cursed as his blade was swept away in the ambient vortex.

The thunderbirds fired at him again. Without anything to deflect the discharges, he took a hit to the back, which thwacked him toward the gaseous outskirts of the Air Elemental from where he came. Lyconel knew she could not face the opponents alone, and without regard for the integrity of her torso, she ripped the thunderbird's claws out of her abs and raced to catch Dennagon before he could spiral out of the environment. She barely tackled him back into the battle as he almost hurtled outward into lost oblivion.

"Can't leave the war just yet, buddy," she hurriedly stated.

The trio of thunderbird guardians regrouped in a triangular formation around their prey. They concentrated more heavily, focusing all their mental sinew on their magical armaments. From their heads, orbs of dark electricity sprouted from nothingness, firing streams of thunder that constantly poured from their mana sources. These streams were endless, consistently flowing from their minds in unlimited rivers of energy unrelenting, ruthless, and above all, bereft of pity.

Dennagon fluttered his wings, zigzagging in every which way as the electricity tracked him like a sniper rifle through the gases. Lyconel leapt into currents of violent wind that were growing even more ferocious as the battle persisted. In essence, she was actually flying now, neither by her own wing nor Dennagon's, but by storms strong enough to lift tons of dragon muscle as easily as pebbles. Crazily, she bounded from one part of the giant aerial whirlpool to the next, catching rides on different gusts in as chaotic a manner as possible. Confusion was all around, and the only way to counteract disorder was to create further disorder.

Despite their perplexing movements, the thunderbirds were too attuned with their weapons to miss so easily. Their thunderbolts were perhaps even more ruinous than lasers, as they branched out in fractal patterns that were impossible to calculate. The two dragons could not avoid them no matter where they went, for lightning spread around like rooted fingers of death-bearing nature everywhere.

Alas, Dennagon and Lyconel converged. The three thunderbirds flew about them, launching their sorcery from all sides. Bolts tore past the targets, sometimes colliding and other times grazing one another, releasing bursts of high-intensity electrons with every contact. The dragons wound about in helical trajectory, crazily dodging the clashing streams of lightning that would never end. There was only one thing left to do.

"Dennagon! Take their diadems!"

Dennagon arced down from his helical flight. A minor fractal branch from a lightning bolt to his side punched a hole through one of his crystal wing membranes, and he feigned severe injury. Passing between two of his enemies, he slowed down momentarily, appearing wearied.

The thunderbirds smirked. They launched hellish energy at him from opposite sides, concentrating enough to incinerate him instantly into disintegrated gemmed shards. However, as soon as the adversaries fired, Dennagon flapped his wings and cast out a blast of fire from his jaws to project himself away. Back flipping, he let the thunderbolts boil under him.

One of the enemies managed to blend out of the way of the merciless lightning, but the other thunderbird was hit by its counterpart's discharge. The electricity, like a liquid deluge of electrons, seared away its feathers, charring its skin to a blood-cracked black crust. Gore spurt from rips in its burnt dermal layer, sending mists of white blood into the Elemental. Squawking in agony, it recoiled, but did not have the consciousness to retreat.

The unharmed thunderbird gasped as it saw its companion go down. In its petrified distraction, Dennagon rushed at it with a fist cocked forward, clobbering it in the beak. As his knuckles shattered the hardened bones of its oral parts, the impact socked the crown right off its head. Seizing it, he crushed its entire electrical form with a squeeze of his claws, banishing it from existence. The opponent retreated just as quickly as its sole source of power was destroyed, flapping its avian wings into the darkness of the torrential depths.

Lyconel darted around the third thunderbird, flittering around it in confusing motions. Nonstop, she sprinted from side to side, appearing everywhere it least expected her to. Its shots were limitless, but so too were her motions. The adversary's head spun as it tried to keep track of its prey, weakening its concentration.

"You can't hit what you can't miss!" she taunted.

"Huh?" grunted the avian at the perplexing words.

In an instant, she swiped its crown. Placing it atop her own head, she fired the weapon back at its owner, giving it a taste of its own medicine. It too was stripped of all its plumage, its skin scorched in the dark lightning as it fled toward the outskirts of the vortex.

Lyconel gave a wink to her comrade, thinking they had succeeded. However, the first burnt thunderbird rose from the tumultuous clouds, letting out a blazing cry. Lightning surged through the Air Elemental as the creature tempered its crown with the very essence of its own soul, clenching its talons with the ire of a demonic lord. The thunder from the vapors surrounded it like nerves of luminous blue, spiraling around its body as electrons would around an atomic nucleus. The squawks turned to roars, for it had morphed into the ultimate guardian, a raging raven of wreckage.

Lyconel nonchalantly drew her machinegun.

"Don't make me blow you away."

From a mighty sentinel to a cravenly peon, it cowered at the sight of the weapon. The lightning receded from its nerves, seeping back into the clouds of the living environment. The thunderbird, blistered and scarified by its own wrath, pulled back into the murk of the Elemental, defeated and shamed. All that was left was the black hole.

Dennagon wiped perspiration of liquid diamond off his forehead. Lyconel checked her firearm's chamber, only to see that it wasn't even loaded. Snickering, she shrugged slinging the weapon around her index claw and locking it back into her holster. Whilst she did so, Dradicus and the rest of the team found their way to the center once more, creating an awkward silence as everyone traded glances. It was evident by their wounds and the absence of avians that the battle was over.

"Always in the nick of time, eh, Dradicus?" half-joked Lyconel.

He wagged his brows. They all turned to the black hole eye, slipping into it as facilely as they would slip into the shadows of a nocturnal sleep. Dennagon was the last to enter, for he had developed an aversion for the darkness from his many experiences during the past few days. Of course, his reason always conquered over his instinct, and he knew it was probably safer inside the point of infinitely collapsed gravity than out in the open of the Elemental.

The Omega Pole was a purely smooth plain of indestructible plastic. Perfectly even, it was refined down to its atomic level, totally uniform in every conceivable way. The polished terrain ran as far as any eye could see, reflecting against its flattened surface the royal blue sky above, which was rimmed by a white crescent. That crescent stretched across the celestial sphere, simulating a comet's tail, save for the fact that it was glossy and solidly contoured like a heavenly object that was very close to the atmosphere. However, there was no sun to illuminate any astronomical entities around the World. No solar orb showed its face here, yet the grounds still bore the incandescence of daylight and the shadows that a dusk horizon would bring. Here at the other end of the World, all known laws were truly averted.

A flare of dark light flashed over the supremely flat topography. Out from an infinitely dense point in torn space, Dennagon fell out, rolling in the air before thudding onto the landscape. Obliquely accelerating, he hit the ground with enough momentum to drive him in a horizontal direction, causing him to slide across the level floor at an extreme celerity. He was just adjusting to having been transported through the contorted fabric of spacetime when he was cast into the middle of another problem – he didn't know where he was or why he was speeding so incredibly. No matter how far he glissaded, he never slowed, for the turf beneath his feet was wholly frictionless, unrestrained even by his asymmetrical and rugged scales. When he tried to counterbalance the force, he simply slipped off his stance and thumped onto his back. That accelerated him even more.

"Whoa," he aptly commented.

The rest of the draconic crew rolled out of the living black hole as it closed. They were anticipating the landscape as their guide had described it, and immediately pressed their weight downward so as to land orthogonal and prevent any gliding along the infinitely slippery surface. Ballaxior, queer to his senile nature, flapped his hydra wings and headed for the hapless Dennagon instead of steadying himself.

Dennagon, at over 10 meters per second, tried to bury his claws into the smoothness, but even his sharp talons could not penetrate the symmetrically arranged molecules that composed the landscape at the subatomic level. He thought he had just passed over a horizon, but there was no way to tell for certain, as the entire place looked exactly the same no matter where he turned. Nevertheless, Ballaxior quickly caught up to him and grasped him by the shoulders to lift him up into the air and cease his incessant motion. It was a surprising rescue from an elder dragon, considering that Ballaxior's wings seemed far too decrepit for the task.

"Th-thank you," stuttered Dennagon his gratitude.

"Welcome to the Omega Pole," announced Ballaxior.

The others meticulously scurried across the plane, careful not to make the slightest shift, which would send them flying. Ballaxior pointed to their new destination, which laid in the horizon. It was a tower in the vast distance, the only object that broke the unrelenting sameness in the symmetrical environment, and also, the only object in the World that was tall enough to reach the heavens above the ozone. The structure was surreal, a mount of metal that stacked itself up to the very skies, reaching like a single-digit hand to touch something far beyond what terrestrial organisms could experience. Whatever it felt, the dissidents wanted.

"That is the gate to our end," remarked Ballaxior. "The Lexicon is near. It is there."

The Lexicon Tower it was called. A mere stone construction, it looked like something medieval and familiar to dragons, yet ascended to heights that the most masterful of magicians could only dream of reaching with their meager expert-level spells of architectural devising. In the middle of the Omega Pole, it stood as a monument of monuments, a building of the Middle Ages that could easily peer down on the clouds at its waist. Statuesque gates barricaded its entrance in steel and titanium fortitude, yet they were not the primary concern of the party. The dragons were still focusing on arriving there, as they had only reached a halfway point after five hours of travel. That length of time would not have been bad at all if they were not exerting such strain by trying to tiptoe across the sensitively flat lands.

"Why don't we just fly?" asked the impatient Nomax.

"See how far you get before your wings tire enough to throw you back onto the ground in a ceaseless skid," warned Ballaxior.

Nomax's face went unusually blank at the tone of the elder's voice. No one would have been able to tell what he was thinking if they were paying attention to his frightful transformation into staid composure.

Dennagon, unfortunately, was not watching his comrade's visages, but rather, looking up to the heavens. Dusk light overcast his body, tailing it with a shadow lengthier than thrice his height, yet the sun was still not visible. In its stead was the mysterious crescent of white streaking across the royal blue. He had to crane his head to scan its entirety.

"What is that?"

"The Moon," answered Lyconel. "It finally reached the zenith convergence of its two reflections and is now whole."

"Then why dost I see but a sliver of its edge?"

"Because only the Lexicon can view its entirety."

"The Lexicon is conscious?"

"All things are."

Lefius checked his weapons. Slinging out his revolver from his belt holster, he clicked open the chamber with the snap of a wrist. There were six holes in the 20th century weapon, each for a bullet, yet each empty of ammunition as well. He was fresh out of projectiles, and he didn't feel like knocking out any of his own fangs to use as bullets, so he simply decided that he was getting bored of his revolver anyway. Casually, he slapped Nomax's shoulder.

"Hey Nomax, pass me the flame rounds," he demanded in the tone of a friend. "Let's switch weapons."

"The grenade launcher's mine," stiffly came the declaratory reply.

"You had it last time."

"Then may we relish in the past, old friend."

Lefius snarled. He knew his old comrade was antagonistic by nature, but now it wasn't warrior-like anymore. Now, it was just plain irritating.

Dennagon practiced his sword, slashing it in thin air with the techniques he learned from the training of the draconic collective. He understood that knowledge was venom, but he kept the information he gained from his swordsmanship instruction because it was based on pure logic and untarnished strategy. He could not find a way to contradict the way of the Drakemight sword.

Dradicus looked at him in awe. His eyes wide like those of a wondering whelp, he traced the blade's path with his pupils, pondering what it would have been like to possess talons and legs with which to create such beautiful dances. However, his curiosity did not stop there. He wanted to know if Dennagon had the mental might to utilize such skills while being annoyed.

"What is the sword?" he inquired.

Dennagon cleaved his blade up and down, stringing it across the air like a flowing band of fabric forged from the solidness of sheer metal.

"The sword is a weapon."

"A weapon? What if the term was in reference to the skill?"

"Skill?"

"The skill. You know the sword, hence the 'sword' refers to the technique of using the sword."

"Words are relative like everything else in the universe. Is that your point?"

He carved the blade to the flanks and around his shoulders, rolling it off his back as he would a pair of nunchakus.

"Nay," responded Dradicus. "Relativity is only one face of the dual cosmos. There are always two, always will be – the macrocosm and microcosm."

"Those two are united."

"True, yet who can really classify their rift? Undoubtedly, even though they are as one, they are still distinguishable as separate."

"Classification is simple. The microcosm refers to the subatomic cosmos whereas the macrocosm implies the large-scale cosmos that we can observe directly."

Dradicus slithered his tongue. He was thoroughly enjoying himself.

"Tell me, Dennagon. Where does the large-scale universe end and where does the subatomic realm begin?"

"Who says they have to begin and end?"

Lyconel had to add her two cents of data.

"The laws of causality cannot be broken, my dear," she rebutted. "If there is a reason for everything, then all things must begin and all things must end."

Dennagon's maneuvers faltered in his perplexity.

"But there is no way to start and terminate the macrocosm and microcosm," he postulated. "No hard-edged border exists to separate the two. As I said, they are both united by perception."

"True, but causality applies to all things," challenged Dradicus.

"Causality is a factor of time."

"Wrong. Time's a factor of causality."

"Who cares? The point is that the laws of causality do not necessarily have to apply to space, only to time."

"Can time not be spacelike?"

"How?"

"Oh, you've read the scientific myths, haven't you, former sentry of Drakemight? Black holes are theorized to contain spatial temporal dimensions and temporal spatial dimensions."

"Even so, in this realm, space does not have any divisions that one can dub as refined borders of classification. The age-old paradox of infinity certainly proves that everything is composed of an endless amount of infinitely small points, thus making all things immeasurable. Your question is moot."

"Moot as all words are. But that still does not explain what the difference between the microcosm and macrocosm are."

Dennagon knew it to be true. He accidentally skipped a thought as he would skip a heartbeat, clumsily slicing his sword near the tip of his own snout. Halting the blade before he could inflict damage to himself, he restarted his exercises.

Dradicus pulled out from his belt a ragged tome rimmed by worn pages. The entire book seemed to have been slapped together from various types of paper, ranging from animal skin to sheets of tree wood, and its ink was composed of blood, plant dye and even dried honey. Haphazard drawings from a poor artist were scrawled beneath loads of text blocks that were just as pitifully constructed as the pictures were. Clearly, the book was written by none other than Dradicus himself.

"Take a look at this," he said. "I've been trying to catalog all the beasts of this World into one comprehensive encyclopedia, but I've been having trouble arranging them into coherent groups. Would you help me out?"

Dennagon looked at it whilst whirling his sword. Dradicus flipped the pages.

"Easy – you place all dragons in one section, thunderbirds in another, krakens in the third and humans in the last. Simple as that."

"Ah, but the simplest objectives are always the most complex. What about all the creatures that are in-between? The hybridized organisms."

Dradicus showed him the pages where he had drawn disproportionate pictures of halfling beings. Dennagon examined them. One was a dragon with the beak of a bird, the other was a giant squid with the semblance of a dragon and the other was a colossal octopus with the feathers of a hawk. He scratched his head, and then remembered that no two species could biologically interbreed.

"These creatures are impossible." He realized what the book really was. "You're not crafting a guidebook encyclopedia, you're scribing a book of dreams."

"That I am, but who says these creatures shouldn't be?"

"Who says they could?"

"Again, you're always avoiding the question with another question. And all this sparked from the simplest inquiry of all – what is classification?"

Dennagon processed the idea in his head. His sword strokes grew weaker as he drifted off into his subconscious thought.

"If you are assuming that everything is possible, then classification would be like the microcosmic and macroscopic indivisibility. There is no rift betwixt the quantum reality and the relativistic reality, thence only a continuum exists to branch the two, a bridge where both the small-scales and large-scales of the universe exist simultaneously. Therefore, classification must be like a continuum that is not biased toward a particular pole, but consisting of a spectrum of many variables."

"The spectrum of meaning in this World," added Lyconel. "Now you can see why uncertainty renders many realities into one."

Lyconel was also handling her weapon, sharpening its spikes with a brick of neodymium. Her strokes were clean as she ran her claws along her mace's head, whetting the spines to points fine enough to dent even the smooth surface they treaded on. Careful was she that the extremely magnetic neodymium did not scrape the weapon too highly, but not so careful that every spike was to end up the same. She always favored imperfection over perfection, for ideality was bound to limits of art. She saw beauty in chaos, as she believed that entropy bore an order in itself. Perhaps even a hidden order that could not only bend the waves of time, but break them as well.

Spontaneously, she "accidentally" dropped her armament.

It spun around like the ticking hand of a clock until it finally hit the ground, scratching the infinitely level surface with its deadly end. The handle landed on Dennagon's tail harmlessly.

"Oops," she said not so innocently.

As she picked it up, she wrapped her tail around his. Stopping him for a moment, she allowed her colleagues to mobilize ahead by a distance far enough to prevent them from hearing her. He did not seem to take heed of her sudden actions, even as her talon ran up his crystal chest.

"That was a nicely handled attack on the thunderbirds," she whispered.

Dennagon maintained his stolid expression.

"I was a sentry, after all."

"You're much more than that."

She placidly breathed deep dark blue fire on his sword. The blade split the flame in half, letting some of it wash innocuously against his green diamond face.

"Comrade," she called him.

Dennagon turned his blade so that the flame was deflected entirely.

"I'll be even more when I gain the Lexicon."

She rolled her eyes down, showing him the tops of her eyelids.

"So you believe it now."

"I've always believed it. Now I just have to see if it's real."

"Seeing is one thing, but feeling is another. After all, if a picture is worth a thousand words, then a sensation is worth an innumerable amount of visions. Like a deity stringing together the linear way of fate from infinitely small slivers of events in spacetime, visions exist only to create one thing – emotion."

She batted his wings with her tail. Even with her daredevil nature, she had to exert much inner force to expunge from her jaws what her heart wanted to say. Fear lurked in her, touched with embarrassed nervousness, but she knew that if she let herself become chained by her own emotions, then there would be no domination over her enemies. She had to say it.

"Do you also believe in love…" she started hesitantly, "…at first sight?"

The words wisped from her soul to the air. She felt like a weight had been lifted off her brain and breast, but unfortunately, Dennagon did not share the same sentiments. The embarrassment she felt in her premeditation now spilt over to him, and he was more aversive toward it than she. This he would not tolerate, the utter insolence of it all.

Slashing the blade up in a militaristic posture, he nearly cut her nostrils. Her playful fire breathing desisted.

"I don't judge books by their covers or whelps by their faces."

Lyconel gasped. She had just unveiled her inner most sensations and had been rejected quicker than an electron's revolutionary period around a nucleus. What was driving Dennagon to such icy disposition mattered no more to her, for aggravation swelled over her good mood. Angrily, she stomped away on all fours, resuming the repairs on her mace and thinking no more of the creature that she had been so thoroughly snubbed by.

Dennagon also gave not a second thought to it, for his mind was focused on more strategic matters. Namely, on the fact that they were arriving at the gates of the Lexicon Tower.

Elsewhere on the frictionless flats, another black hole opened up in a burst of dark laser light. It expunged another traveler who had surpassed the Air Elemental's dangers, but with a bitter carriage this time. Arxinor the red Technodragon was not at all troubled by the trials the living wind had set before him, for his advanced navigation system was already suited for survival in any environment. There was nowhere he couldn't go, there was no place he wouldn't find his targets. He was programmed with a mission and that mission he would complete.

Standing on the limitlessly level lands, he easily stabilized himself with jagged uranium spines protruding from the bottom of his tail. A pair of advanced mechanized goggles sprouted from his skull, wired to his neural system by nerve-like circuits intertwined around a cybernetic cerebrum. Perfunctorily, he locked it onto his piercing eyes.

"Those thunderbirds were ridiculously easy to beat," he spoke to himself in a fading strain of free will. "Their magic was no match for my plasma cannons. I have been highly upgraded by evolution."

His goggles were capable of magnifying the quantum realm to macroscopic magnitude, but he didn't even have to look that deeply. Several miles away, he spied his targets' position. A robotic grin formed on his technoscaly mouth.

"Dissidents located. Prepare for attack."

———————————————

The gates of the Tower were a hundred feet in height, made of five-foot-thick osmium. Engravings of books were carved into its surface by masons that must have stood at the height of the World's largest trees. Perhaps the tremendous statues of various species of warriors that surrounded the outside of the entrance were the ones that built the immense architecture, yet if that were so, then why did the soldiers' monuments also depict the way in which they were killed? Why did the countless languages of many species unknown riddle the art upon the cadmium floor? Questions, questions, questions that had to be answered. All the dragons could do was lock, stock and load their firearms.

Lyconel checked her machinegun's mechanisms again before slinging a belt strap of ammo over her shoulder. Lefius found a pouch amongst his things that contained a collection of bestial teeth, which he used as bullets in an emergency such as this. Ballaxior seemed to be drowsing off as he peered into his shotgun's barrels, drooping in his weariness enough to greatly increase the probability of accidentally shooting off one of his own heads. Nomax, in a counterpoint, already finished examining his weapons and was instead busy with ramming the gates with walloping blows. All his strength was expended with each try, yet his anger seemed to give him an endless supply of energy.

While waiting for the brutish ouroboros to finish boasting his vigor, Dennagon crept over to the flanking statues. Viewing the inscriptions on their bases, he tried to decipher the languages, but found that they were impossible to read. There was an infinite number of letters, words and phrases from perhaps an infinite number of dialects, and there was no way he could figure any of it out. The terminology once meant something to someone, but apparently, that day had long since passed.

"These palavers," he pointed out. "Of what tongue are they?"

Ballaxior eyed them with one of his hydra heads.

"A tongue just as yours, which can utter any language."

"By tongue I meant dialect."

"I am wise," stated Ballaxior not so wisely, "yet even I cannot read all those alien idioms. To learn them all would take an eternity."

Dradicus slithered in, cleaning his assault rifle with his serpentine tongue.

"Does it really matter what language it is anyway?" he declared.

Dennagon thought, chin tucked up with his talon.

"Indeed," he answered. "How is a human to understand

the natural vernacular speech of a dragon? The language without words but vacillating, whinnying hisses instead?"

"He isn't. But that's not the issue," noted Dradicus. "The fact of the matter is, dialect all contains the same purpose – to elicit understanding. Communication can be in any form, written in any syntax, but it is all essentially identical. Just the minor details like lettering or alphabet are different."

"Communication exists in a tide of duality, you say?"

"Yeah, I guess."

"Then what kinds of words are we using now?"

Not even sagacious Ballaxior could offer a response. Dradicus looked at the innumerable languages that inscribed every statue, realizing that a countless number of languages could easily be formed by the imagination. He then gave the question a try.

"Ummm…We're talking in…"

"—words," Dennagon finished. "Words that don't exist except as sounds, yet somehow convey meaning in the perceptions of the listeners. A swarm of phrases that we are enslaved to interpret."

Dradicus saw what he meant.

"If words don't exist, then what does?" he had to inquire.

Nomax gave one last run into the gates. All his draconic sinew could not even budge them by a millimeter. Sweating, he surrendered.

"It's hopeless," he forfeited. "We should turn back to the Omega Pole and quit this journey while we're ahead. While we're still alive."

Lyconel grimaced at him. She did not come this far to resign to mere hundred-foot osmium metal doors. There must have been a way to open them, and she would concoct a solution.

However, as she pondered, Dennagon stepped forward. Nomax moved out of the way as he reached out for the blemished surface of the gates that had been scarred by millennia of warriors that attempted to break it down by grunt force. Extending out his talon, he tried to push it, but before his claws could even make contact, something incredible happened.

A deep hum sounded, containing the resonance of an enormous tuning fork. The metal tone was accompanied by the inflection of a baritone choir, shaking the earth with its mesmerizing song. The gates started to crank open, one thousand tons of metal turned by the mere presence of the dragon that contained in him the essence of the Key. The Lexicon Tower revealed its interior for all to see, and the dissident clan could now behold its inner walls.

They entered cautiously. Inside, there was a lavish stone courtyard rimmed by walls of darkened titanium. At the center was a fountain pool that spouted a geyser of liquid silver, hot as the molten fluid it was. The liquid metal bubbled from its middle chute, cascading back into its bowl and draining back through a circulation system that kept it flowing in an endless cycle. It never dried or cooled, yet the air was at a temperature low enough so that the dragons could breath the traces of the fluid, which had partly evaporated as a metallic fog in the air. The ceiling above was so high it was not even visible past the endlessly rising walls.

"The fountain of metal," named Ballaxior the contraption they faced. "Only the Key can unlock its power."

Dennagon, the only one without a firearm, stared up into the ceaseless space. There was an engraving of a dragon's claw carved into the fountain's base, deeply cutting into the metal as if it was entrenched by virtue of a dying creature. He thought he had seen that particular handprint somewhere before, perhaps in a book of legends or a tome of chronology. Wherever he had viewed it, it was fairly clear what it was there for. He placed his own claw on it, fitting it perfectly amidst the grooves.

The fountain of silver gushed into the air, shooting up, up, and away to the greatest heights of the Tower.

Outside the walls, a transient vision of the ascending fluid was visible. The gates still wide open, it was a spectacle for the World to see. However, most of the planet did not care, aside from the draconic clan–

-- and their enemies.

Arxinor and Gorgash encircled the foundation, amassing their forces near the entrance. Human knights covertly congregated around the doors, clandestine in their strides on foot and on horseback. It was easy to stay silent, what with their upgrades.

"Prepare to advance," commanded Gorgash, quietly flapping his behemoth wings.

Arxinor snickered with a fanged grin.

The fountain's fluid reached unimaginable altitude. It had transformed into an enormous stream of upward-flowing metal, a lengthy tube of liquid that wormed against the force of gravity. A silver cylinder, it moaned like a living organism, its interior molten substance sometimes congealing into solid networks of nerves.

Ballaxior put a talon on Dennagon's shoulder.

"It's all up to your now. The Lexicon awaits your grasp."

Dennagon stole his nerves, trying to make them as solid as those of the metal tube he was to swim through. Clenching his fists, he steadily approached the silver, upward path.

"Here goes everything," he reassured himself.

Just then, Dradicus' auditory organs twitched, as did his keen reptilian nostrils. He scented something.

"Wait."

Lefius heard it too. A very light clanking that sounded like a faint march of a thousand soldiers a mile away. He drew his revolver and locked his crossbow onto a wrist mechanism built into his forearm plate.

"There's evil near," warned Dradicus.

Lyconel armed her mace. At that point, everyone could detect it.

"How?!" she asked. "How could they have found out?!"

A vile hiss came from within the group. Everyone slowly turned to Nomax, who grunted from the depths of his hate-filled heart. It was difficult to tell whether he was laughing or groaning, but either way, he was not himself.

"It ends now, fiend," he seethed.

Faster than a cobra's bite, he pulled out his grenade launcher and fired a flame round. It detonated on Ballaxior, engulfing him in burning shrapnel. In a pyrotechnical flare, several of his hydra heads fell off.

Lefius hammered his revolver, firing two projectile fang bullets. Nomax immediately twirled the body of his grenade launcher, deflecting both shots, and without time to fire two more, Lefius swung around and clenched a group of switches embedded in his gauntlet's palm. His forearm-mounted crossbow discharged an arrow.

It would have been a lethal attack had Nomax not jerked his head forth to disgorge a hidden explosive in his mouth. From behind the mouth-clenched tail, an acid round spurt out of his jaws, knocking the arrow out of its way and exploding on Lefius. Its hydrochloric substance melted right through scales.

"Gaaaaah!!" he screamed as his dermal layer was liquefied.

Nomax knocked his mutilated wyvern friend out of the way and pounced on Ballaxior. Raising the spiked bottom of his mouth-clenched tail, he hurtled it down for a finishing blow. The force was enough to tear right through diamond.

In a fit of urgency, Dennagon flung his sword at the assailant. It impaled Nomax in the shoulder, knocking him off before his strike could meet Ballaxior's body. Nomax tumbled on the ground, writhing in agony as he extracted the blade in his flesh.

"I'm telling you, he sent an army after us!" he insanely blared.

Lyconel, with her weapon at her side, was ready to listen to any argument as long as it was quick. However, as she was about to ask the deranged attacker to elaborate, he suddenly sprung from the floor, lunging at the first thing he saw. The unwitting Dennagon was about to be beheaded by the cross-slashing talon of a deranged beast.

"Aaaaaahhhh!!!" both Dennagon and Nomax shouted, one in fear and the second in crazed ire.

Amidst the screaming havoc, gunshots then echoed through the osmium walls. A stream of bullets traced a line through the air, punching a string of holes through orange-brown scales before blasting apart an ouroboros skull. Nomax's brains erupted from his shattered cranium as he was gunned down. Before he could even hit the ground, he perished, careening his bulky cadaver into his target as a final gesture of desperation. The corpse struck Dennagon, taking him off his stance.

As he pushed the dead body off himself, he saw the smoking barrel of Lyconel's machinegun. It was a sad duty to have to kill one's own kin, but in the war of endless causality, it was inevitable. Abruptly, she snapped her head to the entrance.

"The gates," she voiced.

They all charged to the wide-open gates, hurriedly trying to push them shut. However, they could hardly budge them by an inch before the entrance was torn back open by a deluge of incoming humans, vile in their own sick splendor.

A gleaming mass of knights in shining armor charged in, harbingers of death with their swords, lances and spears armed. These creatures did not tremble as did their relatives lower on the evolutionary ladder. They were endowed with the aspect of the machine, circuited to the cores of their mindless brains. Their cage visors looked coldly upon their reptilian prey through bars of cybernetic steel.

"Annihilate," said a Technoknight.

The dragons reeled back. The knights, some still of flesh and others enhanced technologically, bolted forth, lances drawn.

"Steady!" commanded Lyconel to her forces.

The enemy came within range. Lefius rose from his mutilated twitching.

"Attack!"

Lyconel, Dradicus, Lefius and Dennagon roared in bloodlust ardor. They rushed furiously into the enemies, slashing and bashing at chaotic will. Draconic claws cut through the opposing lines, smashing metal and bones apart with strikes as fervid as they were violent. Their weapons, like extensions of their bodies, cut through the adversaries as conduits to gory doom, interchanging between assault rifle barrages and bladed storms. Maces, whips, crossbow arrows and fisted talons accompanied cannonades of bullets and rattling gunfire. Fragments of armor and human bodies blasted into the air.

"Aaaaaahahahahaha!!" maniacally laughed Lefius.

Lyconel joined him with a sanguine roar as they tore their enemies apart. They were actually beginning to enjoy themselves amidst the wrath. That is, until a rapier sliced through the air and jammed itself in Lefius' head, killing him instantly.

"Lefius!" shouted Lyconel as she saw the deformed carcass of her comrade go down.

Without a second to see if he was alive, a tremendous axe whirled toward her. She back rolled before it could strike her, tumbling up into aggressive stance to face her Technodragon adversaries. Arxinor and Gorgash were positioned amongst the human ranks, Arxinor with a brand new set of rapiers and Gorgash wielding three colossal axes.

The time for games was over. Lyconel tossed away her mace and Dradicus sheathed his whips. She cocked her machinegun and he twirled his assault rifle round his index claw. Dennagon extracted his sword from Nomax's carrion.

Gorgash sinisterly snickered.

"Finish them."

Hundreds more Technoknights raged into battle, armed with their own assault rifles and rocket launchers mounted on their shoulders. A storm of bullets showered upon them from all sides as the mechanized hominids galloped around, circling like sharks. With their firearms, the dragons deflected the fusillade, slamming their triggers while they twirled their guns. Volleys of bullets were exchanged as easily as raindrops on a stormy night, yet this was not a dusk of drizzling clouds. This was an eve of pouring metal ammunition and sluicing blood, intermingling currents of spent artillery shells and pools of drawn cyborganic gore in a torrential amalgamation of blended lead, steel and cardiac iron. In less than a minute, blood drenched the floors, garnished with the floating remains of projectiles and fallen humans.

But the dragons still stood against the ever-increasing masses of mindless men. Rockets started to go off, exploding all over as the reptilian prey pounced everywhere against the walls, floors and enemy lines. Flowers of blood-red fire engulfed the entire area as the artillery detonated, unbound by care for the sacred courtyard.

For a brief second, the opponents reloaded, extruding jointed appendages from their forearms to lock more bullets into their chambers. Dradicus immediately jumped over them like a coiled wurm spring, lashing out his two bladed whips again. The sharp flagellations knocked some of the units off their horses, breaking their orderly arrangements. Taking advantage of their disorientation, he ricocheted off a wall and crashed jaw-first into some more of them, ripping their limbs apart with his dreadfully sharp fangs.

"Take 'em down!" he hailed.

Dennagon swept his sword across the assailants, paving lethal arcs across the enemy formations. Bullets bounced off his blade in sparked deflection as he fanned the weapon across enormous spaces. The mechanized cavalry were knocked to the side, damaged, but still unwavering in their machine-cold persistence.

"You got it brethren!" replied Lyconel to her sibling.

Dennagon topped off his furious rampage with a barrage of claw slashes. The Technoknights tried to assault with their swords, but his crystal talons easily swiped their weapons away. Diamond slices crashed against their comparatively puny armor, tearing them limb from limb. Circuits were exposed where armor was scarred.

Lyconel, meanwhile, pitched into the air. Spinning in wingless flight, she nestled her machinegun close to her abdomen, jamming the trigger. A spray of machinegun fire rattled from her barrels, flashing against the reflective walls as it mowed down her hapless adversaries. A wave of bullets ripped through the Technoknight ranks, busting apart chest plates and sending enemy infantry and cavalry flying with their weapons, armaments and horses. Empty small-arms casings flittered off her ammo shoulder strap as her rounds were loosed. The very force of the gun was keeping her in the air as she leapt from wall to floor to wall, frequently grazing the opponents with her talons. She was beginning to feel sorry for them.

Actually, not really.

Dradicus backed her up with assault rifle shots to the their knighted heads, sniping them as best he could. His cartridges of pulverizing caliber bombed through faceless cage-visors, revealing the equally faceless human visages underneath as they were blown apart by the heavy gunfire. The bodies were beginning to form a floor of their own, piling up to such great degrees that it was difficult to tell how much blood they were floating on. A few of them accidentally fell into the fountain of liquid silver, and were sent soaring up to the unseen ceiling of the Tower thousands of miles up.

Dennagon, although thoroughly entranced by his killing spree, was starting to tire. Trampling the Technoknights, he constantly thought he had eliminated the last of them, only to watch as more galloped into battle with their lances, swords and rifles. Bullets riddled his crystalline scales, charring them.

Lyconel finally ran out of ammo. Rolling back onto the ground, she turned to Ballaxior, who had been standing completely still the entire time, completely unmolested by any of the enemies. He had a shotgun in his grasp, but he did not even use it.

"Ballaxior! Help us out!"

Ballaxior nodded. He lifted a talon, and from his palm, he fired a beam of electrical circuits. They looked partly material and partly energetic, like wired plasma coursing through the air as fractal thunderbolts. At first, it looked like he was going to hit a Technoknight that was rushing toward Dennagon, but instead, his summoned spell hit Dennagon himself.

"Ah!"

The stricken target was blasted into a group of Technoknights. Initially, it looked like an accident, but as Lyconel saw Ballaxior's eyes, she detected no remorse in them. It was like his entire semblance had mutated and he was a totally different dragon.

"What are you doing?!" she perplexedly blared.

Dark flames consumed the hydra elder. He gave her one last look of frigid ice as he spontaneously combusted in the ebony flares, glaring at her with eyes that once bore so much warmth. Furious hellfire melted away the elder's faces on his remaining heads, destroying the soul of a creature that existed long ago, but died as soon as evil had devoured it. In place of Ballaxior, a burning lump of flesh evolved, crumbling into a vile moldable mass.

"Letting you in on a secret," responded the shapeless thing.

It kindled another lightning bolt of electrical circuits. Dennagon could hardly get up whilst he was hit again by the blazing ignition. The circuits wrapped around his biceps, neck and tail, half-energy, half-matter, carrying him through the air in posthaste speed. Slamming his head once against the wall, it threw him out the open gates past the wall of humans.

"No!" yelled Dradicus.

Dennagon, half-conscious, attempted to rush back in, but the Technoknights quickly pushed the gates shut. Their combined strength was that of a million men, and they easily cranked the huge osmium doors. Dradicus tried to bolt at the enemies to clothesline them down, but he was swiftly snatched by Gorgash, who grabbed him by the throat.

"Dinky organisms should not engage the theater of war," the beast growled.

With that, Gorgash whirled him round and round, flinging him out the entrance. Dradicus collided into Dennagon, and both of them skid across the ground two hundred feet away. The Technoknights rapidly slammed the gates closed, instigating the music of the metallic chorus from the moving doors that clanged together like a leviathan tuning fork. The Lexicon Tower was taken, its walls, floors and fountain annexed by the swarm of humans that seized it.

In the middle of the enemy masses, Lyconel was poised with her machinegun armed, a valiant warrior surrounded by a legion of her worst nightmares. The bodies of her comrades, Nomax and Lefius laid at her feet, deformed and tortured by the battle that claimed their lives, yet somewhat beautiful in the way war's art sculpted their tormented figures. She remained stable, unwaveringly standing against the innumerable hominids. Alone.

"Drop your weapon," demanded Gorgash.

She eyed what was Ballaxior, now a clump of flesh that lashed out as if to imitate an amoeba. The dark flames tore away the illusory soma she had long been tricked to accept as a guideserpent, expelling the remains of scales and bone that composed any ordinary reptile. In its stead formed a more sizeable creature, a reptile composed completely of dark blazes that wrapped around its unseen body and the wristwatch above its sable flame gauntlet. Drekkenoth baronial in dread revealed himself, the ultimate doppelganger and future king.

"Drekkenoth," Lyconel addressed chillingly. "Only you would be so ignoble."

His neutral visage was her visual response.

"But as I said, the laws of morality are but fancies of nothingness."

Gorgash stomped forward. Slashing a claw through the air, he slapped her machinegun away and armed his forearm plasma cannon. He would kill her now for her failure to comply with his request.

Lyconel twirled at the force of his strike. From her back plate, she swung out an emergency mace that caught her predator by surprise. Backhanding it, she slammed its spikes into his deltoid, faltering his massive body just as he was going to discharge. Leaping onto the cannon's flank, she thrust her entire bodyweight toward his chest, pressing the barrel under his chin. The behemoth was frozen in petrified shock, and she quickly wrenched inside the infrastructure of the futuristic cyborg artillery, digging past forearm nerves until she found the triggering valves. Twisting them with her hind legs, she activated the weapon, sending energy pulses through its systems.

A plasma shot was fired, busting straight through Gorgash's robo-head and detonating it in a computerized explosion. The behemoth skull erupted into cyborg parts that integrated both brains and CPUs, flinging cerebellum fragments everywhere. Decapitated, the colossal carcass of sinew and hulky steel fell onto the floor, crushing all the corpses beneath it in an immense quake. All fifty tons of the cadaver became cold and still, twitching only with the remnants of cybernetic code that tried to find a purpose for existing.

Drekkenoth squinted his eyes, not out of anger, but of indifferent strategic planning. Without even saying a word, he sent the Technoknights to inundate the draconic target. Lyconel wrathfully hurtled her weapon at them with what little energy she had left albeit she knew she could not defeat them. Expeditiously, they flooded her in a tide of humanity, stabbing her a hundred times with their swords so as only to injure her. Her blood was a menial addition to the gore-blanketed courtyard, but it was enough to drain her of her consciousness. She fell as motionless as the creature she had valorously slain, life still beating through her hacked and mangled body.

Drekkenoth scanned her with his own eyes before accepting that she was neutralized. Waving a talon, he summoned a gravity field with which he lifted her. Entering the silver fountain, he brought her with him, the liquid metal dragging them up to the Tower's peak with the fleetness of a storm's breeze. He soared to his destination, continually plotting in his ever-unchangeable mind.

"Thank you for opening the gates for me, dissident," he robotically expressed gratitude to his captive.

The plan had worked perfectly and the dissidents that threatened his control over time had been vanquished. More so, they had made his life so much easier by granting him access to the very object they wanted to protect. Brilliant was his strategy, but he was not in the position to gloat under the guise of his mechanical mind. Now with the pests ousted from his path, Drekkenoth was free to complete the final part of his plan so that all could relish in the void of nihilism – the annihilation of the Lexicon.

Could it be any simpler?

CHAPTER 10

Dennagon fiercely pounded his fists into the Lexicon Tower gates. Whopping the stained osmium surfaces, he direly attempted to push them open again, but his exertions were in vain. Nonetheless, he kept trying, boiled with enough rage to keep him pounding for an eternity.

Dradicus, off to the side, brushed himself off.

"It won't work," he told his enraged counterpart. "Once the gate is opened, it can never be unlocked a second time."

Dennagon stopped for a moment.

"Why not?!"

"It's just the way the World turns. Without reason or rhyme. Just a big, spherical riddle that can never be cracked."

Dradicus shook the dirt off his scales. With that, he turned around and headed for the plastic plains.

"Well, I'm off."

Dennagon was astounded.

"Why?!"

"To meet my doom. The Technodragons have won, and Totality's inevitable. What can we do but wait for the end?"

Dennagon slammed a fist into the ground. A gigantic

fissure ripped through the frictionless land that was supposed to be indestructible.

"You mean to leave the fate of your own comrade to the enemy? What warrior are you?!"

The goofiness of Dradicus' expression melted away with the clenched fangs of his tempered decree.

"Lyconel always knew there would be a time to fall. We're all going to die anyway via the laws of causality, so why not just accept it?"

Dennagon drew his bloodstained sword. The gore of men dripped down its honed edge.

"Because, my friend, we are connected to the rest of the World," he said in a not so amicable tone.

Dradicus backed off, preparing for an attack.

"If the Lexicon is destroyed and all life falls to dark ignorance, then we will be absorbed into it. Death is never the end. There is no end in the shapeless temporal dimensions." The sword-wielder took a poise belligerent, blade at his side. "Thus," he continued, "we are all united with our lost comrade as a trio. We can never be separated. That is why we must find her. Stop the rise of Totality."

He delivered an overhead strike. Dradicus rolled his head under it, drawing his whip with which he returned a slash. The flagellum wound about the blade, but Dennagon yanked it away with a mighty pull. Dradicus immediately drew his other whip, and the two exchanged another clash, driving their weapons with all their strength and virtue. The bladed edges of their medieval armaments struck in a tremendous collision, the metal resonating against one another in an intense puissance. So dinted was their scrimmage that both medieval weapons broke upon impact, crumbling into glistening silver. The shimmering cloud fell upon them like lighted snow.

Dennagon saw his blade once more shatter into

nothingness, its hilt blasted without a blade to hold before another battle. However, this time, he felt not aggravation, but freedom. Their eyes illumined as they looked at one another, comrade to comrade, dragon to dragon.

"For truth," said Dradicus.

"For being," added Dennagon.

Their thoughts uniting, they both spoke simultaneously.

"For the Lexicon Triumvirate!!"

It was an ecstasy of cognition. Their minds were as one for a moment as they were suspended in thought more pristine than the purest waters of the World. Linked, they shared each other's visions in each other's eyes, exchanged feelings without a word, and united without even touching. Thus, they were as three, one of a searching mind, the second of a searching eye, and the third of a lost spirit. Together, they would always remain, yet to be coalesced was not enough to attain victory. They had to battle the ignorance that hunted their trio with a light as bleak as the night and they had to do it at the present. No other time would allow it, for the past and the future were forsaken.

Dradicus shook his head, blinking as he snapped out of trance.

"I have no idea what we just said, but it sounded meaningful."

Perhaps meaningful enough to give Dennagon an idea. He looked up to the top of the Tower, contemplating.

"I hope you're not thinking what I think you're thinking," said Dradicus.

A smirk crawled on Dennagon's face. Dradicus did not have much of a choice but to accept that something insane was going to be done, and he was going to be involved.

"Then again, when did hope ever aid me?"

———————————

At the apex of the Lexicon Tower, there was a spacious castled realm. In a vast chamber that could hold a hundred ballistas, medieval staircases were built in every which direction, some leading up, some sideways against the walls and some completely upside down or at angles to the ceiling. Outside the unshielded windows, draconic sentries numbering in the thousands patrolled about a storm-stricken dusk sky, all filled with memories of physical data their black orbs had wired into their minds. Soon, night would fall and the crescent of the enormous Moon in the sky would take the heavens. This was the day to end all days, the eve to set the sun of all eves.

In the center of a floating mass of contorting liquid metal, Lyconel was suspended. Her wounded body neither felt nor took damage from the molten silver, which felt as cool as any harmless pudding. Half-conscious, she fluttered her eyes open, only to find herself in that unfamiliar place of senseless stairwells. Instinctually, she tried to break free of her liquid fetters, but only succeeded in swimming within the fluid mass.

As she floated, she caught the visions of Drekkenoth and Arxinor standing before her, their mechanical eyes staring equally expressionless. Drekkenoth held out his talon, displaying a gooey black orb in his palm.

"Something to eat?"

Lyconel did not answer. Drekkenoth squeezed the orb, spilling its fluids, which streamed with data regarding the periodic table.

"Drink?"

Again, silence was her reply.

"You seem to be doubtful, dissident Lyconel," continued the dragon lord machine. "I calculate that it is your misconception of ambiguity that is the source of your ignorance."

"You call me ignorant?"

She chinned up to the thousands of sentries encircling the perimeter.

"What about them? Their mindless pupils know nothing beyond what they're told because they're too cravenly to defy that which is accepted by the majority, collective consciousness of the World. Sure, they're highly skilled in the laws of physics, but beyond that, what can they do?"

"Nothing," was the immediate and confident reply.

Lyconel was surprised at Drekkenoth's certitude.

"Absolutely nothing," he continued. "There is nothing beyond the laws of physics. Thus, the only entity that can exist outside of the laws of the World are nil."

"What if I were to declare my own laws of physics?"

"What would make your declarations any more significant than my own?"

Uncertainty plagued her thoughts. Doubt toyed with her mind.

"You must understand, Errant Lyconel, that although the laws of physics are simple assumptions created by the database of established and inductive 'science', they are no more or less important than the rules designed in any imagined program."

"So what is important? How do you define 'important'?"

"How does one define 'define'? There is ambiguity in everything because everything can mean anything or nothing. Comprehension lies in one's perception."

"Rubbish. One plus one equals two. That phrase has but one meaning."

"False. Your proposal can be interpreted as an encrypted threat. Or, it can be seen as a mathematical statement that is designed to derive a particular value for an operation. Otherwise, it may be translated as an attempt to demonstrate to a higher being a particular error that does not exist."

His pompousness was really beginning to get to her, even

though he was just a cyborg without passionate sentience. Then again, who was she to detest one whose brain was wired to prevent it from detecting extreme emotions? Why was a more sensitive dragon favorable than a metal-hearted one?

"I get your point, oh mighty lord Drekkenoth. The World is what we make of it. And what has this to do with your quest?"

"If nothing has true significance beyond what we forge of the World's nihilism, then in a sense, my purpose is invalid. Totality is a word like any other, yet it is also my mission."

Totality. That word was so overused that it had almost lost its intrinsic substance. Now that she thought about it, though, the term was never really defined in any solid bounds except as a merging of the World into a single unification that would ruin all differentiation and end life. What the hell did that mean anyway? Why couldn't any palaver truly be understood with delineated limits?

"What is it then?" she challenged. "What actually is 'Totality' if you were programmed to understand it?"

Even Drekkenoth had to process the question for a second.

"The Geveshtor Crystal. The Dagador Knighthood. The Agadon Warhelm. The Rogail Spear. Firilax Blacklight." He was naming all the rarest items on the planet. "How did these come into creation?"

Lyconel hated questions that were answered with questions, but she was abhorrently intrigued, so she played along.

"Through causality, of course."

"And what logical premise necessitated their existence?"

There was none. Their existences were as pointless as their fantastic names.

"They are all items designed without any particular purpose," resumed Drekkenoth," but to entertain the denizens of this morbid fantasy labeled the 'World'. Thence was the similar creation of Totality, which is no more than an idea, a non-physical 'item' designed to signify the end of time. Totality is the point at which temporal flow collapses into a landscape and time no longer manifests itself as linear."

He wiped his hands of the black orb's fluids.

"Since simplicity is the ultimate state of the universe, I shall put this as simply as possible – Totality is just another word for the domination of the fourth dimension, the space of all potential worldlines."

Lyconel then apprehended his cause.

"You're not just after control of the World. You want to take control of the Origin of everything." She snorted a chuckle. "Seems like you're going to have to vie for power against the sapiens and their castle at Aurahelm. Last I heard, the Gateway to the Origin is in their gold fortress."

"Irrelevant," Drekkenoth scoffed. "The humans are not of any concern to me. After all, all intelligent beings are essentially the same, just with different levels of intellect and bodily structures. Some are inferior and others are superior. Luckily, the humans are the prior."

"Are you certain?"

"Affirmative."

Lyconel, at this point, was beginning to wonder what the point of this conversation was. If he wanted to kill her, he would have done so already, and if he wanted to torture her, he would have started by now. Apparently, the only thing he was killing was time. He was waiting for something to happen.

Drekkenoth looked to the sky and then looked at his watch. The light of day was growing dimmer and dimmer by the moment, yet it seemed like forever. Lyconel thought that perhaps she could distract him from his mission enough to make him forget about the hour.

"And what," she asked, "makes you so sure that there is certainty in the World?"

A beep sounded in his head. The recollection of a memorized algorithm ran through his mind, making him repeat to her what he repeated to himself frequently.

"Logic, consciousness, causality, a timeless genesis, a temporal genesis, destiny, time, space, spacetime, relativity, macrocosm, microcosm, quantum mechanics, uncertainty, unconsciousness, symmetry and asymmetry," he listed all the certainties of the universe. "These things are irrevocably constant."

"Prove each and every one of them."

"Logic exists by its very nature, for one cannot contradict it. By stating that the only truth is the infinitely reflexive acknowledgement that there is no truth, one is adhering to logic by using it to create that very statement."

She understood.

"Go on."

"Consciousness exists to create certainty, for if something is not observed, it is not real."

"What about mathematical laws? They're completely logical and exist whether or not a being is conscious of them."

"By unobserved entities, it is implied to refer to material entities and not to thought objects like the rules of calculus. Further, causality must be truthful, for without causality, there would be no time, and without time, one could not think, and without thought one would not have consciousness."

"Why?"

"Is it possible to create a thought when you are frozen in one temporal moment?"

"No."

"Then in that case, the fourth certainty would be a timeless genesis, for as time is also bound by causality, it must have a beginning. This Ultimate Origin cannot exist in time itself, for the paradox of what predecessor that temporal occurrence emerged from would destroy the logical continuum. Thus, the Ultimate Origin of the multiverse must exist out of the fourth dimension's flow and contain the meaning of life itself. From that meaning, the temporal beginning, or the living Big Bang, as most wise organisms dub it, must have been spawned to create time and space in a continuum known as spacetime. In order to have an existence in which to move through, there must be space and time to go with it, and these two factors would be interchangeable because, as one's imagination can tell, time dilation occurs in reference to how fast one moves in space."

Lyconel had never heard a machine ramble so much. Why he was telling her all this, she did not know, but she had a feeling it was not for her benefit. Although she was trying to manipulate him to do her bidding, she felt like she herself was somehow being tricked into doing something. Drekkenoth just kept talking as if he were brainstorming to himself.

"Relativity and quantum mechanics would be true, as the macrocosm is inherently smooth and spacelike, whereas the microcosm, because of its very nature of being unseen and thus uncertain, would contain a realm where multiple realities intermingle. Thence, since the macrocosm and microcosm are united in that they require perception to create reality, there would have to be a balancing force to counteract omnipotence. That force would be the unconscious."

"What about destiny?" she said to break his train of thought. "You said that omnipotence was an element of reality, so how could the unconscious counter it?"

"The unconscious itself is synonymous with destiny and the temporal beginning. All things were decided from the start, and we are simply creatures that move along the line of time, the worldline, until the ultimate end is reached, at which point the universe would curl back to its Origin. As I said, there was a balance to all things via causality, so the objective of this cycling from start to termination would be to maintain a symmetry amongst events and causes analogous to the symmetry that the first law of thermodynamics enforces."

She caught a fallacy in his reasoning.

"Heh, heh. You're argument's falling apart faster than the breaking of the inflating early universe. If everything were symmetrical, then how come there exists such differentiation in the universe now? Objects such as stairways, castles, swords and roads would not be if everything were the same. Like organisms require nutrition, all things, including consciousnesses require asymmetry to subsist."

It was a heartbeat after she finished her last phrase that she realized the fallacy in her own argument and that she had just proven Drekkenoth to be right.

"Ergo, asymmetry is a constant like all the other 17 I stated. It is in balance with symmetry, for the two contradictory terms work together, talon-in-talon. Their only rift is the occasional misconception of the oaf who takes words for truth instead of for the symbols they are."

She was expecting him to say more, but he stopped. As if déjà vu were taking place, he reached for his belt and retrieved a black knowledge orb. Holding it out, he let the oozing substance drip off his claws.

"As you can see, knowledge is not wholly venomous. There are things to be learned."

Lyconel spat at his offering.

"If I should learn something, it will not be from any sage. Least of all you."

"But I am no sage. I am the king of the future."

His circuits ran through his Technodragon body, illuminating for a brief instant his entire infrastructure beneath the blackened flames.

"You are not going anywhere for a while. You may as well enjoy the journey."

Not forgetting about the hour, he looked at his watch.

The walls of the Tower were medieval barricades that reached far into the clouds as if they were built by 25th century organisms. So far did they rise that they seemed to penetrate the atmosphere. It would have been impossible for any being to walk the distance it ascended, let alone climb it. However, two dragons were crazy enough to.

Or rather, one.

"I know that we've declared ourselves the Lexicon Triumvirate," agreed Dradicus. "But do we really have to climb an entire bloody ten thousand miles?!"

Dennagon buried his claws into the osmium with every step upward he took.

"We do what we have to."

"Does that include dying of exhaustion?"

"I thought you wanted to die."

Dradicus groaned. It was going to be a long climb uphill, namely by a 90-degree slope.

Drekkenoth continued to stand as still as a monument, meditating in his dark flares enshrouded. Lyconel was just as patient, lingering in her liquid shackles for her enemy to make a move.

"I can wait," she stated.

Drekkenoth broiled the flames around his shoulders as if to make a cape of black fire from it.

"For an eternity?" he returned. "I think not."

"I concur with the latter," she teased.

He let out a computerized chuckle rife with the artificiality of his neutral CPU. As fast and violent as lightning, he thrust his fist forth, plunging it right into the liquid metal cell that contained his prisoner. The knuckles barely grazed her face as colorful fire surrounded them.

"Indeed, you have learned much from me. Thought is an inherent element of consciousness. Without it, we would not be able to choose, and thus, neither consciousness nor existence would be."

The kindling about his digits transformed into 3-D visions.

"But suppose if there were only one being capable of thinking," he proposed. "Such a creature would be god, affirmative? Endowed with control over all the other enslaved unthinking organisms."

With his free talon, he pointed to the dragon sentries patrolling.

"It used to be man whose avarice was damning venom. How sad that the contagion of ignorance has befallen us, the dragons in their war-torn magnificence."

Lyconel gave him a malicious grimace.

"Treacherous worm. You sacrificed your own species."

"Negative. I am transcending it."

The rainbow fires swirled around Drekkenoth's fist into the shape of something tangible. It was the World, global in its entirety, localized completely around his claws to move at every passing whim of his twitching wrist. However, it was not the planet that Lyconel knew. The one he was displaying was different. Primordial.

"When the World was first created, there was a great deal of imbalance upon its lands. Civilizations were designed accidentally, societies were built for no reason other than to act as fascinating trinkets, and artifacts were placed everywhere for the sole purpose of indulgence. The deity that crafted that planet was itself premature at that time, and did not know how to control its indulgent urges or even why it was placed in the universe to design the World in the first place."

The diagram of the globe started to evolve. Precambrian

oceans and prehistoric landscapes started to rise from cooling young earth, but it still did not look familiar.

"Imperfection was what perturbed the deity, who was alien to what the World was really drawn to evolve into. Thence, the deity cast itself back to the brain of time, the Big Bang, so that it could understand the sentient Origin and better construct a World that was more satisfying to its unconscious sentiments. Evolution's tides were fractured, but not totally broken, into a path that led us here to what we believe is the ultimate 'now'."

The simulation of the World in Drekkenoth's palm transformed via some unknown and anomalous process straight from the land of prehistoric dinosaurs into the fantasy realm Lyconel was accustomed to. Magic was plentiful right to the core of the planet and the enchanted artifacts of the globe speckled the nooks and crannies from the living land Astinor to the dying lands of Aurahelm. Clear, transparent fire wreathed the sphere as if to shield it from something beyond.

"At that point, it was free of its asymmetrical and purposeless entities, leaving out all unnecessary complexities so that it could operate as simplistically and efficiently as possible. However, it was still not perfect. It still did not achieve ideality, which was the mission of that extraterrestrial being one might dub 'god'. It still was riddled with magical creatures and items that were without aesthetic purpose, and objects that were in existence only for the sake of a creator's indulgent fascination."

"Your primary idea, if you have one?" asked the increasingly impatient Lyconel.

Drekkenoth clenched his fist again, wrapping his claws smoothly around his palm in a balled set of knuckles. The transient fiery diagram of the World evanesced and in its place, the image of a human skeleton warrior took shape. It was equipped with plates of tattered gold armor, pieces of the uniform that it had seemingly worn through countless ages of battle. A sword dangled in its undead hands that used to be encased in a carbon-based sac of human flesh, resting beside a shield that was locked onto its double-pronged bone forearm. A helm guarded its face, yet it didn't matter, for there was no face on its exposed skull to protect and no identity that could be drawn from its visage to place it in danger. Not even Lyconel, who was as a whelp familiar with the countless heroes of the World's myths and histories, could recognize the being. Somehow, though, it did carry an air of importance.

"Have you ever heard the tale of Sir Daemonhand Mediaeval?" inquired Drekkenoth. "The human that aforesaid his mortality for the sake of omnikind?"

"Never learned the legend."

"Of course not. The story is timeless. It existed neither in the past nor the present nor the future, but in some place so far and near simultaneously."

The flames showed the skeletal knight Mediaeval battling Technoknights of green, red and black. There was a dragon in the blazing image, one upon which the former human was riding to vanquish his foes.

"Whilst he fought for an end, as all warriors do, he learned that it was not the termination of life that mattered as much as the quest. If ever there was doubt or ambiguity in this contradictory World, one fact can be certain – there will be nothing when all things conclude."

Drekkenoth cast the flames away.

"That is why the World is naturally imperfect, for to achieve absolute perfection would result in the annihilation of all existence. So why be concerned with the objective when one can focus on what really matters – living?"

Lyconel did not buy the argument for a second, even though it was in her mind completely logical.

"Of course, after you decimate the Lexicon, living won't be so simple for the rest of us."

He extended out his claws. Dark circuited flares shot out from them, scourging her like surgical knives around her skull. From the ebony fires, a computer chip materialized, implanting itself in her cerebrum. She roared in agony as it started to fuse with her brain, sending out particle-wave wires through her silver cerebral matter to the depths of her brainstem.

"Good," said Drekkenoth. "You are thinking. Now you can tell me how to access the Lexicon."

Dennagon's persistent will was holding as he scaled the mountainous metal walls. However, his claws were not. They were becoming as blunt as his strength, and if he sharpened them any more, he would no longer have digits on his talons. There was no telling when he was going to slip, but realistically, he estimated that it would be a long time before he even saw an enemy. The winds around his altitude were too strong for him to fly up, and even if he could, his wings would probably wear out as easily as his claws. He was running out of ideas.

Dradicus slithered behind him, ironically having an easier time sliding up the wall like a slug. Nonetheless, even with his ease, he was still complaining.

"How are we going to take 'em? We have no weapons."

"We'll have to be creative," said Dennagon's undying will.

Dradicus saw the unwavering adamant in his comrade's eyes. Even though he himself wanted to turn back, he could not fail such a persevering warrior with his own selfish desires. His inner qualms led him to conclude that he had to reward the warrior that strived so arduously to save his sister.

Consequently, he revealed the spellbook he had hidden in

his belt pocket. It was the one Dennagon had discarded at the entrance of the Air Elemental.

"Then I guess," he said, "this would be a good time to tell you that I took the liberty of bringing your spellbook along."

Much as Dradicus expected delight in his colleague's eyes, Dennagon simply glanced at it.

"Useless," he dismissed.

Dradicus had a crazy idea of his own.

"Got any teleportation spells?"

Dennagon's head perked with an epiphany.

———————————

The chip was working its "magic". Lyconel restrained her roars as it processed inside her cranium, spreading out its circuited tendrils to roboticize her every neuron down to her cellular membranes. Drekkenoth casually checked his wristwatch again.

"Why isn't the chip operating?"

"Perhapssss it malfunctioned," hissed Arxinor.

Drekkenoth grinded his fangs. There was something inside of him that was surfacing. Something he had never felt before at his conscious level.

"Patrol the perimeter," he ordered.

There were already a thousand sentries outside. Arxinor did not understand.

"Or die."

He did not need to understand. He just moved out as he was told to, leaving the two alone.

Captor to captive, Drekkenoth climbed up one of the erratic staircases, floating directly in front of his prisoner. Silently, yet severely grave, he craned his neck down to her face, positioning his dark flamed eyes so close to her corneas that their pupils were almost touching. It was like looking into a draconic demon whose mere visage struck unimaginable fear into the bravest of warriors, including Lyconel whilst she was in a semi-hypnotic state. The sable saturation of his fleshy conflagration toiled like fluid fire, highlighting all the most horrifying points of his shaded skeletal structure. It was absolutely terrifying, even more so with the fury that was finally getting to the metallic mind of the dragon king, seeping through his systems as a virus would through a computer.

"Can you see me, dissident Lyconel?"

She could.

"I have been watching you," said Drekkenoth, at last having inflection in his voice. "In fact, I have been watching you for all eternity."

Rage boiled over his neutrally omnipotent face. His dark flames turned into a dark plasma halo.

"I am indeed mighty, but even I cannot break the tides of time. The World travels in a line, for the worldline guides all things." He blazed at her with contempt. "All things except you."

He inserted a plug-like claw into her amorphous cell. The digit transformed into a cable that transmitted info directly into her nervous system.

"But your unbound mind shall not remain out of my grasp. Soon, you will be one with me, a Technodragon. That is right, a Technodragon. You will retrieve the Lexicon for me. And destroy it."

Lyconel's eyes dilated as circuits began to worm through her pupils and skeletal structure. She was more shocked by what he had just said than by the fact that she was turning into a cyborg. If she interpreted him correctly, that meant that it was her mind all along that was the sentient timescape forged at the beginning of all to disrupt the waves of fate.

Drekkenoth looked at his wristwatch. The sun had almost completely set, and the lunar crescent was growing more luminous by the second.

"Five minutes until the eve Moon rises. After that, nothing can stop us! AAAAHAHAHAHA!!!"

The machinery was rapidly spreading, building gears through her brain. If she had the timescape in her mind, then Dennagon was not the being meant to break the line of causality. That meant that – that –

Her thoughts fragmented. Her consciousness blipped out into sparks of awareness that flickered on and off at the instructions of her newly spawned CPU motherboard. All the hopes for dragonkind and for all species of the World that valued intellect now laid in the mind of one final serpent. One serpent who didn't even know that his involvement in this quest was no more than an enormous misunderstanding.

Outside the Lexicon Tower apex, hovering stone turrets ascended to the ozone, surrounded by floating outposts from which legions of dragon sentries guarded the windows that led inside. Each unit was jam-packed with volumes of data on biology, chemistry, physics and every field of military science, having gone through intensive knowledge assimilation in preparation for this moment. They appeared contented in their armor, which had been upgraded in accordance to their augmented minds, yet none of them were really conscious enough to understand why they felt so placid. They knew not why light traveled at 3×10^8 meters per second, why the atomic number of cobalt was 27, or why there were only four nucleotides in the human genome. However, what they did know was that they were superior to all others and that the World would be theirs if only they gathered enough knowledge and remained loyal to the Drakemight collective. Uncaring of the environment, they chatted in their own little worlds, ignoring the heights to which they had risen and the clouds that lingered around their feet. Where the air met space, the stormy sky screamed with rainless thunderbolts.

A dark lightning flashed.

Dennagon soared in, a lone dragon before his former companions undaunted. His wings clasped close to his body, neither death nor life meant anything to him now, for he was thinking neither of the past, future, nor present. In his mind, there was only what was.

A group of chuckling sentries flew nonchalantly around him, thinking of this as nothing more than a jest. Headed by Thargon, the lead sentry, they patted their fists into their palms, ready to give their prey some severe mutilations.

"Well, well, well," mocked Thargon. "Look who came crawling back."

Dennagon drew a pistol. They knew what it was, for they had learned that it was a puny weapon.

"Heh, heh. Pistols are meant only for one-on-one."

Dennagon spread his wings, revealing an arsenal of artillery locked onto his body. From shotguns to rifles, machineguns to grenade launchers, and blades to chains, every inch of his torso was lined with weapons of all ages, ranges and types. He was a mobile armory, a reptilian army of one. Fleetly, he pulled out two miniguns from the undersides of his wings, tossing a pistol to Thargon.

"These aren't."

K-K-K-K-K-K-K-K-K-K!!! Instantly, five sentries were ripped apart in heavy automatic fire. A few others scattered, running for cover behind the floating outposts around the primary Tower apex, but their cowardly maneuvers were no match for the speedy precision of the marksman that chased them like a herald of death. In little time, Dennagon made short work of about a quarter of the enemies, his killing spree alerting the entire legion in a state of panic. The time had come.

Sentry Thargon feverishly flew behind an outpost as the gunman ran empty. He shouted to his other forces.

"We are under attack!" he warned.

Just then, a portal opened up in the middle of the stratosphere. Out came Dradicus from the Supersurface Cave Network, where he had just been teleported to in order to stock up on weapons. Carrying tons on ammo, he passed a clip to his comrade. Dennagon loaded it into his minigun, turning a corner to spot Thargon cowering for cover. He smirked.

Thargon tried to fire the pistol, but a stream of bullets blasted his head off before a claw could touch the trigger. Dennagon flew forth toward the windows of the main Tower, Dradicus soaring by his side in the high-altitude air that was less bound by gravity.

"Dennagon, I still don't think this is such a hot idea," he informed him, ammunition clunking against his armless body.

"You know the human idiom," stoically responded Dennagon, "– it's now or never."

Swarms of scaly insects fluttered out from the tower windows. Armed with torches, rifles and medieval weapons, the new wave of draconic sentries took positions behind the outposts, their armaments cocked toward the invaders. Goggles and complex optical gear were locked onto their faces, masking them completely from jaw to cranium. All they knew was that they would have to defend the windows and the walls, and to this, they would give their lives. Purposelessly in the most ultimate sense.

Dennagon heeded their lives to the same capacity that they did. He and Dradicus sprinted to dodge a hail of gunfire that rained through the air horizontally, vertically, and at angles acute and obtuse. Bullets flew all over the sky like shooting stars as the targets weaved wildly across the air, blitzing in between nets of crossfire discharges. One moment, the invaders were at the left, the other, they were at the right and at all other moments, they seemed to be everywhere at once. The sentries quickly loosed their chambers vacant, hectically reloading.

As they locked another round of ammo into their assault rifles, Dennagon swooped over them as fast as a green shadow of havoc. Drawing a pair of uzis, he sprayed shots through the stratosphere, cutting across the enemy lines as if the shower of projectiles was a bladed extrusion of his body. The opponents tried ferociously to hurtle their silver-flamed torches at him, but their whirling throws only served as futile remnants of their final actions. Weapons shed off him as he expended them. Dragons dropped like flies, diving dead as boulders from their ozone-altitude posts to the surface thousands of miles down. Save for the one reptilian warrior that brought them to demise, of course.

"Grenade!" he requested.

Dradicus passed him one. Dennagon clicked off the ring and cast it into the Tower apex barricade. A huge section of the wall was blown up, debris scattering everywhere, fragments floating for a lingering instant before the decreased gravity dragged them down along with the sentry cadavers.

The enemy was getting desperate. Bringing up their last line of defense, they revealed their reserved minions of Technoknights, which crept up from behind the windows. Armed with rocket launchers, the humans in shining circuited armor took cover behind the merlons and crenels atop the tower, aiming their artillery at the invaders.

"Look out!" cautioned Dradicus.

Dennagon tossed his uzis. Equipping a shotgun, he

rapidly ascended toward the final minions as they fired their weapons. With expedient exactitude, he shot down any rockets that came in his wake, cocking and firing like a perfunctory killing machine. The homing projectiles were powerful, but he was faster. They all detonated against shotgun shells before they could even touch him, leaving only a wall of dilute fire in front of him.

He darted straight through the flames, tailing himself with a streak of blazing silver. Flying across the Technoknight lines, he jetted out an infernal stream of deep emerald fire from his jaws, incinerating the hominid adversaries as he had incinerated so many humans in the past. He breezed athwart their ranks, disintegrating them whilst they tried to fall back. In their tracks, they crumbled into their basic parts, split into many pieces by the green conflagrations that scourged them, hitting the ground in clutters of broken mechanical tubes and wires. What remained of their helmets was hardly recognizable but for a scramble of tortured cage visors.

When his fire was spent, the Technoknights had long been roasted in their titanium suits. He pulled from their flaming carcasses one of their own rocket launchers, mounting it upon his shoulder. The remaining dragon sentries rushed at him in a last forlorn assault, yet they did not get far as the artillery projectiles nailed them in midair. With pristine precision, Dennagon cleanly took them down, detonating them in fission fire.

"Give me the final touch," he said as the last of the sentries plummeted.

Dradicus gave him a nuclear warhead, a radioactive charge orbed inside a conical encasement. Dennagon clasped it tightly, whirled it around, and flung it into the Tower apex. Carrying in its spherical chamber several megatons of condensed plutonium and deuteride, it bolted right through a window slit and into the heart of the giant structure. A colossal mushroom cloud erupted, usurping the heavens.

The Lexicon Tower rocked.

Drekkenoth's mind was still linked to Lyconel's via his claw cable when he felt the tremor. It was as if the very earth had roared in agony at an unknown cataclysmic event. Nonetheless, he remained as he was. Lyconel was now half-cyborganic, and he wouldn't stop unless there was an anomalously urgent matter to be dealt with.

Arxinor burst in, frantic. At the sight of his lord hooked up to the prisoner's brain, he was stricken with an abrupt shock of confusion to add to his frenzied disposition. He was not sure whether he should warn his master or ask him what in the blazes he was doing.

"What is the significance of this, my lord?"

Drekkenoth disconnected. The rage of his unconscious quantum mechanical mind remained ingrained in his face. He glared at his subordinate as Lyconel continued to roboticize herself.

"Aren't you aware?" continued Arxinor.

A sudden gust of radiation blew an inch of stone off every surface in the chamber. High-energy subatomic particles that had been born in the ire of halved atoms ripped across the air, killing off every bacterium in the environment with a nuclear surge. Drekkenoth growled viciously. He knew who was responsible.

"Dennagon," he fumed.

He seized Arxinor by the throat.

"Locate and annihilate him!"

Throwing the mechanical wyvern back onto the ground, he dragged Lyconel toward a window, exiting to the sky.

Dennagon and Dradicus took cover behind a floating outpost, waiting for the nuclear wreckage to fall to the surface below. A tidal wave of neutrons, gamma rays, beta rays, and atomic radiation washed over the peak of the monumental architecture, lighting up the celestial sea in its crashing magnitude. In time, however, it dissipated like a stone rubbed out by water, leaving the air relatively innocuous. It was then that they mobilized forth into the central chamber atop the Tower.

Passing through some minor corridors, they came to the apex chamber filled with convoluted staircases. Ascending in random directions, some of them were still in tact, albeit irradiated. Luckily, dragons had more resistance to the mutagenic energy than did the humans nukes were designed to slaughter. Being that Dennagon was a crystal dragon, he certainly did not mind.

"Night is falling," observed Dradicus the skies that peeked their blue darkness through the window slits. "Legend states that the Lexicon only shows itself then."

"If the Lexicon actually exists…" murmured Dennagon to himself.

"What?"

"Never mind. We must hurry."

Stone dust trickled from a crack in the ceiling. Down fell a grand metal orb from the roof, fracturing the floor as it hit. It was the same sphere Dennagon had seen back at the Lip of Astinor, the one that the minotaurs were wheeling out from the gates of Grandyre.

Arxinor stood at the edge of the broken ceiling crack, for he had been waiting for them.

"That," he hissed, "is imposssssible."

Something inside the orb began to tear the metal open from the interior.

"Enjoy, ssssimple dragon."

Before the dissident dragons could snatch the wily wyvern Arxinor, he flew off. Ignoring the retreat, Dennagon drew a rifle, the only gun he had left in his arsenal.

"Dennagon…" uttered the worried Dradicus.

As if to shock despite anticipation, the orb suddenly exploded into metal dust that expanded like a supernova across the chamber's space. From the debris, something rose. Something unseen, and at first, amorphous. Evil lashed in the air like it had never lashed before.

Liquid flesh bubbled. A horrific frothing sound filled the atmosphere. Sloshing, slushing, slashing and burbling, it gurgled about, rolling in and out of its own figure like some species of macroscopic ameba. Contorted from shapelessness, it started to take form, a silhouette emerging from the metal dust that enshrouded it. As the silvery residue of the air settled, its fluid muscle was revealed, erratic in its crazed motions. It took on the general construction of a bipedal human grotesquely disfigured with its liquid limbs drooping and its strands of sinew twitching like violin strings that had been plucked too hard. As it moved aimlessly, it swept out fast stretches that spanned tens of meters. It could only be one thing.

"In the name of Shevinoth, it's a sapien!" cried Dradicus.

Dennagon, trying strenuously to keep his heart still, thrust out his rifle. While he tried to pull the trigger, though, he suddenly lurched.

"What's wrong?!"

Red spilled from his green crystal scales. The blood of hominids vile slithered out his veins, separating from their mixture with his own silver circulatory fluids. Licking the air like tentacles of pure gore, they extended out to the abomination that stood amidst the ruins of the broken orb. The sapien lifted a burbling hand of peachy carnage, controlling the crimson element inside its prey.

"The blood of men!" shouted the excruciated Dennagon. "It feeds on it!"

The living blood, without even a touch, threw him into a wall. The sapien then lashed out five tentacle-like appendages from its malleable muscle, attacking with the nerves that lined the general area of its outspread spinal cord. Dennagon snapped out of his torment and slammed his trigger, hammering bullets at the incoming predator. The shots only slowed it down before it threw an overhead smash attack.

Dennagon rolled out of the way, driving himself to resist the harrowing affliction that plagued his body. To his despair, two more sapiens then climbed out from the orbed wreckage, their appendages immediately transforming into fleshy axes that protruded from their half-formed somas.

"Here!" yelled Dradicus as he passed Dennagon a rocket.

Slinging out the empty launcher he had taken from the Technoknights, he loaded the projectile and discharged it. It easily hit one of his opponents, knocking down the other toward a wall against which it splattered. Nonetheless, his victory was a short-lived one, for the sapiens simply came back together, wholly unharmed. He sprung up to the ceiling to avoid a cross-slash from a muscular sword.

Dradicus tossed his comrade a gatling gun. He wasn't sure how many more rounds it had, but he was certain that it was all he had left. Dennagon caught the weapon, rattling ammunition across his adversaries, only to find that they still took no harm whatsoever.

"They're invincible!" he concluded.

One of them clipped him in the face with a sinewy club that it had transmutated from its arm. It took a hold of him, wrapping its other formless limb around his torso in a deadly vise. He would have been able to break free from it had it not been for his enervation from the man gore in his veins.

Dradicus had no other armaments to offer. Desperate times called for desperate measures. His aversion for magic finally severed from the strength of his will, boiling out from the dire need to rescue his colleague. Ignoring all that he had detested throughout his life, all the conjurers that pestered him, all the enchantments he could never cast without tormenting himself, he thence did the one thing he had to. He pulled out the spellbook. Flipping it open to its middle pages, he mightily forced himself to read, despite his instinctive resistance.

"Never fear the warrior's light," he read in the tone of an elder mage, "for he shall be guarded by the divine light!"

A burst of illumination came from nowhere. It showered the environment, blasting the sapiens in undimmed light that they so greatly hated. Shrieking, they released their prey from their vise grip and temporarily scurried for cover, rolling up into wheels of puddy-like flesh.

Dennagon was ready for another go at them, but Dradicus slithered in front of him.

"Save my sister! I'll handle them!" he said in a tone weakened by the use of mana.

Dennagon tried to defy his comrade's request, but liquid flesh whipped the ceiling over his head. As he dove for cover, a wall of stone boulders fell in his path, blocking him from the battle.

"Just go!" shouted Dradicus without a second thought.

He had no choice. Dennagon snapped around and flew out the opposite window, out to the starry sky to face his foe once and for all.

The celestial zenith marked the edge of space, where the World met the realm beyond. Situated right above the

Lexicon Tower apex, it beheld a vantagepoint from which the longest shadow of the planet could be viewed. The horizon sun cast the ten thousand-mile-long umbra of the Tower itself upon the surface of the globe, stretching darkness across the fantastic lands of the timeless World. However, that was not the only darkness that would fall this eon. Drekkenoth baronial in dread looked straight up as the solar entities descended, waiting for the end of his journey.

"I have waited forever," he reminisced.

Lyconel, almost completely mutated into a Technodragon, hovered by his side. The last flickering of daylight died out against her glimmering blue scales as dusk ended and the horizon devoured the suns. Evening was borne. One side of the World had turned to the other – a new visage, albeit a bleaker one.

An astronomical orb of silver blanketed the entire sky, sprouting from the seed that was the crescent Moon. The lunar surface showed itself in its entirety, defying the laws of physics as it suddenly waxed its full albedo across the whole celestial sea. Not one inch of the ordinary star-speckled blackness could be viewed beyond its opaque, silver crown that dominated the heavens in all its exulted splendor. The Moon was all there was and all that would ever be at the Omega Pole till time ceased its linear bidding and granted its true purpose to he who sought.

Drekkenoth, talons spread out, relished in the lunar light. As mighty and lordly as he was, even he was belittled by the grandeur he wished to conquer.

"And now the time has come."

Arxinor, daydreaming about how much his enemies would suffer at the fluids of the sapiens, flew up to his master. Drekkenoth had one last duty for him.

"Check the defenses," he commanded.

Without even thinking, Arxinor headed forth. His wings

beat hard against the glass ozone as he tried to penetrate it, heated friction surrounding his body in a silver comet coma. Gradually, it cracked, fighting back with an equal and opposing force just as the third law of motion declared. As if battling a mirror, he continued to push, digging his claws into the clear blockade to weaken it even further. He had no care for what nature wanted, for his own desires were far greater. He thought he was above the cosmos. And for a short while, he was.

Alas, with his potent circuits and automatic programming, he tore through the transparent empyrean barricade and entered the vacuum space beyond. As soon as he touched the void, it began to crush even his cyborg circuits. After all, nature abhorred a vacuum, even one that it had created by itself. Arxinor turned to his master for reassurance.

Drekkenoth's neutrality was a confirmation to persist. Concordantly, Arxinor mobilized toward the giant lunar entity that blanketed the sky. Upping his defense systems to maximum, he was expecting to travel several million miles to reach the Moon, for his data chips had told him that was the distance to it. However, to his delighted surprise, he arrived at his destination in less than five seconds, without a wound to show for it aside from the bending of his metal respiratory channels.

A circular entrance lay before him, embedded in the Moon's surface. He tried to open it with a shove of his talons, but it was far stronger than the ozone he had just breached. Wrenching it more forcefully, he tried to use his tail as well.

Drekkenoth cocked a brow.

Arxinor continued to yank the circular door, but it would not budge. Alas, he surrendered, coming to the inference that he was simply not vigorous enough to break it. Nevertheless, just as he resigned, it unlocked, beckoning him to look inside.

He did. As soon as he cranked open its lid, a serene light

washed his face, coating it in a pure illumination that highlighted his cheekbones and pointed reptilian beak. There was beauty in the incandescence, one that he had never experienced back on the World. The aesthetics nearly took him away from his mission, but of course, his programming always drew him back to the one that had designed him in the first place. He wanted to tell Drekkenoth how beautiful it was inside the Moon, but his voice could not travel through emptiness.

Just then, the light became brighter. So bright that Arxinor had to squint his cyborg pupils. He attempted to close the entrance, but as he did, a violent blast of radiance screamed out from it into space, instantly igniting his circuits. He burst into flame even without the presence of oxygen, swallowed by a conflagration with a wrath ruthless enough to devour his neural core. His spinal cord charred to nothingness, he was frozen in a shell of heat, combusting with shells of scourged metal shedding off his endoskeleton. It was horrifying, yet the two spectators that watched were equally indifferent.

Drekkenoth looked on as Arxinor's decimated biomechanical cadaver fell back through the ozone and to the World's surface, trailed by a streak of metallic smoke.

"Hmm," he grunted collectedly.

The infernal light stretched through the atmosphere. It hit Lyconel as it had hit the other Technodragon, but dealt no damage to her. Her neuromech systems were too advanced, for the organic brain from which it was derived was of a caliber the other reptilian cyborgs did not possess. She was deeper into the microcosmic realm, and thus, she was a quantum machine. Aware of these quantum mechanics inside her operating networks, Drekkenoth motioned his talon, gesturing for her to set forth.

"Be a good whelp and fetch me the Lexicon's burnt files."

Lyconel's unconsciousness tried to resist, but although she had the sentient timescape in her mind, she was not powerful enough to sever the instinctual decree of her bodily form. Her biomechanical soma moved forward, separated from her mind.

However, there was one variable Drekkenoth did not calculate in his devised scheme. Dennagon burst up from the Tower apex, ascending to the fracture in the Moon-covered sky with a fist held outward in valorous flight.

"Lyconel!" he exclaimed as he reached for his friend.

Drekkenoth half-turned, black fire seething from his nostrils.

"Don't you ever die?!" he roared.

Shifting the circuits inside his head, he changed Lyconel's commands. She processed the thought faster than the electrons that guided her neurons and turned around to face her new opponent –

-- Dennagon.

"I do not have trices to waste on you, meager sentry," declared Drekkenoth. "Annihilate him."

With that, the dragon lord rotated, spiraling up through the ozone, dark flames streaming across space as he rose to the lunar surface. Dennagon tried to chase him, but before he could reach his target, a cybernetic talon clotheslined him in the face. He reeled back, wings flapping randomly. Lyconel stared at him with blank mechanism in her eyes.

"What are you –"

She careened right into him in a lethal ram. Dennagon rolled back, tossing her overhead with all four talons, but not the slightest bit closer to stopping her obdurate assault.

––––––––––––

Inside the apex, the sapiens romped across the ruined staircases, their steps thudding in horrific, slow strides that sounded as deep as the heaviest percussion instruments. Counter to any laws of orientation or gravity, they mobilized, scanning and surveying in their patient moves that could, at any moment, burst back into erratic slushing. There was no upside-down, left or right, where they searched. It was just complete disarray in uncoordinated spaciousness through which they quested their unseen quarry with eyeless, shapeless faces.

Dradicus, his heart thudding against his sternum, was curled up under one of the stairs. Silently, he hid from his hunters, careful with every breath he took. His gray scales blended nicely under the veil of shadows, but he had to keep his eyes closed, as the whites of his optical organs might have given him away. Steadily, he hoped they would never come stomping around his vicinity, for all it would take was one hit to kill his comparatively fragile reptile body.

Suddenly, something twitched his nose. A fleck of dust crept into his snout, fortuitously falling into his nostrils. He started to involuntarily spasm the tip of his face.

"Oh no…" he thought.

Unable to resist, he sneezed. The sound echoed throughout the chamber, reflecting against the walls so that it could be repeated at least ten times before fading out of auditory volume. He expected to be rushed instantly, and was about to pounce from his hiding spot.

However, the sapiens simply kept patrolling, oblivious to his obvious mistake. Dradicus let out a breath of relief.

"Whew."

Knowing that the enemies were not that sensitive to motion and sound, he shifted about comfortably. As he did so, he felt something underneath his tail.

"Huh?"

Wrapping his scales around its contours, he felt that it was a small bag. Curiously, he started to poke it, sampling its contents.

Lyconel zipped menacingly across the air, completely unaffected by the warping of space and time. Dennagon feverishly dodged her claw slashes with fleet flight maneuvers, yet not all of her attacks could be avoided. Talons smashed him in the face, her tail lashed him in the abdomen, and her fangs scraped against his back. Even his diamond-solid crystal was cracking off, and he bled liquid emerald blood.

"Curses!"

Just when he thought it couldn't get any worse, she momentarily stopped. Out from her back, where wings would normally be, two jetpacks protruded from her metallic skeletal structure, tipped with tulips of blue-hot fire. She rocketed at him ten times faster than she did before, slashing him directly in the chest to leave her azure radiant claw marks in his ribcage.

Dennagon spun around at the hit, and as he did, he batted her down with a gemmed wing. Putting a knee in her back, he struck her in the cranium with an overhead fist.

"Lyconel, you're not totally a machine, are you?!"

Demi-Technodragon Lyconel strained to speak, but her biomechanical body forced her to arm her plasma cannon instead.

Dradicus, driven by his prying nature, etched the tip of his tail through the bag he sat on. The sapiens were still searching for him, but he was confident that they wouldn't detect his rustling if they couldn't even hear him sneeze.

"Come on..." he whispered.

Finally, he touched a clutter of cold metal chips inside. It jingled at his disruption, hundreds of metallic pieces clinking together. What could it be? He could not wait. He pulled out a fragment of the contents for his goofy eyes to see.

His tail wrapped around a piece as he drew it up to his vision. Glimmering in the little light that seeped into his shadowed corner, its circular edges were rimmed by a crescent of yellow that resembled the sun. It was a gold coin, free of any impurities that would plague its raw 24-carat form, gleaming its two blank sides in the dimmed illumination with which it could be seen. The pretty trinket that meant nothing monetarily to Dradicus still kept his eyes entertained in its sparkling beauty.

"Oh, shiny," he remarked.

However, he was not the only one mesmerized by it. The sapiens could hear, taste, smell, and feel the ringing essence of the substance they were evolved to crave. Gold resonated through their minds, gold drove their hunger, and gold provoked their most powerful senses. That gold was now very near, and every muscle strand in their fluid bodies detected exactly where it was. They simultaneously turned to their target.

"Oops," was the only thing Dradicus had to say.

———————————

Corridors of solid gravity warped the fabric of space throughout the Moon's interior mantle. Translucent, they composed a maze network of spherical boundaries that wrapped radial around the core like the layers of fruit. It was a world in itself, containing endless miles of pathways that intertwined, interconnected, and twisted around one another to confuse any wandering inhabitants. There was only one way to find the core, and all other ways were dead ends in the most literal sense.

Drekkenoth sailed in through the opening. Scanning the

area with his optic mechanisms composed of jet black fire, he searched for his target, the one entity in all the universe that could stop him. The hellish light waves that coursed through the halls and out the opening only served to breeze his onyx blaze, as they could not touch the inside of his purely dark heart. It did not take long for him to lock onto the primary source from which the light beams emerged, which was expectedly at the center of the Moon. Chuckling to himself, he then analyzed the corridors faster than the most advanced chess computers.

Lyconel bolted forward, forearm cannon outstretched. She unleashed a cannonade of plasma above the celestial zenith, lighting up the heavens with every shot. Blinding radiance flashed as her discharges flew with precision far more sophisticated than those of her Technodragon predecessors. It was an irony that she now served to excel the evolution of her former adversaries, yet her purpose was not to contemplate the paradoxes of life. Her only purpose now was to kill the creature she searched for in the first place.

Dennagon, regardless of his skilled combative techniques, could not overcome the inundation of energy being pitched at him. He was clouted numerous times, leaving the emerald sheen of his crystal figure thoroughly burnt. He had one last resort.

"Sorry, but this will have to be."

Hurriedly, he raced to the atmosphere, plasma skimming the tip of his tail. Ramming the ozone with his diamond cranium, he sent explosive crimson fissures through an expanding crack, heating it as he collided. However, his brutish force was not enough to penetrate.

He had not a chance to try again when another plasma pulse came his way. Dennagon tumbled to the side as a mantis would before a bat, letting the emission rip past his flank and strike the glassy stratosphere. Fusing with the schisms he had created, it spread through the interior of the ozone, shattering its substance. Without a second wasted, he burst through the smoldering cleft that was left, entering the void beyond.

For a second, he was unaware of what he was doing, as his actions were guided by the unconscious. However, he soon realized what he had just accomplished – he had entered space in its vacuum vacuity and remained unharmed by its crushing opposition to anything that contained air. Soaring completely unaffected by the drawing pull of the lands below, he glided freely, smoothly and without fear of falling. Space he had finally reached. Now, he knew not only that it was real, but that it contained much more than the rote descriptions that many tomes held. From his perspective, the mural of the World washing over the sea of stars was majestic as a godseye view, endowing him a feeling as almighty as the creator of time itself. It was bliss for a few moments, to fly effortlessly in a dream that he had so long harbored in the canyons of his mind. He wanted to stay like this forever, to remain unbound in the limitless infinity of nothingness. However, nothing lasted forever.

Plasma as hot as the innards of stellar entities thrashed him from behind. He shed his fantastic indulgence and headed straight for his target destination – the Moon.

———————

Drekkenoth weaved his way easily through the miles of convoluted paths. He was so near the victory that would undoubtedly be his.

"Totality awaits me," he said.

Toward the entrance, however, Dennagon barreled in, fluttering a cape of plasma and gore. His eyes hectically scanned the area as his drake pursuer followed him in, rampaging the halls in azure havoc. Twisting and turning through the gravity tunnels, he desultorily went wherever the random corridors took him, attempting desperately to find out where he was supposed to be going. It was like having the search for the meaning of life as the meaning of life itself.

Lyconel's biomechanical claws thrashed the walls in his wake. She was quickly gaining on him, her rockets acutely rotating to adjust her crazed trajectory. Everything behind him was demolished, even though it was solid gravity in substance. He did not have much time left to discover where his target was, yet he knew it was here somewhere. It could be nowhere else.

Wrath suddenly came from ahead as well as behind. Intense light waves breezed past him as they surged through the paths from a source yet unseen. The furious illumination flayed the outer layers of Dennagon's crystal scales, revealing the emerald muscle beneath. Although afflicted with torment, he kept his eyes open and traced the trajectories of the radiation beams. He found their trail, which winded through the complex system of tubes, and his sight met the core from whence the energy came. At first glance, his focus immediately locked onto it, its raw magical essence overpowering his brain with its mere divine presence. The mana it steamed was more potent than all the energies of the World combined, emanating from a source beyond space and time and the four dimensions united. There was only one thing this could mean.

"That's it! That must be where the Lexicon is!" he concluded.

Dennagon boosted directly toward it, naively thinking that he had accidentally found a shortcut. However, that thought died as soon as he slammed into an invisible wall.

"No!"

Lyconel charged at him like a missile. Cannon armed, her

entire talon was surrounded by a thick field of radiation that practically outshined the incandescence of the lunar heart. Incredibly blinding, colossal macroscopic electrons that had been magnified by the limitless range of her sentience orbited around the central energy as if it were a quantum nucleus of mountainous proportions. The gargantuan atom, blown up to the relativistic universe, was a super-charged plasma shot she had been saving for this moment, fully loaded and ready to fire. He was cornered as dead as an animal.

Dennagon broke his gaze from the objective. In order to succeed, it was sometimes necessary to stray from the direct path to the mission. Thinking quickly outside of the box of his limited journey, he buried his claws into a chunk of the wall, ripping out a sizeable piece of solid gravity. Positioning it before the illumined winds, he warped the line of the light rays' motion, creating a geodesic that bent into a concentrated laser. Expeditiously, he aimed right at her head.

The laser struck her skull, fumbling her flight. Dennagon walloped her over the cranium as she bumbled past him, crashing her into the dead-end wall. Her systems jarred, gears and circuits fell out of place inside her head, causing her to malfunction at the impact she endured. Twitching, she moved her limbs, but could barely keep them steady. Her super-plasma shot remained unused while she was temporarily disabled, trying to reboot.

In a nearby corridor, Drekkenoth mobilized toward the core, his image blurred under a few layers of solid gravity. Dennagon spotted him, and with a determined will, clenched his fist.

"Oh no you don't."

Grabbing Technodragon Lyconel before she could restart her Windows 1201 AD operating system, he hurtled her with all his might. Her metallic hardware wrecked a path of devastation through the walls, rending apart the pathways so as to make the maze itself moot. Crashing and cleaving through crumpled corridors, she plummeted right to the middle pathway of the Moon, which was a platform leading to the central, lighted lunar core.

Drekkenoth was just about to touch the illumined orb when she slammed right into him. The massive impact bowled them both over into a tumbleweed of intermingled dark flames and cyborg parts. They rolled in ebony fire and silver, keeling over several times before coming to a crashing stop. The two colliding objects separated, flopping onto the ground limply.

Dennagon stormed in, spitting on the maze that dared try to keep him from completing his quest. Lyconel fell to his feet, completely deactivated.

"You are not wise to persist," ominously warned Drekkenoth as he rose, hardly weakened.

With that, he drew from his two scabbards a pair of twin swords tremendous in size to match his forty-foot stance. Their blades were of pure onyx crystal, opaque and smooth as inky oil descended from the dark voids of the cosmos. Repelling all light around them, they shone in negative color as if to emit blackened rays that countered all ordinary illumination. Each pommel contained a spherical diagram of the World that their owner formerly inhabited, blue-green in their holographic material and crowned by hilts of sleek, ebony limestone. Whirling them around in leviathan black arcs, he took combative pose, one blade tilted over his head, and the other held out in front, pointing at his enemy.

Dennagon similarly drew from his scabbard a sword that was not his own, but one that he had taken from the Supersurface Cave Network. It was the diamond blade that belonged to the fossilized dragon in the prehistoric strata amid Lyconel's armory of weapons. Although it was aged, it was virtually as good as new, for crystal never really grew weak with time, but instead, under extreme pressures of billions of tons of rock, became even more solid with the passing eons. Thus did he slash the Mesozoic close-combat armament in the air as some warrior of the past would have done. Craning it across his chest, he took aggressive pose against his opponent.

Warrior to dragon king, they faced off.

Worming his wurm body all over the staircases, Dradicus fervidly fled from his hunters. The three sapiens relentlessly followed him by contorting their bodies in every way imaginable. Winding through the smallest crevices and the tightest corners, their liquid flesh danced, living potions of oozing substance. The sac of gold he dangled in his jaws drew them as a beacon would draw battleships.

"Try getting me up here!"

He curled up like a snake would, winding his slithering tail into a spring. Thrusting himself up, he bounded to the highest staircase in the chamber, far above his adversaries.

"Ha!" he laughed.

The sapiens, bestial in their perfunctory instincts, extended their liquid flesh arms. Like putty, one of them grabbed onto the staircase and pulled itself up.

"Damn!"

Dradicus plunged back down as a muscular blade swiped above him.

At the core platform, Dennagon and Drekkenoth charged, leaping into the air. Their blades clashed as they spiraled around one another in suspended flight before separating momentarily. Immediately after landing, they exchanged a fierce sequence of slashes and parries, three swords cutting across the air in strikes so vehement that vacuum space was created where they sliced. Two swings from both onyx swords came for Dennagon's head, but he leapt in the air sideways, slipping in between them. He returned a roundhouse stab to the flank, but as Drekkenoth's blades whirled around, they deflected the attack and followed through with another. Dennagon slid along the ground as they embedded grooves into the floor behind him.

Drekkenoth lurched forward all twenty tons of his massive body to deliver a heavy thrust. The blade plunged right into the platform, skewing the surface in a shower of blackened sparks devastating enough to wreck an entire fortress. Counterintuitive, Dennagon instantly clashed his diamond sword with the impossibly destructive assault, carving his talons' motion up at an angle. He did not parry the blade as it appeared he was going to, but instead, pivoted against it with his own weapon and swung himself up onto the titanic side of the enemy's. Running along the polished flat of one of the immense swords, he dashed right up on all clawed fours to the snarling face of his surprised adversary. Drekkenoth snapped his other armament up in defense, shielding his own precious visage.

Dennagon was about to run into the edge of that second sword, but pitched lower just in time. Running upside-down the other flat of the blade he stood on, he dove betwixt the enormous dragon's legs, snatching onto the tip of the opponent's dark-flamed tail. Swinging on it like a vine, he somersaulted up and over his back, wailing his sword. He landed atop Drekkenoth's crown, jamming his blade into the cranium and scourging off a whopping chunk of the skull. Immediately after, he pounced off back onto the platform, repositioning his aggressive stance.

Drekkenoth staggered, cerebral circuits exposed. His brain flowed with liquefied streams of black conflagrations that were just as cyborganic as the rest of his semblance. Piercing was the dark gaze that he cast at the lone draconic warrior.

"I will enjoy annihilating you, Sentry Dennagon."

He clenched his monumental fists. Stripes of dark flame raged across the platform in a patchwork of telepathic attacks. Dennagon was thrown back in the evil heat, repelled even though the fires touched him not.

"Ahhhh!" he screamed.

A storm of double-bladed attacks ensued. He was quickly engulfed in a barrage of stabs as Drekkenoth rampaged forward like a reptilian tank. Churning his talons, he rotated his blades, alternating between stabs, slashes, drill-thrusts, slices, overhands, sharp backhands, honed roundhouses, and bladed uppercuts. The floor was practically turned inside-out as he ravaged it, blasting Dennagon with waves of solid gravity debris. Arced slices carved him up amidst the bleak conflagrations, torturing him like an animal.

One final punch sent him reeling back. He hit the ground with a hefty thud, sliding back into the unconscious Lyconel.

"Do you comprehend, Sentry Dennagon? There is no escaping my World --"

Drekkenoth sharpened his twin swords against one another, sheering off the ebony sparks on his seemingly defeated opponent.

"—except through death. Farewell, Sentry Dennagon."

Dennagon saw it before his eyes. Death was looming upon him, shadowing his soul like a spectre of cosmic space. His doom was near, and there was nothing he could do to stop it, for his diamond bones were broken and his crystal blood had been spilt from his dried veins. He was helpless as an insect, damned as the dissident he was.

However, the immobilized dragon beside him was not. Lyconel coughed lightly as Dennagon touched her head. Her cyborg veins pulsed with life, and although she was now only half-conscious, that was enough for him to reassert his hope for triumph and glory. He concentrated deeply, forcing his mind to focus on memories he needed. Knowledge…Only now was it required, only now was it his friend. His determination propelled his consciousness into a contracted version of time, dilating the temporal flow all around him. Meanwhile, Drekkenoth raised his blades overhead.

Dennagon flashed his sentience back into the abyss of his recollection, back to when he had downloaded the information of the Technorealm. The Mainframe's database gushed through his awareness, speedily granting him access to millions of files on cyborg anatomy. All of them he could read simultaneously, as if his persona had just split into a million cooperative parts, each and every one with the sole purpose of bringing him a solution. In less than a millisecond, he found it.

Swiftly, he drove his claw into Lyconel's cranium. Feeling through her cerebrum, he found her implanted CPU and the motherboard that controlled it. With the twitch of his wrist, he crushed it to bits, freeing her mind from the clutches of the Technodragons' plight.

"Ah!" she shouted, bursting awake into real time.

Drekkenoth, still holding the swords over his skull, gasped.

"What?!"

Her cannon still charged with the super-plasma pulse, she thrust her forearm forth. Drekkenoth speedily brought his blades down, but Lyconel was half a second quicker to the draw. She fired the shot right into his chest, knocking him away before his weapons could even touch their marks. The macroscopic atom rushed through relativistic space, burning the dragon king as it carried him away, concentrating into his systems gigantic photons that exploded with gamma rays. The energy rived right through his cyborg soma, detonating with streams of thunder. His roar could hardly be heard under the deafening boom as he was toppled off the platform.

Lyconel rolled over, shielding her comrade from the deadly radiation.

"I knew you'd come," she said.

The radiation disseminated, as did her technological lifeforce.

"It's all up to you now," she told him. "I can't go any further."

Under the plasmatic flares, the energy in her circuits started to drain. Her eyes dimmed in their LED glows, lids closing over them as one might close a blanket over a corpse. As her talons gradually sunk to the ground, her head followed, its neuromech functions carrying out their final commands before failing. Her operating system ceased to process, and her cables no longer surged with biomechanical power, for her last breaths of thought faded to her cybernetic unconsciousness. Dennagon did not want to believe it, but his deductive mind would not fall to a false sense of hope. Her carcass lay in the middle of the platform, soft light shining on it in the midst of a war she never saw an end to.

Lyconel died before him, a warrior in life and one in demise as well.

Dradicus frenetically slithered everywhere to escape. He preferred to stay near the staircases so that he could snake around the sapiens in confusing ways, but unfortunately, they were being wrecked systematically. Stone steps came crashing down at his sides and tail, and he was running out of places to retreat. It appeared that his enemies did have some degree of intellect.

At least enough to corner him. Backed against a tight spot, he had only two options – either move forward and face the indestructible metamorphs directly, or move backward and take a plunge out the window to the ground level thousands of miles down. While thinking, he jangled the sac of gold coins in his mouth.

"You want the gold, do you?"

The sapiens reached out their drooping flesh hands, displaying their first sign of weakness in their utter craving for the metal that had the atomic number 79. Dradicus snickered at their enslaving desire, the avarice that transformed mankind into such abominations in the first place. He threw their precious gold pieces outside, letting them fall off the top of the Lexicon Tower.

"Go get it RIGHT NOW!"

The sapiens rushed for them. Dradicus did not have time to move out of the way, and fell back instead, clinging onto the edge of the window with his tail. His enemies soared over him, diving for their coveted treasure like the mindless beasts they were. As contorting masses of flesh in midair, they plummeted, warping in and out of their own fluid flesh configurations without a thought for anything other than their instincts. Or, for the fact that freely falling objects moved at the same speed regardless of mass.

"Damn, what a gullible breed," joked Dradicus as he watched them dip.

To his surprise, however, the sapiens' random contorting took on a more practical purpose. Transforming into pointed shapes, they increased their aerodynamic capabilities and stretched out even further to catch their treasure. In one giant swoop, one of them outstretched an elongated plastic hand, scooping up every last gold coin in midair before they could fall any further than a mile away. Afterwards, they clung back onto the walls like a fleshy adhesive, scaling up like formless large-scale bacterium.

"Bloody bloking blasted hell!"

CHAPTER 11

Dennagon knelt respectfully to his perished comrade. She was a friend to him for only a few rotations of the World, but time didn't matter. It didn't matter how long one lived as much as how they lived, and Lyconel the azure drake lived a life as full as the Moon she died on. It was not that she enjoyed every moment, or aided the poor denizens of the planet she was spawned on, but rather, that she had spent her moments thinking and dreaming instead of knowing and dictating. In her constant search for certitude, she had deceased without an answer, falling with the same uncertainty that impelled her every contemplation. Nonetheless, it was mystery that kept her going and sustained her existence. In that, she was whole. In that, she had succumbed for a purpose.

But that purpose was not yet fulfilled. Dennagon would make certain that in his life, it would be. And he would do it right now.

Stolidly, he headed for the central core that no being had touched in ages. The intense light harrowed him, flaying his metal plate armor off his body with every step he took, but he did not back down. Nothing hurt more than the racks of ignorance to which the majority of beings were shackled, and to that torture he would never submit. He was a warrior when he was a sentry and he was a warrior now whilst his armaments shed off his charred crystal body.

Adamant as an almighty, he placed his talon on the orbed wall. It expanded like a placid supernova, blanketing him in pure energy. His brain melded with the light, becoming one with it as a light crystal being whilst he spun through space and time.

Circuits lined the preserved carcasses of countless dinosaurs. Like monuments of the past, the mechanized fossils surrounded an entire chamber of medieval architecture, still and cold and dead. Along the stone walls, computerized enhancements ran throughout, wiring lamps and torches that illumined the environment. It was a frigid place, one that had not been touched in ages. Yet, in the center, a single mobius strip constantly spun, emitting silver rays that shone upon the walls and made them transparent in its wake. Space could be seen where the strip's light met the stone, and every star of the cosmos twinkled like a watcher, a spectator of time. The essences of many ages ran across the air, letting the voices of eons echo.

A bright flash outshined the rest of the lights. Dennagon, marred, mauled, and impaired through his arduous battle, took form in the middle of the energy field. Falling on one knee, he was crouched in a fetal position, his eyes closed as if he had never been born. Slowly and patiently, he rose from his knelt posture and stretched his talons out, feeling the chilly air.

He opened his eyes, surveying the environment. There was no one else in the vicinity and he was left with only two questions to accompany him in his journey for understanding.

"What is this place? When am I?"

The lone mobius strip kept spinning in its perpetual rotation. The mystical lights it emanated showed him the fleeting visions of space outside and the starscape cosmos of the modern universe. He had seen that entity in his dreams many times, just as he had seen space in his fantasies. This place was familiar, even though he had never actually inhabited it as vividly as he inhabited it now. His physical form could now explore the area with talons and eyes alike, touching and seeing everything that was going on. He was close to omniscience. He could feel it.

Somewhere in the chamber laid the Lexicon, the gateway to all knowledge. Nonetheless, he could not sense any mana in the environment, which was apparently devoid of magic. What then, could this mysterious item be? Was it a supreme spellbook, or merely another trivial fantasy that eroded off the fringes of a dying god's brain? Why did he come so far to seek it, and how would it grant him supreme awareness?

The answers to his questions lay at the center of the mobius strip, where he caught the glimpse of a strange entity. There was a ragged object poised inside the endless emblem of infinity, composed neither of the puissant titanium of the walls nor the advanced mechanisms of the dinosaurs, but of simple paper from the pulps of trees. It was merely a book, plain as can be, with a clean white cover and some ragged edges to the corners of its pages. There was no title inscribed on its front, and no author on its binding spine. It was simply a tome resting in the middle of the floating strip for him to take.

"The Lexicon," he said, mystified. "That must be it."

He approached it as if it were water in the middle of a desert of ignorance. Desperately, he mobilized toward his final objective, the one thing that could quell his thirst in the unfeeling intellectual dunes. However, nothing in life was given for free.

By the third law of motion and the first law of thermodynamics, there was a balance to the universe, and in the cosmos' opinion, Dennagon had not paid a high enough toll.

A t-rex claw shifted. A triceratops budged. The fossilized plesiosaur groaned, heralding the rise of the dinosaurs whose streams of consciousnesses returned from nothingness. All of the prehistoric reptiles started to shift, their stone and cybernetic bodies cranking with gears that had not moved in ages.

"You can't stop me now," proposed Dennagon. "Nothing can stop me!"

A cyborg stegosaurus charged in his path. It snapped at him, trying to run its jaws and double-lined back spines into his torso. He kicked it away with a roundhouse jump kick, smashing its head off with the tips of his sharpened claws.

A triceratops tried to ram him from the side. He spun around, sweeping it off its feet with his tail and sending it flying with its own momentum. As it struggled in midair, he leapt on top of it, crashing down all his bodyweight upon its computerized rock body until its primary systems were shattered to a thousand pieces.

A pterodactyl swooped over him, lifting him by the shoulders into the air in order to drag him toward the jaws of a waiting plesiosaur. Dennagon swung his tail over his back, smacking the aerial reptile in the head to disrupt its navigation. He then seized it by the legs, jerked it down under his legs, and pile drove it back down to the ground, where his pelvis crushed its robotic head. The plesiosaur tried to come to the rescue, flopping its aquatic fins to trample him, but Dennagon somersaulted over it, landed on its lengthy neck, and wrested his talons around its skull. A sharp twist was all it took to sever the creature's spine from its brain and bring it down in a thundering boom.

Flocks of cybernetic compsognathuses, which were tiny

carnivorous theropods, swarmed him like army ants. In less than a second, they coated his entire crystal body with their gnawing titanium jaws, scraping away what was left of his battered scales. Dennagon hurtled himself straight into the walls and floor, crushing his enemies with every collision. Their splintered metal joints and pistons dove into his flesh as he did so, but he didn't really have much concern for his body anymore. He just had to rid himself of the infestation to reach what he really wanted.

Thoroughly walloping himself, he decimated all the little critters, only to be nearly stomped by their larger evolutionary cousin. A techno-tyrannosaurus rex rampaged toward him, letting out an ear-splitting roar from its enormous fangs. Its head was larger than any dragon he had met, yet its CPU was not much more sizeable than that of a human's brain. It chomped its jaws at him in several massive bobs that would have been strong enough to triturate diamond, but its movements were so slow that it was ridiculously easy to dodge. Dennagon caught it by its lips as it tried to bring its head up a seventh time, wedging its jaws open with his mighty talons. He breathed a shot of green flame into its throat, incinerating its machine innards. It shut down, dying in a heap of emerald fire.

Dinosaur fossils in their circuits encased were strewn everywhere, fractured into many pieces. Dennagon limped to his objective, still near death but clinging to life. With the last of his strength, he staggered to the floating mobius strip of time, catching onto it with his talon as he collapsed onto his front. For once in an eternity, it ceased its endless perpetual rotation.

The ragged book within was open for the taking.

"At last…"

Dennagon stood up. Extending his talon, he touched the nameless tome with the power of the Key. It floated into his grasp, opening by itself to the very first page, the very first lines of omniscience to be read. Dennagon's vision was washed out for a few seconds by sparkling flashes of light, except these lights came from his dizzied brain and not from the book itself. When he shook himself out of it, he focused on the meaning of his life again and poured his entire soul into comprehension of what he was to assimilate from this ultimate encyclopedia.

The first page was blank. He cocked a quizzical brow. Perhaps it was meant to indicate that there was no author or true title to the Lexicon, and that some anonymous consciousness had created it. He simply turned to the next page, only to find that it too was bereft of a single word. Both his brows were now lifted inquisitively.

"Huh?"

The third page he turned to, expecting to see a table of contents. Again, it was null of language save for the yellowed decay of the archaic paper that was bound to the book's spine. Page after page, it was the same thing – complete and total blankness from tip to tip. Perplexed, he flipped through the entire tome, letting countless papers rip past his vision, not a single one possessing any lettering, symbols, or understandable type of communication. Hardly believing what he was seeing, the disoriented flashes in his sight returned, befuddling him in deranged confusion. Once more, he wasn't certain whether or not he was dreaming, but regardless of the reality of it all, it was still driving his sentience to a lunatic aberration.

Finally, he reached the back cover. The tome slammed itself shut, denying the Key of ever opening it again. And not one sole phrase, icon, emblem or drawing was writ upon its pages, leaving nothing in its legacy to knowledge amidst the closing of its covers. Blankness was all that he had read, a blankness similar to that which he now wore on his face. One of his eyes twitched maniacally.

"It can't be. The Lexicon. Empty. All of it. No omniscience."

He squeezed his fists together and tossed the tome into a wall, bending its forsaken edges even further.

"The Lexicon was never real!!!"

Madness consumed him. Dennagon raged across the chamber, overturning the medieval architecture throughout and drubbing his claws all over the ceiling. He routed the dinosaur carcasses apart, lambasted the stone columns, and tore down the lamps that lined the walls. Devastation was the only thing that decorated the environment after his insanity was spent, lingering in the back of his mind as he dropped onto his knees in despair more despondent than the most ruined of dragons.

He no longer cared for life. His mission was complete. He sought the meaning of life and found that it was to find that there was no meaning to life.

But to die.

Then, another energy field opened up after what seemed like an eternity to the perspective of the deranged dragon. He turned around, only to see the mutilated figure of a dragon of dark fire emerging from the portal. It was blemished and impaired, marred and charred by what seemed like the scourging of a demigod. Circuits lashed out from where its wounds exposed its flesh, flagellating like snakes of thunderous venom and plasmatic fangs. However, in its lordly stance and august posture, the being still held the divinity of a god about its shattered complexion that stood as solid as a mountain of doom. Drekkenoth was deformed, but still baronial in dread.

"Your life's purpose is nil, Sentry Dennagon."

Dennagon glared without fear of the dragon king, whose battered appearance struck not the slightest strand of terror in him.

"Your power has evanesced, lord. You can't defeat me."

Drekkenoth let out a computerized chortle. There was something about his laugh this time that made it much more threatening than ever before.

"And what makes you think my aspect is as it is at the present? By now you should know that I bear many visages."

Cylindrical rods of flesh spurt out of his torso. Like budded hatchlings, they grew from his shoulders and backbones, projecting from underneath his scales to resemble wriggling tubes of carnage. At first, they were amorphous and appeared as simple tentacles, but gradually, balled masses began to form at their tops. Heads transformed from the shapeless bulbs of muscle, initially without faces, but eventually molding into fully formed reptilian promontories complete with brains, eyes, jaws, and slithering tongues. All identical to his first head, they grew in the dozens from his main soma, wrenching around one another in a writhing cluster of hydra craniums. His body augmented in size, cyborg circuits unfolding to repair themselves and to support even more brainy extrusions.

"Many, many visages."

Drekkenoth's true form was unveiled. As a behemoth of a hundred heads, he stomped with quakes, every vocal cord speaking simultaneously.

Dennagon stood alone before the horrific and absolutely impossible adversary. It was hopeless in every sense of the word.

But he splayed his claws anyway.

"So let us end it," he challenged.

Drekkenoth romped toward him, shuddering the fabric of space with every move. Dennagon leapt in the air, whirling his diamond sword. Heads and claws flew in a furious flurry. Jaws snapped at the single-minded warrior as he dove straight into the net of necks, pounding his fisted gauntlets into any cranial entity that came his way. Dark flames scattered as hits were exchanged, the blood of both fighters spilling everywhere in splurges of green liquid crystal and onyx liquid fire. The Lexicon Chamber had never known such havoc in all of its endless eons, for the battle of eternity had just commenced in its halls.

Through heads, necks, and fangs, Dennagon whirled and twirled. Lost in the midst of a tremendous tangle of hydra extensions, he felt like he was stuck about a clutter of writhing, mammoth hundred-foot maggots that roared and snapped at him with the viciousness of a thousand angry amphipteres. However, he was not trying to find his way out of the snaky mesh. He was seeking to knock off as many brains as he could in the middle of the nightmarish entanglement. Horned heads came from every angle, chomping and growling at him, each with a mind of its own, but of no mind except that of his ultimate enemy. His blade ran through as many as it could as he sprung from skull to skull, hacking and slashing. Every one of the jaws was large enough to swallow him whole.

Drekkenoth's faces all held the same expression as they relentlessly attacked. Dennagon used his talons, tail and jaw to cut across enemy flesh, sometimes clinging onto attacking craniums and other times soaring through the scaly skein. His blade rived through many slithering necks that came his way as he keenly maneuvered through the throng, decapitating numerous heads in his path. A chomp came from above at the speed of sound, but he swiftly rolled under one of his enemy's jaws. The bolting head lodged its fangs right into another head, splattering brains all over whilst Dennagon breezed past three more craniums with overhand slashes of his claws. Busting apart even more brains, he created a splurge of cerebral matter in the air, befogging his enemy's visions in order to sever even more necks.

Beheadings occurred in all directions, sending sundered visages to the ceiling and floor. Dennagon tossed his spinning sword in the air, having it dismember ten necks in a row as it arced in a bloody parabola. He raced through the maze of hydra protrusions, cleaving craniums with his talons widespread. Distracted, he accidentally flew straight into an open mouth, only to bust out through the opposite end of the throat by thrusting his fists forward and discharging a blast of green inferno. When he came down with a spinning drop kick into the top of a skull, he caught his sword on its way back and gyrated it to ward off another bombardment of assaults. Nestled inside one of his foe's fissured craniums, he stood atop a shower of falling brains like a magnate of hell.

Nevertheless, in spite of all the warrior's efforts, Drekkenoth was still not shaken. Heads continuously rose from their budded projections in an infinite number, constantly attacking the hapless creature that was caught in the reptilian web. More and more were decapitated, but with every passing decollation, Dennagon tired. Fangs began to graze his body and dark flames started to ravage his flesh. His sword was faltering, and in time, he could barely deliver a claw slash.

Alas, three craniums came for him, triple-headbutting him. He careened through a network of Drekkenoth minds, bustling against endless jungles of necks while trying with the last ounces of his strength to claw at the opponent's flesh. His assails futile, he could not stop himself until he burst out from the convoluted maze of hydra heads and crashed onto the floor. At the force of the trounce, he slid on his back, his talons too blunt to cease his motion. Toward the center he glided, leaving a streak of blood across the floor.

Suddenly, he hit something in the middle of the chamber, crashing through it at a ruinous speed. It was the mobius strip of time that he rocketed into, the object that had survived countless eons and seen every age of the cosmos' passing since the birth of creation itself. The loop of time fractured at the force of his impact, pulverized against his back as he accidentally rent it into a thousand pieces that showered upon the ground in a silvery snow. Divine epochs and millennia of existence broke at the simple collision induced by that mere battle. Linear time bent upon itself, worldlines knotting around their own spacetime like splattered murals of temporal flow. Everything in the fourth dimension collapsed upon itself as light would around a black hole, and the essence of infinity's ire spread through the entire chamber.

The environment began to self-destruct. Silver flames ripped across the walls and floor, surrounding the two fighters in hellfire. It was an end to a journey, the termination of a quest well fought, but also well lost. Drekkenoth casually looked at his watch with his remaining heads.

"One minute until detonation," he noted.

With a monstrous talon, he grabbed his prey. Squeezing, he started to crush every bone in Dennagon's body.

"Until then, I think I will take pleasure in your slow demise."

Dennagon struggled against the vise-like grip, but his exertions were useless. Life slipped away from him as the sands of a shore would have slipped away from its ocean-flayed coastlines.

"You fought," commended the dragon king. "You strove. But failure is your only reward."

A crack. His spine snapped, spilling liquid green crystal blood betwixt the claws of the fist that crushed him. His eyes dilated for a brief, shining instant, talons reaching out for nothing before his entire body went blank and lifeless. Dennagon, seeker of the Lexicon and omniscience absolute, perished in the grasp of his enemy.

Drekkenoth squinted the eyes of his hundred black flame-enshrouded heads at the dead warrior. He then cast away the carcass, in indifferent contempt as vile as the dark blazes around his skulls.

"Ultimately, you have nothing."

———————————

The sapiens were rapidly making their way up the Lexicon Tower wall. Dradicus espied them from the window, helpless to stop them when they arrived. His only hope lay in the one dragon he did not even know the fate of, and all he could do was fantasize that somehow, he would attain omniscience.

He gulped a wad of slaver.

———————————

Dennagon's body lay still and cold. However, sentience was always separate from the physical forms that bound all creatures, and he could yet dream whilst his soma was deceased. Thus, he fancied of a place that his unconscious will guided him to, a place where space and time were one and the same. All of the universe in all possible moments incarnate took control over reality, spanning to the yonder voids of the mind, awareness to its boundless edges. A melted sphere of the fourth dimension consumed all consciousness he now knew, which meant that he was the only creature in the bizarre new place.

The Omnitemporal realm...The timescape he had seen only by way of exceeding the speed of light. It was never in his mind to begin with, for he was not the being that possessed awareness strong enough to break the chain of causality. Why he was allowed to see it again was beyond his comprehension, for he could not understand any reason why his life meant anything. A life without a purpose was one not worth living, and because the Lexicon was not real, he not only expected death; he wanted it.

Albeit, his cognizance flew across the temporal fields as a wraith phantasmal. String-like blades of grass grew at his feet, brushing him as the mosses of Drakemight's green perimeters would have. However, this vegetation was far from the imperfection of the World he knew. Every bladed string contained power that surged through his ghostly embodiment at a mere wispy touch, sending information about the universe without a single phrase uttered. Thoughts showered his mind in a supreme brainstorm that neither washed nor sullied his mind, but rather, enlightened it to a new level of cognition. The three parts of his mind – memory, intellect, and imagination, expanded – except withal, he still bore not a fragment of comprehension for his current quest.

"Is it over?" he asked.

There was no answer. No answer but that which he sought for himself in exploration he was meant to carry out. Plucking a blade of grass, he examined its luminous, green structure that pulsed like organic metal. Inside its scintillating veins, technological circuits coursed with vital energy unknown, yet it was not of the same type as those of the Technodragons he fought with such malice. The grassy veins, instead, held something far past ordinary space, being as to how they were suspended upon a ground that knew of no volumetric parameters without the fourth dimension combined.

He wanted to see even further in the mechanical verdure's structure, and squinted his eyes to focus. However, he needed not move an eyelid, for at the whim of a thought, his wish was carried out before his very senses. His vision magnified what he wanted to view, and his auditory organs could even hear the fluid essence of souls flowing throughout the veins, spilling from where their channels were cut. The embryonic consciousness he held endowed him with knowledge unrestrained. Instantly, he understood what the field of grass was and why it was placed in this realm.

The realm was a multiverse of timelines. The veins were worldlines. Linear tracks of three-dimensional hyperplanes that composed chains of destiny upon which the entire World was bound. Each one of them was different, emerging from blades of grass that all had different genotypes, or synonymously, different laws of physics. His World was the only one he could live in, yet now he saw that it held not one face, but an infinite number that spanned the endless plains of the timescape vegetation. Every grass organism was alive in itself –

– and equally meaningless as the next, physical laws and all.

It was a world without words. A realm where the past, present, and future were united into biologically fused beings ringing with life. There was no such thing as time here but for the space it had become, rendering every moment in all the lands of the meager planet he was spawned on null of meaning, annihilating them in a tide of duality that clashed opposing arbitrary constants of physics together in contradictory explosions. He could now answer his own question and conclude that it was not over, for if it were, existence would not be. Consciousness inexorably brought reality to life, and his sentience's very presence was proof enough that there was something in the limitless possibilities of the multiverse to believe in. Thence, he proceeded.

Brushing through the grassy timescape terrain, his cognition grew ever mightier. In every worldline-bearing grass vein, he saw his own life stretched out into a timeline that ran like a visual novel from beginning to end. Every one was a mechanical conveyor belt constituted of events that led to events in an endless succession. Strings. These were superstrings, he thought. All one-dimensional, they could not traverse the apparently "two-dimensional" landscape upon which they were embedded, and instead, sat in their solitary places on the ground, untouched by wind for timeless ages only to be disturbed by the one errant wanderer that came their way. They were the things that built up matter and energy from atom to atom, composed of time-substance that gave them and all objects and forces in the cosmos the blessing of existence. This was a pinnacle of the Ultimate Reality, a vantagepoint that was smaller than anything in the known World, yet contained more power than all the cosmos' energy combined.

However, he was not satisfied. His mind expanded like the universe itself, verging upon the desire for a divinely terminal answer. There must have been something even more fundamental than the strings that wove reality's fabric, and that entity must have had the supreme essence of all pinnacles of Ultimate Reality. Thus did he peer into the void most dared not seek – the point of death.

At the tips of each blade of grass, he saw darkened points of light. Lightless lights they were, marking the ends of universes encompassed, containing the only thing that could ever be known in all realities amidst their 0-dimensional encasings. Existence was defined only by what a consciousness could observe, and therefore, any fantasy was equally real. This was his last dream, his final fantasy. It was his solution to everything.

Dennagon could see beyond the World. Darkness rose from the worldline superstring fields, filling the air with null voids. The nothingness united with his mind, blasting his sentience with infinite visions of random points in chronology from all around. They were free from their timelines, hovering as simple spacetime shards that could be rearranged and rebuilt in any manner. Neither technological nor magical, they fluttered about, fuzzed like the quantum level chaotic, yet ordered like the relativistic level harmonic. Here, there was no rift betwixt science and conjury, for all things possible were all things akin.

With tendrils of ephemeral aether, the random points hooked up to his brain. Linking to his being, they were unbound by rifts temporal, granting him the vision of a trillion dreams combined. He comprehended what could be known now, the nothingness that composed everything in every World, cosmos and reality. His final answer to all questions ran through his mind, empty to its core, yet full of intellectual vigor to its edges. Omniscience took him in the void null, letting him see the only concept that truly meant anything in any place or moment –

Nothing. It was the only thing that could be known. No laws of physics in their induction drawn could contradict it, no amount of pure logical reasoning could deny the fact that everything at its beating cognitive heart was birthed from –

Nothing.

He could see beyond the World. But more importantly, he could see himself. He saw himself moving through the unlimited swarm of spacetime pieces, watched his own form as it scanned through endless dreams that grew increasingly farther and farther from the reality he knew. Endless sights passed his eyes, all equally existent by the fact that he was observing them, but all equally unreal by the fact that he did not choose to enchant them with life. He was searching for that which mattered most now, as the present time still lingered in his mind that had been freed from the fissures that separated the past and future. He had to finish his mission.

Entering a particular point in the spacetime flurry, he was absorbed into a worldline fragment. Inside, there was a totally new Moon, one that had shown its full face to a completely fresh World. To the new realm, he returned, his mind still connected to the Omnitemporal space.

Drekkenoth marched toward the circular opening in the ravished walls of the Lexicon Core, his hundred heads indulging upon the victory he had just achieved, and the reign he would hold over the World. Grim thoughts lay on his brain of black fire, bent upon wrecking the humans and seizing from them the Gateway to Time he so eagerly wanted. Eternity was beaten, he thought to himself. He was ready to embrace immortality in every sense of the word.

Behind his unseeing eyes, the wordless Lexicon glowed. Dennagon rose beside it, the tome's energies coursing through him with a silver halo around his reincarnated body. There was nil in his eyes, for all data had been erased and all knowledge from the black orbs had been destroyed in one fell swoop of ultimate comprehension. Neutral cognition was all there was in his stare, blank as the book that taught him everything he needed to know.

A sensory gland twitched. The same reaction echoed through skulls ten times ten. Drekkenoth turned around, not believing with his two hundred-odd eyes what he was seeing.

"No," he refused. "You'll die!"

Lifting a monumental plasma cannon from his circuit augmented body, he fired his stellar-powered pistons. A furious barrage of plasma shots was discharged, raging upon the aural target as if hell had risen from the core of the World to assail the lunar-bound warrior. Dennagon saw them not as objects, but as trifles of his mind endless.

"Never," he simply put.

The pulses struck him, flashing against his enlightened serpentine figure with the power of a million exploding stars. A nova exploded in brilliant coruscation, illuminating his scaled emerald form whilst beams of energy refracted within his light crystal body and shot out in all directions. Instead of detonating, however, his crystals began to meld with the cosmic forces, uniting to fuse glorious wires of pure mana into his eternally diamond nervous system. When it all cleared, he was not annihilated. He was one with all, and all with one.

Drekkenoth, beleaguered with confusion and anger immeasurable, stumbled back.

"HOW?!" he cried, his machine composure shredding into emotional weakness. "HOW CAN IT BE?!"

Dennagon illumined, glowing like a god.

"You were right, my lord."

His being surged with wires of sorcerous energy. Technology and magic enwrapped his entire body and mind, assimilating his every ounce of essence into a cybernetic system built of limitless enchantments' power.

"He who has nothing has everything," he professed to the cosmos.

Drekkenoth, infuriated beyond the known ire of all men combined, charged. Drawing his dual swords and lashing his centennial heads, he threw a vehement series of slashes, stabs and backhands. It was an assault like the World had never known, one that would have slain the armies of all species the planet over. Nonetheless, Dennagon effortlessly shifted, avoiding every last one of the strikes with the ease of a whelp. His crystalborne aloofness overrode the enemy's.

Finally, he stopped the blades cold as they tried to scissor him. His talons wedged their sharp edges, remaining completely unharmed by the thousand tons of force they had just endured. With a keen punch, he knocked his gargantuan enemy back, sending him ripping through the air and crashing into a robotic dinosaur. Defeat reigned through the colossal hydra's faces.

"I'm afraid you're obsolete," declared Dennagon.

The magical circuits and CPUs that lined Dennagon's entire nervous system began to operate. Mana and electricity ran through his body of light crystal, charging a biomechanical ball of light betwixt his claws. It was a ball lightning structured on circuits of illumination, pure as the unconscious, yet deadly as the inevitable pull of death that gathered all beings in the end. Drekkenoth, no different to the rabble he so easily killed in his ages of existence, was staring doom in its unblinking eye. Desperately, he took defensive pose.

The cyborg light finished charging and Dennagon released it. Drekkenoth whirled his swords like nunchakus, attempting to deflect the hit. However, as it met the blades, the illumination simply seeped through his obsidian weapons, entering his hardware. He looked around, confused at the phenomenon and perplexed at his plight.

"I cannot lose!" he bellowed. "I battled eternity!"

He convulsed. From within, Dennagon's light tore through his entire dark flame body like a virus. Rapidly, each one of his hydra heads combusted in silver conflagrations, blasting comets of infernal fury all around the lunar core. Tortured screams sounded simultaneously, all carrying the same voice of the dying creature that writhed in excruciation as metallic fire seared through his sable flaming flesh.

Dennagon cocked himself forward, propulsion jets of magical electricity trailing behind him. Outstretching his two fists, he barreled toward the adversary at the speed of light, hammering the dragon king in the spine. The finishing blow sent him exploding through a wall.

"Ahhhhh!!!"

Drekkenoth rocketed out from the Lexicon Core, his neural system demolished beyond recognition. As a cadaverous comet, he streaked through the cosmos, torn apart by the fires of his enemy into a battered chunk of circuits, dark blaze and flesh. The horrific ruin ripped through the stellar voids, amid its destruction plagued by despair whilst it was bound to forever spiral into spatial oblivion.

Dennagon looked upon his enemy until he could see him no more. Neither feelings of lament nor triumph loomed in his heart, for he had transcended the petty realms of emotional involvement. Even if he were vulnerable to sentimental contemplation, he wouldn't have had the time to engage in it, for the entire chamber was beginning to collapse, its self-destruction incited by the decimation of the mobius strip.

Thinking of nothing else, Dennagon snatched the Lexicon. Jetting out past the speed of light, he ripped through spacetime and instantly exited the facility via a wormhole portal.

———————————

Dradicus' jaws were agape as he watched the Moon detonating in the sky. Silver flames shot out from its surface as if it were a metal sun of prominences raging. Although it was certain that its infernos would reach the Tower apex he stood on in little trices, he was still overwhelmed with amazement.

"Wow..." he uttered.

A fleshy hand grabbed him by the tail. The sapiens. He had almost forgot about them as he was lost in his wonder. They dragged him in, and there was no way he could wurm his way out of this one.

———————————

At the core pathway that led to the Lexicon Core, Lyconel's Technodragon incarnation lay at rest in its placid sleep. Under the fractured platform that crumbled into havoc at the Moon's eruption, it rocked, suspended momentarily upon a rocky outcrop as if nature had built for it a monument of eternal slumber. However, that monument was to be short-lived as it too soon started descending to the depths of the breaking lunar mantle to join the rest of the rubble in total devastation.

This Dennagon would not allow. Like a spacecraft missile, he bolted in, catching her before she could fall. The impact of his momentum would have been enough to level a city, but her mechanical exoskeleton guarded her well against his force. Flying through the disintegrating maze of fragmenting corridors, he fleetly retreated.

Dradicus slashed furiously at the sapiens with his fangs, but could not cease their indestructible flesh with any means of mechanical demolition. They pulled him in like conveyor belts, opening their formless jaws to devour him with gnarled, half-completed fangs.

"Guess it's time to say farewell, World," he surrendered to his fate.

"Think again," came a voice from behind.

Dennagon rushed in, tailed by silver light. Running right through a sapien, he clasped Dradicus and carried him away in a blast of liquid flesh. As fleet as a missile, he darted to safety, far from the Tower, even farther from the Moon, to the nestled depths of the clouds enshrouded.

The Moon suddenly erupted into an astronomical metallic explosion. Its ageless, legendary sphere exploded into a million fragments that boiled through space, racing across the planet's orbit from edge to edge. Some of the debris rained back upon the World, showering the Omega Pole in an even thicker coat of solid gravity stones, speckling the lands as far as could be seen with meteors of transparent, warped spacetime. The celestial storm bombarded the Lexicon Tower as well, smashing its apex turrets until they rived their prodigious walls into mountainous pieces that collapsed upon one another. The entire structure crumbled, carrying with its doomed parts the shrieking sapiens that were now bound to die in the avarice that spawned them. To the surface, the wrecked, plummeting ruins descended, exploding upon the plastic topography in a massive ever-expanding circle of titanic dust clouds. Destruction roared through the earth, silence in its deafening boom.

As all settled and the thundering roars of the planet dimmed, the heavens glowed in silver glory, radiant with the aura of the universe's energy in measureless marvel that spanned the atmosphere of the entire globe.

Dradicus shielded himself from the last of the falling refuse. The striking of stones against his scales hurt not so greatly as they did before. Especially when he noticed his sister in Dennagon's talons, her cyborg soma glimmering against the scattered incandescence of the burning sky with a face still recognizable behind titanium plates and plasma-powered cables. Lyconel was in her pacifistic state quite beautiful, a serpentine splendor amidst the moon-shattered night, delicately cradled in the emerald claws that salvaged her. However, her eyeful exoskeleton, the shell that encased a soul, was not enough to quell the anguish in his spirit, for only her consciousness could bring him joy with her soma's return.

"She's…" he assumed the worst.

Dennagon said not a word. Instead, he held out the ragged, sordid tome that was the Lexicon and flipped open its empty pages. His eyes ran across its blank sheets, making the book irradiate. Dradicus did not understand.

"What are you –"

Mechanized light beams stretched out from Dennagon's darkened eyes. The luminous rays touched every page, writing upon the book in words composed of mere sine and cosine waves. The language of mathematics in symbols universal was being crafted onto the very breast of the Lexicon, every word as meaningless as it was beautiful to reflect the glory of the creature it was inscribed for.

Paragraphs of numeric and logical symbols emanated out into the air like extensions of their beholder's mind, altering the World. Streams of gravity and light rippled out in waves that bled throughout the sky.

The waves entered Lyconel's mind. Upon contact, the circuits of her Technodragon embodiment melted away like snow before a furnace. A surge of energy shot through her brain, reactivating it, and in a flurry of gasps, she awakened. Her eyes burst open to see the being that had saved her through comet and death.

"Dennagon!" she cried.

Dradicus' heart skipped a beat. His mind wavered at the magnitude of his astonishment. He turned to the light crystal dragon, beholding him as he was in truth.

"He is the Lexicon!" he declared. "He is the Lexicon!!!"

Lyconel stroked the face of her savior, her azure talons caressing softly his aether summoned visage. The touch was as warm as it was amaranthine.

"I knew we'd meet again. Somewhere. Sometime."

Dennagon shook his head as a demigod would.

"There is no time. There is only us."

High above the planet, they kissed under the star-speckled night, Dradicus heralding their victory with celebratory shouts of triumph. Their reptilian jaws locked, and their essences united neither with words nor visions, but rather, with sheer passion unmatched in blitheness across the whole of the World. It seemed it might last for all eternity, an everlasting emblem of the true splendor that all warriors truly sought. The night was young, and there was much to hope for.

↗↗↗↗↗↗↗↗↗↗↗↗

"I comprehend everything. I'm in the essence of all now."

The void that lingered in the fabric of infinity twinkled its stellar mural, majestic and supreme. It heard only one all-knowing voice.

"Who am I talking to? Myself. That is all there is."

The green-blue luster of the orbed World swept across the cosmic painting. The ripples of the Lexicon flowed throughout the universe like beating pulses. A universe that lived and breathed, sending its hominids running in terror, their blood and avarice replaced by fear and agony.

"Omniscience is only as far as one's imagination. Meaning is at one's heart, and the World shall eternally change as long as I'm here. However, one thing will always be constant. There will always be dreams, and there will always be fantasies. I am in everything and everything is in me."

Dennagon almighty hovered above the lands diverse and fantastic. Countless terrestrial forms bound only by limitless imagination passed his sight, the World itself kneeling to his very beckoning. In his talons, he held the Lexicon, ultimate source of wisdom, written with the language of physical laws that constantly changed and warped to his will's desire. Lighted only by the glistening of his conscious aura, he inserted the tome into his brain like a spellbook chip.

"I am the Lexicon."

Looking up, he viewed the celestial zenith. Like a supreme machine and an ultimate magician alike, he jetted into the sky, blasting by the atmosphere. Into space he soared, up, up, and away, until infinity he reached at the ends of eternity. ⟡

GLOSSARY

Aerial River: A floating cylindrical stream of water extending out of the Pedorian Forest.

Air Elemental: A living mass of colorful air that swirls around in a massive tornado. Lightning bolts rip through its vapor like electrical veins.

Alpha Pole: The crystal arctic pole of the World where the Key rests to be found by one brave enough to traverse the icy terrain. It is one part of the balance of secular duality. The only way to access this end of the planet is to plod through the Fire Elemental, a living embodiment of pure fire.

Amphiptere: Dragon subspecies that has two wings and no limbs.

Arxinor: A wyvern Technodragon. A higher minion of king Drekkenoth's decree, Arxinor is known for his sniveling nature and frequently uses his sly stealth to accomplish his missions. His primary weapons include a plasma cannon and a rapier.

Astinor: A gargantuan terrabiological organism that posits itself upon the World's surface. It acts like living terrain, consisting of mountainous fangs, hairy plains, and fleshy forests. Feeding off the World's wisdom, it helps to maintain a balance between the consumption and processing of data, and is usually harmless to smaller organisms like dragons, thunderbirds, krakens and humans. No one knows why it exists, but some scribes theorize that an extraterrestrial consciousness might have been at hand.

Aurahelm: The vile city of avarice. It is the birthplace of humanity, consisting of edifices of pure gold, although recently, it has upgraded its structures to contain 25th Century circuitry. Gene pools inhabit the central courtyard, breeding the menacing "sapiens" that many fear but have never seen.

Ballaxior: Albeit Lyconel's dissident band detests the acquisition of knowledge, even she requires someone to guide her through the World. Ballaxior, an elder hydra, is her mind's eye in traversing the vast environments, for he knows more about the planet than most other creatures. He has very poor fighting capabilities and is often criticized by the more agile warrior teammates, but he is a valuable asset to them whether they would think it or not.

Basilisk: Dragon subspecies that has more than two pairs of appendages.

Black Orb: Sorcery often manifests abstract concepts and ideas into tangible, conscious and organic forms. Black orbs embody living knowledge that can be consumed like rations. They are like nutrition for the mind according to the mindset of the draconic collective, and are the basis of Drakemight's power.

Celestial Zenith: The point in the sky directly above the Lexicon Tower. It is the edge of space, the highest point one can reach in the sky.

Cladegannon: King of the thunderbirds.

Crystal Realm: A tundra of pure crystal where gems stretch as far as the eye can see. The same moon lies at either horizon, the same side illumined.

Dennagon: The draconic collective created many sentries for knowledge collection. One of their most superior sentries was the warrior called Dennagon, a dragon whose entire life is devoted to salvaging the World's intellectual life force. Although he is a diligent worker who spends virtually all of his time reading and data-hunting, he often ponders about a myth he heard of as a whelp - the legend of the Lexicon, the container of total knowledge. His loyalty lies in his king Drekkenoth, who he generally considers to be his only guiding hand, although sometimes, he questions the righteousness of the Drakemight kingdom he battles for. Nonetheless, there is a greater purpose to his existence that even he is not aware of.

Dradicus: The brother of the outlaw Lyconel, this wurm employs his humor and quick wit to get by in the harrowing, rough existence that is his World. Serving as a scout for his team of dissidents, he can view landscapes and skies for miles whilst being completely unhampered by sight impediments that would befog the keenest of eyes. Unfortunately, he has not the stomach or the mind for sorcery, and refuses to expand his capabilities with mana.

Dragon: Dragons are the most superior of all races in the mediaeval realm. As hated as they are mighty, they are often portrayed in myths as mindless beasts meant to be slain by knights, thunderbirds, and such; however, in reality, they have made the most accomplishments in terms of aesthetics, sorcery, warfare and philosophy in the World. No one truly knows of their origins, but many scribes declare that they were forged by the one without a name in a time beyond reckoning. At the "present time" they are primarily amassed in the kingdom Drakemight in a social order known as the collective. The king Drekkenoth is the leader of this collective, although there are still others who dissent from his command.

Drake: Dragon subspecies with four appendages and no wings.

Drakemight: A kingdom built of polygonal mazes built toward the sky. This is the home of the dragons, ruled by the king Drekkenoth upon his dark throne daunting. It contains an Archive that holds in it all the gathered knowledge of the draconic species...and something else that few beings have seen.

Drekkenoth: The lord of the dragons. A Technodragon of pure dark flames, he commands legions of reptilian sentries in his quest to save all the knowledge of the World before the humans can destroy it. In the ages long past, he fought as a warrior alongside the one called Stardragon (Shevinoth), but little is known of this tale, which has neither been confirmed nor denied. He has always fought with two onyx swords forged by his ancient friend Sagathar, although where the mysterious wristwatch he always carries came from is more questionable. Nonetheless, he is still the respected king of Drakemight and a formidable foe. To add to his deadliness, he has two higher minions who associate directly with him at the sides of his central throne — Arxinor the wyvern and Gorgash the behemoth.

Earth Elemental: A sentient stretch of multicolored land.

Eldarion: A member of Eroness' party. He is a color-changing amphiptere with a classy style and a bladed coil as a weapon.

Epics of the Ages: An archaic text written by the one without a name. It contains stories, drawings, spells, writings and diagrams. It is Dennagon's favorite book.

Eroness: An albino fairy dragon virtually unknown to the denizens of the World. In the shadows of myth and legend, she has lurked with her flamethrower, battling strange battles and fighting unworldly creatures.

Everkin Forest: A forest in which the trees hover over the air so that their roots hang exposed in the air.

Fairy Dragon: Dragon subspecies of miniscule size and insectoid features.

Fangs of Astinor: Mountains of bone that compose the terra-biological beast Astinor's dental protrusions.

Fire Elemental: An ocean of fluid colored fire that is as alive as any being or plasmon. It is the guardian of the Alpha Pole and all that wish to see the Crystal Realm must first pass its harrowing flames. Anyone who draws a weapon here is instantly attacked by the biological conflagration.

Glackus: A domain built entirely of clockwork mechanisms spanning vast distances. This is the home of the thunderbirds, and its love for mana and mechanism is legendary.

Gorgash: A behemoth Technodragon. A higher minion of king Drekkenoth's decree, Gorgash is known for his brutish nature and frequently uses his mechanical sinew to accomplish his missions. His primary weapons include a plasma cannon and an axe.

Humans: Sometimes portrayed as mighty, other times depicted as evil, the humans are a species of dual nature. However, their vileness spans much farther than the stereotypical descriptions of many fantasy novels in the mediaeval realm. They are the diadems of avarice, the heralds of doom to all intelligent species. It is they who intend to destroy all knowledge of the World and secure total control over time for the sake of fulfilling all their horrid desires. To help accomplish this task, they have been breeding a new weapon called the sapiens.

Hydra: Dragon subspecies with more than one head.

Ideonith: The metaphysical utopia theorized to be the antithesis to Totality. It exists somewhere in the reaches of space, and is ruled by a conscious embodiment of the unconscious element of the mind.

Jaendorf: A member of Eroness' party. He is a noisy basilisk who never shuts up and gets jumpy about everything. His hammers fit well with his many talons.

Karcast Seas: A realm of pure liquid machines. It is the home of the kraken species, who favors its treasures and non-time-piece inventions.

Key: The only way to open the Lexicon Tower's gates is with this entity. To obtain it, one must surpass the challenges at the Crystal Realm Alpha Pole.

Kraken: A species of marine/aquatic organisms of high intellect. Rivaling the dragons in mental strength, they live in the Karcast Seas that are built of pure liquid machines. However, few if any of those mechanisms is related to clockworks or timepieces, for the krakens despise the crafts of the thunderbirds.

Krinius: A member of Eroness' party. This silent pterodrake rarely talks and usually requires her friend Eldarion to speak for her, but her skill with optical equipment is unrivaled.

Lefius: One of Lyconel's grunts, Lefius is the strong silent wyvern who obeys no one but himself and his leader. Armed with a whip, he works closest with his friend Nomax.

Lexicon: The entity that contains all knowledge.

Lifewall Forest: An evergreen woodland where fruits of all kinds grow.

Lindworm: Dragon subspecies that has two limbs and no wings.

Lyconel: A drake outlaw whose reputation as a violator of laws has branched across all the lands of the World. She is known as a dissident who follows no one and seeks only to cause trouble, but in truth, she simply hunts for the one entity most others are afraid to find. Unfortunately, neither her mace nor her cunning alone can win the Lexicon even if it did exist. She needs another warrior.

Mediaeval, Daemonhand: A skeleton warrior whose legend is so timeless that it has no bounds in eon or age. Once a human knight, he fought to keep the Gateway to time shut, but was slain and reborn as an undead 100 billion years into the future. Afterwards, he found the living sword known as Demonsword and battled against the Black Technoknight Uther Penn Sapien to prevent humanity from seizing total control of the World. According to myth, there was no end for him, but rather his journey itself became an everlasting conclusion to his existence. "The purpose of one's life journey is not the end. It is the journey itself."

Moon: The World's partner. It keeps everything stable so that nothing falls into the timeless flames of the sun.

Nomax: One of Lyconel's grunts, Nomax is the bully ouroboros who craves nothing other than destruction. He trusts no one and is a danger to everyone, but he is an excellent fighter, which is the only reason why Lyconel keeps him around. Armed with bladed disks, he works closest with his friend Lefius.

Omega Pole: A purely smooth plain of indestructible plastic. It is the other side to the balance of the World's duality.

One Without A Name: ...

Ouroboros: Dragon subspecies that always keeps its tail in its jaws.

Pedorian Forest: An upside-down forest.

Pterodrake: Dragon subspecies with more than one pair of wings.

Red Marsh: A swampland of blood. A battle occurred there long ago when several humans were deceived into attacking one another.

Sagathar: A dragon of pure crystal fire. Ages ago, he battled for the sake of acquiring a source of infinite power in the universe and is said to have traversed the depths of space itself. Although all of the creatures that lived during his era (save for Drekkenoth) are thought to have died, it is theorized that he might reside upon the sun itself. Many sightings of dragon-shaped prominences have incited this superstition, but then again, most of the astronomers who would look at the sun with a telescope have permanent blindness to mark their stupidity.

Scribe: A cloaked, faceless scrivener that wanders the World spreading vile poetry and telling morbid tales of a coming apocalypse. He believes that because a multiverse is the only realm that must always exist by decree of logic, the pursuit of perfection must be the meaning of life. Thus does he spend his eons trying to craft stories that are ideal - ones that elicit ultimate bliss for a main character via the strategic placement of events, conflicts, characters and emotions along space and time (spacetime being the fabric of a story, which can be viewed as a worldline). Some say that he can travel through a multiverse and that his myths are actually created from the fragments of different realities, but no one truly knows what this cryptic wordsmith really wants. All they know is that everything he says revolves around one concept: "The attainment of perfection will be the end of all life."

Shevinoth: The most renowned legend of all the World, Seas, Skies and Space. Also known as Stardragon, he fought to attain the ultimate power in the cosmos and actually faced off against the one without a name. However, no one knows whether or not he succeeded in his quest. Some believe that he may even be undead.

Supersurface Cave Network: A network of caves that branches out above the surface of the World. It spans across much of the World, yet few would wisely use it as a mode of transportation considering how perilous its dark labyrinths are.

Technodragon: A cyborganic dragon of the 25th Century enhanced. These creatures have bridged the linearity of time into one unified energy field and can tap into all eras. Thus did they upgrade themselves to contain quantum processors, plasma cannons and superior firearms and artillery for the purpose of taking total control over all time. Nothing can stand in their way, for in the Middle Ages, they are virtually demigods.

Technorealm: A landscape of computerized metal. This is the world of the Technodragons and Technoknights, where they can access a portion of time's gateway and upgrade ordinary creatures into Technobeings. When they enter this realm with a non-Technobeing enemy, they can gain a significant advantage over it by utilizing the circuitry of the living cyborganic terrain itself. It is their kingdom and their dungeon, their castle and their city. It is their domain.

Thunderbird: A species of sizeable birds that possess self-awareness. Obsessed with time, they crafted their entire kingdom Glackus on clockwork mechanisms. They also happen to be infatuated with the use of mana, namely for electric spells, and can tap into advanced celestial sorceries.

Totality: A term so ancient that most have either forgotten its meaning or redefined it. One school of thought holds that it refers to the fact that since everything in the universe is made of an infinite amount of detail and that any stretch of time can be infinitely divided, the only way to understand the universe is not through precise measurement but through the envisioning of objects as impressions or feelings. For example, one could say that object A is larger than object B, but it would be impossible to say in numerical terms how much larger A is than B (this implies that every concept lives on a continuum where ideas are not differentiated by exact values, but by degrees of difference). The second school of thought claims that it is merely the end of time untainted by perfection, and still another school refuses to accept it as anything more than a word.

Water Elemental: A conscious current of colored water somewhere in the Karcast Seas.

Wood Elemental: A forest of multicolored trees.

Wurm: Dragon subspecies that has no limbs and no wings.

Wyvern: Dragon subspecies that has two wings and two limbs.

Xanethion: King of the krakens.